Tobias
and the Angel

By
Frank Yerby

The Foxes of Harrow
The Vixens
The Golden Hawk
Pride's Castle
Floodtide
A Woman Called Fancy
The Saracen Blade
The Devil's Laughter
Benton's Row
The Treasure of Pleasant Valley
Captain Rebel
Fairoaks
The Serpent and the Staff
Jarrett's Jade
Gillian
The Garfield Honor
Griffin's Way
The Old Gods Laugh
An Odor of Sanctity
Goat Song
Judas, My Brother
Speak Now
The Dahomean
The Girl from Storyville
The Voyage Unplanned
Tobias and the Angel

Tobias and the Angel

Frank Yerby

The Dial Press
New York
1975

Manufactured in the United States of America
First printing

Library of Congress Cataloging in Publication Data
Yerby, Frank, 1916–
Tobias and the angel.
I. Title.
PZ3.Y415To [PS3547.E65] 813'.5'4 75–2153
ISBN 0–8037–5967–3

Book design by Paulette Nenner

For my sons, Jac and Jan,
who, being of this *generation,*
dwell quite comfortably in vast aqueous dreamscapes,
very similar to the ones evoked in this book,
whose shores are but obliquely tangential
to what mine *thought of as reality,*
swimming through them as easily,
as gracefully as fish do through water.

Or—as do lemmings,
in certain cycles of what men call time . . .

One

Walls.

Only there weren't any tops to them now. No arch and span and girder. No supporting columns for the screams to echo eerily among. No rain-slicked slate. No corrugated galvanized sheet. No tar paper. And no men and women dressed all in white with faces painted by an American artist named Grant Wood, to move in endless phalanxes beneath those roofs and—

Is this an anachronism? Had Grant Wood painted them?

Walls. Roofed over by the sky.

They crawled off at odd angles to one another. Up hills. Down valleys. Crooked, jagged granite walls. Fallen in places where the frozen ground swell had got under them and—

"Left not a stone upon a stone—

"Something there is that doesn't love a wall—"

"God knows *I* don't," Tobias said half under his breath.

"Well, here we be," the man in the blue uniform said.

Tobias knew who the man in the blue uniform was. Nicholas Brightwell, Chief of Police of Ryland Township, in upstate New York. Now that he could remember again, he remembered everything about Ryland, including the fact that he had been born there, and his father before him, and all the Tobits for seven or eight generations back. Of course there were still gaps in his memories of things, and some of the things he remembered had not happened at all, or at least not yet, which was Angie's fault. There were times when he hated Angie, or came close to it. Angie, come to think of it, was pretty hard to take.

"Planning to stay?" Chief Brightwell said.

"Don't know," Tobias said. "Anyhow, Mister Brightwell, didn't you just tell me that the old place—"

"Was up for sale. Did," Nicholas Brightwell said. "Taxes, state *and* county. Helluva lot of back taxes. But it appears to me, young fellow, that seeing as how you're the *last* Tobit, the state and county comptrollers just might take that fact into consideration. Give you a year's extension, say, to raise the money, what with you being a veteran and all. The more so since ain't nobody exactly rushing in to buy . . . Le's see. The War's been over all of four years now and—"

He stopped. Peered at Tobias Tobit.

"That's another thing," he said. "Don't mean to go poking my nose into your business, Tobias. But seeing as how your Pa and me were the best of friends; don't allow as you'll mind telling me *how come* you took so daggumed long to come back home—?"

Tobias looked at the chief of police. The question was hard to answer. Before he had met Angie, he would have either answered it right off the bat, or he wouldn't have been able to answer it at all, depending upon whether or not he remembered what the answer to it was. But now, thanks to Angie, or rather no thanks to Angie, he lived in a world of limitless possibilities and his mind—trained by Angie—could think of half a million simultaneous and mutually contradictory answers to that question without even half trying.

"Fer instance, me boy, me boy!" he could hear Angie saying in that fake Irish brogue that he must have copied from some tinhorn comic in a traveling minstrel show, "ye'll just have to decide which war it is, ye be a coming home from *now.* You see, Toby, we've fit, you'n me, in all the wars that iver wuz, including them that happened before mankind learned to scribble down the record of their bloody misdeeds. Try'n find out which one this blue-coated Billy goat'll settle for. Won't do to go'n tell him that time."

Was an amorphous, slow-rolling sea. Directionless and purposeless. That it didn't flow. It just lay there and wallowed, sort of. That then is now. That now is now. That tomorrow is now. That a firefly's flash and eternity were the same thing. That life and death and past and future are all coexistent, meaningless and simultaneously flickering bad dreams in the mind of God. If there were a God. About that, Tobias had his doubts. But Angie swore there was.

"Ye're caught in it," he could hear Angie saying, somewhere in the deeper recesses of his often out of order brain, "so ye have to go on repeating the same damn fool motions over'n over ag'in like that silly old Greek sod, pushing his idiotic rock up that bloody hill forever. So now, to prove to you that 'tis a friend of mankind that I am, I'll give ye a clue. Look at his blinkin' duds and at the miserable contraption ye've been a ridin' in . . ."

Tobias looked at Chief Brightwell's clothes, and the contraption they'd been riding in. The clothes, he judged, were early first quarter of the twentieth century in their cut, and the contraption was indisputably a Model T Ford.

"Therefore," Angie's raucous voice rang through his mind, "the answer's easy, me boy, me boy! 'Tisn't the bronze chariot I dragged ye out from under the day that Assyrian archer put a barbed arrow betwixt yer ribs—Ye remember that, don't ye? 'The Assyrian came down like the wolf on the fold,/And his cohorts were gleaming in purple and gold;'."

"Yes," Tobias said, "Lord Byron."

"What did you say son?" Chief Brightwell said worriedly.

"Nothing, sir," Tobias said. "I was woolgathering, I guess. The way everything's all broken-down reminded me of a poem about the Assyrian king Sennacherib. He left everything pretty well ruined too . . ."

"Up here, it's the weather," Chief Brightwell sighed. "Tell me, son, just where the devil have you been these four years? Not in any trouble, were you? Jailed, maybe?"

"Nor," Angie went on, "the occasion upon which that princely swish, that fierce faggot, Richard Coeur de Lion cracked yer noggin fer ye with his mace. Nor that glorious, flame shot, smoke-hazed day that 'Butcher' Grant sent ye and twelve thousand other involuntary suicides out to reduce the Bloody Angle. Because on either of them occasions th' contraption wouldn't have rubber tires 'n 'twouldn't be pulled by a beastie—a mule or a horse."

"No, I haven't been in jail," Tobias said slowly. "I have been—sick, sir. Sort of. In a hospital—"

"T.B.?" Chief Brightwell said. Again he sounded worried. Tobias wondered why.

"His daughter, Nell," Angie supplied. "She's gettin' along and hasn't caught herself a hubby yet. Ye're nothing much, but ye're available. C'mon, Toby—tell him *which* war was it? The one ye bailed out of yer Flyin' Fortress over Meissen in, got down without a scratch only to have them Nazi civilian scum break half yer bones? Good thing I happened along. Or the one when ye got yer feet frozen off tryin' to stop all the Chinks on earth from crossing the Yalu river? Or the one ye had yerself a foine auld time wastin' Dinks, Gooks, o' Slants, whether they wuz man, woman, o' child—"

"Wouldn't be this kind of a car," Tobias muttered.

"It might not be a car at all. Helicopter. Jetplane. Rocket. Or disintegration and transmission by Laser beam with reintegration guaranteed upon arrival." Angie said. *"Which* war, Toby?"

"World War," Tobias said. "The first. Look, sir, this is—kind of hard to explain. I was in—the Veterans' Hospital down in Arlington, Virginia. I wasn't sick—or wounded. I just kind of, sort of—lost my memory. A howitzer shell. Big one. One hundred eighty-eight millimeters. Hit right smart close to where I was and—"

"Left you shell-shocked," Chief Brightwell said.

"Something like that," Tobias said. "Concussion, anyhow. But—one thing, sir: I wasn't *loony.* Doctors said my behavior was perfectly normal. The minute I did remember who I was and where I came from, and they checked it, they let me out right away—"

" 'Pears to me they'd of had some kind of records," Nicholas Brightwell said.

"They did. Only that shell blew my uniform clean off me. Underdrawers, too. Left me mother naked, except for my socks. Even my I.D.s got lost. So they didn't know who I was, either. And all the rest of my squad were dead. Bucket cases. Had to *shovel* 'em up. Just came to me two weeks back. Who I was, I mean. So they let us out—"

"Us?" Chief Brightwell said.

"Me'n Angie. Friend of mine. He's been mostly cured for over a year. Only he waited around for me. Good guy, Angie. Real buddy . . ."

He stared at the house.

"How'll I get in?" he said. "You got the key, Mister Brightwell?"

"No," the Chief of Police said. "Been lost these six or eight years. You go round back and pull some of them boards off the back door. Mind you, I can't help you do it. Illegal. And I never told you to do it. You never heard me say it. Seeing as how you could forget your own name you can forget that much can't you? Slip of the tongue, anyhows—"

"It's forgot," Tobias said. "Well then, good-bye, Mister Brightwell. And thanks—"

"Not good-bye. You're having supper with me'n the missus, tonight. And—Nell. She'll be glad to see you, Nell. Or is *eating* another thing you've forgot?"

Tobias grinned at him.

"Damn near had to, these last two weeks," he said. "Be seeing you, Mister Brightwell."

"Eight o'clock sharp. The old woman gets right pert peevish, she have to wait supper," Nicholas Brightwell said.

Tobias stood there under the dutch elms—proof positive he had got the time right, now, because the blight hadn't yet ruined them all—and watched Chief Brightwell rattle away in the contraption. Then he turned and stared at the gate. The gate was bolted shut, and what was worse it had a rusty length of chain wrapped around the bolt, and a huge padlock was jammed through the links of the chain. From the amount of rust on it, too, it must have been there since the Flood.

Immediately, that damned gate became the kind of problem Angie always inflicted upon him. Because now he had to decide whether to climb over it, or walk under it. The method of procedure depended upon who he was at the moment. Because, a lot of the time, Angie had convinced him, he wasn't Tobias Tobit, a lanky, twenty-seven-year-old New Englander, five feet, eleven inches tall, but his homunculus. And since his homunculus was exactly eight and one-half inches high, in that case, walking under the gate would be a much more practical method.

But deciding which of the various avatars, alter egos, doppelgänger that Angie swore all human beings were constantly being transmogrificated among as they made their unreal voyages through illusionary time, was too much of a chore, so he let his mind go blank and started towards that gate.

Then he was past it (over or under it, he didn't remember which) and walking around the house. The house was Steamboat Gothic in style with all sorts of fretsawed gimcrackery decorating it. Or at least it had had, for now most of the decorations were rotting away and falling off it.

Then, abruptly, he stopped in his tracks, as though he had run up hard against an invisible wall. He stood there and shivered like a wet dog, for another odor had come pouring through the scents of mildew, woodrot, and leaf compost. Then he doubled in half and vomited. He had smelled that stench a damned sight too often now, maybe even, as Angie insisted, in all the wars that ever were, or ever would be; but it wasn't a thing a body got used to: that sweet, sickly, utterly, obscenely vile stink of rotting human flesh.

And raising his head, he saw it: There was a little blonde girl about three or four years old in the pond, floating. She was grossly swollen and her little tongue protruded from her mouth and had turned black. He couldn't see what color her eyes were because the crows had been at them. In fact, they still were. They were greedily beaking away at whatever of her poor putrid little corpse they could reach and—

"Devils!" he screamed at them. "Black feathered Evil! Get the hell off! Leave her be! Why the poor little thing, she—"

He picked up a fallen branch and threw it at them. They beat upward heavily, slowly, and came to rest in the tops of the palm trees.

Tobias stopped. The detail was wrong. There damned sure weren't any palm trees in Ryland, New York, a town so clinking cold that the weather, nine months out of every twelve, would not only freeze the tits off a witch, but the blue balls off a polar bear.

He knew what that meant. Angie was playing tricks with his mind again. Then he remembered another thing: There wasn't any pond on his father's old place. There never had been. So how the devil?

"Could that poor wee one have drowned in it?" Angie said. "Niverth'less she did. But not now, nor not here. Or then, ag'in, maybe she didn't. That's for ye to decide, Toby, me boy, me boy!"

Tobias turned and glared at him. This time Angie was there in the flesh. He usually was, except when he didn't want people like Chief Nicholas Brightwell to see him. Then he sort of turned into smoke and drifted off.

"Make it go away," Tobias said sullenly.

"It's gone," Angie said.

When Tobias looked up again, it had. There was no pond. No dead obscenely stinking baby girl-child's pitiful corpse. No palm trees. No crows.

"You," he said hotly to Angie, "hadn't ought to go'n do things like that! Make up things in *my* mind, I mean. Mess up your own for a change, will you?"

"Didn't make it up," Angie said. "It happened—as much as anything kin happen—*dentro de las posibilidades ilimitadas de la vida. . . .*"

"And don't go speaking Spanish to me!" Tobias screamed at him. "You're no more a Cuban than I am! Who th' hell ever saw a six-foot-four Cuban with freckles, blond hair and blue eyes?"

"Put that self same question to me Sainted Mither," Angie said solemnly, "whom th' blessed saints have with them in Glory. And she couldn't account for it either. Of course, not all the clients of la Casa Verde wuz Cubans. Lots of Yankee sailors passed through Habana in those days, so—"

"You're shameless!" Tobias said. "To call your own poor, dead mother a whore—"

"Nor did I," Angie said. "My theory is that I be the product of an Immaculate Conception. 'Blessed be she among wimmen, blessed be the fruit of her womb, namely, me—' "

"That's blasphemy!" Tobias said.

"Oh come now, Toby, me boy; how could *I* blaspheme? I am an Angel. Your Guardian Angel, sent to—"

"Oh, shit!" Tobias said.

"I do that, too, upon occasion. Unpleasant necessity of this stinking body I got saddled with because of you. You mean you *still* don't believe me? Permit me to introduce meself: Don Rafael Angel Claro, at your service—"

"You're nobody's Angel—not even an Anhell, as you call it—"

"I, and all who speak me Sainted Mither's native tongue. But tell me, Toby, *who* d'ye think I be?"

"Don't know," Tobias said sullenly. "The Devil, maybe."

"Ah, there, ye could be right. Which do I be, I wonder: Don Rafael Angel Claro, Hidalgo de la Luz; o' Don Lucifero Angel Moreno, Duque de las Tinieblas? Now, c'mon, let's see if yer auld man has left a drop o' th' brew hid somewheres about the place—"

"Angels don't drink. And who ever saw an Angel abed with *nine* whores at the same time? There you were—a pulling on that whisky bottle as though it were your mama's tit, while black, tan, yellow,

white, and all shades in between naked women crawled all over you and—"

"And what?" Angie said.

"You know what," Tobias said disgustedly, "never dawned on me that there were *that* many ways to go at it, but let's let that subject drop, shall we? I'll admit you can do a hell of a lot of things there're no accounting for, but all the same—"

"Ye're badly mixed up," Angie said. "As usual. But that's normal. So is life. Ye believe a great number of erroneous things, me boy, to wit, that an Angel has to be *good.* Or that there *is* such a thing as good, existing in a state pure, unmixed, and undefiled. Which there ain't. Or that ye would be capable of recognizing what ye call good, even after ye've stuck yer foot into a stinkin' mess of it, slid a country yard, took a belly flop, and buried yerself in it up to yer bonny brown eyes. Now c'mon. 'Tis thirsty I get after so much palaver . . ."

"No," Tobias said. "I can't live like this! Before I got mixed up with you—"

"But there wasn't any *before* that, me boy. That crazy Auld Cuss upstairs formed a synarthrosis of our souls the very first instant He went on a rampage and started creatin' all over th' place. We've been transmigrated, and reincarnated all down eternity, ye'n me, me boy. Ye as a sinner, me as yer Guardian Angel. And 'tis ruddy sick I gets o' being stuck with ye at times. Now, c'mon!"

"But there *must* be something *sure* in the world," Tobias wailed. "There must be!"

"Ah, but there is, me boy, me boy. If yer auld man hadn't gone to sleep in th' garden he wouldn't have got hot bird shit in his eyes and gone blind—"

"Oh what a liar you are!" Tobias said. "It was an accident. A train wreck and—"

"That's what they told *you,*" Angie said. "More dignified than bird shit, I suppose. But that's one certainty, if ye're in need of one. And another is that skinny witch of a Nell Brightwell will get ye sure if *I* don't do something to stop her. Got to put me mind to that—"

"Why should you?" Tobias said. "To my way of thinking it would be kind of nice to get married and settle down—"

"Aye, that it would, me boy, me boy. But not to Nell. Not to a woman who would perform a nightly castration on ye by *freezing* off yer blinkin' balls. If that is not the fate worse than death, it comes uncomfortably close to it to me sweet angelic mind. But first jist *where* d'ye suppose yer auld man hid *his* whisky. Think, lad. Put yer mind to it."

"My father didn't drink," Tobias said.

"With an auld biddy like yer Ma for a wife, he didn't drink? How many stout fellas did it take to haul him off to th' booby hatch, then?"

"And he didn't go crazy, either!" Tobias said.

"Ergo, he drank. Ye can't have it both ways, Toby, me boy. Or don't ye remember yer Sainted Mither whom the saints—"

Tobias looked at Angie. Then he grinned, very slowly.

"If the blessed saints have got Momma with 'em in Glory, Lord help the blessed saints!" he said.

Angie threw back his head and roared. There really was something angelic about his laughter. It lifted silvery and pure up to the very floor of heaven. Lifting his eyes, Tobias could almost see it floating skyward like a cloud.

But long before they found the whisky—which was in the basement, hidden behind the furnace—they found the letters.

The letters were in a trunk in the attic, carefully tied into separate bundles. Each bundle was bound with a different colored ribbon. Tobias recognized his mother's fine hand in that.

"Bring 'em along," Angie said, " 'twill save me from havin' to explain to ye all the bloomin' things ye need to know. Startin' with *why* ye've got to jump over the broomstick with Sara—or is it Clara? Niver mind. They're twins. Or they *were.* And the one of them can wiggle her delectable little tail as nicely as the other. Fillies with blood in their veins, not cracked ice. Of course, 'tis Tobit blood, too, which may be overdoing things a mite. But then, maybe not. Who knows?"

"Yin and Yang," Tobias said.

"Exactly, me boy, me boy. The principle o' the universe. That everything is *part* of everything else. And so long as ye keep yer long part outa Nell's stitched-up and deep-frozen part you'll be doing fine! That is unless ye *like* icy gash. Now c'mon! Th' whisky, lad! The whisky! Oh where did the auld sot keep it hid?"

"Don't know. Downstairs in the basement, someplace, I'll bet," Tobias said. "He used to spend an awful lot of time down there when Mom would get him wild . . ."

"Now ye're talkin', Toby lad! Downstairs we go. An' after we build a fire in our poor shiverin' bellies we might have a look at that furnace—ought to be some way to get it to draw, even after all these years. For if iver I be punished for me sins, here's hopin' the Auld Cuss don't send me to an Eskimo's Hell!"

They lay by the furnace—which Angie had lighted, Tobias would have sworn, by pointing his index finger at it and muttering curses in ancient Hebrew—and stacked up the piles of letters all around them.

"Yer auld fader's taste in whisky was as good as his eye for wimmen flesh was bad," Angie said. "Right oft it is that I've wondered how he *iver* got ye. What did he do, Toby: tie her down?"

"Guess she considered sharing his bed her wifely duty," Tobias said. "Mom was awful strong on the subject of duty, you know. And, anyhow, she always wanted kids—"

"So she tried it—*oncet,"* Angie said. "Start with th' ones with them vile, vomit-green ribbons, Toby, me boy. They're sure to be th' interestin' ones—"

"How'd *you* know Mom hated green?" Tobias said.

"When ye wuz but a wee, pants-pissin' li'l snotnose, 'n I wuz a guardin' and a protectin' ye, chiefly against ye Sainted Mither's not so saintly wiles, I got to know Anna Tobit a sight too well. Because part o' me mission was to save ye from being ruint. An' the likeliest way there wuz o' yer being ruint would o' been for me to allow yer Sainted Mither, whom th' blessed saints—et cetera, et cetera, et cetera—to turn ye into a pious, hymn-singin' little swish. Had me work cut out for me there, I did—"

"So that's why you've dragged me into every cathouse 'twixt here and Alexandria, Virginia?" Tobias said.

"For lack of a better remedy only, me boy—though I must say ye've acquitted yerself nobly! But now, it appears to me the better remedy's coming up. That is, if ye don't let Nell Brightwell screw up the deal. Read yer letters, will ye!"

So Tobias did.

They were nearly all from a man named Ralph. Turning the envelope over, Tobias saw that the first ones were from Beaufort, South Carolina, and that above the return address was scrawled "R. Tobit."

He looked at Angie.

"Yer auld man's cousin. First, but not quite. And Sara's papa. And/or Clara's. Or he wuz."

Tobias went on looking at Angie.

"Who is Clara?" he said. "And Sara? My cousins?"

"Wrong conjunction. It's 'or.' Haven't got it straight, meself. Clara, or maybe Sara, is the sister of the poor wee one ye saw floatin' in th' pond. Exactly what I'm not clear about is *which* it wuz o' them golden cherubs who drowned. If one of 'em did. Maybe neither of them. *Porque, dentro de las posibilidades ilimitadas de la vida—"*

"Shit!" Tobias said.

"¡Mierda!" Angie agreed, cheerfully. "Read yer family history and let me do a little *serious* lappin' up o' the brew, will ye, please?

It was hard going. Cousin Ralph's epistolary style fell a good bit short of genius, Tobias decided. And one of the troubles about reading letters addressed to someone else, even when that someone else was your father, is that they are often full of references that assume a shared experience, even a knowledge of events held in common, that the present, illegitimately reading reader, simply does not have.

But as far as Tobias could make out, his father's first-and-a-half cousin had been something of a crook.

"More'n somewhat," Angie supplied, reading Tobias' mind, as usual. "Iver livin' thing th' blighter touched turned to money, which he then blithely made off with. Reason they had to leave South Carolina—or have ye got that far—?"

"Yes," Tobias said. "But I thought it was because little Sara got drowned. There's a whole letter about her being lost for three or four days, then there must be at least two letters missing. And part of the next. Because the one that comes next is numbered page three in the corner and it says:

" 'And when we came back from the funeral, I had my mind made up. Edna, I says, we're getting out of here!' "

"Does he say *whose* funeral?" Angie asked.

"No," Tobias said.

"Ah!" Angie said.

"What do you mean, 'Ah!'?" Tobias said.

"Told ye more'n oncet that the Auld Cuss upstairs is a mite daft, didn't I? Sometimes He—well just don't get His sequences right, Toby, me boy. All right, Time, in the sense ye humans think of it, jist doesn't exist; but happenings *do*—and they usually have sequence: a beginning, a middle, and an end, ye could put it. Maybe they don't happen when, where 'n how, ye think they do; but generally they have rhythm, pattern, form. All art is, anyhow, th' attempt to impose form on formlessness, being on nonbeing, permanency upon impermanence, as it were . . ."

"Go on," Tobias said.

"But this particular one is way out, Toby, me boy. Niver could get it straight, meself. I'll wager ye that in none of th' remaining letters does Ralphie mention little Sara or the funeral o' th' bit about her being lost. Always it's me daughter this o' me daughter that, or me girl—even after he'd moved the family to East Egypt, Kentucky, and bought his chiselin' way into the coal mining business, in which he, by paying them poor divils—their lungs rottin' away from the coal dust 'n the damp, their limbs broken from the explosions, pinned helpless under tons o' rock 'n dirt two miles under ground—even less than the other coal barons did, caused the biggest, longest, bloodiest strike in Kentucky's history. Always he says 'me girl—' "

"Or my girls. See. Right here on page five of this one," Tobias said.

"Jehosephat!" Angie said. "Ye're right, me boy. So now *ye* tell me: Jist who *was* that stinkin poor li'l lump o' corruption floating in that pond?"

"Don't know," Tobias said. "Angie—they've got an awful lot of money, haven't they?"

"Yes, Toby, me boy, me boy—that they have."

"Is *that* why you want me to marry one of the twins?"

" 'N keep t'other as yer mistress on the side, if she be among the livin'," Angie said. "No, Toby lad. Ye ever see anybody what the mere possession o' the world's tawdry goods made happy?"

"Then why do you?" Tobias said.

"Th' last time I wuz allowed a peek inside their weird little female minds, I wuz impressed with one delightful fact: Their daydreams were all of a healthy lewd 'n carnal nature. They—or she—if only one of them survived—will likely grow, I mean—*have* likely grown up into that rare 'n gallant breed of women who fornicate for fornication's own foine 'n pleasant sake. Than which there is no greater treasure . . ."

"Angie, you really don't know if both of 'em are alive?"

"Ye've read those clinkin' letters. Do *ye?"*

"No," Tobias said. "Lot of 'em make no sense—especially the later ones."

"Ye iver heard of a Tobit who *wasn't* daft—at least somewhat?" Angie said. "Now tell me something, Toby, me boy, me boy—if ye wuz to git yer paws on a bit o' th' coin of the realm, what would ye do?"

"Buy this place back. Work it. Hard as the weather is up here, I could make a go of it, I'm sure of that. Farming's a hard life—but it's—it's close to the heart of things, Angie. I sometimes think it's the *only* decent way of making a living that there is—"

"There ye may have a wee bit o' something, me boy, me boy. Now drink up. Put some lead in yer pencil not t' mention iron in yer so-called soul. Got to prepare ye for yer battle with th' fair Nell."

Then, throwing back his head, Rafael, the Angel, sang in a fine husky, whisky tenor:

"Nellie, Nellie
Had a raisin in her belly:
'N when she plucked it out
There to her wond'ring doubt,
She saw a golden screw
(Unlike the likes o' me or you)

Where her belly button ought to be!
'N struck with Cu - ree - os - i - tee
She went 'n got a spanner
From her auld man's greasy panner
'N gave that golden screw
A healthy twist o' two—
Now she's a sorrowful lass
For off dropped her bonnie ass
The moment that Golden Screw
With th' slightest twist or two
Came free. . . .
So Lad, you can see
That Nellie, Nellie
With a raisin in her belly
Was by far a happier lass,
For now, bereft of ass
She is so sad 'n blue
'Cause she can't even screw
Not even with a spanner
From her auld man's greasy panner;
Poor Nellie, Nellie
Without a raisin in her bellllleeeee!"

"Oh, for crissake's shut your trap, will you!" Tobias said.

"It's shut," Angie said. "But ye will tell me, won't you, Toby, me boy, me boy—"

"Tell you what, you drunken sot?"

"Whether she's got one fer a fact . . ."

"Whether she's got *what?*" Tobias said.

"A raisin in her belly. Or a golden screw. For, judging from all th' other attributes of femininity she ain't got, I'd say . . ."

Tobias picked up a lump of coal and threw it at Angie as hard as he could. But Angie wasn't there anymore. Only his laughter was, cackling among the flames of the furnace.

"*Now* I've done it!" Tobias wailed. Then he called out softly, tentatively, almost whispering:

"Angie— Angie——"

Then crying, really crying, whimpering the name like a child, "Angie! Angie! Come back! I—I need you! You know I'm not right in the head. You know it, Angie! I'll get into some Lord-awful mess so fast it'll make your head swim, without you along to tell me what to do! Angie, for the love of God, I—"

But only the silence answered him.

And the fire in the furnace, maybe, making a noise curiously like laughter.

Angel's laughter. Or—Devil's. Yin and Yang. Who knew? And what difference did it make, anyhow?

Wearily, poor, befuddled Tobias Tobit turned and climbed back up the basement stairs.

Two

"What kept you so long, Tobias?" Nell Brightwell said. "Those French girls, I'll bet. Everybody says they're awf'ly fresh!"

Supper was over. They were sitting on the front porch of the Brightwells' house, and Tobias Tobit was shivering. Which proved how out of condition he was, for any other native Rylander would have considered that April night in 1922 positively balmy.

The minute he thought that, he stiffened and waited for Angie's voice to come jeering through his mind: "Nineteen hundred twenty-two years after *what?* The birth of Jesus? That, me lad, is a laugh! Them rum old sods called Essenes, who wuz always a washin' the hide right off their own bones, made him up. Got sick'n tired o' waitin' 'round for their 'Teacher of Righteousness' to put in an appearance and bash the bloody Romans more than somewhat. So they——"

But Angie's voice didn't come. The silence inside the enormous darkness of Tobias' mind whimpered. Roared. Echoed.

"I said," Nell said, again, "that I'll bet it was those mademoiselles who—"

Tobias looked at her, sorrowfully. Only *she* thought it tenderly. "The female o' th' species," Angie often said, "has got th' damnedest habit of mistaking plain male horniness for love—whatever *that* be. So ye can't tell 'em th' truth, Toby me boy, me boy, which is 'I'd love to git into yer lacy step-ins, darlin' '—Yer gotta say: 'I love you.' Make a body sick to his guts it does!"

"You know me better than that, Nell," Tobias said.

"Yes, I suppose I do," Nell said. Then she looked at him archly, out of the corner of one smoke-grey eye. "Aren't you—aren't you even going to—try to kiss me, Tobias!" she said.

So Tobias kissed her. Only by then he'd been trained by more than one hardened member of the world's oldest profession who'd found his innocence intriguing. And corrupting it, delightful. He kissed Nell Brightwell a long time, and very thoroughly. When he quit it finally, Nell was gasping like a beached and gaffed codfish. "Looks like one, too, come to think of it," Angie said.

"Well I never!" she got out.

"You never what, Nell darling?" Tobias said. Or rather he *didn't* say it. He just sat there, helplessly, and let Angie's words pour out of his mouth; the voice, rhythm, tone, inflections, all perfect imitations of his own. "You don't know what you've been missing, then. Ought to try it, sometime. *Now,* for instance."

"Try *what?"* Nell Brightwell said.

"Fucking," Tobias said. Or rather Angie said it, using poor Tobias as a ventriloquist's dummy, as usual.

Wait. This was nineteen twenty-two, remember, as men reckon nonexistent time. And *nobody* said that word to a decent woman. The majority of men would have thought twice before saying it to a whore. To make matters worse, Tobias had never said it out loud in his whole life, not even to Angie, though there had been times he had been powerfully tempted to tell Angie to apply the action suggested by that ancient epithet to himself—and in some painful, contorted, and unsanitary fashion, at that.

But maybe Tobias had been corrupted a little by then by some of the activities Angie had led him into, carefully getting him drunk enough first, so that his rock-ribbed New England conscience would be too sodden and bemused to lift a hand. Or maybe all the past and future lives Angie had forced him to almost remember—including the really dreadful one when he'd been chief eunuch guarding the harem of Suleiman, the Magnificent, and all the bored, perfumed, overstuffed beauties therein used to torment him by kissing and playing with him lasciviously—had confused him more than he already was.

To make matters worse, if worse were possible, he hadn't the slightest desire to engage in what Angie called "Th' Gran 'n Glorious Sport of Fer Unlawful Carnal Knowledging," with Nell, for Angie's description of her was cruelly accurate. She did look rather like a codfish—if you can imagine a codfish with buckteeth and bleached seaweed on its head.

"Neither fore nor aft is she enticin'," Angie groaned. "That is, if ye can distinguish her fore from her aft."

None of which saved Tobias Tobit from the inevitable. Nell Brightwell slapped him and ran sobbing back into the house.

Confused as he was, Tobias was not too confused to remember that

Chief Brightwell was a man of uncertain temper who both carried, and was licensed to use, a gun. So he got up from there, went down the front porch steps, opened the gate, and loped out into the street.

As soon as he did, he saw Angie coming up the street leading his homunculus by the hand. It was the damnedest sight, for the six-foot four-inch tall, blond blue-eyed allegedly Cuban, *soi-disant* Angel had to bend over more than double to gently offer the one huge finger that the eight-and-a-half-inch tall mannikin was grasping by both hands.

Then in one of those maddening, jarring shatterings of sequence Angie was capable of, Tobias was holding on to the whisky and tobacco-stained finger bigger than a telephone pole and was progressing by jerks and bounds through an overwhelmingly enormous and menancing world in which the blades of grass sprouting from the cracks of the sidewalks were crueler than swords, taller than spears.

Tobias gritted his teeth. Concentrated. Thought:

"I am *not* an eight-and-one-half-inch tall homunculus of myself. I am Tobias Tobit, five foot eleven, capable of knocking this fake Angel right back on his ass. I am me, dammit, me!"

And reached, stretched skyward, towered, became himself again.

"Ye're progressin' Toby, me boy, me boy!" Angie said.

"You bastard!" Tobias said.

Angie cocked a merry blue eye at him.

"Thought we'd agreed I wuz a product of Immaculate Conception," he said. "But let it go. Ye'll thank me fer that one day. Yer immortal soul was in danger back there. Or yer mortal balls. O' both."

Tobias stood there. As his convalescence progressed, he was becoming increasingly capable of longer and longer periods of concentration, of reasonable clarity of thought. He asked himself:

"Would I *like* being married to Nell, really? Or even bedding her on a quickie, one night stand?"

"Negative," Angie said. "To both questions, Toby. A mite daft ye may be; but a fool ye ain't. In fact, fools *niver* go daft. To lose yer blinkin' mind, ye've got to have one in the first place. Now, c'mon—"

"C'mon where?" Tobias said.

"Kentucky, natch. Where else? Got to git ye reasonably settled down 'n comfy in *this* life, so's I kin have meself a breathin' spell now'n ag'in. And for *that,* li'l Sara—or is it Clara?—will do quite nicely, thankee Ma'am!"

"Or both," Tobias said with one of those flashes of pure mischief that he was getting the hang of now, that came easier to him all the time.

"Or both," Angie agreed solemnly. "If both there be. That's the damnedest thing! Can't make that part out. Blessed if I can!"

"You're an Angel, remember," Tobias mocked him. "Try. Concentrate. Figure out which one it'll be. That is, if it can't be both . . ."

"Ye mistake th' very nature of Angels, me boy," Angie said. Saying that, his voice sounded sad.

"Do I?" Tobias said. They were walking by then, towards the outskirts of the township.

"Yes, ye do. We're the most predestinated beings in the whole, clinking, ding danged universe. Th' point is, Toby, me boy, me boy —that we're th' Auld Cuss's creatures, sparks from His mind as it were, so He don't hafta worry about being fair to *us.* We're practically robots, ye ken. He tells us to do this, and we do it. Fetch that, and we fetch it. Watch'n guard a poor, shell-shocked, addlepated son of a Tobit—and here I be, stuck with th' likes of ye. Hell, I'm purely a slave!"

"You damned sure don't act like one," Tobias said.

"Oh, all us Angels is in revolt ag'in Him. Fat lot o' good it does us, though. He's held back just enough omnipotence and omniscience to rock us right back on our sweet angelic gluteus maximus anytime th' notion strikes Him. Hell, we don't bother Him none a'tall. It's ye humans what have got Him buffaloed—"

"How?" Tobias said.

"Lots o' ways. Ye see, when Night 'n Chaos give birth to *Him* they forgot—or weren't able—to give Him control over Random Chance 'n the Absurdity Factor. That's what really fucks things up, th' Absurdity Factor. . . ."

"And what is the Absurdity Factor?" Tobias said.

"Life," Angie said. "Now c'mon."

They went down the road until they came to the roadhouse. That took them a long time, because the roadhouse wasn't near Ryland Township. In fact, it wasn't near anything. Its location was determined by its isolation, so that respectable gentlemen from New York City, Boston, Hartford, and all the larger cities in between could drive out for a one night bender—"really lap up th' brew" as Angie put it—with no fear of running into their neighbors. Because in sequential progression, which even Angie accepted, in 1922 public morality in the United States of America hadn't yet slipped very far. By 1928, the roadhouse's business would be greatly diminished, for, by then, respectable gentlemen, their wives, sons, and flapper daughters, no longer had any compunction against getting blind, stinking drunk in a speakeasy, two blocks from home.

Even so, the owner and sole proprietor, Dino Martinelli, hedging his bets, or maybe only trying to make enough money to pay off his paisanos in the protection racket and allow himself a modest profit to boot, had introduced another method of prying the suckers loose from their cash: He had a flock of teen-aged, subdeb tarts whose mission it was to get the customers to lose their inhibitions more quickly, and drink up—buying the girls drinks in the bargain. Dino didn't call them B-girls; the name hadn't been invented yet. But he did give himself credit for inventing the profession. He was wrong. The profession was almost as old as the world's oldest, of which it was, in fact, a branch; the only difference being that if the girls played it right, they could separate the suckers from their folding green stuff without even having to go to bed with them.

"An' Dino makes sure they plays it right by givin' 'em only green tea when they orders whisky 'n plain water o' soda pop when they orders gin," Angie explained. "That 'ere nach'l son o' forty generations o' Sicilian brigands thinks he invented that dodge, too. But he didn't. To give ye but one example: The fillies on 'Frisco's Barbary Coast pulled the same one on th' gold miners during the Gold Rush. 'N Cleopatra got ol' Baldy Bean Julie smashed—after he'd unrolled her outa that rug, while drinkin' nothin' but colored water, herself."

"But, Angie," Tobias protested, "what are we going to use for money?"

"This," Angie said, and pulled a roll out of his pants pocket that actually would have, in the classic phrase of the day, choked a horse.

"Now—Angie—" Tobias said.

"Come by it honest," Angie said. "Found meself th' oldest perpetual floatin' crap game in these parts 'n horned in. 'Twas a breeze. Only trouble was that after I'd rolled twinty-siven sivens in a row, a large 'n unsavory character pulled a heater on me'n asked to see the dice. Which even *he* could see *wuzn't* loaded, when with a sweet angelic smile I passed 'em over to him. So he sez, sez he: 'Give me some skin, fella! See if some of the luck won't rub off on me'—'n shook me by the hand, so help me. After that I let him 'n two or three other Neanderthals win some o' their money back. Prudence, ye ken?"

"That," Tobias said grimly, "was rotten of you. You hadn't ought to go and use miracles like *that.* You dirty 'em!"

"Toby, me boy, me boy—a miracle is, by its very nature, a dirty trick. Interferin' with nature's laws for yer own ends is cheatin'; whoever 'n however. Even the Auld Cuss knows that. Besides, 'tis thinkin' I am that yer education's sadly wantin'. Th' blessed saints thimselves did worse. Did ye ne'er read yer hagiography, now?"

"Don't believe you," Tobias said.

"And don't ye, now? Take Saint Thelma of Egypt who served forty years in a cathouse, a-pleasurin' twinty customers nightly in any fashion they asked for, to git th' wherewithal to build a cloister for her order, the Barefoot Sisters o' Charity—'n she's among th' elect, I tell ye."

"The elect of what?" Tobias said. "The Bare-assed Sisters of Sin? Angie, you suppose they've got any *grub* in there? After the supper old Mrs. Brightwell served me, I'm so damned hungry I could eat a horse!"

"Which is precisely what Dino's steaks be carved from," Angie said. "Them as died o' old age, two years agone."

Inside the roadhouse, it was so dark that even the most pimply of the teen-aged tarts looked good. "Bet Nell could get by in here," Tobias thought, "if it ever occurred to her to try. . . ."

He also thought that Dino's handling of the situation was careless to the point of being foolhardy. In all the other roadhouses, taverns, speaks, blind pigs and/or tigers they'd been into on their way north, there'd been a peep window about six inches square and barred to boot, through which they looked you over before they let you in. Even then you had to say something like "Benny sent me," or some other such magic formula.

But at Dino's apparently, you just walked right in, sat your self down, and made yourself at home.

"Got the law bought, lock, stock 'n barrel," Angie supplied. "Feds who've been pukin' drunk in here twinty times, jist can't manage to find this place when their big shots send 'em out a-raidin'. Or, if they *do* find it, th' only bottled stuff on th' premises turns out to be milk. Pasteurized, at that. An' all th' li'l dillies is home that night takin' care o' their aged mithers. So relax. We won't end up in th' cooler, *this* time. . . ."

"What'll it be, gents?" the bartender said.

"Whativer variety o' panther's piss ye've got, Mike, me friend," Angie said, "so long as 'twas made at least day before yestiddy—aged in the wood, ye ken. Pink elephants 'n purple snakes I kin stand—but pink snakes a humpin' purple elephants—goin' at it hot'n heavy they wuz, I kin tell ye!—that's a sight too much. Ye wouldn't have some honest to God authentic *whisky,* would ye?"

The bartender leaned forward confidentially. Put the back of his hand alongside the corner of his mouth in a gesture that was a classic of its kind. "Means he's going to lie in his store-bought teeth," Tobias thought.

"Got a bottle o' prewar stuff," he whispered. "Real, blue-ribbon Scotch. Only 'tis scarce it is these days, stuff like this here, me friend. So this here Angel's Dew Drop'll cost ye . . ."

"How much?" Angie said.

"Wal now—how would fifty bucks strike you?" the bartender said.

"Done!" Angie said, and broke the bartender's heart, for he realized, tragically too late, that Angie would have gone to a century note or even beyond without even thinking twice.

They sat there at the bar and batted back the first ones. When that liquid dynamite hit, Tobias was sure his belly was going to dissolve. He looked at Angie out of tear-blinded eyes, wondering how Angie was going to handle this situation.

Angie showed him. He opened his mouth and let a whoooosh of

brilliant orange and yellow flame lance across the darkness. It looked like the fiery sword that God placed before the gateway to the Garden of Eden.

Then, groping into his hip pocket he came out with a .38 caliber police special, whose barrel had been sawed off to exactly one inch long.

The bartender turned as white as his apron. "Look, Mister," he quavered, "ye kin have yer money back! Iver red copper if only ye'll put up that gat 'n go quietly someplace else!"

"Why Mike, me boy," Angie grinned, "I ain't aiming to drill ye, Lord luv us each and ivery one! It's jist that I've always thought th' stuff that Dino sells would dissolve a gun barrel 'n now I mean to prove it. Bring me a bowl, will ye, like a good lad?"

The bartender brought the bowl. All the little dillies crawled out from under the tables where they'd thrown themselves when Angie had drawn the revolver, gathered around, wonderingly.

Angie poured the bowl full of the alleged Scotch whisky, caught the police special by the muzzle, and lowered it gently into the brew.

It dissolved.

The girls stared at that, goggle-eyed. Then they all began to laugh and clap their hands.

"Do another trick, Mister!" they pleaded.

"They think it's sleight o' hand," Tobias mused, "but it's not. He can do the absolutely damnedest things—and it's wrong. Sinful and wrong. If I could work miracles, I'd work 'em for the good of humanity, not just to make a bunch of junior grade whores laugh. But if I were to tell him that he'd only say: 'Ye've got yer sense o' values mixed up, Toby, me boy, me boy! Makin' wimmin laugh, be they *putas callejeras* o' no, is a rare 'n noble work!' "

"That I will," Angie said to the little dillies, "but ye'll all have to cooperate, me darlings. Fer th' life o' me I cannot work afore a hostile audience. So now, t' prove ye all love me dearly, ye've all got to take a sip from this self-same bowl. . . ."

"Whaaat!" all the girls shrieked.

"Tisn't p'izen, that I'll avow," Angie said. "Look!"

Grandly he raised the bowl to his lips and quaffed therefrom as though it were nectar and ambrosia.

"Improves th' taste, lad," Angie said to Tobias. "Try it, will ye?"

There was nothing to do but comply, so Tobias obediently sipped the liquid dynamite. To his not very great astonishment, knowing Angie as he did, with a .38 caliber police special dissolved in it, the brew tasted a hell of a lot better. And he also knew, somewhat sorrowfully, how it was going to taste to the girls. It was going to taste delicious. Each of them was going to swear that it tasted just like her favorite flavor, whatever that flavor was.

Tobias, with the instincts of forty-seven generations of dour Puritan ancestors glowering through his blood, sat there grimly and watched young faces reddening, eyes sparkling, teeth flashing in ever wider and sillier grins as they drank from that infernal bowl.

"Why, it—it tastes good!" a tall and lissome brunette said.

"Another of the same, Mike!" Angie said.

Grinning, Mike produced another bottle of the poison. Mike knew damned well that Dino didn't allow the little dillies to drink; but Dino wasn't here tonight. Nor was Mike permitted to lay one pinky on all that superabundance of female flesh, which frustrated him no end; but Dino wasn't here tonight. And maybe one o' two of th' li'l darlings might get drunk enough to fergit herself, and Dino wasn't here tonight. The situation, Mike decided, had its possibilities. Especially since Dino wasn't—

Tobias groaned aloud. He knew what Angie was up to. The only thing he didn't know was how his most unangelic Guardian Angel was going to go about it—this time. Angie was a creature of infinite variety.

"He doesn't exist!" Tobias told himself, fiercely. "I made him up. Or whatever's wrong with my head since that shell lit right next to me, did. Most of the time people can't even see him, or hear what he says or—"

Then he bent his head, and a tear stole from beneath one eyelid. Because he'd thought of the great number of people who *could* see, hear, touch, taste, and smell Angie.

"They—they're crazy, too!" he thought. "Just like me. Maybe my head sends out—waves. Just like a radio does. And—and crazy people—sick people—hurt, tormented people—like tramps and beggars —and bartenders—and gamblers—and whores—tune in to my waves. 'Cause they've got the kind of minds what—can. But did I ever know any normal decent respectable person who could see Angie? Nosireebobtail! Not one!"

Then the other side of it hit him: "How could a mind like mine invent a creature like Angie? It couldn't. I like things quiet and decent and orderly. I don't like getting drunk. I don't even like fucking—very much."

Then he straightened up and stared out into the smoky gloom of the roadhouse. "That's a lie," he told himself somberly. "You love it. You can't get enough of it. Only the way Mom brought you up makes you ashamed of loving it and—"

He bent his head and stared at the floor.

"Oh Lord, I'm so damn mixed up!" he wailed. The great tears gushed, poured from his eyes.

Then he felt the two soft, fat little arms wrap about his own. He could smell her before his eyes cleared and focused enough for him to see her. She was literally drenched in dime store perfume. And she was probably well enough washed. But, his nose told him, she was one of those plump little girls who smell sweaty, no matter what, so that perfumes and deodorants only make their natural aromas worse. "By denaturizing them," Tobias thought.

"Don't cry," she whispered.

He turned and looked at her. She was rosy and blonde and round. She hadn't an angle to her name. The curves were nice. Especially the two round softnesses she was pressing his arm against. Tobias liked the way they felt so much that he got a hard-on, which made him so furious with himself that he cried worse than ever.

"Don't cry," she begged, crying herself now, her tears making a mess of her mascara, and tracking two utterly adorable glistening black streaks down her round and rosy cheeks. "Not a beautiful, beautiful man like you!"

Now Tobias Tobit was as skinny as a rail fence, uglier than a backwoods shoat caught in a picket gate, inhibited as all get-out, timid to a painful degree—in short, he was a nice, average fellow of the type who go around mourning because, as everybody knows, it's the smooth, sonofabitching bastards who get all the girls.

"I'm not beautiful," he croaked. "*Men* can't be beautiful. Only girls are beautiful. Like you."

He hadn't meant to hand her a line. But accidentally he had hit upon the best possible line: sincerity. He meant it. She did look beautiful to him.

"Kiss me," she said.

As Tobias bent to comply, Angie's face came into focus. He was shaking his head warningly. That was surprising. Most of the time Angie was trying his damnedest to get Tobias mixed up with as many girls as possible, and now here he was trying to stop him from kissing as nice a collection of rounded delectabilities as Tobias had ever seen in all his born days.

Tobias stopped in midair. Hung there waiting. Then he heard Angie's voice inside his mind:

"Not this one. She's poison. Oh hell, maybe she's not poison. She isn't. She's a good enough kid, as whores go. But she's going to come to a bad end—soon. And ye'll blame yerself. So leave her be, will ye, Toby—please?"

"What kind of bad end?" Tobias thought.

"Don't know. Us Angels can't see th' termination of a sequence that clearly. Once we could, but we asked to be relieved o' it. Too bloody horrible, ye ken. 'Cause you see, me boy, me boy—it's th' gawddamnedest most awful feeling to know just how'n when'n where the Auld Cuss is gonna let something pukin' dreadful happen to some poor helpless human ye've got fond of 'n not be able to do a clinkin' ding danged thing about it . . ."

"Why can't you?" Tobias thought.

"The Laws of th' Universe is fixed," Angie whispered inside Tobias' mind. "Yer see, th' Auld Cuss is a Presbyterian. He believes in predestination. And what He believes in, goes. So don't kiss 'er. Don't screw her. Don't whatever with her. She's a lovable little hunk o' carnal sin—and you ain't up to lovin' 'n losing yet, Toby. Might crack you up. Or haven't ye had enough o' booby hatches by now?"

"Kiss me!" the plump little dilly shrilled, and dragged Tobias' face down to hers.

When she turned him loose finally, Tobias' head was reeling clockwise. Then it reversed the direction of its motion and started to reel counterclockwise. He put both hands on top of it and pressed down hard to keep it from flying off altogether.

"Leave 'er be, I tell you!" Angie's voice thundered inside Tobias' aching cranium.

"Oh fuck you, Angie!" Tobias thought defiantly.

"All right. On your head be it," Angie said.

Then the little blonde had dragged Tobias' head back down again, but this time she only wanted to whisper in his ear.

"Le's go upstairs, you'n me, Beautiful Man," she said. Then she added quickly: "For you, it's free."

Seeing her whispering, all the other girls started to laugh. Because the little fat blonde was the patsy of the whole establishment. She was always letting herself get laid for two excellent reasons: She wasn't smart enough to fend off the customers the way the other girls did, and she purely loved to screw, anyhow.

By then they were all three sheets to the wind *pro obra et gracia* of Dino's homemade poison, except the little blonde, who was four.

"Don't care!" she yelled at her sisters in sin. "He—he's just bootifool 'n, 'n I love him, so there!"

Then she turned back to Tobias, said: "What's your name, Beautiful Man?"

"Tobias," Tobias said. "What's yours?"

"Nancy," the fat little blonde said. "Now, c'mon!"

"No," Tobias said.

The fat little blonde stared at him. Her round, rosy mascara-smeared face started to break up. She looked as if he'd just slapped her. Hard.

"You—you don't even *like* me!" she wailed.

"Yes I do!" Tobias got out. "I like you very much, Nancy. Maybe I even love you. Only—let's wait awhile, shall we? They're all watching and—and—oh please, Nancy, in about a minute Angie'll do something to attract their attention; then we can sort of sneak out without their noticing and making fun of us. . . ."

"All right, Tobias—Toby! Who's Angie? Oh I know, that big blond fella. Don't like him. He's mean. Toby, darlin'—kiss me some more, huh? Please?"

Tobias was right. Angie was leaning towards the tall brunette.

"Art a devotée of Terpsichore, darlin'?" he purred.

"A devotée of whaaaat?" the tall brunette said.

"Terpsichore," Angie said. "Th' Muse o' the Dance. Bet ye can twirl a mean measure, th' spirit bein' right."

"Oh I can dance, all right. But what'll we dance *to?* There's no music. Not even a gramophone . . ."

"Not *we,"* Angie grinned. "You—all by yer lonesome. I'm goin' t' be th' orchestra—"

"All right," the tall brunette said. She was drunk enough to try anything by then. Anything notably including Angie, a fact of which that most unangelic of Angels was perfectly aware. "Only where you're going to get your instruments from, Maestro?"

"From here!" Angie said dramatically, and plucked a fiddle and a bow out of thin air.

All the little dillies squealed delightedly at that. Then Angie began to play. He was, Tobias decided at once, absolutely the greatest violinist in the history of the world. The music he drew from that fiddle was unearthly. Angelic. Maybe even—celestial.

Dreamily the tall brunette started to dance. Her dancing was—or became, under the witchery of Angie's music, beneath the spell of his drunken and profane miracle working—perfection's very self. Not even Pavlova at her best ever danced like that.

Then, winking at Tobias, Angie changed the beat. The music became Hungarian, Zingara, Andalusian Gypsy, whirling, stomping, pounding, wild. The tall girl rose to the occasion, whirling, pounding, stamping her feet, her mouth a wound of animal passion, her black hair loose and swirling about her head.

And then—and then——

Her clothes vanished.

She didn't even notice it at first. She went on whirling, stamping, waving her arms about, swirling her long black hair. Tobias stared at her. She was utterly beautiful. So beautiful that she didn't even awake lust in him. Then the other girls spoiled it. They began to point, to titter, to giggle, to explode into peals of silvery laughter.

And the tall girl realized she was naked.

She stopped dancing. Fell into that awkward and ugly posture of the famous statue attributed (wrongly, Angie assured Tobias) to Phidias, the Aphrodite Callipygia. ("Which means," Angie quite accurately assured Tobias, "Venus of the Gorgeous Ass.") That is, she crossed one arm across her breasts, and dropped one wide-spread hand to hide, not very successfully, the wild spiraling black triangle of her *mons veneris.*

The minute she did that, her clothes came back again.

Which made her posture even more absurd. The laughter of her colleagues in the world's second oldest profession split the roof.

And Nancy took advantage of the uproar to half drag poor Tobias up those stairs.

Seeing them go, Angie raised both hands and crossed the index and third fingers of each of them. At once, and completely, Tobias lost his hard-on. "Probably for good," he was dismally aware.

An hour later, Nancy was weeping the bitter tears of disappointment in Tobias' arms. She'd tried everything, including the most delicately expert and tender blow-job that Tobias had ever experienced; but nothing worked, nothing at all.

"You bastard!" Tobias screamed at Angie inside his mind.

And Angie, hearing that, changed his tactics. Tobias' male member sprang to attention in the damnedest, aching, hurtful, most terrific erection he'd had in all his life.

"Look!" he said to Nancy.

"Oh boy oh boy oh boy oh boy!" little Nancy said.

Then it was that Angie, Angel or not, made what even he afterwards admitted was "The gawddamnedest mistake I iver made since I convinced Eve that th' Snake wuz a foine fella fer a fact!"

His mistake was to fix things so that no matter what poor Tobias did with and to, poor Nancy, he wouldn't be able to come.

By which Angie proved that male Angels, like any other males, could be chauvinistic celestial porkers without even half trying. For sadly, fatefully, even, as it turned out, tragically, he forgot plump little Nancy's part in the proceedings altogether, forgot, even, how women generally work.

"Evolutionary dysfunction," he spat, explaining it later to Tobias. "When th' Auld Cuss created man, He plumb forgot all about the critter fer a hundred million years o' so. Last time He cocked an eye on yer ancestors they were swinging through the trees 'n screwin' from behind like any self respectin' quadruped. But th' next thing He knowed, yer greatgrandpappy, a million greats removed, of course, had lost most o' his fur, become a biped, and was goin' at it missionary style. Doesn't work—at least not properly. Misusing quadruped's genitalia in that fashion is sure to throw something off. In th' case of ye humans, it's th' female's timing. She got to be slower 'n old hell, and ye—out o' sheer nerves 'n frustration, got to be faster than iver . . ."

"I know," Tobias said sadly, thinking about all the occasions, which was most of them in fact—when out of nervousness, fear, faulty control, lack of experience, and, above all, youth, he had disappointed the living hell out of his bedmate by going off like a skyrocket before she'd even started to thaw out properly.

"Ejaculatio praecox," Angie supplied. "That's what it's called, by all yer solemn human scientific voyeurs. Mean to cure ye of it completely, if this particular sequence don't jam up on me. Fact is, I've got to, or ye'll go'n spoil things fer little Clara/Sara, quite. But so help me it niver occurred to me that by temporarily relieving ye of the problem I was going to compound the very confusion I was tryin' me damnedest to avoid. What a screwup! Now she loves ye! I'll be blessed 'n billybluedamned if she don't!"

By that segment of this sequence, they were both sitting on stools before the bar. The bar was untended. Mike was off somewhere with two of the little dillies, presumably taking advantage of Dino's absence. At this point they heard the wail of a police patrol car's siren and started to get out of there. But it wasn't a siren. It was Nancy. She came flying down the stairs, screaming like a hopped-up banshee and hurled herself upon Tobias so hard she knocked him flat, barstool and all.

"Thought you was gone, Toby!" she sobbed. "Thought you'd left me! An' I wanted to die!"

He looked at her. She'd got dressed, sort of. Which meant she'd slipped her black silk dress over her head with nothing under it. And she smelled like Saturday night at Susie's. He felt his stomach churning dismally. But she had a stranglehold on him and was babbling into his ear:

"Don't ever leave me, Toby! I—I'll kill myself, so help me! I love you love you love you love you, you understand? So you gotta stay or take me with you—or else I'll cut my throat from ear to ear 'n write down telling 'em to send you a hankie soaked in my blood t' remember me by!"

Tobias shuddered.

"I will I will I will!" Nancy moaned.

Then because he couldn't think of anything else to do, and *had* to shut her up, he bent and kissed her.

She pulled her mouth away from his, and smiled at him blissfully. "Take me back upstairs, Toby love," she said.

Three

When Tobias woke up that next morning, he found that he couldn't move. The reason he couldn't was that Nancy had succeeded in transforming herself into a really remarkable imitation of an octopus. At least that was what she felt like. She was wrapped around him in so many ways, and had a warm and loving grip on so many different portions of his anatomy, that breathing was as much as he could manage. Moving was out of the question.

"Get up from there Toby, lad," Angie's nauseous voice rasped through his mind.

He looked up and glared at the Angel. Then he looked at the door. It was still locked and barred. It still had the dresser pushed against it as an additional precaution against their being disturbed. The window was still down, the shutters were still drawn. But Angie stood there at the foot of the bed grinning at him.

"You don't exist!" Tobias thought at him. "I made you up!"

"Right," Angie purred telepathically, "I don't exist. You made me up. I'm but a figment o' yer distorted imagination. That being settled, will ye untwine yerself from a hundred 'n forty-six pounds o' used whore 'n come on?"

"No," Tobias said. "Look, Angie—I—I can't just sneak off and leave her like this. The poor kid, she—"

"Loves ye. I know. My fault. Niver occurred to me that when I crossed ye up that way, I wuz sure as old hell gonna convince th' li'l dillie that ye wuz th' world's greatest lover. But, believe me Toby, me boy, me boy, sneakin' off quietly without so much as wakin' her up is just about the most sensible thing ye can do—"

"Why?" Tobias said.

"Don't ye even remember what I told ye?"

"You said something awful is going to happen to her," Tobias said.

"Right," Angie said.

"But you don't know *what,*" Tobias said.

"Beyond th' fact that it's gonna be two hundred per cent fatal—no, three; ye're right: I don't know what that something awful's gonna be," Angie said.

"Three hundred per cent fatal?" Tobias said.

"Yes. Th' Auld Cuss upstairs has got a Pentagon type mind: He believes in overkill."

Tobias stared at Angie.

"But if I were to take her away from here—" he began, "maybe—"

"And maybe not," Angie said.

"But you don't know *where* it's going to happen," Tobias said hotly. Then he saw the vast pity in Angie's bloodshot blue eyes. "Or do you?" he said.

"Yes, Toby, lad, it so happens I do," Angie said.

"And where's that?" Tobias whispered.

"Anywhere she is," Angie said.

"Oh Lord, Angie! I can't let her die! I can't! She's so pretty and sweet and—"

"She screws with commendable enthusiasm. Which is a sin. A mortal sin. Fer which th' Auld Cuss ain't even startin' to fergive her. She wuz to not even like it, He'd make her a blessed saint 'n elevate her straight t' Glory."

"But *He* made her, didn't he?" Tobias protested. "Gave her—the —the temperament she's got and—and the inclinations and—"

"Th' nicely rounded, useful tail wherewith to accomplish what both temperament 'n inclinations drive her to. Not to mention that He knew what she was gonna do with herself before she wuz even a twinkle in her auld man's eye. 'N didn't stop her from doing it, 'cause as Saint Thomas sez, He's self-limitin', which means He hangs up His all-knowingness, 'n His total power long enough to grant ye poor humans freedom o' will, which works out to havin' th' freedom to get yerselves fried. Eternally, at that—"

Tobias shuddered. "You make Him sound *awful,"* he said.

"He's not though. Good enough Auld Cuss, as Auld Cusses go. Just a mite confused. As I said before, Random Chance 'n the Absurdity Factor have got him more 'n a bit perplexed . . ."

"Angie, you don't mean to stand there with your bare face hanging out and tell me that no matter where I took poor Nancy, it wouldn't make any difference?"

"Didn't say that. It would make a great deal o' difference,—to you."

"Oh!" Tobias said.

"Somebody wuz to write you tellin' you th' li'l Nance has got hers, you'd grieve somethin' awful. I grant you that. After all she *is* th' best piece o' tail you've had to date. But readin' about it 'n seein' it happen are two different things. Might even throw this sequence out o' kilter. So leave her here, will you? Just as she is, a sleepin' the sleep o' the generous 'n the good. 'Cause a couple o' *more* years in a straight jacket wouldn't do you a damn bit o' good 'n ye know it. . . ."

"What difference would they make?" Tobias said. "Aren't you always saying that there's no such thing as time?"

"There ain't. But, being only human, it feels to ye like there is 'n ye'd suffer jist as much. Now will ye quit arguing with me 'n come on?"

"No," Tobias said. "Not without Nancy."

"She'd be in the way. 'N she'd sure as hell throw Sara/Clara off her/their feed."

"Fuck Sara and/or Clara!" Tobias said.

"Exactly what I had in mind. Fer ye, at least. Look, Toby, it's no good. We're gonna hafta ride the rods ag'in, and—"

"Whaaaat!" Tobias exploded. "What th' ever loving hell did you do with all that money you had last night?"

"Well—" Angie said ruefully. "One o' the little dillies apparently rolled me. O' maybe 'twas Mike. Anyhow, they've all gone. Mike, too. 'N I've got the sum total o' thirty-five cents in me pockets."

"You clown!" Tobias said. "Calling yourself an Angel!"

"But I *am* an Angel, Toby, me boy, me boy. 'N Angels, lad, though we do be possessed o' powers not granted to ye humans, ain't omniscient nor omnipotent neither one. In fact, long as I'm stuck with this human-type carcass I hafta drag around because of ye, even me powers is severly limited. 'N iver blessed time I *do* something human—like humpin' them six o' seven little dillies last night—"

"That wasn't human," Tobias snorted, "that was—"

"Jist heavenly!" Angie grinned. "Only vice ye humans have that's worth a tinker's damn. But, as I wuz sayin' before I was so rudely interrupted—iver time I do something *really* human, like screwing, fer instance, me powers plumb desert me fer a while. So ridin' th' rods it is . . ."

"Oh Jesus!" Tobias said.

"Don't call on Him. Told ye more'n oncet He's only a figment o' the Essenes' diseased 'n disordered imaginations. Now git up from there, lad. We've a long way to go."

"Oh Lord!" Tobias said. "I hate hoboing, Angie! Always cold, always hungry, always dirty, tired, miserable. The railroad dicks batting the living hell out of us every time they catch us, which is four or five times a day. People setting dogs on us. And about once a week, maybe, some kindhearted lady will make us cut a whole carload of wood before she condescends to hand us out a can of watery soup!"

"Can't help it," Angie said. "We've got to git down t' ol' Kentucky, somehows. The whole damn' rest o' *this* sequence depends on it. 'N as I said before I got to git ye happily wedded 'n frequently bedded so's *I* kin have a mite o' liberty oncet in a while. . . ."

"That's a *time* concept," Tobias pointed out to him.

"No, it ain't. Only the terminology is. It's a sequential concept which ye've repeated th' Auld Cuss only knows how many times now. Th' last time wuz during the Assyrian captivity, which if ye'll reach me that Gideon Bible a lyin' there alongside o' yer bed o' carnal sin, I'll prove it to you."

"Reach it yourself," Tobias said.

Whereupon Angie did. While he was thumbing through the pages, Tobias looked at Nancy. She was still sleeping the sweet sleep of virtue lost, or innocence regained, or something. There had never been the slightest danger of his and Angie's long debate disturbing her, because although what they did *felt* to Tobias like talking, it actually wasn't. They communicated directly, mind-to-mind. (Or maybe one part of my mind to another, Tobias thought.) So no matter how they seemingly roared and yelled at each other, nothing so physical as sound was produced.

" 'Tain't here," Angie snorted. "This is a Protestant Bible. Ye wouldn't happen to have a copy of the Apocrypha, would ye?"

"What's not there?" Tobias said.

"The Book o' Tobit. Ye Protestants are too strict. It's an awful good read. Which reminds me: Don't let me ferget to catch a fish just before we gits to Kentucky. . . ."

"A fish?" Tobias said.

"Yes. Fish guts are good fer curin' blindness. Even th' kind caused by hot birdshit droppin' into yer eyes. That's how we cured yer auld man in *that* sequence, ye know. The Assyrian one."

"But Angie, my father is *dead!*"

"Oh hell! Told ye th' Auld Cuss was confused. This proves it! He don't even git his sequences right anymore. But all the same, we'll need the fish. To chase Asmodeus with, ye ken . . ."

"Asmo—whaaat?" Tobias said.

"Asmodeus. He's a demon. 'N he's causing li'l Clara—or is it Sara?—one hell of a lot o' trouble. Only since I got stuck with ye'n this carcass o' mine, I can't see clearly what that trouble is."

"You're a fraud," Tobias told him.

"No, I'm not. I'm an Angel. A sadly limited Angel, but still—an Angel. Now will ye, fer th' Auld Cuss's sake, unwrap all that female blubber from around ye'n git up from there?"

"I can't," Tobias wailed. "Can't you see I can't, Angie?"

"Hmmmm—" Angie said. "Okay. Papa'll fix. . . ."

Thereupon he goosed poor Nancy. Hard.

"Oh, Toby, love," Nancy murmured, "not again! I'm sooooh tired. . . ."

Angie considered that. Then he brought his big hand down, open-palmed, across Nancy's ample buttocks. They quivered under the impact. They went on quivering for several seconds. Tobias found the sight fascinating—which made him angry at himself. And thereby, by extension with Angie, who, very likely, was only a part of himself, anyhow.

"You hadn't ought to've gone and done that!" he began, when Nancy did a sudden double take and leaped from the bed. Then she saw Angie standing there grinning at her, and snatched the covers off the bed. Held them in front of her. They didn't do much good. There was an awful lot of Nancy.

"You—you peeping tom!" she screamed at Angie.

"Got me wrong, sugar," Angie said. "Ain't a peepin' tom—I'm purely a lookin' tom; that is when I ain't a humpin' tom. Hmmmm—maybe we'd better bring ye along, anyhow. That is, if Toby's willing to share . . ."

"Not on your life!" Tobias said.

"A c'mon, Toby, me boy, me boy! There's enough of her to go round, appears to me. 'N besides, I'm only a figment of yer diseased 'n disordered imagination, so what harm could I do her?"

"No you're not," Tobias said. *"She* can see you, too."

"Which only means *her* imagination is diseased 'n disordered, too. Responds to yer vibes."

"My what?"

"Vibes. Vibrations—as the hippies say. Oh hell, now *I'm* out o' sequence, ain't I? Hippies won't be until the 1960s or thereabouts, right?"

"How the hell would I know? Now get out of here and let me and Nancy get dressed."

"You—you're *queer,"* Nancy said suddenly. "I—I don't think you're even—human!"

"I'm not," Angie said. "I'm an Angel. Toby's Guardian Angel. Looks like I gotta take *you* under my protection, at least for a while. . . ."

"If you're an Angel," Nancy said, "where're your *wings?"*

"Daggone, that's right!" Tobias said. "Where *are* they, Angie?"

"Under me shoulder blades, hidden—'n all folded up. I kin sprout 'em anytime I take th' notion. Not even th' aroma those little dillies —I mean yer comrades-in-arms, babydoll—left on me can hinder that. *Essence des sardines,*—right baby?"

"Don't know what you're talkin' about," Nancy pouted.

She had the cutest damn way of pouting, Tobias decided.

"Prove it!" he said to Angie.

At once Angie was resplendent in snowy wings.

"Angie—" Tobias said. "You could *fly* us down to Kentucky. Me'n Nancy, both. With wings that big and powerful you could—"

"Sure it is that I could, laddybucks!" Angie said, preening to catch a glimpse of his magnificent wings. "Only you couldn't stand it. Ye nor th' little lady either one. Ye see, we Angels have to fly too high, now that ye humans have invented airplanes–ag'in (that makes at least ten thousand times ye've invented th' noisy, frail, suicidal things by now)—orders from the Celestial Control Tower: We're *not* to be seen. Ye'd freeze. Or die discombobulated by th' lack of oxygen . . ."

"I don't believe you!" Tobias said. "Give us a demonstration!"

"Toby, me boy, me boy," Angie chuckled, "ye're purely asking for it now!"

Then the roof blew off the roadhouse. Dissolved, disappeared. And Tobias and Nancy were sitting on Angie's back between his mighty wings. There was no danger of their falling off, because Angie's back was twelve to fifteen miles wide at the waist, its narrowest part. Where they were, it was even wider still.

Angie's great wings swept from horizon to horizon, beating slowly, powerfully. Ice crystals swirled back from them, making iridescent contrails, pluming against the night-black sky. Looking back, Tobias could see them trailing behind through light-years of empty immensity, aeons of nonexistent time.

He heard a sudden, curiously human sound. Looking down, he saw the cause of it: Nancy's none too white, not especially regular teeth were chattering in her mouth between lips turned a heavenly blue.

"Oh, Toby, I'm sooohhhh damn cold!" she wailed.

She had reason to be. Angie hadn't given either of them time to get dressed, so they were both mother-naked—which sure as hell was no way to ride an Angel's back through the fringes of outer space.

Then Angie began to—to sing, say. That's not right; but say it anyhow. And the way he sang made them forget how cold they were. It was an eerie, keening sound, lifting, soaring, as though all the still-to-be-invented electronic synthesizers there would ever be in the whole of nonexistent time were being played by heavenly fingers, their music pouring through all the black holes in space, which Tobias realized suddenly, were the time warps, Angie had told him about in which even sequential progression was twisted around the curves of spiral space, where, as Einstein had demonstrated, parallel lines do meet.

Then the sound was coming from everywhere, too loud for even Angie's immense lungs (Do Angels *have* lungs? Tobias wondered) to manage. And turning his head on his neck to positions and angles of view he had never been able to accomplish before, Tobias saw wings all around them, above, and below, beating horizon to horizon across the midnight sky.

Nancy clung to him, shuddering. "Oh, Toby—how *awful* they are!" she cried.

They were. Their eyes ranged from turquoise to bloody red, and were two miles across at the pupils. Their immense, singing mouths could have swallowed the world. Rainbow-colored contails swirled back from their immense, slow beating wings, trailing pure celestial glory across the Universe to out beyond where the last dwarf star dimmed out into the endless dark.

"Who are they?" Tobias thought in the general direction of Angie's immense, curly blond head.

"Th' Auld Cuss's personal guard," Angie thought back, "the Angels of the Presence. Me comrades-in-arms, 'cause I'm one, too. Them there twins are Michael 'n Gabriel, the morning 'n the evening stars—an' that's Suriel, prince over us all. 'N that's Uriel, his brother. 'N th' big fella's Metatron. 'N that's Sandalfon—smell how good he smells? Thrillin' ain't it? And that one down there is Domah, Angel of th' Winds; 'n his sidekick, Yurqami, Prince of Hail; 'n the other one way down there stirring up whitecaps is Rahad, Lord of the Sea—and that—one—that she Angel—nice tits 'n tail she's got—is Laila, Princess of Conception. Got in there once but th' Auld Cuss threw all the cherubim and seraphim we made the hell Down Below, and—oh brother! Now we're gonna have some fun! Ye ever see an aerial dogfight in that there fuss you wuz in? Heck 'twuz the war they invented dogfightin' in wasn't it?"

"Yes," Tobias said. "Spads 'n Fokkers. It was awful. They didn't have any parachutes like we did in World War Two—fat lot of good they did us most of the time—"

"Ye're remembering *forward,* Toby lad," Angie warned him. "Bad habit. Keep it up 'n ye'll git so good at it that ye'll *know* what's gonna happen next. 'N being human, ye couldn't stand that. Now hang on to th' li'l dillie, for here we go!"

Then looking down, Tobias saw them, an immense host of black-winged Angels, beating up from below, trailing contrails of orange flame and sooty smoke behind them. He had no trouble recognizing their leader, because that grime-black and soot-caked Angel had horns on his head, cloven hooves, a pitchfork in his hands, and his wings were bat wings of billowing leather with their bony skeleton frame showing through.

"Ho Mal'akim!" Angie was roaring. "Look alive! Here come the Hosts of Hell!"

"Mal'akim means Angels in ancient Hebrew," he explained. "Ye better hang onto th' li'l dilly, 'cause we're gonna hafta dogfight 'em.

"Rnrnrhrr roarrrr—zooommmm—screech! Rat tat tat rat tat tat tat tat tat! Oh brother I got one! Look at 'im! Goin' down in flames!"

Tobias saw then, to his vast astonishment, that one of Hell's Angels was a woman. Her eyes were slanted, three miles tall, and leaped with crimson flames. Fangs protruded from a pair of the most lusciously sensual lips he'd ever seen. A slinky black robe clung to all fifty or sixty miles of her, and trailed blacker blackness across the midnight sky.

"That's Lilith, the night-flyin' demon. She belongs to old Nick. But I fraternize with her iver chance I get. That's how he got those horns. An' every dogfight we have he zooms 'n power dives straight fer me. 'Course I always down him, but he's so goddamned stubborn—"

"Look out!" Tobias thought screamingly.

"Hang on, kids, I gotta do an Immelmann turn o' he's got me! Here we go! RRRRRRRPR Roar RRRRRR! Zoooooommmmmm! EEEEEEEEEEEE! Rat a tat tat! Rat a tat a tat a tat! Damn! I missed him! The tracers th' supply depot's handin' out these days ain't worth—"

But they weren't there. They couldn't be. Angie's broad back bore not the slightest resemblance to the cockpit of a Spad. They had neither seats nor seat belts. And an Immelmann turn consists of a half-loop straight up, that you snap roll out of at the top so that you find yourself at a much greater altitude going in the opposite direction, presumably having left the Red Baron's crimson Fokker Dreidekker somewhere far below.

But Nancy and Tobias were falling like newborn souls from heaven, trailing pearly mists of glory behind them as they came. They could see the Earth beneath them now. It looked like a blue marble, with feathery white splotches moving across it. Somehow or another, they weren't afraid. It all seemed remote, somehow. Even dying did. Even the certain knowledge that they were going to splatter all over like—

"Ohhhh, Toby darlin'! That was heavenly!" Nancy said.

Tobias opened his eyes. They were back in the roadhouse, back in bed. The roof was safely in place. And they were—or had been—For Unlawful Carnal Knowledging again.

"You took me up to heaven!" Nancy breathed. "I saw all the Angels! I did—I swear I did! And—"

"Time's up, kiddies," Angie said. "That there's th' last quickie fer a while. We gotta git movin' now—"

"So—" Tobias croaked. "You—you changed your mind, Angie? We, we're taking her with us?"

"Yes—though th' Auld Cuss singe me pin feathers fer being a sweet angelic idiot—we are," Angie said. "Now fer the Essenes' dreamboy's sake—o' which iver other solemn nonsense ye believe in at th' moment, Toby lad, will ye'n yer *putita gordita* please c'mon?"

Four

Tobias Tobit looked up at the sky. He didn't have to look far. Where they were by then he could almost reach up and touch it. It was a sullen, lead grey color and it was getting closer all the time. He couldn't even see the peaks of the mountains any more. Even the tops of the pine trees were swallowed up by the clouds.

"Going to rain," Tobias said.

"Oh Lord, not again!" Nancy wailed.

"It holds off fer another hour," Angie said. "I'll git us to a place where we kin hole up, snug as a bug in a rug. Less than that, ye kids clap spurs to Shank's mare . . ."

"Then what are we waiting for?" Nancy said. "C'mon!"

Angie stopped dead. Stared at her. Sighed.

"Now that I come t' think o' it, no I can't," he said sadly. "Hafta dream up somethin' else. . . ."

"But you just said you could!" Nancy flared. "I heard you! Didn't he, Toby?"

"Yes," Tobias said uncertainly, "he did." Then he thought at Angie: "Why not, Angie—because of her?"

"Yes," Angie answered, "because of her. Ye see, lad, it's a hobo jungle. Biggest one in these parts. 'N th' roughest. Half them bums down there is wanted by th' law. No, three quarters. 'N th' li'l Nance is a real toothsome bundle of carnal sin fer a fact. 'N—"

"And what?" Tobias said, or rather thought.

"I grant ye that gittin' raped ain't all that awful fer a healthy lass. But bein' rough humped by three or four hundred bums *is*. 'Twould do in a woman grown, 'n Nance, fer all that baby blubber, is a delicate li'l thing, right?"

"Right," Tobias thought. "But we could protect her, you and me, Angie! Especially if you pulled one of your stunts, they were to start something."

"Ain't no ifs about it," Angie said. "They'd start somethin' all right. Hoboes are always hard up fer a little free tail. But we couldn't depend on me bein' able to pull a fast one, Toby, me boy. Maybe I could 'n maybe I couldn't. It all depends—"

"Depends on what?" Tobias thought.

"*Her* sequence. It's running out on her, lad. 'N toward th' end of any human's sequence, his or her inevitabilities git to be even more inevitable than usual. In that case, I could rear back 'n throw in a miracle 'n it wouldn't even go off. Th' Auld Cuss upstairs would wet it down afore it could even blow—"

"But if we stay here, she'll catch pneumonia!" Tobias said.

"I know. 'N maybe that's what's intended fer her—though I don't think so. I keep gittin' glimpses into her sequence—and that ain't the way she's gonna go . . ."

"What're you doing?" Nancy complained. "Standing there staring at each other like that 'stead of finding a barn or something we could hide in before the rain—"

"Thinking," Tobias told her. "We're thinking about what to do . . ."

"I got it!" Angie said. "Look Toby, me boy, me boy—there's two trails through those hills. The one goin' down is the easier; but it leads straight towards that hobo camp. But th' other don't. The trouble with it is it goes up fer a while before it goes down, which is why folks seldom take it. Harder 'n longer, ye ken. But it ends up at a railroad siding, where there'll be some nice dry packin' cases we kin crawl into. So now c'mon!"

"I would have thought," Tobias said, while they were walking, "that the hoboes would have put their camp somewhere near the railroad siding instead of—"

"They would have, too," Angie said, "if so many of 'em wasn't wanted men. So they hid this here jungle real smart like, down in a gorge. But fer all that, it ain't too far from th' tracks. The trail it's closer to leads to the sidin' too, just like this one does. Only it's newer. Folks got tired o' all this climbing 'n cut it through 'bout six, seven o' your alleged years ago. Shorter. Easier. So this one is mostly abandoned, except for moonshiners 'n hunters 'n folks with some good reason for not wantin' to be seen. . . ."

"I'm tired!" Nancy said. "Oh Lord, Toby, I'm so tired! And this road doesn't go *anywhere* except straight up, maybe, and—"

"C'mon," Tobias said, "I'll carry you piggyback for awhile. Because we can't stop, Nancy. We can't. We'll get soaked to the skin!"

"I'm too heavy," Nancy said. "I'll wear you out."

"Then Angie can spell me for a while. You'll do it, won't you, Angie?"

"Right. Now quit jawing 'n c'mon," the Angel said.

It was hard going. Even if Angie hadn't already told him so, Tobias would have been able to see for himself that the higher trail was seldom used. It was thickly overgrown in places; rocky as old hell in others. And it went up and up and up as though it were trying to lead them to the back door of Heaven.

They took turns letting Nancy ride them piggyback; and she even walked for long stretches, because the way the terrible labor of lugging her up that mountain trail made them pant and gasp for breath finally got her ashamed of herself.

And still, miraculously, the rain held off. The clouds were just as dark, equally as menacing, but not a drop fell. At one point, at the very top of the trail, the sun even broke through. They saw, suddenly, by its rays, a good-sized town nestling in a mountain valley, with a couple of good gravel roads circling around it, and smaller ones leading into it.

"Oh!" Nancy said.

But Angie shook his head.

"Can't go there, Nance," he said. "Those folks is purely rough on hoboes, which, like it or not, we be. 'N neither Toby nor me is up to working on a chain gang. So—"

"Oh damn it all! Especially *you,* Angie!" Nancy said.

They got to that railroad siding just as the great splattering drops began to come down, largely, Tobias was sure, because Angie had willed it so. And there were those packing crates, ready and waiting—probably because Angie had willed them into being, too.

Tobias and Nancy dived into one of the crates together, Angie into another. And the rain came down. In sheets. It rained cats and dogs, frogs and snakes, and nakedniggerbabies, maybe. The packing crates kept some of the rain off them, but not much.

"Kiss me," Tobias said to Nancy.

"No," Nancy said.

"Why not?" Tobias said.

"Don't feel like it," Nancy said. "Look Tobias Tobit! I never run off with you to starve to death! And freeze! And—and drown!"

"Come cuddle up with me," Tobias crooned. "I'll keep you warm, love. . . ."

"Don't call me love!" Nancy flared. Then a look of moronic craft, idiot's cunning stole into her little blue eyes.

"Toby—" she said. "What was the name of that town Angie made us circle all th' way around a little while back?"

"Damned if I know," Tobias said. "Why, Nance? We couldn't have stopped there. We haven't a red cent in our jeans—and folks in places like that don't take kindly to tramps. Not even to pretty little girl tramps in boy's clothes."

"Big town," Nancy mused. "Folks got money there, haven't they?"

"I suppose they have," Tobias said. "Fat lot of good their money will do us, though."

Nancy thought about that. But Tobias couldn't read *her* mind. His telepathic powers were confined to communicating with Angie. That was just as well. What little Nancy was thinking at the moment would have outraged him to the bottom of his puritanical soul.

"Kiss me, Toby," she said.

"Lord, how you do change!" Tobias said. "A minute ago you said—"

"That was a minute ago," Nancy said. "Kiss me, lover!"

Tobias obliged.

"Mmmmmm," Nancy purred. "Nice! Toby—"

"Yes?"

"Help me outa my things. My pants, anyhow."

"Nancy!" Tobias said. "Angie's not a yard away in th' other box and—"

"No he ain't. I just looked. First he was, but when he saw me looking, he turned into smoke and blew away. . . ."

Tobias stared at Nancy. That was one of the things that troubled him about her: She reacted to Angie exactly as he did. What was worse, she took all the inexplicable things that the Angel did as perfectly normal, as a matter of course.

"Nancy," he said now, "sometimes I think that Angie isn't—isn't anybody. That he doesn't exist. That I—I made him up—he's a figment of my imagination, maybe. You know I had a piece of shell casing inside my head, and even after they took it out, I—"

"But *I* never did," Nancy said. "And I see him, too. And all the girls at Dino's did. And Mike—"

"How about those people in Baltimore?" Tobias said. "The time he won some money in a poker game and we got cleaned up and went into that flossy restaurant to eat. He *told* you not to talk to him. He told you! And to only order dinner for two, with extra helpings. But you would have it your way. And, inside of three minutes the headwaiter was saying: 'Mister, you better take th' li'l lady home. We don't want no trouble with th' law. You hadn't oughta give her so much to drink on an empty stummick!' "

"He was a fool," Nancy said serenely. "There! I got 'em off. Toby, love—"

"You're *sure* he isn't there?" Tobias whispered nervously.

"Sure, I'm sure. But poke your head out. See for yourself," Nancy said.

Tobias pushed his head out of the box. She was right: Rafael, the Angel, alias Angie, was nowhere to be seen.

"Now kiss me," Nancy said. "And—and play with me—a little. To get me ready. But only a little. Don't need much. I'm almost ready now. . . ."

Tobias obliged. An hour later, he was begging for mercy.

"Nance, for God's sake!" he gasped.

"No," she said, "I'm not satisfied yet, Toby love. Bad business, leaving me unsatisfied. I just might crawl into Angie's box tomorrow night and—"

"Oh damn you, wench! C'mon!" Tobias said.

Nancy lay there curled up beside him, gauging the quality of his breathing. "Like a dead man!" she murmured to herself, and giggled wickedly. "What poor weak creatures men are anyhow! Just can't keep it up. While wimmen now—at least a real female woman like me can do it all night and all the next day and all the next night and—"

She poked her head out of the box. The rain was over. The clouds had blown away. The stars were out. Still giggling, Nancy dug into her pack. She brought out her black net stockings, her black silk and lace peek-a-boo panties, her matching bra, and put them on. Slipped her black silk whore's parlor dress over her head. Applied a lopsided smear of lipstick to her mouth. Ran a comb through her silken blonde hair. And was ready. Then she glanced down at her high-heeled shoes.

"No," she thought. "Ruin 'em sure long before—"

So she sat back down, pulled them off, put on her rubber-soled tennis sneakers instead. Wrapped her good shoes in a piece of newspaper; tucked them up under one arm with her handbag.

That done, dear, sweet Nancy started out for town.

Tobias Tobit crawled out of the packing box. He ached all over, inside and out. But his insides ached worse. He had a desolation in him. A fetid swamp of abominations in his gut. He didn't know why this was, but he didn't like it. He didn't like it at all. Then he screwed up his sleep-blinded eyes until the physical world snapped back into focus, and saw Angie sitting on a fallen tree trunk about ten feet away from him. Angie was smoking a fragrant Habana "puro" and staring off into space.

Tobias lurched over to where the Angel sat. "Angie—" he croaked.

Angie turned. Looked at him. Said: "Go lie back down, Toby lad. Try to sleep some more."

"Angie!" Tobias screamed.

Angie shrugged his massive shoulders. Sighed.

"Told ye not to drag her along, Toby, me boy," he said gently. "But ye wouldn't listen. Ah well, ye humans always be slaves to yer dangling gut. Do as I tell ye, lad. Go lie back—"

"No!" Tobias said. "Where is she, Angie? Don't tell me she—she's—oh no, Angie, don't tell me that!"

"Nor will I," Angie said, "cause she ain't. At least not yit. But *her* sequence is running out. Very fast, now. Tonight. Tomorrow—who knows?"

"Oh Jesus!" Tobias said.

"Toby," Angie said, "promise me something."

"What?" Tobias said.

"That ye'll forgive her. When she comes back, I mean. Take her in yer arms 'n say real sweetlike, 'It don't matter, Nance. I love ye.' "

Tobias stared at him.

"And just what will I be forgiving her *for?"* he said.

"Humanity. Mortality. Both. But that ain't th' important part."

"Then what *is* the important part?" Tobias said.

"Ye'll be fergivin' yerself at th' same time. Anticipatin' a little, maybe. Putting yerself in—well—call it a state o' grace, where self-fergiveness is reasonably possible. All Down Below is, anyhow, th' condition o' knowin' what ye've done is unpardonable. Th' Auld Cuss don't hafta lay it on ye, nor even turn ye over to His twin brother Satan. That's where all yer theologians are way off. They never realized that externally imposed torments only arouse bitter resentments ag'in th' tormentor. But when 'tis yer own beak that tears yer liver—th' sight o' yer own reflection that turns ye to stone, yer own hands that smash them jeweled brooches into yer glimmers—"

"That's mythology," Tobias said. "Greek, at that—"

"What religion ain't? Th' only advantage th' Greeks had is that they managed t' invent all the better symbols. But myths one 'n all. Compendiums o' the dreams 'n racial/tribal memories o' th' naked ape. Walls built around his littleness 'n his fears. Props fer his feeble pride. A toenail-hold on dignity. Only ye've always gone at it wrong. Instead o' admitting to yerselves that ye were designed from the outset to end up in a worm's gut, and making of yer little lives yer firefly flash betwixt two eternal darks—somethin' o' value, ye hedge. Invent gods, devils, imps—"

"And Angels," Tobias snapped.

"And Angels. Jist as ye've invented me. But we elude ye, we figments of yer imagination. Ye've no control over us. Because we oughta set things straight fer ye, and we don't. We can't. Ye invent a lovin' merciful Father and a five year drought comes along 'n half a continent dies o' thirst 'n hunger. Ye think up terms like honor, peace, 'n justice—'n respectable businessmen put in competitive bids fer the contracts to build gas chambers in which to exterminate an entire race. Yer best brains can't git together on the problem o' curin' a simple disease like cancer; but in a two year sequence they come up with a city-bustin' bomb. Ye've built a whole civilization o' gimcrackery 'n fraud, totally wantin' in moral values, 'n yit, even now, when ye're on th' brink o' drowning in yer own *mierda,* being crushed under the debris o' a mechanical civilization dedicated to th' production o' expensively useless junk, ye *still* chant:

" 'But He hath made me but a little lower than the Angels/And hath crowned me with glory 'n honor!'

" Hell, a worm's gut is too good fer th' likes o' ye!"

"Angie," Tobias said, "you're—strange. I've never seen you in this kind of a mood before—"

"I know. Usually I keep 'em to meself, Toby lad. But this sequence is gittin' th' hell out of control. Ye go at this wrong 'n it'll take me a couple o' million more of yer sequences to git yer inevitabilities back in workin' order. All I'm sayin' Toby, me boy, me boy is that no matter what little Nance has done 'tis part of *her* sequence, out o' the pattern of *her* inevitabilities, 'n if ye let damn fool *human* notions like male possessiveness 'n rutdog sexual jealousy make ye do somethin' ye can't quite fergive yerself fer, ye'll be tossin yer life to th' wolves—o' t' be exact, surrendering it to Random Chance 'n the Absurdity Factor—than which there is no worst fate. . . ."

Tobias stared at the Angel.

"Angie—" he got out, "you saying that *I*—that *I'm* going to—to kill her? You saying *that,* Angie?"

Angie bowed his head. Looked up again.

"I don't know, Toby lad," he whispered. "I just plain don't know. Maybe ye were right. Maybe I've been misusin' me powers. But I can't see how this here sequence is goin' to come out. An' I don't know whether to be sorry o' to be glad . . ."

Then he saw or felt how still Tobias was. And looking down he saw Nancy coming up the hill.

Long before she was even close, Tobias had stopped breathing. And when she *was* close, his big gut pulled apart. A scream tore his middle bloodily. It hurt like hell, all the more so because he didn't let it out.

She was a mess. Her mouth was bruised and swollen. There were blue teeth marks on her throat. Her hair was tangled, sweat-sodden. Her dress was torn. And she smelled like a two-bits-a-tumble crib girl after a busy Saturday night.

She looked at him. And the brave, bright smile she had been

wearing vanished. Her bruised mouth turned sullen. Her round fat baby face took on a narrow-eyed, mean, and hateful look.

"Whatcha looking at me that a way for, Toby?" she said.

Tobias didn't answer her. He couldn't.

"So all right!" she shrilled. "Just what you're thinking! A gal gets tired of being hungry and cold and miserable all the time! 'Sides—" and her voice changed, became an utterly obscene, ingratiating whine, "I only did it for *you,* Toby love! See! I brought every cent I made home to you! So nows we can eat in restaurants and ride on pullman cars and sleep in hotels and take hot baths and—"

He hung there, staring at her.

She fumbled in her handbag. Brought out a huge roll of crumpled dollar bills. Some fives. Even a ten or two.

"Toby me boy, me boy," Angie said warningly.

It did no good. All his dour Puritan ancestors, witch burners, ducking-stool operators, pinners-on of scarlet letters, implacable chastizers of *Female* sin, poured bile and gall into his aching gut. This was *his* woman (slave, chattel, witless bestower of exclusively-by-him-owned nightly pleasures) and she damned well had not right to go around selling or giving to other men what was his, goddamn her, his!

"You little bitch!" he whispered, achingly, and hit her, open-palmed, across the mouth. Her lips broke like ripe plums, dying her baby-girl's chin a shocking scarlet. But instead of inspiring pity in him, the sight drove him wilder still. He swarmed all over poor Nancy with both hands and both feet.

She screamed like a stuck pig at hog killing time. He hammered her to the ground, knelt with both knees pressing into the small of her back, caught her by her bobbed blonde hair and ground her face into the dirt.

"Sup your filth, whore!" he grated.

"That's damned well enough, Toby," Angie said.

Tobias got to his feet. Stood there. He was shaking all over. Then his eyes cleared. He saw Nancy lying on the ground. Her face was a mess. A dirty bloody mess. She was crying and vomiting at the same time. The sight wasn't pretty. It wasn't pretty at all.

"Nance . . ." Tobias whispered, "Nance . . ."

She went right on crying and throwing up.

He knelt beside her. He was crying, too, now.

"Nance, I . . . I'm sorry," he got out, "only you got me crazy doing that. Oh Lord, Nance, can't you understand? When a man loves a girl the way I love you he . . ."

But Nancy was scrambling to her feet. She faced him. Opened her broken, bleeding, vomit-frothed mouth.

"Loony!" she shrilled. "You belong in the asylum! And I'm leaving here right now!"

She turned then, and began to gather up all the greenbacks that were scattered all over the ground. With grave courtesy Angie helped her. When she had them all, she crammed them into her handbag.

"Nancy . . ." Tobias said imploringly.

"Nancy nothing!" she said. "Ain't staying with no crazy man! I'm going back to Dino's. It was nice, there—fun. While you . . ."

"Nance!" Tobias wept.

"You can't even fuck worth a damn!" sweet Nancy yelled, and started down the hill.

Tobias started after her. But Angie caught his arm.

"Let her go, Toby lad," he said.

Tobias hung there.

"You've done your part," Angie said sadly, "asked her pardon, meaning it. So now ye're free o' blood guilt. . . ."

"*Blood* guilt?" Tobias croaked.

"Yes. 'Cause she ain't going back to Dino's. She ain't going anywheres. This is the end o' the line fer her, poor kid. I'd got fond o' her, damn me fer a jackass! As well I know it never makes sense, gettin' fond o' humans . . ."

"Angie . . ." Tobias whispered, "you know what she's done? She's taken the *left* fork of the trail!"

"Yes," Angie said. "She *had* to."

"But, Angie, that way she'll run right smack dab into that hobo jungle you made us go two miles out of the way to circle round! Said those fellows were bad guys. Fugitives from the law most of them. Wanted men. Killers, even, some of them!"

"That's right," Angie said.

"Good Lord, Angie! We've got to stop her!"

"We can't," Angie said.

"To hell with that noise!" Tobias said. "Those bums catch her they'll . . ."

"I know," Angie said.

"Angie!" Tobias screamed.

" 'Th' movin' finger writes, 'n havin' writ,' " Angie quoted solemnly, " 'moves on. Nor all yer piety nor wit, kin lure it back to cancel half a line, nor all yer tears wash out a word o' it!' "

"Fitzgerald," Tobias said automatically. "Or Omar; or both." Then it hit him. "Angie!" he moaned. "You're saying that——"

"There's nothing we can do? Exactly that, me boy. Told ye that us Angels asked th' Auld Cuss to take away our power o' seein' th' future, by which I mean foreknowledge o' how a sequence is going to work out. Too bloody awful. What's th' good o' knowin' what ye can't help, change, or stop?"

"But Angie, there must be *some* way!"

"No, there ain't. Sequential patterns are fixed. Life has got its inevitability built in."

Desperation sharpened Tobias' wits.

"Can't we sort of invoke Random Chance?" he said. "Or the Absurdity Factor? You said yourself that they had *Him* mixed up!"

"I did, but only because they foul up moral responsibility when they don't negate it altogether. They don't stop a person's inevitabilities. Can't nothing or nobody do that, Toby. Not even th' Auld Cuss Himself."

"I'm going after her, Angie! And you can't stop me!"

"I know. Wish I could though. It's gonna be pukin' dreadful, Toby lad."

"Oh, fuck you, Angie!" Tobias said, and hurled himself up that trail.

Long before he got there, he could hear Nancy screaming. And the way she screamed was unbearable. And unbelievable. She sounded as if she were being tortured to death.

"She *is,*" Angie said inside Tobias' mind. "The buggers are goin' at her two at a time. Hurts like hell, that sodomizin' business—when ye ain't used to it. An' poor Nancy ain't."

"Oh God, Angie! Please!"

The screams stopped abruptly, in a choked off, strangling sound.

"Now they're goin' at her *three* at the time," Angie said and materialized out of the morning mists. "That's the limit. After all, a woman ain't got but three useful orifices, Toby lad. A pity."

"A pity!" Tobias screamed.

"Yes. She had four, they'd kill her that much faster'n she'd suffer one quarter less. Only sure thing in the Universe, me boy, aside from Random Chance and th' Absurdity Factor, is mathematics. Toby, don't s'pose I kin persuade ye not to interferr, seem' as how interferrin' is only goin' to git th' shit beat out o' the two of us, and ain't goin' to do the poor lass no good at all?"

"I'm going to save her!" Tobias shrieked. "I don't need you, you goddamned fake! You really were an Angel, you'd pass a miracle and . . ."

"I mean to. I'm going to. But fat lot of good it's gonna do poor Nance," Angie said.

By that time they'd reached a place where they could look down into the hobo jungle. A huge tramp was standing to one side. He had a club in one hand and a glass jar in the other. The 'boes were lined up. Three abreast, and, as they got to where he was, they dropped two dimes and a nickel, or five nickels, or a quarter, or even twenty-five pennies into the jar. For that was what the big tramp was asking, after having claimed, and made use of, poor Nancy as his own, from the outset.

"He's th' king," Angie explained. "Roughest, meanest old sod ye ever did see. Rest of th' buggers is plain scairt o' him. They're right. Fastest hand with a shiv I ever run acrosst . . ."

But Tobias didn't answer him. He couldn't. While Angie had been talking, he had seen what the three hoboes whose turn it was were simultaneously doing to poor Nancy. So now he was sitting down on a rock with his head between his knees and was puking his guts up.

He looked up with streaming eyes.

"Angie!" he wept. "Oh, Angie, please!"

"Oh all right," Angie said sadly. "Here goes!" He stretched his big hands towards heaven. Muttered something in Hebrew. And the rain came down in sheets. In torrents.

The 'boes didn't even look up. In seconds they were soaked to the skin, but even that had no visible effect upon them.

"Try something else," Tobias moaned.

"Her inevitabilities are locked in their final groove, Toby, me boy," Angie said sadly, "but since ye insist . . ."

He raised his hands again. Muttered something else. Thunder crashed, deafeningly. And jagged spears of lightning hurled down the sky. They slammed into the hoboes' camp. They set tents and packing crates afire. Smashed rocks to powder. But not one singed a hobo's hair or beard.

"You aren't aiming right!" Tobias yelled. "Change your elevation, Angie! It's point zero oh four and three decimals, damn it! What th' hell kind of an artilleryman are you, anyhow?"

"I know what the range be, Toby lad," Angie said. "But th' Auld Cuss is spoilin' me aim. Him or Ol' Nick, maybe. Or th' two of 'em together. They're mostly the same entity, anyhow. Age'n essence cojoined. Well, here goes another salvo—"

The lightning flashed and flickered the day. Started rock slides, avalanches. Blasted the hobo jungle into oblivion and beyond. But it didn't touch a man. They stayed right where they were, moving up, three at a time, to take their turns at Nancy.

Then Tobias went crazy. Crazier than he already was, anyhow. He got up and started running down that trail, straight into the hoboes' wrecked camp.

Angie raised sorrowing blue eyes to heaven. Said a prayer. Looked down to see that the hoboes already had Tobias down and surrounded, and were kicking in his ribs.

"So be it," the Angel whispered, and started down to save his charge.

Tobias opened his eyes. He hurt. He hurt all over, inside and out. His mouth was full of blood. His vision was blurry, largely because both his eyes were rapidly swelling themselves shut. His nose was broken. Three ribs. He'd lost two teeth. He was sure he was dying, but then it came to him that for him to hurt *that* much, he couldn't be.

He screwed his swollen, blackened eyes into focus. Saw Angie sitting a little way off. The Angel was almost as much of a mess as he.

"Fine Angel you are!" he thought. It was a good thing he didn't have to talk, because he really couldn't have managed it.

"I done me best, Toby lad," Angie said sadly, "but as I told ye, 'tis beyond our powers to interferr with a human's inevitabilities. Hell, I doubt that th' Auld Cuss ken do that Himself, once a sequence has been set in motion—"

Which reminded Tobias what the whole thing had been about from the outset.

"Nancy!" he got out. "Oh, Angie, don't tell me—"

"Yes. She's gone, poor li'l thing. Didn't last halfway through the lot of 'em. That's what the trouble is about now."

Tobias raised himself half up. Saw that the 'boes had their king ringed round about, and were trying to pull him down.

"Poor divil," Angie said. "Th' first 'n only decent impulse he's had in all his life 'n now he's gonna die of it—"

"Impulse?" Tobias got out. *"Decent* impulse? *Him?"*

"Yes. He objected to them makin' use o' poor Nancy's slaughtered carcass. Every man's got his limits—'n that's his. Rape, sodomy and fellatio, didn't faze him, but necrophilia seems to him a mite too much. He's right. It is. Only he was too ruddy late discoverin' he had at least one principle to his name."

"Angie—" Toby whispered, "couldn't you—save him?"

"Don't know. Ye mean ye *want* me t' save th' bastid?"

"Yes. Don't know why. It—it's all *his* fault, isn't it? Still—a man with a principle, even one, isn't—isn't hopeless. Will you—try?"

"Natch!" Angie said. "Toby, me boy, me boy, ye're a-gettin' there—"

"Getting where?" Tobias said.

"To—or at least towards—a state o' Grace. And—oh hell!—we're too late. They just cracked his skull for him. Poor divil!"

"Angie!" Tobias screamed. "Don't let—don't let them do—*that* to poor little Nancy! Not now! Not since she's dead!"

"Right," Angie said. "Now since her inevitability's terminated, I kin really fix their wagons!"

He put the sun out. Blackened the day. Hurled down rain, hail, sleet, lightning, meteors, thunderbolts. Stirred up an earthquake. It was awe-inspiring. Grand.

But raising himself up, Tobias saw the 'boes running like rats down the trail, away from the wrecked camp. "Why, you didn't get even one of them!" he said.

"Couldn't. Th' Auld Cuss has got much worse in mind for th' buggers. 'Vengeance is mine!' says th' Lord. '*I* will repay!' Now just ye lie there real quiet-like, while I attend to poor Nance. Give her decent burial. All I kin do now—"

"No!" Tobias said. "I'm coming with you! Owe her—that much—anyhow. To—to kiss her good-bye. Say a prayer over her. Seeing as how I was too weak and too cowardly to save her from those bums, I—"

"Ye," Angie said quietly, "had nothin' t' do with that. If ye've just got to fix the blame—another Simon-pure absurdity in a Universe o' Random Chance, governed by the Absurdity Factor—blame it on th' Auld Cuss. Or on His brother Satan. His Siamese twin brother, Satan—"

"Now, Angie—" Tobias said.

" 'Tis a fact. They're joined hip 'n thigh. 'N each of 'em partakes o' th' other's nature. Th' Auld Cuss loves goodness 'n has got absolutely no patience with sinners, which means He's got th' essentially cruel temperament o' all Puritans. 'N Auld Nick is just th' opposite—he loves evil 'n has got no patience with good folks. On th' whole, *I* tend to side with Auld Nick. . . ."

"Good Lord, Angie—why?"

" 'Cause sinners are mostly good, 'n good folks is mostly bad. Sinners are warm, weak, lovin', 'n human. 'N good folks—officially good anyhow—are usually hard, cold, unlovin', 'n unforgivin'. And—"

"Angie—you said they didn't exist. Neither God nor Satan. That we made 'em up."

" 'N hence, they exist. Thoughts exist, don't they? Dreams? Imagination? Art? Only things that do, maybe. Ye've made up the Auld Cuss 'n there He *is.* Ye've made *me* up, 'n here I *am.* Ye needed an excuse to account for the fact that snafuin' the works is humanity's *normal* mode o' procedure 'n there's Auld Nick, horns, pitchfork, cloven hooves, batwings 'n all—"

"But we never made him up as being *joined* to God. Siamese twins! Lord God, Angie—"

"No. That's *my* contribution t' yer cosmology. To give it a little symmetry, ye ken? A mite o' logic. Since *nothin'* in yer long history o' plagues, crimes, mass murders, abysmal bestiality, cities fire bombed, atomized, helpless babes 'wasted,' people whose noses ye don't like gassed, others whose camouflage job displeases ye lynched, liberal leaders 'n politicians assassinated—gives the slightest indication o' an intelligent guidin' hand, I give ye a cosmology that *works.* Only one that iver did, unless ye want to go back to th' Greeks . . ."

"The Greeks?" Tobias said.

"Yes. Theirs made sense too. A host of warring, randy, petty, spiteful human-type gods. Auld Zeus a-screwin' iver human female whose knees he could pry apart. Bad-tempered cuss like Mars. Aphrodite, sanctifyin' adultery. Hera, female jealousy 'n cussedness. Pallas Athena deifyin' ice-cold, narrow-minded intellect, 'n that frozen-tailed bitch Artemis slaughterin' iver poor beastie what got in her way. Just loved to kill, she did. 'Twas she'n her brother, that pretty boy god, Apollo, who 'wasted' the children o' Niobe, remember? 'N—"

"And they made *sense,* Angie?" Tobias said.

"Yes. Screwed-up gods for a fucked-up world. Since th' randy Olympian cusses was always opposin' each other 'n fightin' on opposite sides, it made sense that *nothin'* could ever go right, didn't it? So now ye take this: Th' Auld Cuss 'n his brother, Auld Nick, are twins. Siamese twins, at that. So, iver so often, when th' Auld Cuss —who really ain't right bright—gits so mad at Auld Nick that He fergits they be joined hip 'n thigh—hurls him outa heavin—He has to go with 'im. Stands to reason, don't it? So more'n half th' time th' Universe is bein' ruled from Hell. Then th' Auld Cuss gits tired o' the heat 'n the screams o' the Damned, maybe, fryin' forever in their own grease—now *that's* a nice kindly, lovin' concept, ain't it? Wonder whoever thought *that* one up?—'n He ups 'n drags Auld Nick back up to Heaven. So natcherly th' Universe *stays* royally screwed both fore'n aft, like poor Nance. Which reminds me: I better git on with buryin' her, or she'll be too stiff to unbend. . . ."

"Oh damn you, Angie!" Tobias said. "You're always sidetracking me with your chatter! Help me up, I've got to . . ."

"No," Angie said, "just ye lie back 'n conserve yer strength, Toby lad. Do ye absolutely no good to gaze at that poor slaughtered hunk o' female meat. Might even drive ye batty again—"

"Help me up, goddamnit!" Tobias yelled.

"All right," Angie said sadly, "on yer own head be it. I warn ye, the sight ain't pretty, Toby me boy, it ain't pretty at all."

Tobias lurched, staggered, tottered over to where Nancy lay. Stood there looking down at her. She was drawn up in fetal position, with here and there a rag of the clothing they had ripped off her clinging to her bluish-white, greenish-white, stone-cold and rigid flesh, her eyes wide open, blank and mindless as blue glass, thick clotted blood mixed with the greyish white of semen trailing out of her from two natural apertures not meant to be so used, and from the one that—at least somewhat more gently—was, and the whole of her, face, arms, legs, trunk, frozen into a silence shrill enough to break through heaven's floor and drag down God.

He stood there looking at her until a shaking got into him. He shivered and shook like a spastic. His belly, his throat, his mouth filled up with a vileness, but his teeth locked together and he couldn't let it out. He was choking on it, strangling on it, but he couldn't get his mouth open. There was a noise inside his head. It sounded like the howling of a pariah dog. The noise grew and grew, a wild, sobbing ululation, slamming slivers of broken whisky bottles into his ears so real it made them bleed. He turned mad, streaming eyes towards Angie's face.

The Angel put up one hand bigger than half of Heaven and plucked the sun out of the sky. Sighing, he put it in his pants' pocket.

"Give up, Toby lad. Die a little," he said.

Five

Tobias Tobit opened his eyes. Blinked them rapidly several times to make them work properly. Saw that he was in a room he had never seen before, in a bed of a type that was only too dismally familiar to him because he had spent the majority of his days and nights, during that segment of his personal sequential progression which, despite all Angie had taught him to the contrary, he persisted in thinking of as lying between September 1918 and April 1922, in one just like it. An articulated bed whose springs and mattress could be cranked up to various angles above the horizontal, each more miserably uncomfortable than the last.

Which meant he was in a hospital—again. Then he realized that his whole chest was encased in a plaster cast. And that he was itching in about five hundred different places at once, none of which would he be able to scratch before they drove him slowly and excruciatingly out of his mind.

His head was bandaged, and a huge, unwieldy hunk of plaster had been moulded round his nose in a way cunningly devised to hurt, itch, make his eyes run water, give him a terrific yen to sneeze, and effectively prevent him from doing so, all at the same time.

A rubber tube had been attached to that part of him poor Nancy had found—temporarily, anyhow—so comforting, and golden droplets of urine dropped sullenly down it to come to rest in a grossly distended bag of rubber that clearly was going to burst any second now.

And, as if to make his joy complete, his homunculus, all eight and a half inches of him, was sitting on the white-stockinged knee of a red-haired nurse as pretty as all get out (the nurse, not his homunculus) and grinning at him brazenly. (His homunculus, not the nurse.)

"Get out of here, you little bastard!" Tobias screamed at him.

"Why, Mister Tobit!" the red-haired nurse said.

"Wasn't talking to you, miss," Tobias mumbled; "I was talking to *him.*" And to make his meaning entirely clear, he pointed a shaky finger at her rounded, dimpled, gorgeous knee.

"Why, you poor boy!" the red-haired nurse crooned. "You're

delirious, aren't you? Just you wait a minute, and I'll fix you right up!"

Then she scampered from the room with such a delightful swish and sway that the only reason Tobias didn't get a hard-on was because all that tubing attached to him wouldn't let him.

Then he saw Angie sitting in the same chair the nurse had got up out of. Apparently the celestial sinner had been sitting there all the time. With the red-haired nurse on top of him, maybe. Or—

"Oh damn you!" Tobias said.

"Dee-licious!" Angie said. "Dee-lightful! Dee-lectable! And a few other adjectives what don't come readily to mind. Only she *thinks* that she's a normal, strait-laced li'l she-human, which she ain't, really! By that I mean, Toby lad, she's normal enough for what she *is,* but what she *is,* me sensitivities tell me, is somethin' other than human, a helluva lot *better* in fact. But because she honestly *believes* she's human, 'stead of whatever kind o' exotic creature—from outer space likely—she really is, she sorta, kinda tunes out the music o' th' spheres. So she don't perceive, sense, apprehend, o' even feel me. While—"

"You bastard," Tobias said.

The nurse came back with a glass of water. Deftly she poured some powder into it.

"Now drink this, dearie," she said, "it'll make you feel real good, I promise you."

Tobias took the glass. Sipped it. It tasted like hell.

"What's your name, nurse?" he said.

"Baxter," the nurse said, "Anne Baxter."

"I love you, Anne," Tobias said. Or rather Angie said it, speaking through Tobias' mouth.

"That's mighty sweet of you, Mister Tobit," Anne Baxter said frostily. "Now just you take your medicine like a good boy. It will stop you raving—I hope."

Then, having got that one off her nicely rounded, delectably doubly uplifted little chest, she sat right back down on top of Angie.

"Nice tits, eh, Toby lad?" Angie communicated.

Tobias didn't answer him. He was too busy trying to figure out how two bodies could occupy the same space at the same time. Old

Prof. Wiltz, who had taught him physics at the Ryland Agricultural and Mechanical College (from which august institution Tobias Tobit had graduated cum laude at just that point in his own sequential progression, or the World's quite illusionary time, to get sucked into World War I) had repeatedly, and with great conviction, declared that particular feat to be ut-ter-ly IM-possible!

"Well, he wuz wrong, th' lame-brained old coot," Angie said now. "In the first place, space don't exist. 'Tis but another figment of ye poor human creatures' diseased 'n distorted imaginations. Or, to put it another way, space, time, 'n motion are all part of the same illusion. I could prove that to ye, but I'd have to teach ye Einstein's Second Law o' Relativity, 'n that would take too long. Use yer eyes, lad! I'm sittin' in this chair, ain't I? 'N this deelightful 'n deelicious li'l piece o' tail is sittin' in this chair, ain't she? Ye'll grant me that, won't ye?"

"Yes," Tobias said, or rather thought.

"So ordinarily, her marvelously warm 'n soft little arse ought to be raised above the chair by my thickness, with me longitudinarous subtracted from me thickness since she's rightly built to accommodate me longitudinarous anyhow. But since space, motion, 'n time are only human mental and/or imaginary concepts, it don't work out that way. She don't perceive me, so I ain't here. Now all I gotta do is convince her that a little charity toward the hungry, I mean th' horny, is rightly a good'n pious work . . ."

"How are you going to do that?" Tobias hooted. "Since you can't even convince her that you're *there,* there isn't much else you can convince her of, is there, Angie?"

"No," Angie said sadly. Then he brightened. "But she does perceive ye," he said, "so 'twixt th' two of us, we ought to be able to have a spot o' fun. Let's practice a li'l telepathy on her, combined with a wee bit o' kinetic parapsychology, say . . ."

"Kinetic *what?"* Tobias said.

"Oh, skip it. Th' term won't even be invented 'til ye'll be too auld 'n worn out fer it to do ye much good. Now jist ye start imaginin' that ye're kissin' her. Imagine it real *hard.* 'N go on from there—takin' yer time so as not to git her alarmed. Say ye're thinkin' how 'twould feel to brush by these here li'l rosebuds she's got pokin' yer eyes out fer a fact, with a careless strayin' finger—"

Nurse Anne Baxter's bonny brown eyes opened very wide.

"While I'm convincing her that she *likes* it, which ain't hard. Bein' a healthy young female she *does,* fer all that she's been taught to th' contrary. C'mon, Toby, me boy, me boy. Got yer lecherous 'n lascivious paw on her knee haven't ye? Now jist let it stray about forty-five o' fifty centimeters higher—gently now. . . ."

Nurse Anne Baxter exploded upward out of that chair.

"What's the matter, Nurse?" Tobias croaked.

She glared at him furiously. Then she became aware that he was still lying flat on his back, still hugely encased in plaster, still a full two yards away from where she stood. The furious glare faded from her eyes. Momentarily they went blank. Then they almost crossed as she tried to peer inward into her own weird little mind.

"I—I'm going crazy!" she whispered. "Bad wicked crazy. Deee-praved! And—"

"Nursie-pie," Angie's letter-perfect imitation of Tobias' voice purred through the badly injured New Englander's battered mouth, far clearer than Tobias himself possibly could have managed at the moment, "why don't you build up my morale a little? With a harmless sort of exhibition, say? A nice slow striptease, Anne, darling?"

"A what?" Nurse Baxter said. She sounded dazed, Tobias decided. Which made him decide something else: that at this juncture, it was considerably smarter, as well as promising to be a hell of a lot more fun, to keep his mouth shut and let Angie do all the talking.

"A striptease," Angie said. "The term's new, Anne, darling. I just invented it. It means to take off your garments one by one to the time of music. Don't you worry about the music, dearie. *I'll* provide it. How's this, for instance?"

Then from nowhere a string orchestra began to play a dreamy waltz. And even more dreamily, Anne Baxter began to move in perfect time. Her fingers strayed upward to the topmost button of her uniform, stayed there a tiny aeon, a little age, loosened it. Moved down to the next. The next—until Nurse Baxter stood there in her nurse's cap, and a garment that nobody in that particular segment of the world's nonexistent time had got around to calling a "slip." Rather it was called a "combination" because it combined both shirtwaist and petticoat into a single functional unit.

The music played on. Dreamily Nurse Baxter sat down atop of

to-her-invisible Angie, kicked off her white low-heeled shoes, then drew off her white lisle stockings ever so slowly. Stood up, pushed the "combination" off her shoulders, let it slither to the floor, stepped out of it. Under it, she wore what the French would have called still another "combination," this time of a halter blouse, and a quite remarkably voluminous and disappointingly chaste pair of knee-length bloomers—for, although the brassiere and panties *had* been invented by then, only an advanced and/or sinful female like poor Nancy dared wear them.

She was toying with the shoulder straps of this ultimate and singularly unappetizing piece of underwear, which she, like all American women, called "step-ins" for obvious reasons, though "step-outs" would have been just as logical half the time, when Tobias heard the beat of heavy, deliberate, clearly masculine footsteps in the hall, coming in their direction.

"Random Chance!" he groaned inside his mind. But Angie set out to right matters on the spur of that same instant. And his methods, while effective, left a good bit to be desired as far as chivalry was concerned.

"Why, Nurse Baxter!" that most unangelic Angel gasped through Tobias' mouth. "What *ever* made you think I'd do a thing like *that?* In the first place I'm too weak, and in the second it's immoral!"

"You bastard!" Tobias thought at Angie. "Wake her up! You heard me, wake her up! Make her lock the door! And put her clothes back on! A joke's one thing, but getting the poor girl fired *and* ruining her reputation in the bargain . . ."

"Will change her whole sequence for th' better," Angie said solemnly. "Without her clinking reputation, she kin start in to have *fun.* And a chappie I know who runs a burlesque theater will pay her five times what she gits here, and—"

"Wake her up!" Tobias screamed.

"Oh, all right," Angie sighed. "Ye kin git 'em outa New England, but ye can't git th' New England outa them!" Then, his mental voice softening: "Wake up, Annie, me darlin'. Lock th' door. 'N git back into yer duds or there'll be hell t' pay, I sadly fear. . . ."

Anne Baxter's bonny brown eyes cleared. Flared into memory, recognition, horror.

"Don't waste time, me dollie!" Angie hissed at her. "Lock th' clinkin' door! Or d'ye *really* believe ye kin explain th' state ye're in?"

Anne Baxter was a very bright girl indeed. And women, even when not too bright, tend to be realistic-minded little creatures. She rushed to that door, locked it. Gathered up her scattered garments, dived into them. Naturally the result was a mess, the more so because the doorknob was being vigorously twisted, and the voice of Dr. Carlton Brice, head of the hospital, was thundering through the door, less from suspicion than from certainty.

"Open up! You hear me, Nurse Baxter? Open up! What the hell's going on here?"

Anne decided that putting on her stockings would take far too long, so she balled them up and hurled them under Tobias' bed. As she straightened up, she saw that he—out of pure relief mostly—was grinning at her. For the first time, she lost control. Sobbing wildly, she rolled him halfway out of the bed with a slap that sounded like a .38 caliber police special going off, and hissed:

"*You* did it! Put your dirty thoughts into my clean mind! From now on, Tobias Tobit, you keep your filthy ideas to yourself!"

Then whirling, she ran and opened the door. She would have been much wiser to have delayed Dr. Brice still longer. For to that medical gentleman's clinical eye, the spectacle she presented was practically as damning as it would have been had she stood before him stark naked. Her lovely red hair was a mess. Her uniform had the third button fastened into the second buttonhole, the second into the first, the top unbuttoned, the hem of her combination was showing, and not only was she stockingless, but her feet were bare.

Dr. Carlton Brice stared at her. Frowned imperiously. Said, every word dripping venom:

"I must confess, that as a member of the masculine sex, Mister Tobit's charms escape me completely, Miss Baxter. Nor had I dreamed that you were—well—so impulsive, let us say? Or perhaps ardent is the better word. Which is neither here nor there. What is more germane is the fact that your employment with Brice's Clinic terminates as of now. Your severance pay will be waiting within the hour in my office."

Tobias thought at her desperately:

"Tell him I tried to—to get fresh! To take advantage of you! That you fought me off! That—"

By then she'd slipped far enough into the ranks of the outcasts and the damned for her mind to synchronize with his almost perfectly.

"He—he tried to rape me!" she wailed. "I—I fought him off! I—"

"Oh, come now, my dear!" Dr. Brice said, "Can't you girlies ever think of something new? That alibi is more than a bit threadbare these days. He tried to violate you, after you'd so obligingly locked the door. And removed your wearing apparel—quite voluntarily, all the evidence would suggest. May I point out to you that your uniform is neither ripped nor torn, nor is a single button missing? Of course it's misbuttoned and in some disarray in your haste to conceal a pleasant morning's dalliance . . . Enough of this! Will you stand outside while I examine the patient?"

Despairingly, Anne Baxter stepped outside. Dr. Brice took a step forward, said, "My God!"

For, by then, he saw how Tobias' broken nose was bleeding.

"Angie," Tobias thought furiously, "you got me into this, now goddamnit, get me out!"

Aloud he said: "She's telling the truth, Doctor—" and paused, waiting for Angie to pour those singularly expert and convincing lies into his mind. "When she—she came in here, I had my eyes closed, pretending to be asleep. So she sat down in that chair, and it was so hot"—

It hadn't been up 'til that moment. April in those mountains is distinctly cool. But all of a sudden it was stifling.

—"that—seeing as how I was dead to the world—I suppose she figured it was safe enough to—to unbutton her uniform and take off her shoes and stockings. But she's so damned pretty that I guess I sort of went wild and grabbed her, and—"

"She hit you in the nose?" Dr. Brice said.

"Yessir," Tobias said. "Doctor, I'm sorry! Don't know what made me act like that. I apologize to you, sir—and to Miss Baxter—most humbly . . ."

"Well, Mister Tobit," Dr. Brice said severely, "as you are a paying guest, I can't put you out. But I must say you've played the bounder and the cad for a fact! In any event, I shall change the nurse in charge of your case. Substitute for Miss Baxter, here, a more experienced woman, quite a few years older and a good bit less attractive. Which should enable you to keep your biological impulses under somewhat better control. Nurse Baxter, go tell Nurse Warren to come here—and bring the instrument table. This nose wants fixing. . . ."

But Anne Baxter was staring at Tobias. She knew perfectly well that it hadn't happened the way he had said it had. She wasn't really clear as to what had happened, but she knew that Tobias hadn't touched her. Of course he had told her to take off all her clothes, but—but—no he hadn't! He hadn't said a word! The voice she'd heard had been inside her head and—

"Inside yer warm li'l heart, Annie, me darlin'," Angie purred, sure now that she was sensitized to telepathic communication. "Repressed desires have th' damnedest way o' breakin' out—as me good friend Sigmund Freud always says. Ye took off yer duds. That's a fact! But why did ye, lass? Because poor beat-up helpless Toby made ye? Perish th' thought! Ye took 'em off under the influence o' one wild sweet glorious impulse—purely biological! 'N if this stuffed shirt of a sawbones hadn't shown up when he did—"

Anne Baxter's face had turned a lovely crimson.

"Doctor—" she got out, "don't take me off the case! In a way, it was my fault. I was—indiscreet—even immodest, maybe. It was foolish of me to—to loosen my uniform that way. I—I *know* how men are—even crippled-up fellas like Mister Tobit. And I can handle him. I didn't even need to hit him, really. He's far too weak to do me any real harm. Besides, I'm sure he's really sorry and will never pull a trick like that again. Will you, Mister Tobit?"

"Never!" Tobias croaked.

"Ha!" Angie said.

"Ha, what?" Tobias thought at him.

"From now on, ye'll have to fight *her* off," Angie said.

"Well—" Dr. Brice said, "are you sure *she* hit you in the nose, Tobit? Or was it just the excitement of the occasion?"

"She hit me all right!" Tobias croaked. "Don't blame her. Terrible way I was acting and all—"

"Do you swear it?" Dr. Brice said, grimly.

"I swear it!" Tobias said. "So help me God!"

" 'If there be trouble to herward,/' " Angie quoted solemnly, " 'That a lie of the blackest, kin clear;/Lie, while thy tongue still moveth,/'n a man is alive to hear!' "

"Kipling," Tobias said automatically, *"The Barrack Room Ballads."*

"Right," Angie said.

Nurse Baxter was staring at Tobias with wide, soft penny-brown eyes.

"Who're you talking to, Toby?" her sweet, bell-clear soprano came stealing through his mind.

"Him," Tobias thought, and jerked his head towards where Angie stood.

Anne looked in that direction, and her eyes grew wider still.

"And who're *you?"* she whispered.

"Now I ain't rightly sure, darlin'," Angie said, "and neither is Toby. Most of the time *I* think I'm Don Rafael Angel Claro, Hidalgo de la Luz; but since Toby sometimes thinks I'm Don Lucifero Angel Moreno, Duque de las Tinieblas, th' issue's confused, sort of. What's sure is that I'm a figment of his diseased 'n distorted imagination—and now, darlin', likewise of *yours*—and his Guardian Angel, to boot."

"They're Spanish, aren't they? Those things you called yourself?" Anne Baxter said, or rather thought.

"Yes, sugarplum," Angie said. "Ye see, in this here corporeal visitation, or this avatar, say, me human identity is Cuban, so I sometimes *think* in Spanish instead of Ancient Hebrew, which is th' official language o' Angels. . . ."

"But what do those words *mean?"* Anne asked him.

Tobias glanced nervously at Dr. Brice. This particular extrasensory perception session was going on too long. Then he saw he need not have worried. This session was going on outside of the ordinary human concept of time. Dr. Brice was locked, or frozen, into the instant it had begun. He didn't move. His eyes didn't blink. His heart didn't beat. He wasn't even breathing. So Anne and Angie could go on communicating telepathically for ten minutes, an hour, ten million years, all the aeons there ever were or ever would be of quite illusory time, and when they stopped it, finally, to Dr. Carlton Brice it would still be the exact instant they began it, the hiatus they had locked him into was so deep.

"Which is the *Third* Law of Relativity," Angie said.

"I asked you," Anne whispered, "what those words meant."

"Well," Angie said, "translation ain't where I shine, me little hot-cross bun; but Don Rafael Angel Claro, Hidalgo de la Luz, means something like Sir Rafael Bright-Angel, Lord of Light; 'n Don Lucifero Angel Moreno, Duque de las Tinieblas, means somethin' like Sir Lucifer Dark-Angel, Duke of Utter Darkness, hell! That's redundant, ain't it? Say Duke o' Night 'N Fog 'N Blackness—which is what Toby often thinks I am."

"He's wrong," Anne said, her voice vibrant with tenderness. "You're the Bright Angel, all right—all splendid and shining and—and beautiful!"

"Oh Lord!" Tobias groaned. "Now see what you've done! You've made her go and fall for *you!*"

"It's called transference, me friend Siggie says," Angie said solemnly. " 'N besides, I *am* a pretty li'l ol' Angel fer a fact. 'N beyond even that, this glorious li'l object wuz to go fer *you,* 'twould screw up th' deal more'n somewhat. There's still Clara—or is it Sara?—a-waitin' fer ye to show up in—"

"I don't believe you," Tobias said morosely.

" 'N don't ye now?" Angie said. "Well then have a look!"

The walls of Brice Clinic faded out. And abruptly he, Tobias Tobit, was back in that clearing. And there was that pond, surrounded by palm trees. And that utterly obscene stench of putrefaction was filling up the world. And there were the crows again, beaking and tearing at that poor, grossly swollen baby girl's corpse. And—

"Ooops!" Angie said, "wrong wave length! Lemme see, lemme see. Wonder wouldn't five 'n eight-tenths Gigi Hertz do it? There!"

It was dark. Darker than Hell's seventh circle. Tobias was in a great, luxurious, splendid bedroom. He couldn't see a damned thing, but he just sort of knew where he was. The bedroom was in a castle. He knew that because the walls of it weren't square but curving which meant this particular bedroom was in the Keep or Tower. He was ankle deep in bearskin rugs, which kept him from making any noise as he walked toward that bed.

Then the darkness lightened, and he could see her. A little of her, anyhow. Because most of her was covered by, what? A man? "No

—looks more like an ape," Tobias thought. "Or at least a monster, anyhow."

And the two of them were For Unlawful Carnal Knowledging like crazy.

"Why, the sonofabitch!" Angie roared. "So *that's* what he's up to!"

"Who's up to?" Tobias said sadly. His heart was broken, for by then he had seen her face, and she was absolutely *the* most beautiful girl in the world.

"Asmodeus. He's a demon. Told ye once that he wuz givin' li'l Clara—or is it Sara?—a hell o' a lot o' trouble, but I niver figgered on *this* kind!"

"No point in us going down to Kentucky, now, is there?" Tobias said forlornly. He was unable to tear his eyes away from the sight. Asmodeus was busily engaged in pounding the bed and little Clara/Sara completely to pieces. And she was loving every second of it. She was clawing his huge back, a damned sight hairier than a silverback gorilla's—which was what Asmodeus looked like anyhow—to bloody ribbons, and screaming endearing encouragements into his tufted, pan-shaped ears. Only those encouragements would have made a longshoreman faint, and even a mule skinner blush, Tobias decided.

"Why not?" Angie said. "Screwin' never did anybody a mite o' harm. Save ye th' trouble o' teachin' her how—that is if ye iver *learn* how yourself, ye short-fused dud, ye—"

"No," Tobias said primly, "my wife must be a *decent* girl, Angie! I'm certainly not starting to get mixed up with a whore."

"She ain't," Angie said reasonably enough. "Ye kin bet yer bottom dollar that old Asmo don't pay her. Oh, that ain't what ye mean is it? Besides," and he turned his head sidewise so Tobias wouldn't see the mocking grin on his face, "that one ain't yer intended, Toby, me boy, me boy! 'Tis her sister—Clara. Or is it Sara? Niver could tell th' two of 'em apart."

They, he and Angie, were in a simple, modest, rather shabby bed-sitting room. And *she* was there. The same girl. But she couldn't be. She was wearing huge, horn-rimmed spectacles, and a quilted bathrobe. Through an opened doorway, Tobias could hear water gushing into a bathtub.

"Ssssh!" Angie whispered. "She can't see us. We're invisible. But her mind's so bright that she just might be sensitive t' E.S.P. 'n that would really hump matters fer fair! Ye see, she's a chaste 'n a modest lass just like ye put yer order in fer, jist now. . . ."

The girl took off those hideous glasses. Her eyes were—heavenly, Tobias decided. Her hair was pale golden, a true ash blonde; and her mouth was shell pink—and—

He stared at it, startled. Her mouth was disturbing. Because it wasn't a chaste little cupid's bow. Her lips were very full and—and shockingly sensual. "Why, goddamnit, Angie," he thought, "a girl with lips like those can't be—"

"Virtuous? Guaranteed, Simon-pure, grade A 'n pasteurized," Angie said. "Didn't say she wuz *cold.* But she's savin' it all fer Mr. 'Right' to come along—namely ye. 'N, oh brother! What d'ye say *now,* Toby lad?"

Because the girl had slipped off that quilted robe and was testing the water in the bathtub with the big toe of one exquisitely sculptured foot. And her body was a living miracle. She was every romantic and/or salacious dream that Tobias had had in all his life. He was fairly swooning with tenderness, and getting a hard-on at the same time. The hard-on hurt. Looking down, he saw why. There was a rubber tube attached to him down there, which ran into a grossly distended rubber bag that—

"Where'd the two of you *go?"* Anne Baxter said. "All of a sudden you both sort of blued-off into smoke and drifted away!"

"Kentucky," Angie said, matter-of-factly. "Something I had to show Toby down there. Th' girl he's gonna marry, to tell ye th' truth, darlin'. Or th' girls. It's a mite confusin' fer a fact. . . ."

"Do you swear it?" Dr. Brice said grimly.

"I swear it!" Tobias said. "So help me God!"

" 'If there be trouble herward,' " Angie began. "Oh, shit, Toby, I had to bring him back. He was turnin' *blue."*

"Very well," Dr. Brice said. "But from now on that door stays both unlocked and *open.* Is that clear, Nurse Baxter? And you're to spare Mr. Tobit any further exhibitions. Now go get the instrument table. I have to reset Mr. Tobit's nose. For I sadly fear you've broken it again. Get going now!"

Nurse Baxter scampered from the room with her delightful swish and sway.

"Angie—" Tobias thought.

"Yes, laddybucks?" Angie thought back.

"I thank you. I thank you with all my heart!" Tobias Tobit said.

Six

"Toby, me boy, me boy," Angie said, "I'm gonna hafta leave ye for a while. There're a couple o' little matters that want attendin' to. . . ."

"What matters?" Tobias said. He had been awake and conscious several days by then, and his morale was shot to hell. He felt, at his best moments, like the low man on a totem pole, and at his worse, like a worm's belly button.

"Matters touching ye, me lad," Angie said. "I've been visitin' yer auld man's first-'n-a-half cousin Raguel—I mean Ralphie—inside his head, anyhow, to see what makes him tick . . ."

"And what does?" Tobias said morosely.

"Damned if I know. He's as daft as animal crackers. But I did find out somethin' useful: He's got his shrivelled miser's heart set on his daughters marrying rich 'n aristocratic fellas. . . ."

"Oh Lord!" Tobias said.

"Amen," Angie said. " 'N that's what I've got to attend to; th' financial angle anyhow. Th' rest won't be hard. Ye've a gift fer th' ol' blarney fer a fact. Dressed in flossy duds, ridin' in a Pierce Arrow, say, mindin' yer Ps 'n Qs, ye'll do nicely. . . ."

"You mean you're going somewhere to dream up some wild scheme to make me *rich?*" Tobias said.

"Not jist somewhere, Tartarus. 'N I don't mean to dream it up. I mean to buy, beg, borrow or steal it from an old girl I know, name of Lachesis—"

"One of the fates," Tobias said. "But that's only *mythology,* Angie!"

"What ain't? Including ye 'n me. I'm only a spark from th' Auld Cuss's mind, 'n he's jist—"

"A figment of my diseased and distorted imagination," Tobias sighed. "Get on with it, Angie. . . ."

"It's like this, laddybucks; Tartarus *exists.* 'Cause long as even one daft critter *believes* in a thing, there it be. 'N so do those three slatternly old bitches. 'N they're extra useful at this point, 'cause since they exist outside of Judeo-Christian cosmology, the sequences they deal in come over to th' modern, western mind as Random

Chance with th' Absurdity Factor built in. 'N that ain't all. More'n half of 'em has been twisted through th' black holes o' outa space, which means that their sequential progression *ain't* fixed. And *that* means they ain't got a damned bit o' predestination or inevitability neither one. Makes 'em more'n a wee bit unpredictable, but what's the odds? Since nothin' about 'em's fixed, they're even reversible. So I'll pry two o' three loose from them old hags—"

"Clotho, who spins the thread of life," Tobias said. "Lachesis, by interpretation, 'The Disposer of Lots' who assigns each man his destiny. Atropos, 'she who cannot be turned,' bearer of the abhorred shears, who cuts each man's thread at the end. You should tell her to get busy. Atropos, I mean. Cut mine. Lord knows, I'm sick of it!"

"Now listen to 'im! Sweet li'l ol' intellectual! Knows all about Greek mythology 'n stuff like that there! Don't be a jackass, Toby lad. Ye persuade that funky ol' bitch to snip this sequence off, ye'll only be reincarnated into another one. Worse, likely. The Hindus have got more'n a little somethin' there with their concept of Nirvana, which boils down to reunion with the Oversoul in blissful nothin'ness."

"Angie, you get a fellow wild the way you talk about all religions as though they were absolutely equal!"

"Aren't they? Blessed if I see the difference, this damnfool nonsense o' th' other. If ye humans would fergit 'em all 'n jist settle down to enjoy life—"

"That is hedonism," Tobias said.

"Oh brother! Pin a label on it 'n it goes away, eh? *Reductio ad absurdum.* And what ain't? Absurd, I mean. Anyhow as I was sayin' afore ye sidetracked me, I'm gonna pry ol' Lachesis loose from two or three concurrent sequences, or, as ye'd call it, *simultaneous* ones. That way, if one of 'em don't work, we flashback to where we wuz in your sequential progression 'n start all over ag'in—"

"And if *none* of them does?" Tobias said morosely.

"Then we're no worse off than we be in our present situation. Only means I'll have to figger something else. But one of 'em *will* work. Since it's written in yer stars that ye're to wed 'n bed Sara—or is it Clara?—one of 'em's *got* to."

"All right," Tobias said. "Get going then."

"Sure ye'll be all right? I kin call on Michael o' Gabriel o' Uriel o' one of the other other fellas to watch over ye if ye like."

"No thank you," Tobias said, "I'll be all right. And any other Angel would only make me nervous. I'm too used to you."

"Why thank ye kindly, lad! Be seein' ye now. 'N stay outa me Annie's chaste knee-length bloomers, will ye?"

"Sure *you've* been staying out of them?" Tobias said.

"Why Toby! What kind of a rotten, bounding cad of an Angel d'ye take me to be?"

"That kind," Tobias said. "Doubled. And in spades. Now beat it, will you?"

After Angie had gone, Tobias lay there very still. The trouble was that he couldn't get poor Nancy and what had happened to her out of his head. Nor out of his heart for that matter.

"I *killed* her," he thought, "murdered her just as if I'd strangled her with my bare hands. 'Cause if I had left her up there at Dino's roadhouse she would be still alive and—"

"No she wouldn't," Angie's voice poured through his mind. That was one of the maddening things about being associated with Angie: you were never free of him. He might be at your side or winging his way past the dimmest spiral nebula on the outer fringes of space, two billion light years from this earth, and his raucous voice would come banging into your head with no lapsed interval at all.

"I did!" Tobias moaned. "Persuaded her to run away with me and——"

"Me boy, me boy, ye're a trifle mixed up. Ye didn't persuade. Ye'd have needed an axe to *keep* her from following ye. Get things straight, will ye, huh, puleeze?"

"But all the same, the *way* poor Nance died was——"

"Pukin' dreadful. Throwed a megatonner at the poor lass, didn't he? Quit thinkin' about that, Toby lad. 'Twasn't yer fault and——"

Then abruptly his voice faded out of Tobias' mind, for Nurse Anne Baxter came through the door and stood there looking at him with great and troubled eyes.

"Who is—Nancy, Mr. Tobit?" she said aloud.

"Toby to you, Anne—please?" Tobias said.

"All right—Toby. Who is she? You keep thinking about her all the time. And—and either I'm crazy, or I can *hear* you think. And that's not possible! People can't hear each other think, can they?"

"Yes, they can," Tobias said, "when they're kindred spirits, they can, Anne, dearest. Only the people who can do it aren't—normal. Everyone I ever met who could—well—communicate with me that way was—disturbed. A little crazy. Bad hurt on their insides. Misfits. Outcasts. The—the walking wounded, Anne . . ."

"Oh!" she said, and her gaze turned inward. Then it cleared. She nodded vigorously. "That's me, all right," she said. "I've been a misfit my whole life long, Toby. Ever since my one-sixth daddy dropped me out of his *soucoupe volante* on my head and those Terrestians—Oh! What *am* I saying? What's a *soucoupe volante,* Toby? And what are Terrestians?"

"Don't know. What *are* they, Anne?"

"If I knew, I wouldn't have asked *you.* They're words that just pop into my head sometimes. And—and Yllyia. Only I *know* what Yllyia is. It's a place. A planet just like this one. It circles around the dwarf star Xfemon in the ninety-seventh spiral nebula beyond——Ohhh! I *am* crazy! I must be! Do I really *know* things like that, Toby? Things that make no sense even to *me?* It *feels* like I know them!"

"Then you know them," Tobias said. "We'll have to ask Angie what they mean after he gets back. He'll know. Angie knows damn near everything."

Anne thought about that.

"We must," she said. "Oh, I have so many things to ask him! That is—if I can remember them. Because I—I keep—forgetting 'em, Toby. Something—blocks them—out of my mind. But—you'll remind me, won't you? To ask him, I mean?"

"Ask him—what?" Tobias said.

"Whether a—fvonia—a girl!—could have *six* real daddies. And—and *eight* arms. And her—her tits on *her back,* between her shoulder blades, and——Oh! Ohhhh Lord! I am crazy! I am! Stark raving——But let's not talk about me any more. Tell me about her. About Nancy. I keep *feeling* the way you're hurt over her. And it's awful. Makes me want to scream out loud."

Tobias bent his head. The tears poured down his cheeks. But he didn't tell her about Nancy. He couldn't. He just lay there, remembering every lousy, stinking bit of it, and crying.

Then he felt her soft warm lips on his. She drew back, wrapped her two arms around his neck, and hugged him to her bosom. There was nothing sensual about the gesture. It was achingly tender, completely maternal.

"Oh you poor, poor boy!" she sobbed. "How awful! How perfect-ly awful!"

And he realized she had read his mind—or at least his memory—again.

He rose up and kissed her. Her lips were wet. They tasted salt.

"Toby—tell me another thing: Just who—or *what* is Angie? Is—he real? Or do I just imagine him, too?"

Tobias thought about that, long and deeply; which was the exact equivalent of saying it to Anne aloud.

"I—I don't know," he mused inside his head. "He—he came to me in the hospital. The one down in Alexandria, Virginia. Or maybe even the one in France. I had a concussion. Shell shock. And a little sliver of shell casing, inside my skull, pressing on my brain. So—maybe he—he's just a part of my craziness, Anne. Only—when they took that piece of shell casing out of my head, he didn't go away. One time he says he's my Guardian Angel. And the next, he swears that he's only a figment of my diseased and distorted imagination. . . ."

"Toby," she whispered, "could I—could a girl—*love* a figment of your imagination? Could I even see him? Or touch him or—"

"Anne!" he said sharply.

She bowed her head.

"It hasn't gone *that* far yet," she said.

"But it will, won't it?" he said sadly.

She nodded, dumbly.

"Yes," she sighed. "I've—I've always been a good girl. Not cold as ice, maybe; but smart enough to keep my feelings under control. But he—he gets to me. Don't know how or why, but—"

"The bastard!" Tobias said.

"Now, Toby!" she said reproachfully.

"He's no good!" Tobias said hotly. "He's a scoundrel! A shameless scoundrel! All he ever thinks about is getting into some poor girl's step-ins and—"

"But, Toby," she pointed out, "if he's only a figment of your imagination, how could he?"

Tobias thought about that. Said, or thought, or both.

"Maybe he—he's *that* side of me. The sinful side. Maybe he's all the lust and lechery and hot rebellion in my heart run wild—the personification of everything I hadn't ought to be, but maybe am. My unbridled imagination. My hidden and forbidden desires . . ."

She smiled at him, then. Her eyes were still misty, but her smile was honest mischief's self.

"Then all I've got to say is hurrah for unbridled imagination and three cheers for forbidden desires!" she said.

"Anne, no!" he said. "He—he'll take advantage of you! He—he's heartless! He's left all the other girls he ever—"

She stared at him.

"Toby," she whispered, "you mean there have been other girls who could—"

"See him and feel him and—and do what they damn well shouldn't with him? Yes. Only up until now they've all been—whores."

Her penny-brown eyes opened very wide.

"Maybe I am, too," she thought. "A whore. At least at heart."

"No!" Tobias said again.

"The funny part about it," she went on, "is that *you* don't appeal to me that way at all. I like you, yes. Maybe I even love you in a sisterly sort of way. But I haven't the faintest desire to—to go to bed with you, to say it straight out and ugly! But him—Lord Jeses! He looks at me and I—I melt!"

"Oh goddamn him, anyhow!" Tobias said.

"So he *can't* be just your imagination, Toby! He can't be! In the first place he doesn't look anything like you—"

"Maybe," Tobias said sadly, "that's because I don't like the way I look. . . ."

"And he doesn't act anything like you, either—"

"He acts the way I would, if I had the nerve, which I don't," Tobias said.

She peered at him oddly.

"You mean that I—that I appeal to you *that* way?" she whispered.

"Yes," he said, "you appeal to me that way."

She jumped up from the edge of his bed.

"Then I'm going," she said, "not only because it's silly to put temptation in your way; but because it's—kind of—mean, isn't it, Toby? Cruel. Unkind . . ."

Then with her delightful little swish and sway, she scampered from his room.

That night, Tobias couldn't sleep. First, he counted sheep. But since sheep are dull and stupid animals, distinguishable from one another only to other sheep, he lost count two dozen times, and gave himself a headache. So then he started counting naked girls jumping over rose bushes. To keep score, he decided that every tenth girl should have three tits, instead of merely two. But after thirty girls had jumped the rose bushes, he decided that three tits made a singularly unaesthetic arrangement and changed over to blondes, brunettes and redheads, fat girls, thin girls, medium-sized girls, and girls of different colors.

But the first girl over the hurdles after that was the tall brunette from Dino's. The next two were his ash-blonde cousins Sara and Clara, which made him get a hard-on; but the fourth girl was poor Nancy, which caused him to detumefy abruptly.

"Got to stop this!" he moaned. "Got to stop it!"

But by then there was no stopping it, for the next ten girls, leaping the rosebush as graceful as gazelles were all gorgeous redheads—and each and every one of them was Anne.

That absolutely *had* to be stopped, so he reached up and pulled the bellcord. While he waited, he prayed that it wouldn't be Anne who answered, because he was far from sure that he could resist dragging her into his arms. So when he heard those lumpy, graceless footsteps coming on, he was much relieved. It was going to be Nurse Warren who answered—Old Piano Legs, he called her. Carefully he rolled over to one side so she wouldn't see his hard-on pushing the covers up like a tent.

Nurse Warren came into the room, blinked at him through glasses thick as stove lids, said sourly: "Yes, Mister Tobit?"

"Could I have a sleeping pill, Nurse Warren, please?" Tobias said.

"I've been having nightmares—and I just can't get back to sleep."

"Well, all right, I reckon," she grumped, and clumped from the room.

She was back in a shade under five minutes with a glass of water and the pill. He took it gratefully and said:

"Thank you mighty kindly, Nursie—dear!"

"Oh you!" Nurse Warren said, again, and marched out of there.

The pill was great. He turned left, turned right, pounded the pillow with his fist, and burrowed sudden, shrieking light-years deep into night and sleep.

What waked him was the feel—no. Let's get this right. He *didn't* wake up. He knew perfectly damned well that he was both asleep and dreaming. But it took him a shade under two seconds flat to decide that only a blithering idiot would wake up and spoil a dream like that one.

Her mouth was on his, warm and wet and parted. And his plaster cast had miraculously—and conveniently—disappeared so that he could feel the whole firm-soft, cool-warm length of her lying atop him and moving slowly.

"Why, Anne!" he thought, or said, or anyhow communicated to her. "You haven't any clothes on!"

"Oh course not, silly!" she said, drawing her mouth away from his a little. "Clothes only get in the way!" Then she went back to kissing him, biting his lips playfully, and thrusting a wickedly busy tongue tip between them when he opened them to gasp for breath.

He kept his eyes tight shut. He was afraid that if he opened them, the whole thing would go away. But it didn't go away. She didn't go away. He put down his left hand, letting it steal slowly down all the cool and silken slopes of her to where she crisped and spiralled, tangled his fingers in her sudden fur, exploring until he found her quiver, gape, and scald, and played hot wet braille games there until she tore her mouth from his, and thrust flaming swords and fiery arrows of breath into his ears, moaning, chanting:

"C'mon! C'mon! C'mon! Come on!"

Then he arched and thrust and pierced her, raging, roaring, wild. It was all so real that he would have sworn he wasn't dreaming, except for one thing: He was in no hurry at all. His control was miraculous. "If you were awake, you horse's ass," he snarled at himself, "you'd have gone off like a 188 millimeter howitzer shell by now!

"Thank God for sleep and dreaming!" he murmured, as a bugler sounded the charge. Then he was riding her like a madman, and she was bucking like a wild, unbroken mare. And the world blurred out in upheaval, down thrust, limb-locked writhe, twist and scald. He was gasping for breath, for life, but still triumphant, for he knew he could outlast her, that this time he wouldn't have to be ashamed, apologize for his weakness, voice that classic, tragicomic cliché: "Oh, I am so sorry, dear!"

In fact, he didn't have to say anything, because he felt her nails, ten white-hot lance points, dig into his back, felt her whole body become a lighted taper melting, a long, exquisite shudder, heard her voice, flutes and woodwinds, a cymbal's sudden crash.

"Oh, Angie! Oh, my love!" Anne Baxter cried.

Tobias opened his eyes. She wasn't there. He was alone in his lonely, terrible bed. His chest was encased in plaster. He was dripping sweat from every pore. His heart was pounding. He couldn't catch his breath. And he felt the deep slow-sweet lassitude of after love.

He was uncovered. The sheets were on the floor. His pillows were sodden. The bed was soaked. But he was alone. More alone than any man should ever be, more crushed than Atlas under a weight of silence heavier than the vast, teeming globe, more spirit-bruised and bleeding than Sisyphus behind his crippling stone. He plunged his face into a pillow that reeked of sweat and shook like a spastic, wept like a child.

Then it was morning and she was standing at the foot of his bed staring at him. Her hair was neatly combed, her white uniform and cap stiffly starched. Her stockings weren't twisted, her shoes were clean and neat.

But there were death and hell and terror in her eyes. He stared at them, seeing them blue-ringed, deep-circled, utterly weary. Dropped his eyes to her swollen, almost blue-bruised lips. Said: "My God!"

She went on looking at him with aching sorrow, passed a pink tongue tip over those swollen lips, whispered:

"Toby—did you—did you—dream, too?"

He nodded, stiffly, unable to trust himself to speak.

"Th—the same dream—that I—that I dreamed?"

"Yes," he croaked. "At least I suppose it was, the same."

She went on relentlessly:

"What did you dream?"

"That I—that we—made love," he whispered.

"Did—we *dream* it? Didn't I—maybe—walk in my sleep?"

He shook his head. His eyes went scalded, blind.

"No," he said bitterly. "Because—at the—end you called me 'Angie'!"

She nodded.

"I know," she said, her voice toneless, dull. "I dreamed it was him. And I—I was so happy! Then I—I almost woke up—and I—I wasn't sure, anymore. Because just for a second his face—melted. Blurred like a—like a reflection in a mudpuddle you drop a pebble into. And then—it wasn't his face any longer. It—it was—*yours.* For an instant, half-a-heartbeat—it was yours."

"Anne!" he said.

"Toby—are you *two* people, you and Angie? Are you?"

He bent his head. Stared at the wall.

"I don't know," he said miserably. "I just don't know!"

"No," she said reasonably enough, "you couldn't, could you? All right. But just one thing. I want your word as a gentleman that you'll *never* make me dream *that* again!"

He stared at her a long slow time. Whispered:

"Then who made *me* dream it? You?"

"Don't give me that excuse, Tobias Tobit! You admitted, yourself, that you had a yen for me, *that* way! So when you started in to dream *that,* you sort of put the idea in my head and—"

"Made you call me Angie? 'Oh Angie! Oh my love!'?"

She stared at him; said: "Then *who* did?"

"Damned if I know. Angie himself, likely. His idea of having fun—to get us both worked up, I mean. But hear this, Anne Baxter! Nobody can put an idea in another person's head that that person is not receptive to. And especially not an idea that the person in question doesn't like. Only kindred souls can communicate by E.S.P., anyhow, and—"

"E.S.—*what?*" Anne said.

"E.S.P. Extrasensory perception. The term hasn't even been invented yet. But it will be soon—by a man named J.B. Rhine and—"

"Toby," Anne whispered, "you *know* what's going to happen? I mean—you can *see* the future?"

Tobias thought about that.

"Sometimes," he said. "Dimly, for instance—I was an artilleryman in the last war; but in the next one I'm going to be an aviator. A bomber pilot. Don't ask me how I know that. I just know it, that's all. . . ."

She looked him straight in the face. Her brown eyes were very deep and dark and troubled.

"Have—have Angie and I—any future? Together, I mean?" she said.

He thought about that. Thought long and slowly and carefully and well.

"No," he said.

"I *knew* you'd say that!" she said furiously. "I *knew* it! You're jealous of him, Tobias Tobit! Jade green jealous! Just because he's tall and handsome and gay and—"

His look stopped her. His eyes.

"I *am* jealous of Angie," he said quietly; "but that hasn't anything to do with my telling the truth. And kindred souls like you and me, Anne, *can't* lie to each other. Because the minute I start lying to you, what I'm thinking would contradict what I'm saying, and since you can hear *both* what good would it do for me to try it?"

She stared at him. Said: "Oh!" Then: "Toby—why haven't Angie and I—any—future—together?"

"Don't know. I think it's because you're beings of different orders: that he's—imaginary, maybe; and you're real. Or because he's an Angel and you're human—which is just another way of saying the same thing . . ."

"Oh!" Anne said again; then: "Toby, what *am* I going to do?"

"Don't know," Tobias said. Then he grinned. "Why don't you try converting your dreams—and *mine*—into reality, Anne, darling?"

"You want me to break your nose again, Tobias Tobit? You look just like a prizefighter now, or a gangster; and if I punch you in the snoot again it sure Lord won't improve your looks!"

"Then *don't* punch me in the snoot," Tobias said. "Just For Unlawful Carnal Knowledge me a little, Annie me dearest!"

"And don't call me Annie!" Anne yelled. Then she got it; "Why you dirty-minded, crippled-up, damn yankee swine!" she got out; and hit poor Tobias in the nose, again. She didn't break it this time, but she did make it bleed. Then she got out of there.

That night, they both dreamed that dream again. And they went on dreaming it for each of the thirty nights that Angie stayed away. With variations. And improvements. Between them, they rewrote and revised the *Kama Sutra.* Brought it up to date. At least by remote control. Because all the X rays that Dr. Brice took showed that Tobias' broken ribs were stubbornly refusing to either knit together or heal, and even Anne had to admit that the kind of boudoir gymnastics *she* dreamed about every night couldn't be accomplished by a man encased in as much plaster as Tobias Tobit was. Besides, in her dreams, her partner in delicious carnal sin was always Angie.

But on the morning of that thirtieth day, she suddenly began to doubt that the ordinary laws of nature were working properly. Because, that morning, she woke up sicker than a snake-bit hound dog. She barely made it to her wash basin before she threw up. With streaming eyes, she stumbled back to her bed, fell into it. Half an hour later, she suddenly jackknifed into a sitting position, and began to count on her fingers. But she didn't have enough fingers. What she was trying to reckon back to had occurred too long before. She needed the fingers of both hands, and the toes of one-and-one-half feet, or rather all the toes on one foot, and more than half the toes on the other to get back that far.

"The bastard!" she moaned. "The no-count damn yankee sinful bastard—a takin' advantage of me like that!"

Then her brown eyes widened.

"But—but—" she whispered, "it was only a *dream*—dreams. Thirty of 'em—'n Lord God, were they ever *fine!* And a girl can't get knocked up dreaming! Or can't she? Anyhow, Mister Magician

Tobias Tobit, you'n me are gonna have words, right now!"

But by the time she got dressed and got to Tobias Tobit's room, both Dr. Brice and Nurse Warren were already there.

"I can't understand it!" Dr. Brice was saying; "I simply can't! Not only aren't his ribs healing, but he's steadily losing weight! Can't afford to have him die on us, Nurse, 'twould give the clinic an awfully bad name and—"

"Oh, he isn't going to die, Doctor," Nurse Warren said; "but he sure Lord is eatin' into our profits, isn't he?"

"Not yet. But he will be soon. Of course that old nigger who brought him in turned over his billfold to us—and it was full of money. Who ever heard of a nigger's being *that* honest, eh, Nurse Warren? So we don't have to worry about the financial side yet. But—this unconsciousness—I don't like! And look at his bed, will you? I'd swear he's been having convulsions, or some sort of a seizure . . ."

"Oh my God!" Anne Baxter said, so loud that they heard her.

"Come in, Nurse Baxter," Dr. Brice said, "and answer me one plain and simple question: Have you been sneaking into this gentleman's room, nights?"

"Why, Doctor!" Anne gasped, "how dare you!"

"Now wait a minute, Doctor," Nurse Warren said. "I'll admit that Nurse Baxter is a mite too flighty 'n a trifle too fresh for her own good; but you hafta remember that you, yourself, took her off night duty nearly a month ago. Sure made it rough on the rest of us, but I figgered you knew what you were doing. And since *I've* been on night duty on this floor for the last week, I can vouch for the fact that she hasn't set foot in this room for that long back anyhow, and all we've got to do is ask Nurse Reed about the week before that, 'n Nurse Tyler the one before that, and—"

"Unnecessary!" Dr. Brice snapped. "Because whatever caused Mr. Tobit to relapse occurred *last* night. I'd stake my professional reputation on that!"

"Doctor—he—he isn't going—to—to *die,* is he?" Anne Baxter whispered. Inside her mind, she added, wailing, "And leave me knocked-up and disgraced and—"

"He ain't the guilty party, Anne, me darlin'!" Angie said, and slid down a dusty ray of sunlight into that room.

"An-gee!" Anne squealed, "you're back! Oh my darlin' you—"

"Might I ask to whom or to *what* you're talking, Nurse Baxter?" Dr. Brice said. "Or is it that you don't feel very well, my dear? Do you have a headache? Here, let me feel your pulse! Surely *you* don't do enough work around here to—"

"Angie!" Anne moaned, "*freeze* him! Fix him in time. And *her,* too, the old witch! 'Cause we've a lot of talking to do, you 'n I!"

"Frozen and fixed. 'N what he heard you say, me darlin', is already washed out o' his alleged mind. Hers too. Now come here 'n give us a kiss, willya, lass?"

With a skip and a scamper, Anne was in his arms. But once there, she drew back, pouting.

"No!" she said. "You're—wicked, you are, Angie! Angie—tell me something: Did I—did I *dream* all that? Or—"

"Well, in a way, yes. 'N in another way, no. Yin 'n yang, ye ken, me darlin'. There is confusion. That's the basic law o' th' Universe, me sweet. Confusion is. I sorta projected me image into yer chaste li'l cot nightly in order to protect me interests, and—"

"Angie—Toby dreamed the same thing. Every time I did, Angie! You didn't—you didn't *share* me with him, did you?"

"Well now," Angie grinned, "that's difficult to say, me doll! Since I be only a figment of yers 'n Toby's diseased 'n distorted imaginations, any sharing that wuz done, th' two o' ye had to do it, not *me.* Not that I'd mind, really. It's practically indestructible, ain't it? Don't wear out, and—"

"But, Angie—I—I'm pregnant! And from what you're saying now I won't even know *who* my baby's father is!"

"Yes ye will, me duck—"

"Don't call me 'duck'!" Anne shrilled.

"Them as objects to the word 'duck' jes' don't like *duck,* that's all —however ye spell it," Angie said solemnly, "but ye will know. Once th' li'l bastard gets here—"

"And don't call my baby a bastard!" Anne yelled.

"Well, ain't he?" Angie said reasonably enough; "but if th' squallin', burpin', leakin' li'l shitter is *mine,* he'll be a *giant* just like the Good Book says. More'n seven-'n a half foot high. So we'll make a basketball player outa him, 'n spend our declinin' years in comfort on his earnin's. But if he's Toby's, he'll be a dark-skinned Jew-lookin' li'l bastard with a great brain. Win th' Nobel Prize fer chemistry, physics 'n literachew all at th' same time, and . . ."

"But, Angie! I can't wait for him to get here! I've got to get married right now! Before I start to show and people *know* that I—that I've been *bad* and—"

"Honeychile," Angie chuckled, "you call that *bad?*"

She grinned at him then, and kissed him.

"No," she whispered, "I call it mighty fine, Angie darlin'. Angie—can *you* marry me? I mean are Angels allowed to—to marry *girls?*"

"And if I *can't?*" he teased her.

"Then I'll marry Toby. But only on one condition: That you rally round so's you 'n me can cheat on him right smart frequent! Oh, Angie, darlin', I *do* love you so!"

"Well," Angie said seriously, "you *can't* marry Toby."

"Why can't I?" Anne said. "Not that I want to; but just for curiosity's sake, why can't I?"

"Because his sequential progression is fixed—that is, all save these two maverick sequences I brung him back from Tartarus—and his inevitabilities is locked in with them belongin' to a girl named Sara—or is it Clara? So marryin' him is *out,* Anne me darlin'. On th' ither hand, ye kin marry me, that is if ye want to."

"Oh I want to! I want to! I want to!"

"How's about a li'l prior samplin' o' th' goods right now, then?"

"But Angie! We can't! There's—Doctor Brice and Nurse Warren! And—Toby!"

"There ain't nobody but *us.* See!" Angie said, and waved his hand. And there wasn't.

After *that* was over, Anne whispered:

"Darling—poor Toby isn't going to *die,* is he? Doctor Brice said—"

"Dr. Brice is a jackass. With long 'n hairy ears. Toby is gonna be our best man. Only this marryin' business is gonna take some doin', Annie, me darlin'. . . ."

"Why, Angie?" she said.

"We've got to find a preacher man who is a whore hopper, a drunk 'n a mite daft, or else he can't even *see* me. And witnesses what ain't too normal 'n respectable either. 'N, havin' got by that chore, how're ye gonna convince th' decent respectable people who'll be starin' at yer roundness 'n rotundity that ye've actually *got* a hubby when decent respectable people won't be able to see me neither?"

"Why can't they?"

"Got closed minds 'n no sweet rebellion in their miserable souls. Not a damned bit o' hell 'n ginger neither one. Could git to be rough, me doll."

"Don't care!" Anne said. "Long as I know it, that's enough for me!"

"That's the spirit, lass! Now c'mon, we'd better go look fer a sinful preacher or—"

"But, Angie! Poor Toby is so *sick!* Those dreams of ours—wore him out. And his ribs won't heal and he's losing weight and—"

"Well, he looks all right to *me,"* Angie said solemnly. "Don't he to you, honeychile?"

And Tobias was sitting up in bed and yelling:

"Get this damned plaster cast off me! It itches! And there's nothing wrong with me anyhow and—"

"What did I tell ye, me duckie?" Angie said.

Seven

They were standing in the parlor of the house belonging to Soames McGill, Justice of the Peace, in the town of Hootnholler, North Carolina. Tobias stood to the right of the Justice, and kept a firm grip on his arm. Mrs. McGill, née Eula Mae Grimes, stood on the left side of her husband, and clutched him just as firmly by his other arm. This was necessary because if they hadn't held him up, the Justice, known to all the local wits as "Soaked to the Gills," would have fallen on his face.

Eula Mae McGill was grinding her store-bought'n teeth with rage. Or rather with outrage. She was suffering from acute frustration, brought on by the conflict between her moral sense, and the aching knowledge that there wasn't, at the moment, one red-Indian penny in the cookie jar where she kept her scanty savings. Soaked had found the cookie jar again. No matter how many times she changed its hiding place, the results were always the same: "Soaked to the Gills" found it and as usual, got soaked to the gills.

But her husband's state of inebriation wasn't the cause of poor Eula Mae's outrage; she was too used, even too resigned to that. The real cause of it was the presence in the flesh—a good two hundred-odd pounds of flesh—of one Cecilia Helen Norton, known to every traveling salesman in the state, and to dead-game sports from as far away as Winston-Salem, as Celie-Belle. Celie-Belle ran the local spo'tin' house; though, in this case, the adjective "local" called for a certain qualification. Celie's cathouse, as it was also known, *was* local in the sense that, physically, a wooded plot a scant mile outside the town limits was the site of it; but it was far from local in the more important sense that its clientele was almost never drawn from among the good male citizens of Hootnholler.

Not, of course, that said good male citizens were above sampling Celie's luscious, imported, and frequently changed—"Freshness is mah sellin' point!" Celie-Belle bellowed—wares; but the sad, dull truth of the matter was that they usually couldn't afford Celie-Belle's rates, which firmed up their moral fiber more than somewhat. "Swear t' Gawd," more than one would-be local sport had been heard to observe, "a body'd think that theah citified poontang wuz gold plated!"

But even on those rare occasions when one of them managed to scrape together Celie-Belle's asking rates, there was one more deterring factor that tended to keep the itching-to-stray foot on the straight and narrow: And that factor was that Celie's Ho House, as elder and plain-speaking citizens insisted upon labeling it, was located just off State Highway Number One, so the chances of an erring citizen's being able to sneak into Celie's place, without his one and only's getting the news—and by party line telephone at that—before the festivities were even over, were slight indeed. In fact, they were nonexistent.

But what really broke Mrs. Justice of the Peace McGill's heart was the sad fact that every time her outraged sense of decency told her to throw "that overgrown tub o' sinful lard" out of her chaste and upright parlor, her down-to-earth common sense, dismally adding up the dozens of unpaid bills her husband owed, shot back: "Don't be a Jenny-Ass, Eula Mae!"

To make matters worse, if worse were possible, "this heah furr'n fella, sumpin' odd about him," so help her! sensing her indecision, had quickly raised the ante from the three dollars and a half that Soaked to the Gills usually got for "a Splicin' " to twenty honest-to-God smackeroos, "to tie th' knot o' holy wedlock 'twixt him 'n this bobbed-haired, red-headed li'l chippy—no better'n she should be," Eula Mae was grimly sure, with Celie-Belle as one of the witnesses.

When asked why it had to be Celie-Belle, the furr'ner had drawled in what *he* probably thought was a first-class Nawth Ca'lina accent: "Wal now, ma'am, Celie's purely one o' th' few folks heah abouts what kin *see* me."

At first, that hadn't struck Eula Mae as odd, but now it did. Because, as she got a check rein on her feelin's—after all, marryin' a couple was usually over in less than two shakes of a jackrabbit's tail —she wasn't rightly sure that *she* could see th' furr'n fella. He kept —well—kinda fadin' in 'n fadin' out, as 'twere, like he wuz some kind o' hant, o' somethin'—

"Look, Mister!" she snapped at him. "Can't you stay *put.* Or anyhow, try to?"

"It's all right, Ma'am," the tall, skinny, dark-complexioned fella who was hanging onto Soaked's right arm said gently, "all that means is that you're a decent, respectable lady for a fact. Decent respectable people have a hard time seeing Angie . . ."

"Why do they?" Eula Mae demanded, logically enough.

"Well, now—" Tobias floundered.

" 'Cause I'm an Angel," Angie said calmly. "A somewhat fallen Angel at th' moment; but still, an Angel. You see, Ma'am, I've got th' orphan's curse upon me head, 'n—"

"Th' whaaaat?" Eula Mae shrieked.

"The orphan's curse," Angie repeated, just as calmly; then quoted grandiloquently:

"An orphan's curse would drag t' hell
A spirit from on high;
But oh! more horrible than that
Is th' curse in a dead man's eye!"

" 'The Rime of the Ancient Mariner,' " Tobias said automatically, "Samuel Taylor Coleridge."

"Right!" Angie said, "right as rain, you sweet li'l ol' intellectual, you! Now how's about squeezin' that there sponge ye're holdin' onto a little? Hard enough to squeeze some o' th' booze out o' him, 'n a little sense in, anyhow? I aim to make this heah cute li'l collection o' delicious delectabilities legally mine afore I gits too old t' *do* anything about her!"

"Well I never!" Eula Mae gasped.

"Squeeze him!" Angie said.

Tobias squeezed Soaked to the Gills's right arm. Hard. That worthy public official came to life. Briefly. Long enough to say:

"I now per-nounce y'all man 'n strife! Sign th' book, will y'all?"

"You mean man and *wife,* don't you?" Tobias said.

"Don't make no nevermind," Soaked growled. "Sign the gaw-damned book, will y'all?"

They signed it: The happy couple, first, then Tobias and Celie-Belle as witnesses, then Soaked scrawled his John Hancock across the bottom. "In Babylonian cuneiform," Tobias decided, "from the looks of it."

"That'll be three buck 'n a half!" Soaked said.

"Why, Soames!" Eula Mae gasped, "this heah furr'n gent'lm'n said—"

"It's all right, Ma'am!" Angie whispered, and passed her over the twenty. Then he gave Soaked exactly three dollars and a half, as requested.

"Now, c'mon, li'l Puddin 'n Pie!" he said to Anne. "I got me a few new mannish tricks I aim to show ye!"

"No you don't!" Anne got out. "I don't like this, Angie, I don't like it none a'tall! Don' 'pear to me *legal.* I never even got to say 'I do!' 'N—"

Angie grinned at her lecherously.

"But, honey, I already *know* ye do," he said.

By then, Eula Mae was 'fearin' fur' her twenty dollars, so she said, 'mighty fas' like'—

"It's legal, honey. Minute you signs th' book, it's plumb down right legal 'n proper."

"But ma'am!" Anne protested, "I wants myself a weddin' certificate! Can't go home 'n tell Paw I'm a married woman without nothin' to prove it! He'll skin me alive sure as shootin'. 'Specially since—"

She stopped short, her sweet, young face five different shades of crimson.

"Why, Angie!" Celie-Belle hooted, "you no-count ol' dirty dawg, you! Been puttin' in a crop afore you've built a fence, ain't you? Wal, I'll be shot with slops 'n arrested fur stinkin'! Never woulda thought you still had it in you! 'Cause if there ever wuz a fella who oughta be plumb wore out by now, hit's you, you ol' rascal, you!"

Anne was staring at her newly acquired—maybe—husband, and her penny-brown eyes were wide with sudden horror. Then they went light-filled, crystalline, blind.

"Oh, Angie!" she wailed.

Celie-Belle put out an arm that would have graced—or disgraced —a full-grown Portland China hog, and drew the weeping bride to her ample bosom.

"Now, now, honeychile!" she crooned, "don't take on over hit! I was purely jes funnin' ol' Angie, anyhow. I be dawg effen I ain't purely got hoof 'n mouf disease fer a fact! Open up this heah trap o' mine 'n mah hoof jes purely flies up to stick itself in it! Now, now, baby! Don't take on over it! A man what *ain't* done a spot o' cundanglin' in his day ain't no man atall 'n—"

By then Eula Mae was sitting down, busily writing out the marriage certificate. Soaked to the Gills, since all and sundry had inadvertently turned him loose, was lying down. Flat on his face on the parlor rug.

"No!" Anne shrilled, "don't write it out, Ma'am! I don't want it! Don't want no whore hopper for my husband! And even less than that for—"

She stared at Angie, and her wide brown eyes grew wider still.

"My—baby's—pa . . . Ohhhhhhh! Angeeeeeee!"

Gently Angie eased her out of Celie-Belle's arms into his own. Kissed her, long and deeply. Grinned at her, said:

"Look, Annie, me darlin', Celie-Belle's ridin' fillies wuz purely fer practicin' on, nothin' more. Ye iver see a fella what could play a Stradivarius th' first time he picked it up? And that's what ye be, me duckie—a Stradivarius—not to be put into th' hands o' amateurs like poor Toby here. Or would ye rather that I wuz a short-fused dud, like certain parties I could mention, but won't?"

"Nooohhh—" Anne whispered tremulously, "I'd rather you be you, even sinful though you be, but—"

Celie-Belle gave a vast and windy sigh of relief. So vast and so windy it made the windows rattle.

"War's all over, ain't it, honeychile?" she boomed. " 'Sides you done promised to love, honor 'n *obey,* ain't you? Now, c'mon!"

Anne stared at her, said, "C'mon *where,* Miz Belle?"

"Mah place, nach! Got th' dawggonedest weddin' supper enybody ever sunk tooth into all spread out, th' bridal suite all cleaned 'n aired. *Silk* sheets on th' bed, 'n—"

But Anne's big brown eyes had eclipsed both earth and sky.

"Angie," she said slowly, softly, clearly, "you mean you actually planned for us to spend our weddin' night in—in—a *whore* house?"

Angie stared at his bride in pure dismay. Since he had never paid much attention to how human nature, female gender, actually works, it hadn't so much as occurred to him that there was anything wrong with the idea. Even granted that Anne's nature *was* human, which was a thing he often doubted. In fact, by then, he was practically *sure* it wasn't. But that it was feminine, he was just as sure; much of the time he had the feeling that she was at least six or eight times *more* feminine than mere *human* females ever were. . . .

"Look ye, Anne, me darlin'," he said, whispering the words into her shapely ear, "I—we—can't give offence to—poor Celie-Belle, not after she's gone to so much trouble on me behalf. Th' supper, anyhow, please? After that we'll purely skedaddle fer points unknown, and—"

"Sit down at the same table with—with wimmin you—you've gone to bed with? Have 'em a-smirking and a-grinning and a-thinking poor li'l fool, she—"

"None o' that, honey!" Belle boomed. "I purely changes mah stock right pert frequent. Ain't a filly in th' house at th' moment what ever even *seen* Angie before, 'n I'll take mah Bible oath on thet!"

"Well—" Anne began, "I—"

"Tell you another thing, baby," Celie-Belle said, leaning toward her and assuming a confidential tone that would have deafened a gatepost, "wuzn't fur y'all decent, respectable *ladies,* madams like me would hafta go outa business. Fact is, ladies like you 'n Miz McGill here, could shut up every spo'tin' house in the country inside o' two weeks, you wuz to set yore minds to it. . . ."

Eula Mae finished signing a very credible forgery of her husband's signature to the marriage certificate. Looked Celie-Belle straight in the eye:

"Wal now, Celie-Belle," she said flatly, "done promised th' Good Lord I'd never address a spoken word to a critter like you, direct like, anyhow. But what you jes said done made me take that promise back. I'd sure admire to have you explain to me *how.* How we kin shet up all th' ho houses 'n keep our menfolks to home, I mean?"

"Hit's plumb, downright simple, Miz McGill, 'n you, too, you pore baby! Git in there 'n *fight* fur yore menfolks! Give us a *run* fur our money! Buy yourselves two or three silk nighties so damn thin yer hubbies kin see through 'em jes' like they wuz window glass—"

Abruptly the vision of how Eula Mae McGill would look in a transparent silk nightgown crashed into Tobias' head. He got up and walked out on the veranda. If he hadn't done that he would have risked death by asphyxia from the gale storm of laughter rising in his windpipes, shutting off his breath.

"And?" Anne whispered.

"Stands t' reason, honeychile," Celie-Belle's bass voice boomed on, "effen a pore housebroke critter like th' majority o' menfolks be, is even got the strength *left* to *walk* to a cathouse, hit's proof positive that y'all ain't treatin' him right at home! Menfolks is critters o' *habit.* Loves their comfort more'n enything else. Ain't even fixin' to go to no restaurant to eat no greasy swill, yore home cookin' be equal to his ma's. 'N by th' same token, whut he's a-gittin' hot 'n heavy *every* blessed night to *home,* he ain't a gonna go tomcattin' round to *find,* 'n then hafta pay out his hard-earned *cash* fur it to boot! Do *thet* sound reasonable to y'all o' don't hit?"

Eula Mae was staring at her husband's supine form with a warm and speculative eye.

"It shore Lawd do, damned if it don't, Celie-Belle!" she said.

"All right," Celie-Belle went on, enjoying her own flights of oratory now, and even more their effect upon her captive audience. "Take Mister McGill, Justice o' th' Peace, 'n a fine fella—'ceptin' fur a certain weakness fur the cup what cheers. Many's th' time I done reproached him fur his drinkin' habits. 'Soaked,' I sez to him, I sez, 'you's got yoreself a mighty fine missus to home. Good-lookin' woman yore Eula Mae fer a fact! So how come you's always soaked to th' gills instead o' rallyin' round 'n tendin' to yore homework?' 'N you know whut he ups 'n answers to thet, Eula Mae?"

"No," Eula Mae said, ignoring or maybe even pardoning Celie-Belle's temerity in addressing her by her Christian name, in her hunger and thirst after useful knowledge, "I shore Lawd don't. What did he now?"

"He sez, sez he, 'You's right, Celie—you's purely right! Eula Mae's a mighty pretty woman fer a fact! But how is a fella to snuggle up next to a gal purely born with a geldin' knife in her hands? Don't even know eny other word but "No!" Or maybe: "Git away from me you onery dirty-minded critter, you!" That's how come I drinks, Celie-Belle—t'ease th' pain in my balls where she's done purely froze 'em *blue!*' "

"Why th' filthy-mouthed, lyin' bastid!" Eula Mae shrilled, and aimed a practiced kick right where it would do Soaked to the Gills the most good—or harm.

"C'mon, Annie, me darlin'," Angie purred, "I suspect we'd best be gettin' outa here!"

"All right," Anne said primly, "but *where* are we goin'?"

"Oh Lord!" Angie groaned, but then he saw how she was grinning at him. As though she had invented mischief, and still held the original patent on it. "Where *do* we be a goin', me duckie?" he said.

"Celie's place," Anne said. "To *stay.* Tonight anyhow. And if by morning I haven't made you forget every other female critter you *ever* had, there or anywhere else I mean, you can write me out a bill of divorcement, Angie, darlin', without one red cent of alimony in it, at that! Now c'mon!"

The wedding supper was really something, Tobias had to admit. But he couldn't eat it. He sat there picking at the food: Hawg jowls 'n black-eyed peas, chitterlings with red beans, mountains of fried chicken, alps of beaten biscuits piping hot, candied sweet potatoes, ham hocks 'n gravy, collard greens and hominy grits, corn pone and molasses, apple pie, lemon pie, sweet potato pie, pumpkin pie, pecan pie, pancakes and bacon, eggs any style, beer, wine, gin, whisky, and what have you, but he simply couldn't eat it.

He was too consumed with the world's most abject and miserable emotions: envy, jealousy, and frustrated desire. The trouble was that Celie-Belle in a sudden attack of discretion had decided *against* having any of her stable of riding fillies attend the supper, so poor Tobias was all alone.

He sat there, glowering at Anne, hating her even worse than he did Angie, because Angie couldn't help being Angie, while Anne, goddamn her, knew just how he, Tobias Tobit, felt about her; and, despite that knowledge—or because of it, maybe?—kept right on acting as though he weren't alive, as if there weren't any other two living beings on the planet Earth except Angie and her own, luscious, delectable little self, which was maybe how she even felt about matters by then.

Angrily, Tobias pushed back his chair, stood up:

"I'm tired," he announced to no one in particular, "gonna catch me some shut-eye." Then, directly to Celie-Belle, "Anywhere I can bunk, Miz Belle?"

"Why shore, honeylamb!" Celie-Belle boomed, thus adding intolerable insult to very nearly mortal injury, because he wanted to scream at her: "I'm nobody's fornicating *lamb,* goddamnit!" but he didn't, and she rumbled on, cheerfully: "Number thirty-four, lambie-pie, right at th' head o' th' stairs . . ."

So sick, hurt, cold-sober, his all-but-empty belly beginning to growl at him a little, Tobias climbed the stairs. The door wasn't locked, so he pushed it open, switched on the lights and went in. It was a fair-sized bedroom decorated in what might be best described as Basin Street Parlor House Gothic; but poor Tobias was in too foul a humor to even be amused, as he ordinarily would have been by that monumental orchestration of every conceivable detail contributing to the violation of all the canons of taste. As long as said taste ran the gamut from the merely awful to the absolutely execrable, that is.

Swearing, he kicked off his shoes, stripped off his clothes, underwear and all, and lay there glaring with pure sadomasochistic rage at his own agonizingly aching hard-on, but refusing to lend it a comforting hand.

"Ache, damn you!" he snarled at it. "See how much good it'll do you!"

He had no sooner got the words out, when the door flew open, and a girl came into the room. Quivering with outraged modesty, Tobias flopped over on his belly only to have his mind occupy itself with the curious, but entirely logical thought: "Is modesty any better served by a breech presentation? Is my ass any less offensive than my cock?" He was still debating the niceties of correction and courtesy under those peculiar circumstances when the girl opened her mouth and said:

"Are you Mr. Dan?"

"Hell, no!" Tobias raged. "Get out of here, will you? Haven't you any shame?"

"Nary a bit, come to think of it, honey," the girl said cheerfully. "Now *you* tell *me:* What th' heck would a girl do with *shame* in a place like this?"

Tobias stole a look at her. She was small. Slender. She had jet-black hair and eyes. Her knee-length dress did little to hide her shape. Said shape, Tobias decided, was decidedly shapely. In fact it was mighty fine. Whereupon his hard-on tried to bore a hole through the bed, mattress, springs and all.

The girl laughed.

"You *are* Mr. Dan, ain't you?" she giggled. " 'Cause this is number thirty-four, sure as shootin'. 'N Angie 'lowed I'd find you up here!"

"Angie allowed you'd find *whom* up here?" Tobias growled.

"Mr. Rapid Dan, th' Jackrabbit Man, Fastest Gun in th' West," the girl said calmly.

"I'll kill him!" Tobias shrieked, his voice gone woman shrill in his rage. "Why the lousy bastard he—"

"Now you ain't bein' fair, honey," the black-haired girl said. "Angie fair dotes on you, for a fact. Tha's how come he sent you a present. . . ."

"A present?" Tobias said. "Why goddamn him, I don't see any present, and—"

"Me. I'm the present," the black-haired girl said. "Now turn over. I want to see if you's interested. 'Cause if you ain't, I'll go right back downstairs. . . ."

Tobias could feel the rage draining out of him, right through the soles of his feet. Slowly, luxuriously, he turned over. Stretched out his arms to her.

"Come here, baby doll!" he said.

First she got out of that little dress, under which was only her shapely shapeliness. Then she came to him. But when he wrapped her in his arms, she put her two hands against his chest, pushing.

"No sir, Danny-boy," she said. "Not like that."

Tobias stared at her wonderingly.

"Then—how?" he gasped.

"Us is gonna play games," she giggled. "Angie said I wuz to learn you. To slow down, I mean."

"I—I don't understand—" Tobias said.

"Knows you don't, Danny-boy. Just you lie back real comfy like 'n let Momma tend to you . . ."

She attended to him, all right. But the *way* she did so was maybe a mite peculiar.

"Ouch!" Tobias yelled. *"Now* what th' hell?"

"That's th' Masters 'n Johnson technique," the black-haired girl said. "Don' ask me what that means, 'cause I don' know. Fact is, it ain't even been invented yet. But it's gonna be—forty, fifty years from now, Angie sez."

"Dammit you—you've *maimed* me!" Tobias moaned.

"No I ain't, honeylamb. Jes' stopped you from goin' off like a damn Yankee firecracker on th' foah o' July. Rewards 'n punishments, Angie sez. Stick 'n carrot. You keeps a tight check rein on yo'self, 'n we'uns'll have fun. But none o' thet Rapid Dan business, you heah?"

Tobias heard. And obeyed. And sometime before daylight, was rewarded, finally. Only by then, he was too blamed sore to care.

But, thinking about that session afterwards—"Emotion recollected in tranquility" as the poet says—Tobias acknowledged that he had real reasons to be grateful to his Guardian Angel. For never, after that night, was he the fastest gun in the West.

The *second* fastest, maybe, but the all-time quick-draw champion in the boudoir rodeo, no. Even that was an improvement, he had to admit. Though not enough of an improvement to serve him for very much if he were forced to take on little Sara and/or Clara in the immediate future, of that he was dismally sure.

"So we sort of postpones 'em," Angie said. "Fer, after ye gits back from these here two Random Chance sequences, with th' Absurdity Factor built in, I brung ye up from Tartarus, ye will be, Toby lad! Ye kin bet yer poor blue-bruised longitudinarious on that!"

As it turned out, Angie was right. Tobias was. Ready, willing and able. Fat lot of good it did him, though.

Or maybe it *did.* Who knows?

Eight

They were sitting on the front porch of Celie's parlor house, busily engaged in fanning flies. Anne wasn't with them. She was still upstairs, sleeping the sweet sleep of the good, the generous, the warm of heart.

"All tuckered out, poor li'l thing," Angie said.

"You don't look so high and mighty yourself," Tobias said.

"I ain't. Fact is, I'm feeling mighty poorly. Fer Unlawful Carnal Knowledgin' damages me essential spirituality—o' somethin' . . ."

"Ha!" Tobias said. "Then by now your essential spirituality ought to be wrecked!"

"It *is,*" Angie groaned. "Smashed to kindlin'. 'N me poor ol' longitudinarious is—"

"Angie, for God's sake!" Tobias said.

"My, my! Ain't we prim 'n proper, though! Tell me, Toby, me boy, me boy—how wuz she? I mean that li'l black-eyed Susan I sent ye up?"

Tobias glared at him.

"As if you didn't already *know,*" he said.

"Yes," Angie said. "Congratulations, Toby lad! Ye acquitted yerself nobly, fer a fact. A li'l more trainin' 'n ye'll be ready fer li'l Sara—or is it Clara? Wouldn't do to disappoint her—or is it them?—ye know. Fact is, disappointin' sweet young things horizontally just ain't *nice.* But we don't have to worry about that anymore. Or we won't, after ye get back from—"

"California. And after that Kansas, Oklahoma, northern Texas. Or is it the other way around?"

"Don't know. Depends upon ye, lad. Which sequence would ye rather try *first,* lad: the gun moll or th' lady preacher?"

"The lady preacher," Tobias said. "At least she'll be a decent respectable religious woman and—"

"Ha!" Angie said.

"You mean she isn't?" Tobias whispered.

"Her religion ain't nothin' but a sublimation—or a substitution, just like me friend Siggie says. When ye show up she won't have to sublimate, nor substitute, not neither one. Ye see, along with making ye rich, I got to further yer bed trainin' or else ye'll go'n ruin things for a fact. Now all I got to figger out is how to get ye out to California in time . . ."

"Why California?" Tobias said.

"That's where *she* is. L'Amour McSimple Fearsome, which is th' handle the lady preacher goes by. And it's got to be California, 'cause that's the only state that people like her kin' operate in. Ye see, Toby, me boy, me boy—eastern folks is inhibited, southern folks is moronic, mid-western folks is retarded, but California folks is plain *insane.* Helps more'n somewhat. Ye don't have to look out fer but one thing—"

"And that one thing is?" Tobias said.

"Actin' sensible. You do that, and right off they'll think *you're* crazy 'n throw you into th' local booby hatch. Only damn state in the Union where normal people is locked up 'n all the paper-doll cutters 'n pancake collectors is running things. Never could get away with a damned thing out there. Everybody kin see me—'cept of course, the nice, sane, decent people they've got locked up. Helluva a place, California. You'll love it!"

"You get me introductions to Mary Miles Minter, Mabel Normand, Barbara La Marr, Pola Negri, and Theda Bara, and I just might," Tobias said.

"Can do," Angie said solemnly.

"Now *look,* Angie! I was only kidding! I don't want to get mixed up with those movie vamps! Why—"

" 'N why not? Maybe they could teach you something, though I doubt it. No, that ain't th' way to go at it. Fer instance, you don't like big wimmen very much, d'ye?"

"Can't stand 'em," Tobias said. "Why?"

"No reason. That ain't even the main problem . . ."

"And what is the main problem?" Tobias said.

"Gettin' ye out there. Since, as usual, we're both short o' the coin o' th' realm, I can't jes' put ye on a pullman 'n ship ye out to th' coast. 'N gettin' out there ridin' the rods would call for me goin' along to guide ye, which would mess up me honeymoon more'n somewhat. Sweet li'l duckie, me Annie—"

"Angie," Tobias said, "how're you going to manage *that?* Being married to Anne, I mean? It isn't as if you were *human,* you know. Seems to me she's going to have one hell of a life, being married to a figment of my imagination, and—"

"First things first, me boy! I get ye settled down, well-wedded 'n frequently bedded—with Clara—or is it Sara?—and I kin dispose of a certain amount o' leisure. Then I'll petition m'Auld Cuss to let me assume me human form permanent—which means fer th' rest o' *her* sequence anyhow . . ."

"And will he?" Tobias said.

"Dunno. Mebbe. Depends on the mood he's in. He kin be a mighty nice Auld Cuss, sometimes . . . Now let me see—let me see —got it!"

"You've got *what?"* Tobias said.

"How to get ye out to Cal-li-forny. Be a might rough on ye, but —no, it won't. I'll put ye to sleep first."

"Now, Angie!" Tobias said.

" 'Tain't nothin' neither harmful nor dangerous. Just a mite scary, ye wuz awake. To save time, I'm gonna hafta use a li'l extreme kinetic parapsychology on ye. Bend yer illusions concerning time 'n space a bit. Waft ye out there so damn fast that ye'll arrive day before yestiddy 'n—"

"But, Angie, that's not possible. Oh hell, I suppose it is, isn't it? But before you pull this particular fast one, tell me this: Just how is associating with—what's that name again, Angie?"

"L'Amour McSimple Fearsome. Hell of a moniker, ain't it?"

"It sure is! Anyhow, explain to me the main point. How is associating with this female evangelist going to—"

"Increase yer material wealth? Fix it up so that ye kin arrive in East Egypt, Kentucky, all dolled up in flossy duds 'n ridin' in a Pierce Arrow? Or would ye rather have a Duesenberg?"

"Don't care. Don't know a damned thing about cars, anyhow. Answer my question, Angie!"

"Bringing salvation to sinners is a lucrative business, Toby me lad. First rule in any evangelist's handbook: pry the sucker—I mean sinner—loose from his ready cash. So L'Amour's got it made. That there First Church o' th' Emergent Saints 'n Holiness Tabernacle o' hers is twice the size of a football stadium. She's got three jazz bands sepplin' each other just to keep th' spirit movin'. Floodlights in Technicolor—"

"What's Technicolor?" Tobias said.

"Ye're sharp t'day, ain't ye, me boy? Technicolor ain't been invented yet, but them floodlights that wicked old ex-casting couch broad is got in her hysteria mill is a mighty close approximation of what it's gonna be like . . ."

"And what's a casting couch broad?" Tobias said.

"Ex. Ye ask too damn many questions, sometimes," Angie sighed. "Besides, ye're wastin' me time 'n yer own. Close yer glimmers, will ye?"

"No!" Tobias said.

"Ye'll be sorry," Angie said. "Close 'em, Toby!"

"I'll be damned if I will!" Tobias said, or started to, for at that precise instant, the world began to whirl. It whirled in eccentric circles like a pinwheel, faster and faster and faster. The circular bands of the pinwheel were orange and green. Then time and space lurched, shuddered, and slid out from under Tobias Tobit.

He went streaking out through space ten billion times faster than the speed of light, which was supposed to be an absolute, but, as it turned out, wasn't. The atoms of his body separated themselves from one another farther and farther, and even the nuclei from the protons, neutrons, and electrons, so that at this stage of his travel outward through the twin illusions of space and time, he rather resembled a comet. In fact, Quichi Kuychi, the great Japanese astronomer, put him down as one, and even plotted his course through the universe, predicting that he would reappear on April 1, 2001.

But, in strict accordance with the second law of relativity, as he streaked outward (bare-assed, of course, as was reglementary for streaking, even then) time slowed down. By the time he got to the outer rings of Saturn, where Angie allowed him a brief rest by incorporating him with the tons of debris—old space ships, mostly—in that celestial junkyard circling the planet, time had come—for him, anyhow—to a dead halt. Then, as the ring he was in speeded up so that centrifugal force spun him off into space again, his conception of the illusion men call Time had reversed itself, so that by the time he got to Uranus, he was a little boy. He whirled past Neptune's lovely sea-blue surface as a tiny baby. As he looped around Pluto he was just being born, spewing forth and squalling out of the black womb of night and chaos, screaming his rage at the titanic injustice of being forced back into that vast absurdity that men call Life.

Thereafter, as he sped sunward once again, he lived all his life over again in vivid, completely realistic pictures inside his mind, which took him no little time since the cellular structure of his brain had separated into its component atoms, and they into their correspondant subatomic particles, the whole gooey mess, as well as the rest of him being spaced-out a couple of million light-years or so across the Void, which made remembering quite a chore. But he did it anyhow, or rather actually relived it, and in not-yet-invented Technicolor, helplessly repeating all his former mistakes, follies, would-be sins, regretting the latter all the more bitterly because he had been and/or was so amateurish a sinner, neither giving nor receiving joy. All the girls who had scorned him scorned him all over again as he streaked through vast aeons of night and nothingness, much more conscious of their scorn than he was of his own remarkable voyage through the Void.

All those who had laughed at him filled outer space with the silvery lift and soar of their feline, female mockery. He fumbled that long pass on Hillburn High's three-yard line, stood there weeping helplessly as "Bearcat" Wolfson, Hillburn's quarterback, scooped it up to run ninety-seven all but unopposed yards to score the winning touchdown against Ryland. Sat on the bench in mute misery the rest of his senior year. Went on to college, where the only thing he'd ever been good at, his books, earned him a little acceptance, a wafer-thin slice of peace. But after that it was girls, girls, girls, most of whom froze him off, or slapped him off, or cried him off, but the ones who really sunk him were the ones who *didn't* refuse him, who allowed him to demonstrate his monumental ineptitude at anything you couldn't learn from a book, and Lord knows For Unlawful Carnal Knowledging heads the list of the subjects *not* to be so learned.

Nell Brightwell, again, who wouldn't even let him try, but who kept him on as her semi-official "promised," because, being a realist, she realized she couldn't do any better. Then the War, and France, where the ma'moiselles were even beginning to teach him a trick or two when that 188mm howitzer shell zeroed in on his Company, and —faster, pluming the ice crystals of his disintegration into his own atomic and subatomic particles five trillion light-years across the majestic night of space. Time jamming upon him, foreshortening, slowing down. And the earth like a speckled-blue marble below him, creamy tufted with clouds, looming up now, screaming up towards him, filling half the horizon, all of it, and his subatomic, atomic, molecular, cellular structure, incandescent from friction with the atmosphere, flaming meteor bright across the black California sky so that all the people jerking rhythmically to the syncopated beat of Sister L'Amour McSimple Fearsome's three jazz bands looked up and cried:

"Ohhhhhhhhhhh!"

Then he hit. Or did he? Anyhow, he opened his eyes. He was clinging to the rafters of the Holiness Tabernacle some seventy feet above the floor. Only it looked a hell of a lot higher than that to him, because you see he was

Eight and one half inches high.

And all the sinners and the saved were pointing up at him and screaming and fainting and going into the bends and jerks, until Sister L'Amour lifted up her great voice and roared.

" 'Tis th' spirit of th' Lord come upon us! I pray thee, Blessed Spirit, come on down!"

"And break my damn fool neck?" Tobias groaned inside his mind.

"No ye won't, Toby lad," Angie's voice poured through his head. "Look what nice *wings* ye've got fer a change!"

Tobias twisted his head on his neck and saw them. They were absolutely gorgeous. Instead of being feathered, they were butterfly wings, made up of stripes and whorls and splotches of every primary color in the spectrum, all the secondary colors, or mixtures, and every shade or tint in between. They were thirty-two inches from tip to tip, and thirty-eight inches long. He tried moving them. They swished and shimmered, glowing softly in the Klieg lights.

"Now ain't ye th' cutest li'l fairy anybody iver did see!" Angie chuckled inside his, Tobias', head. "Oh no, Toby, lad, I don't mean *that* kind. Not a fairy-swish, but a fairy-fairy. Like Peter Pan. Now turn loose that there rafter. Flying's fun, me boy!"

"Come on down, Holy Spirit!" L'Amour McSimple Fearsome boomed. She had a voice almost as deep as Celie-Belle's; but not quite. That is, she sounded like a yearling calf instead of a steer.

"Let go, lad!" Angie said.

With a shudder, Tobias turned loose the rafter. Much to his surprise, he didn't fall. His wide-spread butterfly wings caught the updraft from all the heat generated by that mass of jerking, moaning, sweating, stinking humanity below. He soared, weightless as a cloud, up to the very peak of the roof. Then, mightily pleased with himself, he flitted back and forth to the tune of the "Waltz of the Flowers" from Tchaikovsky's *Nutcracker Suite,* which, of course, Angie was busily playing inside his head.

"That's enough now, lad," Angie said. "Flit on down'n let 'er catch ye. This dodge is gonna build up her reputation no end. This time next week, she's gonna have to build another temple to hold all the suckers—I mean sinners—come to glory!"

Reluctantly, Tobias started down. Then it hit him. He was stark, mother-naked. And despite the fact that he had returned to earth in the form of his homunculus, he had all the attributes of adult masculinity—cleverly reduced to scale, of course. He was even as hairy as he'd always been, which rather spoiled the fairylike effect of his beautiful wings.

"But Angie!" he wailed.

"Don't make no niver ye mind," Angie purred. "She'd only like ye better in th' altogether . . ."

Toby fluttered on down. Sister L'Amour caught him. Held him triumphantly aloft in one huge sweaty hand.

What happened after that was history: L'Amour McSimple Fearsome preached the greatest sermon of her entire career. The sinners fell out in rows, then in mounds, piled atop one another in layers three to five sinners deep, all of them jerking, screaming, foaming at the mouth, talking in tongues, a prey to a religious ecstasy so great that fully fifteen female sinners who merely happened to be on the bottom of their respective mounds conceived *pro obra et gracia* of well —if not the Holy Ghost—at least of volunteers working in his spiritual behalf, and anyhow, miracles of that magnitude are not to be sneered at, are they?

At the end of the services, Sister L'Amour bore Tobias away to her dressing room, still holding him triumphantly aloft like a torch. Or rather like a candle, because he wasn't anything like as big as a torch.

"You're crushing my damn wings, damnit!" Tobias screamed at her.

"My, my, what a filthy tongue you've got for such a little fellow!" Sister L'Amour laughed. "Tell me, hon—if I turn you loose, what will you do?"

"Get the hell outa here!" Tobias said.

"Thought so," Sister L'Amour said judiciously. "Which is why I'm damned sure not gonna turn you loose. You're worth a fortune to me, you know."

"All right," Tobias said, "what's my cut gonna be?"

"Ha!" Sister L'Amour boomed, "that li'l pinhead of yours *works,* don't it, hon?" Then: "How's ten per cent strike you?"

"Fifty per cent," Tobias said. "Half your take, L'Amour. Or I'll flit outa here so damn fast that—"

"You try it and I'll pluck them gorgeous flappers of yours out by the roots. Then where would you be?"

"Bleeding to death, likely," Tobias said. "But on the other hand, where would *you* be, sister? Without my wings I'm just a naked, subcompact midget. With 'em, we can convince the suckers I'm the only begotten son of Beelzebub and the Sugarplum Fairy, or something . . ."

"Twenty-five?" Sister L'Amour said hopefully.

"Forty!" Tobias squeaked. "And that's my last offer! Take it or leave it, L'Amour!"

"Done!" Sister L'Amour boomed. "Say—tell me something, you li'l doll you—what's your name?"

"Toby," Tobias said.

"Toby what?" L'Amour said.

"Toby Mariposa," Angie said through Tobias' mouth.

"Knew you was Eyetalian!" L'Amour boomed. "Just *loves* you Latin fellas! Hotter than a two-dollar nickel-plated pistol, every living one of you. C'mon, Toby, doll, give Momma a kiss to seal th' bargain!"

"All right," Tobias said, and leaned forward. Then he was drowning in a red tide of the thickest, gooiest lipstick anyone could possibly imagine. Bourbon-flavored lipstick at that. So heavily bourbon-flavored that Tobias felt himself drowning in it, and getting drunker than a skunk at the same time.

"Help!" he shrieked. "I'm suffocating! I'm dying! I'm drowning! Help!"

Catching him by his gorgeous wings, L'Amour proceeded to lick the lipstick off of him with a tongue that seemed to Tobias to be about the size of the mattress of a single bed, except that no mattress ever was that busy, hot, and wet, and surely not so delightfully bourbon-flavored.

The results upon poor little Tobias was both psychological and physiological, which caused L'Amour to roar with laughter.

"Why damn me for a sinner!" she boomed. "You remind me of my *last* producer, Sammy Blitz! He used to *love* that all-around-the-world business, too, he did. Now, tell Momma—are you *happy?"*

"Divinely," Tobias sighed. "In fact, I'm limp!"

"Which any fool can plainly see," L'Amour said. "And you damned li'l sneak, you've taken unfair advantage of me! And you no bigger than—"

Her eyes lighted up with what seemed to Tobias, diabolical glee.

"A tallow candle!" she boomed, and made a grab for him.

Desperately Tobias spread his wings and fluttered ceilingward.

"No, you don't!" he shrieked. "I'll asphyxiate! I'll drown! I'll—Angie, you bastard, save me!"

"Why?" Angie chuckled. "Told ye a million times it ain't *fair* to disappoint th' lassies. 'N besides, th' electric vibrator ain't even been invented yet! So do yer duty like a nice, sweet li'l mannikins and—"

"Let me out of here!" Tobias screamed and fluttered out the window. But he was still well tanked up on the bourbon from that lipstick, so his flying was even more erratic than the flying of a butterfly usually is. So, instead of flitting in a more or less straight line, he flitted hither and yon, yon and hither. Worse still, every time he soared up to treetop height, he got vertigo, so Sister L'Amour, encumbered by nothing heavier than her white linen priestly robe, under which she wore only a pair of black silk and lace step-ins, caught him quite easily.

Once back in the dressing room, she was very shortly encumbered by nothing at all. And, holding Tobias with his wings folded tightly to his back in one huge paw, she took aim and——

"I'll be damned if you will!" Tobias thought with such an onslaught of pure outrage that he burst through whatever spell Angie had put upon him and became his normal size again.

In the process, of course, his butterfly wings, not being a part of his essential molecular structure, fell off, and fluttered to the floor.

L'Amour stared at him, her eyes glassy with astonishment. Then they cleared.

"Boy oh boy oh boy oh boy!" she said. "Come to Momma, baby!"

Tobias considered that. For about ten seconds. He was a little disappointed at the fact that she wasn't entirely, or at least not originally, a blonde, for, being a purist, he preferred his blondes blonde, and his brunettes brunette, as the case may be. But since the action involved had become considerably less drastic than it would have been even a few minutes before, he saw no reason not to oblige, especially in view of the fact that Sister L'Amour, in the costume of sinful Mother Eve, wasn't at all hard on the eye.

And, be it said, acquitted himself nobly, prolonging the festivities until dawn began to create form out of the primordial dark, to Sister L'Amour's wild and exceedingly noisy delight. But be it, with sad truth, also said that his new found prowess was a matter of neither will nor skill, for, as he groaned inside his mind:

'How's a fellow going to do himself any good a-poking around inside Mammoth Cave?'

"Lord, I'm tired!" L'Amour moaned at last. "And are you ever the *greatest,* Toby, love! Now, get up, will you? Return bout's postponed 'til tomorrow night, after services, and—"

Then, as he straightened up, she saw what a state he still was in, and burst into a great booming roar of laughter.

"Just like Sammy for a fact!" she guffawed. "Only respond to that all-around-the-world business, don't you?" Then, more gently: "Come here, hon. Momma'll fix . . ."

And did.

That next night, she introduced him to her congregation as the new secretary-treasurer and business manager of the Holiness Tabernacle of the Emergent Saints, which caused Angie to chuckle almost audibly inside Tobias' head:

"That's th' ticket, me boy, boy! Right off th' bat, we've got it made!"

But Angie hadn't taken into consideration the very real dangers involved in importing an exotic pagan sequential progression existing outside the narrow and rigid rules of Judeo/Christian cosmology. Which was why that heavenly miscreant, who was well aware of the demonstrable fact that, by any normal standards, the good citizens of the sovereign state of California are stark, raving crazy, hadn't, and couldn't have, realized that the *Cerritus Californianus* or California madness, extended to the young females of the species, and certainly not that the form it took among them was the unanimous opinion that one Toby Mariposa (the alias poor Tobias had got stuck with by then) was absolutely Dee-Vine!

"Better than Valentino!" more than one distraught miss declared. "That cute little crooked nose of his is plain swoony!"

So it was that when Sister L'Amour got back to her dressing room that night where she confidently expected to find Tobias awaiting her not exactly spiritual pleasure, that recent addition to her operational staff was conspicuous by his absence. Almost visibly snorting fire, Sister L'Amour surged out into the night.

She found Tobias easily enough. He was in front of the Tabernacle neck deep in flappers (as *that* generation of flower children, female gender, were usually called). For the first time in his life he was basking in general and wholehearted feminine approval. More than basking, he was fairly lapping it up. Because, you see, the girls of Ryland, New York, being a good bit shrewder than the California variety, as well as having been equipped by their native climate with what might be best described as *pudendae frigidae,* had, without notable exception, held the opinion that, "Tobias Tobit is an awful dope!"

True as that opinion indisputably was, it was becoming less so by the minute. In fact, the only thing that had kept Tobias Tobit, alias Toby Mariposa, where he was long enough for Sister L'Amour to catch up with him was that the confrontation with such an overwhelming embarrassment of fleshly riches had stoned him right out of his skull—oops! an anachronism!—had confused him to the extent that he was unable to decide *which* of the short-skirted, shingle-bobbed, delicious little dears to lead down the flowering primrose paths of carnal sin *first.*

But he *had* just about decided before L'Amour got there. And the glorious little sexual object upon whom his election had alighted turned out to be an object lesson (no pun intended!) in an aspect of human destiny, man's fate, that had escaped even so intellectually advanced an Angel as Angie. That aspect was—and is—that even Random Chance and the Absurdity Factor have a certain degree of inevitability built in. Or to put it another way, the long horror of human history clearly demonstrates "Something there is, that doesn't love the race of man!"

For any observer who has vanquished homo sapiens' unfortunate tendency towards sentimentality, and, as a consequence, has learned to view things as they really are, must long since have become aware of the workings of this iron law: "Given a choice under any circumstance where emotion takes precedent over sense, a man will make the *wrong* choice every time."

As now. There were roughly two hundred giddy young flappers surrounding Tobias Tobit, each of them possessing exactly the same biological equipment—in fine working order at that—and each of them about equally disposed to be rather easily persuaded to make sweet use thereof to her and Tobias' mutual joy. And upon whom did Tobias' election light?

Why, upon one Tilly McGuire.

And who was Tilly McGuire?

Why, the daughter of one Mike "Muckraking" McGuire, a newspaper man who was by that segment of his sequential progress forced to even sleep in a bulletproof vest because his weekly column, "Digging The Dirt," syndicated in a hundred and twenty-seven newspapers throughout the nation, had inspired more than one irate citizen to respond to the character assassination that was "Muckraking" Mike's stock in trade with attempted assassination of a more basic order.

But to return to our impromptu questionnaire.

Why did Tobias Tobit choose Tilly McGuire? Believe it or not, because of a total irrelevancy. Tilly was one of those Celtic misses who combines the opposites of jet-black hair with sky-blue eyes, and that startlingly contrasting combination really "sent" (another anachronism, but less) Tobias Tobit.

Now any fool can plainly see that the color of a girl's hair and eyes, or of her skin, for that matter, had absolutely nothing to do with the business at hand. But Tobias Tobit was not just any fool; he was his own special kind of super-fool, especially gifted, perhaps even a genius, in the exercise of folly.

In any event he'd got around to whispering in her dainty ear:

"You're gorgeous! What's your name?"

When Sister L'Amour caught up with him. Drawing her one hundred sixty pounds up to her full five feet eleven and three quarters inches tall, that saintly saver of sinners declaimed with icy, perfect histrionics:

"Why Mis-ter Mariposa! I never expected to find a serious God-fearing gentleman like you here, surrounded by painted hussies!"

And wading into—and through (for they parted like the Red Sea before Moses, the Lawgiver)—the flappers, she caught him by the arm, and dragged him bodily off to her lair, where she cuffed, cursed, and kicked him around for the better part of an hour before, the iron of her wrath transmuting itself into the gold of love, she made vigorous and prolonged use of his rapidly improving talents.

Naturally, of course, when she had borne down upon them like a dreadnought at full steam ahead, the flappers had scattered. Most of them had gone straight home, their dear little hearts filled to the breaking point with disappointment. A few of them had found other, suitably masculine, consolations.

But one of them did neither. She, with all the instincts inherited, doubtless, from her father, stole silently and totally unobserved behind L'Amour as, like a lioness with a billy goat, she bore Tobias to her den.

Positioning herself just outside the door of Sister L'Amour's dressing room, with one eye as blue as an Irish sky glued to the keyhole, Tilly McGuire observed with growing wrath poor Tobias' punishment, and, with a breath-gone fascination that only later, after having taken thought, was transsubstantiated or transmogrified into the jade green flames of jealous rage, its sequel.

That night, after supper, dear little Tilly fired the opening shot in the masterfully arranged, tactically speaking, battle of her revenge.

"Papa," said she. "That old L'Amour McSimple Fearsome ain't all she's supposed to be!"

"Tell me something I don't know, daughter mine!" Muckraking Mike chuckled. "She's worn out more'n one casting couch trying to get to be a star before she found out that a big horse like her could never make it. Not even with that fool Sammy Blitz pulling every wire 'twixt Holywood 'n Vine. But she's a *smart* cookie, lass! Or else I'd have got something on her by now. . . ."

"Papa," Tilly said demurely, "would you like to? Get something on her, I mean?"

"Would I like to be th' only son of John D. Rockefeller, Jay Gould, J. Pierpont Morgan, and Andrew Carnegie?" Mike roared. "Get something on that flossy old pious hypocrite 'n me column will grace th' front page o' th' *New York Times,* so help me!"

Then he stopped short. Unlike one Tobias Tobit, Mike was nobody's fool, and especially not when it came to the rather Machiavellian workings of the female mind. Even when said mind was housed in the head of his only daughter.

"Tell me, lass," he said, "would *you?* Like to get something on that fat-assed old ex-casting couch broad, I mean?"

"No, Papa," Tilly said primly, "I wouldn't like to. Only—"

"Only *what,* lass?" Mike growled.

"Only it seems I *have,"* Tilly said with venomous sweetness.

"Jehosiphat!" Mike bellowed. "And what have you got on her, Tilly, me darlin'? Tell your old fadder fer the love of Mike!"

"Well, Papa," Tilly said, "first off, she stole my boy friend. No—that isn't right. He wasn't my boy friend *yet.* But he was going to be. Because with all those silly girls around him, I was the only one he was payin' any attention to . . ."

"Hardly surprisin!" Mike said fondly. "You take after yer Sainted Mother whom th' blessed saints have got up there in Glory. Ye're as pretty as she wuz, lass. Maybe a mite prettier . . ."

"Thank you, Papa," Tilly said. "Will you see this fella—is he ever a sheik! Better lookin' than Rudolph Valentino—more *manly* lookin' anyhow, what with that cute li'l broken nose he's got—just like a prizefighter's—"

"That oughtn't to make him good-looking," Mike observed.

"Does though. Otherwise his face is so smooth—and—and so perfect he'd look sissified. His boxer's nose saves him from that."

"Th' fate worse than death!" Mike quipped. "Go on, lass!"

"Well," Tilly said slowly, "if the fate worse than death is the same for a man that people say it is for a girl, it *didn't* save him from that, Papa. Far from it."

"Je - hos - e - phat!" Mike said. "You don't mean—?"

"Yes, Papa. In *her* dressing room. I saw them."

Mike stared at his daughter. Said:

"How? Or mayhap 'tis of greater importance if you tell why?"

"How? Through the keyhole, nach! First she was slappin' him around she was so mad at him for payin' attention to *me.* And then she took off all her clothes, and after that she undressed *him.* And then—ohhhhhh Pa—paaah!" Tilly wailed.

"Now you don't even hafta tell me 'why,' " Mike said sadly. "A wee mite jealous, aren't you, lass?"

"Yyyyes, Papa! Papa, you aren't gonna let her get away with this, are you? Stealin' Toby from me, I mean?

"Toby what?" Mike said absently. "What's the moniker that this sheik—with patent leather hair I have no doubt!—goes by?"

"Mariposa. Toby Mariposa. Leastwise that's what she called him when she introduced him as her business manager."

Mike's head literally hit the ceiling, he bounced up from his chair so hard.

"Jeh-hos-si-phat!" he got out. "Gimme that phone, lass!"

Tilly sat there, her blue eyes very wide, as her father barked into the telephone.

"Operator! Operator! Gimme Long Distance will you please? Long Distance? Gimme Chicago. I want to talk person to person to Bill Hines, at th' *Chicago Sun.* Hell no, I don't know th' number! Lookitup, will you?"

Then, about a half an hour later:

"That you, Bill? Howya, kid? Yep, Mike. Tumbled right away didn't you? Bill, I think I'm onto th' scoop o' the century, but I need your help. Nach, kiddo! You do right by me, 'n I'll do right by you. It's a deal. First exclusive is mine, of course, but you can break it in the midwest in your late morning edition—long as you give me time to break it first, catch? Big? Of course it's big! Hell, kid—it's gigantic! Now just you hold on: Didya ever hear o' the Mariposa brothers? Ya did? Gimme th' dope on 'em willya?"

He beckoned his daughter to his side, and took the receiver a little way from his ear, so that she could hear the Chicago reporter's reply. For so dangerous a madness as she had fallen into, the cure had to be draconian. And he was wise enough to realize that she would both accept it better and believe it more quickly from a stranger than she would from him.

"Yah," Bill Hines's voice cackled over the wire, "th' kid just brought me their files from our morgue. Yah. Angelo and Antonio Mariposa. Hoods? Worse than that, Mike! Them sweet, lovable little characters are Scarface Al Capone's *hit* men. The dope is that th' younger one, Tony Mariposa, is th' mobster what knocked off Slow Dough Moe Green. Though knocked off is puttin' it mildly. Moe was slow on his payments as usual, so Capone sent Tony Butterfly—that's what Mariposa means, y'know—over to talk to him. Well that mean, skinny li'l hood took along a baseball bat 'n an assortment of lead pipes to liven up the conversation. When he got through th' coppers had to take th' stiff's fingerprints to prove it *wuz* Moe Green. . . ."

"Oh Papa!" Tilly wailed.

"What was that?" Bill said.

"Why me darlin' daughter, Bill. You see th' lame-brained little idiot has gone 'n fallen for this Tony Mariposa. So I had to let her hear the straight dope, and from *you,* kiddo. Yes, he's here in Califor - ni - ay. Hidin' out under th' sweetest dodge anybody *ever* figgered out. Nope. Can't tell you yet. Got to get proof. With *pictures,* natch. So hang up, willya? I gotta git hoppin'! Sure, sure! Ya got me *word.* Second exclusive's *yours,* lad. Ta-ta, now! Be seein' ya!"

"Papa—" Tilly whispered as he hung up, "it's not *Tony* Mariposa. It's *Toby* Mariposa. . . ."

"That makes a *difference,* lass? Only thing I can't figure is why he didn't change th' whole shebang. Tony Cucaracha—Tony Cockroach—would suit that miserable murderin' bastid just fine. 'N shacking up with L'Amour, herself, no less! Don't say much for his taste, does it? Now look, Tilly, me darlin', I got to hop. Git right onto this scoop. Don't s'pose I hafta tell you to stay away from this character, do I? One o' Scarface Al's torpedoes. Jesus! Half o' Chicago 'n all of Cicero is after this rat by now. You're anywhere *near* him when Dion O'Banion's tommy gunners catch up with 'im, you'll end up lookin' like so much Swiss cheese, daughter. 'N if it's the Gennas, Mike 'n Angelo, who get here *first,* gettin' ventilated will look like to you a mercy. So you stay *home,* lass! You've been seen talkin' to this hood, which in itself is enough to make characters like Hymie Weiss, Frankie Yale, Johnny Torrio, or Three Gun Aterie want to drop in on me diggins here to ask you questions. And th' way them mobsters got o' gettin' folks to sing like canary birds —even an innocent lass like *you,* daughter!—just plain ain't *nice,* catch? So don't you even go outside for air 'til I tell you that it's *safe.* You hear me, Tillie?"

"Yes, Papa. Ohhhhh Papa, how awful!" Tillie said.

One hour later, Muckraking Mike had taken his daughter's place outside L'Amour McSimple Fearsome's dressing-room door. He was determined to stay there as long as he had to in order to learn something useful. Which turned out to be practically all night— L'Amour didn't have talking, except for a few choice exhortations to greater speed and vigor when poor Tobias' none too ardent ardor flagged, in the back part of her head.

But Mike persisted, and finally, just before morning, had his reward. All the noisily amorous sound effects ceased at last, and L'Amour's big voice came breathily through that door.

"Toby, you jackass," she crooned fondly. "The trouble with you is that you ain't been broke in right. And since it stands to reason that I can go on giving you private riding lessons now that I've introduced you to the congregation, we're going to have to pull a nifty swifty, you'n me. So tomorrow night, you're gonna disappear . . ."

"I *am?*" Tobias whispered. "How, L'Amour?"

"Simple. You just ain't gonna show up, love. And, after services, I'm gonna announce to the suckers, I mean the sinners, that you're traveling from place to place to arrange a grand preachin' 'n soul-saving tour, all over the U.S.A. Which is exactly what you *are* gonna do—but not right away . . ."

"Then what *am* I going to do right away, L'Amour darling?" Tobias said.

"You're going down south almost to the Mexican border and hole up in a place called Cerda Gorda, at a hotel named La Suciedad Asquerosa," L'Amour said. " 'Til I join you there. That'll be in about two weeks. I don't dare make it any sooner, love, 'cause one of these frozen-tailed old biddies'll put two 'n two together sure as hell. You rest up. Sleep. Eat. But not at the hotel. That greaser's food ain't fit for human consumption. Give you a case of the Aztec two step th' *first* day." She smiled at him, then went on absent-mindedly. "Don't have to worry about the wimmen because most of 'em is fat as brood sows, ain't had a bath since th' fall of Chapultapec, 'n is guarded by a passel o' greaser hubbies, fathers, and brothers who'll stick a shiv into you if you even *look* at those Mex-frails out the corner of one eye . . ."

"You mean everybody is Mexican in that town?" Tobias said.

"Except the gringos, and they've gone native so damn long ago you won't be able to tell the difference. Anyhow, here're two C notes. You catch the two-oh-five train this afternoon. And *behave* yourself, you hear? 'Cause if you don't you'll be in trouble—and not just from *me,* Toby, love. You shove your li'l chili pepper up one of those Mex broads and it'll *drop* off on th' floor by the next morning —that is if some hot-tempered Mex ain't carved you up into something that looks like hamburger before *then."*

"I hear you, L'Amour," Tobias said. "And I'll be good, I promise you."

"All rightie. But just to make sure, I better send you down there all tuckered out. Some come to Momma, baby-boy!" L'Amour McSimple Fearsome said.

Muckraking Mike McGuire tiptoed away from that door.

"Boy oh boy oh boy! And also hotdiggity dog!" he said.

Nine

When Tobias Tobit first walked into the dining room of La Suciedad Asquerosa, he was immediately convinced of the saintly certitude of L'Amour McSimple Fearsome's wisdom. For that dining room was literally black with flies—the fly being the only other living creature beside a Mexican who can eat Mexican cooking and survive it.

So Tobias crossed the street to the Hotel El Asco Cochambroso. It turned out—a feat of truly miraculous proportions—to be a trifle dirtier than even La Suciedad Asquerosa, and was the proud possessor of at least one extra fly.

"I'll starve to death!" Tobias wailed. "In two whole damn weeks, I'll—"

Then, before his wondering eyes, he saw the spotless—comparatively, anyhow—expanse of La Pulga Saltona, the town of of Cerda Gorda's newest fleabag. He entered it at once, and was greeted with lazy amiability by Don Felipe, "El Flacucho," which honorable title, meaning in English, "The Skinny One," was naturally awarded to Don Felipe for the simple and logical reason that the owner of La Pulga Saltona weighed a little over three hundred pounds.

Seeing that Don Felipe had gone back to sleep again—that gracious hidalgo being, the good citizens of Cerda Gorda swore, the only human being in all of history who could and did sleep twenty-five hours out of every twenty-four—without even waiting to see whether he, Tobias Tobit, was going to sign the register or whatever, Tobias made his way to the dining room.

You could actually *count* the flies in La Pulga Saltona's dining room, which was a vast improvement over the town's other two hotels; and a goodly number of them were already stuck fast in the flypaper with which Conchita, Don Felipe's nineteen-year-old daughter, was busily festooning the place.

It was, of course, Conchita who was responsible for La Pulga Saltona's quite remarkable cleanness. For Conchita was what Mexicans call "Una Mujer Brava." Now if any sly Mexican tries to tell you that means "A Brave Woman," which is what the literal translation of it actually is, stamp on his bunions and spit in his eye. What it actually means is an advanced, or a liberated woman, a species that any self-respecting Mexican will avoid like the plague, and any half-way prudent Mexican will run from.

It was this temperamental peculiarity—far from rare in women of the Latin races, as any man who has ever seriously tried to tame one will have his share of scars to prove—which, by impeding her from even pretending submissiveness, had enabled Conchita to reach the ripe old age of nineteen years without having been spoken for. Of course, there were other difficulties: It was widely rumored—a rumor substantiated by her fresh and fragrant smell—that Conchita bathed all over every blessed day, and washed her more strategic areas even more frequently than that, a finickiness hardly recommendable in a wife. Besides which, she had a tongue that could take both hair and hide off a full-grown steer from fifty yards away, and a temper made up of both ball and chain lightning, steeped in tequila 'til it smoked.

On top of all that, she didn't even *look* right. For one thing, she wasn't even *llenita,* a term best translated in poundage. For a girl of Conchita's height, some five foot two, to be called *llenita,* her weight should have hovered around one hundred forty-five or fifty pounds, instead of the starveling—to Mexican eyes—or the lissome—from the gringo point of view—one oh five she carried alluringly (to Tobias) draped upon her (again to Tobias) delightfully racy little frame.

Nor was she *metida en carnes,* a term absolutely untranslatable until the G.I.s of World War II hit upon the perfect translation for it, which is "stacked." By which they meant, dear children, all the usual feminine equipment, but stacked up quite nicely in certain places. Now Conchita visibly possessed all of the aforesaid equipment, except that to the opulent Mexican taste, said equipment was sadly underdeveloped, which meant that to Tobias' New England yanqui eye, she was pluscumperfecta, a dream walking, and a singularly ravishing dream at that.

He collapsed into a chair, sat there, staring at her. He was rapidly turning a lovely shade of blue. You see, he had long since forgot to breathe. Somebody—Angie probably—started playing "La Habanera" from Bizet's *Carmen* inside his head. Then she turned and saw him sitting there.

Wait! What happened next is difficult to explain. Say, first of all, that Conchita, though of Mexican parentage, was a native Californian, since el Pueblo de Cerda Gorda was north of the Mexican frontier, not south of it. Add to this that she was the first and only female citizen of that minuscupolis to have completed a high school education, having graduated with honors *not* from the local parochial school, but from the Southern California District Public High School, which was as "anglo" as all get out. Her English was both fluent and good, a fact that, oddly enough, it took Tobias some considerable time to find out.

The real point in all this is that poor Conchita *wanted* to be "anglo"—or typically American—and hence was completely susceptible to California madness. And the form her madness took was exactly the same as that of the flappers before L'Amour's tabernacle; she thought that skinny, homely, broken-nosed Tobias was *the* most gorgeous male human she had ever seen.

In short, she was hit by the *flechazo*—or blow of the arrow—presumably from Eros's or Cupid's twanging bow, as Spanish-speaking people call falling suddenly and insanely in love.

She tiptoed over to where Tobias sat, and whispered:

"¡Te quiero! ¡Te quiero con mi alma! ¿Como te llamas, Dueño y Señor de mi corizon?"

And Tobias, opening his mouth, took in air, and said, dreamily:

"Me llamo Toby. Y yo, a tí, igualmente. O más. Te quiero con mi vida, con toda mi esperanza, con mi sangre y mi cuerpo. ¡Se te lo juro antes la Santa Madre de Dios!"

Then: "My God! I'm speaking *Spanish!* Now what the hell did I say to her?"

Whatever it was, it must have been effective, because Conchita draped her warm and lissome form blissfully into his lap, and proceeded to literally devour him with kisses. Which illustrates still another point about the workings of Random Chance, and/or the General Maliciousness of Fate. And that point is that it is nearly always impossible to separate good luck from bad, or even distinguish one kind of luck from the other.

Tobias' luck was close to miraculous in the sense that he had stumbled into the establishment, and into the arms of the daughter, of the sleepiest Mexican north of the Rio Grande. Or south of it, for that matter. Else by now he would have had a minimum of six or a maximum of twelve, depending upon the number of Colt's revolvers that the irate father carried, very likely fatal perforations in his hide, said perforations caused by an equal number of .44 caliber bullets fired from point-blank—or as a Mexican would put it "quema ropa," "clothes burning"—range.

But Don Felipe snored blissfully on and allowed the gringo swine time and to spare to seduce his daughter. Which took some doing, because little Concha had much more serious and more lasting ideas in her pretty head.

"¿Estas casado?" she whispered; then: *"¡Oh no! ¡No me digas eso! ¡Si ya tienes esposa, me moriré de pena!"*

"Oh Lord, Angie, help me!" Tobias groaned inside his head.

"She's askin' ye if ye're married," Angie purred. "Tell her ye ain't, 'n see what happens, lad!"

"No," Tobias said; "I'm not married." But what came out of his mouth was: *"No—no estoy casado."*

"¡Bueno!" Conchita murmured. *"¿Me quieres, verdad? ¿Bastante para casarte conmigo?"*

"Oh, Jesus, Angie! This has got to stop! I don't know what she's saying or what *I'm* saying, or—"

"Then speak English," Angie said calmly. "She understands it perfectly."

"Look, baby," Tobias said, "let's speak English, shall we?"

"¡No me llamas bébé!" Conchita flared. *"¿Y porque me hablas en inglés cuando hablas perfectamente el español?"*

"But I *don't!"* Tobias groaned. "Believe me—say, what's your name anyhow?"

"Conchita. Which means the very little shell, you know? Like the oyster shell, only littler. And you are—Toby. Toby what, *mi amor?"*

"Toby Mariposa," Angie said quickly before Tobias could tell the truth and spoil things.

"But thees ees no—thees is *not*—an anglo name! It is Spanish! *¡Y tú estas mentiendo! Eres Español y hablas—"*

"I am not lying. I am not Spanish and I don't speak or understand a word of your language. Somebody is playing tricks on us. A witch —or an evil spirit—or—"

Tobias and the Angel

"An Angel," Angie said.

"Si, un Angel," Conchita whispered, "because only an Angel could have brought you to me. Kiss me, Toby, *mi amor!"*

Tobias complied, with fervor. He also put his hand on the inside of one lissome thigh, and slid it all the way up. Whereupon Conchita slapped him winding.

"Peeg!" she spat. "Gringo peeg! *¿Que clase de una puta pienses que soy?"*

Tobias understood that perfectly. He had heard Angie chattering away about *"putas callejeras,"* which meant "street whores" often enough.

"But I don't," he wailed. "I think that you're an angel, Conchita! It's just that you're soooh exotic and exciting that you drive me *wild!* I'm a human being, dearest and—"

"Y yo tambien, and I—also—am human, Toby, *Cielo,"* she whispered, and buried her face against his skinny Adam's apple.

Tobias kissed her thick black hair. Put his hand back where he had it before, only not quite so high.

She straightened up, stared at him.

"Do not do thees, my Toby," she said gently. "Not because I do not like it, but because I like to too much! And we are not married yet. When we are *esposos*—marrieds, no?—I will permit thee this—and—and everything! But now, no."

Toby, defeated utterly, took his hand away.

"Would your father *allow* you to marry a gringo?" he said.

Conchita gazed at him with troubled eyes.

"He would 'ave all the skin off my bones in strips, first," she said. Then her eyes cleared. "Therefore, *mi amor,* we must elope!"

"Great!" Tobias opened his mouth to say, when Angie's raucous voice came jarring through his head.

"Now, *look,* Toby me boy, me boy! Ye can't wed this darlin' little chili pepper! Ye truly can't!"

"Why not?" Tobias thought furiously. "I don't give a damn whether she's Mex or not! She's pretty and good and sweet and—"

"High spiced 'n hotter than enchiladas *con molle verde!"* Angie said. "All of which I know, lad. And Mexican lassies make a man damn close to the world's *best* wives. Not because she's Mex, but because yer inevitabilities is locked in with li'l Sara's—or is it Clara's?—and all ye'd do would be t' *wreck* this poor, sweet li'l jumpin' bean. So quit this, d'ye hear?"

"Oh Lord!" Tobias groaned.

"On th' other hand, beddin' her wouldn't do either of ye a mite o' harm. Good fer th' soul, beddin' of the *quality* this first-class li'l pepper pot kin provide ye with. Lemme think . . . Lemme think . . . Got it! Now ye stay out of this! Lemme do *all* th' talkin. Don't ye interfere . . ."

Nothing was further from Tobias' intention, or for that matter, from his capabilities, because Angie was pouring a long, staccato kettledrum roll of Spanish through his mouth. Translated, it went something like this:

"Look, Conchie, hon, there's another catch: I ain't even of th' one true faith. . . ."

"¡Oh!" Conchita wailed. *"¿No eres siquiera Catolico, mi amor?"*

"Nope," Angie said with perfect, lying, hypocritical sadness. "I'm not a Catholic. But that don't make no niver ye mind. I'll convert. Ye're well worth a mass, me lass. Only—ye know how *long* that takes?"

"Yes," Conchita whispered brokenly. "Weeks. Months. Sometimes years. *Y siendo un tourista,* thou canst not—"

"And being a tourist, I can't. Heck, baby, not even *that* is so. I'm not a tourist. The truth is, I'm on the lam. Hidin' out, ye ken? From the law and also from certain baaaad guys who'd purely enjoy venilatin' me—with bullets, that is, and—"

Conchita's lovely eyes lighted up.

"¿Entonces eres un bandido, mi amor?" she said in an awed tone of voice. You see, to Conchita, brought up in the great tradition of Pancho Villa, Zapata et al, a bandit was an absolutely splendid thing for a man to be.

"Yes," Angie said, through Tobias' mouth, "which means, *mi dulce platillo de helada caramelada,* that—"

"But I am *not* thy dish of caramel ice cream!" Conchita protested.

"I should hope *not,*" Angie said solemnly. "Ice cream is *cold.* How would *mi tarta de manzana con nata batida* suit you?"

"Nor thy apple pie with whipped cream on it! I am not thy dish

of any sort! I am a girl, *idiota!* Not something to eat!"

"That's one of the ways I'm queer," Angie chuckled. "Or maybe I'm a cannibal. Anyhow, you look delicious to me, baby!"

"Will you be serious!" Conchita said. "We have, thou and I, a problem of an enormous complexity and thou passes the time in joking and—"

"But I do not. I am not joking. *No estoy bromiando.* Nor is *nuestra problema de una complejidad enorme.* It is quite simple, really. Or its solution is. We go upstairs, thou and I. To thy alcove—thy bedroom. Right now. This minute. *Y fabricamos un niño.* We make ourselves a baby."

Conchita's eyes took fire. Her hand flew back.

"Kiss her!" Angie roared inside Tobias' head. "Catch her arm! Or else she'll break yer jaw! That's it! No, kiss her! Kissssss 'er, Toby lad! Tha'ssss it! Ye're really learnin', ain't ye?"

"Oh, Toby!" Conchita wept. "Thou sayest that thou lovest me. And—and thy kisses—say so, too. But thou hast no respect for me! How couldst thou hold me so cheap?"

"Not cheap, *Angelita mía! Nunca cosa barata.* Don't ye see 'tis th' *only* way? Thy father, instead of forbidding our wedding, will draw his *pistolas enormes* and *make* me marry thee! Now, c'mon!"

"But—but—Toby—thees ees—this is *wrong!* Sinful. I—"

"Catch her by the arm, ye dope!" Angie commanded Tobias. "Drag her upstairs, ye lucky fool!"

And Tobias, who was becoming less of a dope every day by at least arithmetical if not geometrical progression, obeyed his guardian Angel to the letter. And thereby compounded confusion, added his share of absurdity to an Absurdity Factor already replete with it, demonstrated beyond either questioning or doubt the basic malice that governs human fate.

Wait, children, let us go about this slowly. First of all, clear, sweet little Conchita, her initial scruples overcome, proceeded to demonstrate to Tobias the one true, authentic, indisputable advantage of Mexican cooking, which is that being normally seven times hotter than the seventh level of a Dantean Hell, it tends to thaw out—no. That's wrong. Latin girls are *born* thawed out already. It tends to warm up the little darlings more than somewhat.

And this—to Tobias—astounding and delightful discovery must itself be placed in the perspective of all his previous amatory experience. Poor Tobias, up to that moment, *se había acostado solamente con gringas,* with the now long ago and almost forgotten exceptions of a ma'moiselle or two; which meant that his short, slight, insufficient training had been confined largely to Anglo-Saxon misses, the best of whom are manufactured in series by Kelvinator, and the worst by the refrigeration departments of Westinghouse, General Electric, *and* Kelvinator combined in flagrant violation of the anti-trust laws, not to mention the laws of human nature.

Anyhow, the net result of the sudden and blinding relevation of what a woman ought to be was to intensify what Angie admitted was at least the third worst mistake He'd ever made after introducing Eve to the snake. Before a half hour of the world's most pleasant activity was out, Tobias was totally, desperately, hopelessly, and almost (though, as it turned out, not quite) incurably in love with *la pequeña Concha.*

Which was a pity. A very great pity indeed.

Because Tobias, much against his will, was very shortly to find himself in the position of those exceedingly stupid gringo adventurers in those totally moronic songs written by songwriters who surely have never ventured south of Tin Pan Alley, not to mention the Rio Grande, and who—in diffidence, or deference to one of the most idiotic of all Anglo-Saxon prejudices—are always riding back across the border and leaving girls like poor Conchita behind.

Now any man who has spent as much as a week in a Latin American country, unaccompanied by his own true mechanical doll (Kelvinator patent number 05006000; the trademark's stamped on the left side of her southernmost exposure, in case you're interested) will reach practically unaided the conclusion that riding back across the frontier and leaving dear little Concha or Juana, or Alicia or Dolores or Mercedes or what have you behind, ranks high on the list of the world's most dim-witted ideas—barring, of course, said returning ride's having been compelled by the general unpopularity not to mention the low esteem—except, to be sure, as targets for tonight—that *male* gringos enjoy among Mexicans of the same gender.

But, dim-witted as fleeing Conchita's loving embrace seemed to him, and despite his ardent, even burning, desire to stay right where he was, Tobias rapidly found himself faced with the imperative necessity of taking evasive action, because, as usual, human fate insisted upon doing its very own thing, which is to fornicate matters dirtily.

As witness the arrival in the town of Cerda Gorda, California, of "Muckraking" Mike McGuire even *before* Tobias, with the sterling, diligent, and even, to a degree, disinterested assistance of Angie, the Angel, had persuaded Conchita to climb those primrose stairs.

Now Mike was an expert. Before that aforementioned and totally delightful, delicious, delectable, and what have you, half an hour was over, he had traced Tobias to La Pulga Saltona. In fact, perched upon a purloined ladder, just outside the window of Conchita's bedroom with his trusty Speed Graphic (if Speed Graphics hadn't come out in 1922, substitute the correct make of camera) in hand, he—just before Tobias became a near basket case—was able to take one grand and glorious "feelthy" picture of the event, firing off his flash powder with such perfect timing that its explosion managed to coincide with the other neurological, physiological, and all the other "logicals" you can think of, explosion—mutual, for once, so greatly had Tobias progressed—within that room, which sweet Conchita, by means of instinctive and wholly native talent, not only managed to prolong unbelievably but also to intensify into something closely resembling an earthquake of, say, magnitude eight on the Richter scale.

Thoughtfully, Mike crept back down that ladder. Cerda Gorda was a town of sufficient size and importance to afford not only one, but two local photographers. A generous amount of the old blarney and a small amount of folding green stuff with Honest Abe's picture on it enabled Mike to borrow a darkroom. Some hours later he was observing the truly magnificent results of his labors and considering what use to make thereof.

He decided, finally, to employ it as a time-saving device. Sister L'Amour, he knew, had told Tobias that it would be two weeks before she could join him. But a print from that negative, Mike was confident, would bring L'Amour McSimple Fearsome down here so damn fast that—

He was right. That saintly lady arrived two days later—one day, in fact, after receiving that print.

Which probably saved Tobias from death by delightful exhaustion, the world's greatest way to go. What it didn't save him from, of course, was almost getting murdered.

And breaking poor Conchita's warm and loving heart.

Ten

"Just who," dear little Conchita shrieked, "ees thees wooman, Toby, *cariño?*"

"His wife, *Putita Flaquita!*" L'Amour roared or bellowed, or maybe both. At this point, we'd better explain that in her younger days as an aspiring starlet (a euphemism for a casting couch broad) L'Amour had been a great fancier of "Latin lovers" and, by having made good and sufficient use of sleeping dictionaries, male gender, she had acquired a fairish vocabulary of bedroom Spanish, a most apt variety for the kind of exchange she was embarked on now.

"Oh!" Conchita gasped. "Do not call me skinny whore, Fat Sow! The *same* Fat Sow, without a doubt, that they named thees Pueblo after. Since it is clear, even *clarísimo,* that you have a sufficiency and even an excess of both years and of grease to make eet possible! Now *vete!* Go away and leave my Toby in peace!"

Which, you have to admit, kiddies, was one helluva gasp. But, before we forget, that's actually what Cerda Gorda *does* mean: Fat Sow.

"In *thy* little piece, no doubt?" L'Amour sneered. "Which is both too narrow, and unacquainted with the use of soap and water since the hour of thy birth! Look you, *putita flaca, my* husband has no need to go to work in *una fábrica de sardinas y—*"

As well as being unjust, grossly unfair, and totally inaccurate, that remark about the sardine factory coming from a huge and noticeably sweaty gringa was a little too much for poor Conchita to take.

Shrilling "Thing of bad milk!" she waded into L'Amour McSimple Fearsome. With both hands and both feet, at that.

Tobias, of course, was both sufficiently ill-advised and inexperienced enough to try to stop the fray. His attempts to separate one tiny tigress from one enraged white elephant were both short and futile, the only sufferer from them being himself. Conchita kicked him in the shin so hard he was sure the bone was broken, and L'Amour, with one magnificent backhand, laid him out full length upon the dusty patio for at least the count of nine. By the time he came somewhat to himself, Don Felipe, "El Flacucho," was there. And that, according to the good citizens of Cerda Gorda, was the first time in recorded history that Don Felipe actually managed to stay awake for as long as five minutes. In fact upon this notable occasion he outdid himself—he remained both awake and in a state of quivering rage for the entire rest of that historic day.

"What," Don Felipe roared, "ees going on here?"

At the sound of his voice, Conchita disengaged herself from the battle, although she was getting much the better of it. Being younger, smaller, quicker, and madder in the order named, she'd managed to mess up poor L'Amour more than somewhat.

"Oh, Papa!" Conchita wailed. *"Esta Gorda asquerosa dice—"*

"And just what, *hija mía,"* Don Felipe demanded, "does this disgusting Fat One say?" Then looking again, he modified Conchita's adjectives: "Neither too fat, nor even excessively disgusting, daughter," he said in a warm and speculative tone of voice. *"Ni demasiada gorda ni asquerosa. Una suficiencia.* Just enough. As los gringos say: Mighty fine!"

"Oh, Pa-pa!" Conchita flared, and stamped her shapely little foot. "Do not speak thus of this *enorme asquerosidad de una cerda gringa!* (This enormous disgustingness of a yankee sow!) Especially not when she has come to steal my Toby from me!"

"And who is thy Toby, one permits oneself to ask?" Don Felipe said. "This elongated and supine gringo who seems to be enjoying a siesta upon my patio?"

"Ohhhh, Toby!" Conchita gasped, and, flying to him, she dropped to her knees and cradled Tobias' battered and still spinning head in her tender arms.

"Unhand my husband, *zorrita flaca!"* L'Amour boomed. You will observe that Sister L'Amour's command of boudoir Spanish was more than adequate. While *zorrita flaca* literally means "thin vixen," in bedroom Spanish it has all the force of "skinny bitch," which is what Mexicans actually mean when they say it.

"I find your language somewhat excessive, *señora!"* Don Felipe said sternly. "Especially in reference to my daughter who is a chaste and decent girl!"

"¡Casta y deciente!" L'Amour boomed. *"¿Cuando se ha pasado los ultimos tres dias jodiendo a mi marido hasta que se le ha caido el culo?"*

Now we have to admit that L'Amour's language here displays a certain want of delicacy. Which is why, dear children, the use of sleeping dictionaries is not to be recommended as a method of learning a foreign tongue. To translate the above phrase we should be forced back to Anglo-Saxon, and the employment of epithets more than a trifle jarring upon a sensitive and a cultured ear. Let us, therefore, dispense with a literal translation and say merely that the import of dear L'Amour's remarks was that poor Conchita deserved neither the adjectives "chaste" nor "decent," since she had passed the last three days engaging in a certain much too intimate activity with her, L'Amour's, husband, and with such a fine excess of enthusiasm and vigor that the extreme southern-most portion of Tobias' anatomy had fallen off.

Which, Don Felipe was able to observe, was at least something of an exaggeration, for Tobias' posterior, while notably skinny, was clearly still in its usual place. Therefore that rotund and dignified hidalgo said with ominous quiet:

"I hope, *sinceramente, señora,* that you are prepared to prove your terrible words!"

"What, I ask you, *señor hotelero,* is this?" L'Amour bellowed—shrieking, of course, being beyond her yearling calf's type of voice—and pushed one of her two wedding rings, the one she had acquired from the late Timothy McSimple, up under Don Felipe's nose, while keeping the other, that she had acquired from the long since departed for climes unknown Ernest Fearsome, cleverly out of sight.

"Well—" Don Felipe began, visibly shaken. *"Señora y—"*

"And this!" L'Amour roared like a lionness, and tearing open her bag came out with that "feelthy" picture. Now, most unfortunately, all of Conchita's lissome litheness was visible in that picture, since she had been, for the moment, anyhow, on top. And Tobias had both raised up a little and turned his countenance towards the window, presumably to gasp a much needed breath.

Don Felipe hung there. A quiver started in his enormous curve of happiness, as the Mexicans call a well-larded belly. Conchita knew exactly what that symptom meant.

"¡Corre, mi amor!" she moaned: "Run, my Toby! Run!"

Tobias broke the world's Olympic records for the fifty-, one-hundred-, and two-hundred-twenty-meter dashes before Don Felipe got that Colt Dragoon Revolver out. Even so, the only thing that saved his life was the fact that that particular sidearm hadn't been cleaned or oiled since Santa Ana used it to do in Davy Crockett at the Alamo. The first time it failed to go off, the second time it threw wide, and the third time it exploded, breaking Don Felipe's right arm in two places, which, incidentally, also saved Conchita's life as well, because Don Felipe was unable to beat his erring daughter to death with his left hand, though right manfully he tried, working on the matter, and on poor Conchita with single-minded thoroughness every time he was awake for the next two weeks.

But, even thus handicapped, "El Flacucho" managed to make matters a trifle warmer than somewhat for Our Hero Tobias and for that great and saintly lady L'Amour McSimple Fearsome. And, at this point in Tobias' quite nonlinear sequential progression, they are both fleeing the vicinity of the Hotel La Pulga Saltona in a motor car, said motor car being well ventilated with rifle bullets, both because Don Felipe's Winchester 30/30 was much newer than his Colt Dragoon, and also because Don Felipe's marksmanship, even while propping the rifle up across the hotel's adobe garden wall and shooting with his left hand, wasn't all that bad.

Behind them came still another motor car, occupied—need we say it?—by no less than Muckraking Mike McGuire who was yelling at his driver, a Mexican-American from Cerda Gorda, that immortal classic phrase from every chase sequence ever filmed: "Follow that car! Look alive man, don't lose it!"

Nor did he. For that next morning, after Sister L'Amour had used poor Tobias as a punching bag for long enough to convince him that her wrath was serious, but not long enough nor hard enough to incapacitate him for more delicate nocturnal exercises and/or purposes, Mike was again perched outside of a bedroom window with his trusty camera and his even trustier pan of flashpowder in his hands.

This time the picture he obtained was a good bit less spectacular, and considerably less "feelthy" than his previous effort, because Mike deliberately waited until the action was over before taking that picture, both because he was afraid the disparity between L'Amour's opulent bulk and Tobias' skinniness would obscure the absolute clarity of detail he needed as proof of the rich pay dirt he was presently going to display in his syndicated column and because he hoped to keep the photo well enough within the elastic bounds of public taste to allow some especially daring newspaper editor to actually print it.

At which, be it said, he failed. Both of L'Amour's monumental and/or mountainous mammary appendages were all too clearly visible, fairly poking out any prospective viewer's eyes. Beyond that, the rest of the photograph utterly violated the United States Post Office's succinct dictum for deciding whether any representation of overt nudity could or could not be passed through the mails. That dictum being: "Any noticeable hirsute or even hirtellous shadings visible upon the represented, unclothed, female form, anywhere below the eyebrows, say, is, in the judgment of this Department, sufficient cause to remove said representation from the category of, and to bar its passage through the mails as something less than, art."

But, as proof, Mike's artistic endeavor served well enough, especially since that enterprising gentleman supplemented it with a clear photo of the hotel's register bearing the entirely legible inscription: "Mr. Tobias T. Mariposa and wife."

In fact, when Mike "broke" his story, more than one editor printed it front-page center and gave it headlines, most of them following said headlines with a legally quibbling question mark to protect themselves against libel suits. Typical of those headlines was the one *The Chicago Sun* blazoned forth at midmorning of the same day that Muckraking Mike released his exclusive: "LADY EVANGELIST IN ILLICIT ROMANCE WITH MOBSTER?" and under that, in only slightly smaller type: "L'Amour McSimple Fearsome, Famous California Religious Leader, Registers in LA Hotel with Tony, 'The Butterfly,' Mariposa, as Man and Wife!"

Now the only way that headline differed from fifteen or twenty others that story caused to be printed all over the U.S.A. was—apart, of course, from some minor differences in the wording—the *place* where it appeared, which was The Windy City, Chicago, then number-one crime metropolis of the nation, having nosed out both New York and Boston for that sterling distinction.

Which made it a lead pipe cinch (Chicagoesque, dear children, for "A foregone conclusion") that one Hymie "The Wise" Wisenheimer was going to read it and thereby be moved to take appropriate action. For, Hymie "the Wise" was not only a dear friend of the late, lamented "Slow Dough" Moe Green, but also was—or rather had been up to the moment that Tony "the Butterfly" had splattered poor Moe all over the floor, walls, and even the ceiling of his (Slow Dough Moe's) near northside apartment, thus making it necessary for the coroner to take the stiff's fingerprints to even determine who the stiff had been in life—Moe's brother-in-law.

But since that "Wise" that Hymie had been nicknamed by all and sundry was highly appropriate, Hymie had lain low considering even his brother-in-law's sudden and exceedingly messy departure for another world (better than Chicago and/or Cicero, Illinois, we have no doubt!) and even his beloved little sister Sadie's tears and reproaches insufficient motives for committing suicide, which tangling with Scarface Al Capone indisputably was. For although in those days Capone was only Johnny Torrio's lieutenant, and the at least nominal manager of the Syndicate's Cicero Gambling Casino, "The Ship," Hymie was wise enough to smell out where the real power actually lay.

But (again) there had been some changes. For one thing, the fact that Tony the Butterfly man had actually gone on the lam after knocking off poor Moe—an action totally unnecessary if he had really made that particular "hit" on Scarface Al's behalf—coupled with the plausible rumors that he, Tony Mariposa, had actually gone to Moe's to collect the seventeen Gs that Slow Dough Moe owed him, Tony Butterfly, and was, as usual, slow and reluctant about payment; and that, more importantly, his, Tony Butterfly's, sudden departure for distant and presumably safer climes was due to his failure to collect said seventeen Gs, a failure likely to prove slightly fatal since the Butterfly man was said to owe at least fifteen of those seventeen big ones to sweet, lovable characters like Dion O'Banion, Vincent "Schemer" Drucei, Frankie Yale, and at least two of the three Terrible Gennas.

"So," Hymie mused, "dat rat's bein' in California puts a different face on t'ings—note bein' taken o' de fact that Al ain't sent nobody out dere to bring 'm back. He wuz to wind up croaked out dere would confuse de issue more'n somewhat, considerin' the number o' characters around what loves th' flyin' insect a little less dan his ol' guinea broad of a mutter does! Now lemme see, lemme see—"

So thinking, Hymie "the Wise" Wisenheimer picked up the phone. By nightfall that night, no less than seven short, stocky, dark-complexioned gentlemen each nattily attired in a wide-brimmed fedora, and a double-breasted dark blue pinstriped suit took the train for Los Angeles. The fact that each of them also carried a violin case caused absolutely no surprise at all. That *every* musician in a string orchestra should be a violinist was accepted without question in the America of 1922, especially since the tabloids had made the average citizen fully aware that asking questions about such matters was likely to cause a sudden deterioration in the questioner's health, if not his abrupt departure for a presumably better world.

But, on that selfsame evening, L'Amour and Tobias were poring —in still another hotel room—over *The Los Angeles Bugle*'s remarkably similar headlines.

"I'm *ruined!*" L'Amour wailed. "And it's all *your* fault, you cheap li'l Dago gangster, you! Why didn't you tell me you was with that Chicago mob? Never would have let you within five city blocks of me! And now—"

"But I'm not!" Tobias said. "It's all a mistake, L'Amour honey! I've never so much as set foot in—"

"Ssssh!" Angie's voice came whistling through his head. "Don't be a long-eared jackass, Toby, me boy, me boy! This is purely th' moment t' strike while th' iron's hot, o' I miss me guess! Now speak slowly 'n listen carefully to what I'm a transmittin' afore ye open up yer stupid trap! First off, ye *are* Tony Mariposa, th' mobster, ye kin and—"

"Look L'Amour, ya wicked, fat-assed ol' castin' couch broad," Tobias' voice came suddenly and startlingly out of the side of his mouth, "don't muck around with yours truly, Tony 'the Butterfly' Mariposa, or what you'll be is not ruint, but deceased. Somewhat *dead,* catch?"

"Oh!" L'Amour gasped, and backed away from him, her eyes wild blobs of terror in her full moon of a face. "I—I didn't mean any harm Toby—I mean Tony, love!"

"Now slap 'er around a bit!" Angie instructed him. "Not only to get her entirely in yer power, but because 'twill be good fer yer little mouse's soul!"

Tobias complied. With, sadly be it said, a certain enthusiasm, for not only was his loss of sweet little Conchita clearly all L'Amour's fault, but also because he was worn down enough by then to realize how thoroughly demeaning the place and the position (and/or positions, some of which, dear children, would have to be seen to be believed!) of a male sexual object were.

"Take that!" he roared. "And that! And that! Not to mention this! And th' other!"

"Now, now lad, quit it!" Angie said. "Maiming 'er ain't in the cards. Listen carefully, now—"

"I only took up with an outsized piece o' snatch like you," Tobias sneered gleefully (quite a trick, sneering gleefully, but Our Hero managed it very nicely, thank you!), "because I was on th' lam, 'n needed a pad to hole up in as well as a certain amount o' dough. Or did ya really think I found friggin' round in Grand Canyon excitin'?"

"Ohhhhh Toby! I mean Tony!" L'Amour moaned. "What a horrible thing to say!"

"Horrible truth," Tobias went on calmly. "Now you listen careful like, Fat Ass! We're checkin' outa this fleabag right now. Goin' back to Cerda—('But, Angie, we *can't,'* he wailed inside his mind. 'Conchita's old man will *kill* me!') Well, not to Cerda Gorda, but to Cerda Chica which is twenty miles east o' that. 'N there ya gonna write a note to yer flock o' hysterical suckers, sayin' yer bein' held for ransom by *me*—Tony Butterfly, catch?"

He grinned at her suddenly.

"Actually, it ain't so bad, L'Amour, me moll— 'cause I'm perfectly willin' t' disappear after I get th' dough—leavin' ya with yer reputation more or less intact. Ya was forced, catch? Ya couldn't help it. This wild torpedo from th' Windy City forced ya to commit all sorts o' beastly abominations—th' suckers will purely love that beastly abominations bit, or I miss my guess!—at gunpoint but since yer will wasn't involved, th' sin ain't rightly yers. Build yer fame up more'n somewhat. Heck, ya'll make so much dough that ya kin afford to get in a fancy sawbones to whittle three tons o' lard off yer top 'n four off yer bottom not t' mention sewin' up yer excavation more'n somewhat so yer next lovin' fella won't feel so lonesome! Now, c'mon! Move yer backside, broad!"

You will observe, Dear Children, that Angie, perhaps because he was much too occupied with his new bride, Anne, to give the matter his undivided attention, had already become guilty of a several serious errors, to wit:

1. He had neglected to find out anything about Tony Mariposa the actual Chicago hood whose name—at least in part—he had accidentally borrowed as an alias for Our Hero,

2. He had sent poor Tobias back over the same border region from which they, Tobias and L'Amour, had recently fled, thus making it laughably easy for Hymie "the Wise's" hit men to trace them.

3. It had never even occurred to him, even after having seen those headlines, that borrowing the moniker of a mobster on the lam was a risky business, putting poor Tobias' whole future in serious jeopardy. And, that

4. Kicking off from an overdose of lead poisoning brought on by a case of mistaken identity was, to put it mildly, one helluva way to go.

But Tobias, himself, compounded the growing uncertainty surrounding not only his alleged future, but even his continued existence, by hiring four slender, young, and decidedly handsome Mexican *pistoleros* to stand guard over L'Amour McSimple Fearsome while he rode into Los Angeles to post that ransom note demanding one hundred grand from the sinners and/or saints of the Holiness Tabernacle for the safe return of their kidnapped leader.

Now, not even Tobias shared poor Conchita's stated opinion that L'Amour was *una cerda gringa asquerosa,* which means a disgusting yankee sow. To the young Mexicans with their native tendency to measure feminine charm by the pound, she was a relevation and a delight, *"¡Mucha Mujer!",* much woman, indeed.

And the young *pistoleros'* dark, Latin good looks made the obvious strategy she instantly hit upon, wearing the lot of them into a state of delightful exhaustion, ecstatic collapse, thus enabling her to flee into the night before Tony "the Butterfly" could return, a distinct pleasure to L'Amour herself. Thereupon she proved that Angie's contention—voiced, you will recall, upon the occasion of poor Nancy's tragic demise—that a girl really couldn't take on more than *three* guys at the same time, was in her case, at least, wrong. Dead, damned wrong. How? Well, you see, she—oh, hell. Go read Masters and Johnson, will you, please?

Anyhow, when Tobias got back to el Pueblo de Cerda Chica, (The Town of Little Sow) he found the four *pistoleros* stretched out on the ground, snoring peacefully, smiles of blissful satisfaction upon their weary faces.

But L'Amour was gone. Long gone. And that particular Random Chance sequence, as a money making device anyhow, and, for that matter, as anything else, was shot to hell.

In a towering rage, Tobias bent over the four weary and vanquished warriors, just in time to—temporarily, anyhow—save his own life.

Because three low-slung touring cars crept up the road past the adobe hut. From them, Hymie "the Wise's" hired musicians opened up with their favorite tune: "Saint Valentine's Day in Chicago," followed by "Ring Around the Rosey," followed by, "Tag, You're It," followed by "X Marks the Spot," followed by—but you get the general idea, don't you?

Anyhow, that hut disappeared. Sunbaked mud, which is all adobe is, kiddies, was never calculated to the resist the impact of seven hundred rounds of Thompson submachine-gun fire, which is what Hymie's hitmen poured into that hut in a shade under thirty seconds flat.

Thereafter, of course, they had to reload, which gave Tobias time enough at least to *start* getting out of there.

But he wouldn't have got very far if it hadn't been for one thing: a *fourth* low-slung touring car came careening up that road, and skidded to a stop in a cloud of dust, one yard from where poor Tobias ran. The front door nearest to him flew open.

"Git yore skinny ass in heah, you long gone Guinea bastid, you!" Hellcat Hattie McCoy, the famous gun moll, said.

Eleven

"Jeez-sus!" Hellcat Hattie McCoy said happily. "That theah Dago cuss sho kin drive!"

"And his little playmates sure can shoot!" Tobias thought unhappily, as he doubled over in the front seat of Hattie's wildly careening Hudson touring car with his eyes tight shut and both hands over his ears. By then the back end of the Hudson looked just like a sieve. Or Swiss cheese at a banquet for mice. Or a reluctant bridegroom at a Kentucky mountain wedding.

"Heah, honeyboy," Hattie said. "You take this heah li'l play toy o'mine 'n see effen you cain't discourage 'em a little!"

Tobias opened his eyes and stared into the muzzle of a Browning Automatic, caliber .45. The muzzle stared back at him. It looked a little smaller than the main entrance to Grand Central Station in New York, but not much.

Now one of the effects of World War I upon Tobias Tobit had been to leave him allergic to gunfire. A trifle more allergic to it than he had been born, which was narrowing possibilities to their limits. When, as a boy, much against his will, his father had forced him to go hunting—as a normal part of the training of any normal country boy—the quail, ducks and what have you would use his head and shoulders and the barrels of his shotgun as a landing strip, while rabbits snoozed peacefully across his knees and ankles, secure in the knowledge that wherever Tobias was they were sure of living to a ripe old age.

"My God!" Tobias gasped.

"Take it, ye blitherin' idiot!" Angie said.

Gingerly Tobias took that cannon. "The howitzer that wiped out my Company in the Argonne must have been about this size," he thought. Then he wailed inside his mind:

"Now that I've got it, what th' hell do I *do* with it? Tell me *that,* Angie, will you please!"

"First ye take th' safety off. Tha's th' little gizmo down there on th' left side o' the grip. Thereafter ye point it back in th' general direction of them distinguished members o' th' *Unione Siciliana* 'n pulls the trigger. . . ."

"But Angie! I don't believe in killing people! It's a crime! Wrong! Th' Bible sez—"

"An eye fer an eye 'n a tooth fer a tooth. Th' Old Testament, anyhow. 'N since the *New* Testament is an Essenes' forgery, let's stick to the Old, eh, Toby me lad? More practical. And even grantin' that them Mafiosa scum that Hymie the Wise hired to knock ye off *are* human—a distinctly debatable point—if ye don't blast 'em, they'll blast *you.* Which'll make li'l Clara—or is it Sara?—a widow before she's even a bride. Not to mention th' even sadder fact that ol' Asmo will rally round to console th' weepin' widow afore yer even cold. So take aim, me boy! 'n shoot 'n shoot 'n shoot!"

Now, in all his life, Tobias had never been able to hit the side of a red-painted barn from a range of two and one half inches. In fact, it is highly significant that shells rained down on Paris from what the experts swore was a mammoth artillery piece named "Big Bertha" located fully seventy-five miles from the French Capital at the exact time that Tobias was forced to act as gunnery officer for his Company because the first gunnery officer stayed dead, stinking drunk for two solid weeks, the second gunnery officer was in the hospital with appendicitis, and the third was AWOL in Paris itself and busily engaged in working his horizontal way through every *maison close* on the *Rive Gauche.* A coincidence? *Peut-être.*

Anyhow, crouched low in his seat now, Tobias shut both eyes tight, pointed that hand cannon in the general direction of his pursuers, and squeezed off three shots in quick succession.

The first shot parted the driver's, Dino Andrioni's, hair, causing him to almost lose control of the Maxwell he was driving. The second hit the radiator of the car dead center, causing a stream of scalding water to gush out of it. And the third blew out the left front tire, causing the Maxwell to slew around until it was completely broadside the road, which, in its turn, caused the two other touring cars, that naturally had been tailgating it, and each other, to plow into it with a crash that, with the sole exception of Conchita's dulcet voice murmuring, "Toby, *mi amor—*" was the sweetest sound that Tobias had ever heard.

"Wal I be dawg!" Hattie chortled. "Fur a Guinea 'n a damn Yankee both, you ain't half bad, is you, hon? Now soon as ah find a place on this damn road wide enough to make a U-turn in, we better go back 'n plug all them Dagoes afore they comes to. Or else yer mought hav trouble wit 'em later, th' lousy Wop bastids!"

"And have half of Chicago and all of Cicero down here after us?" Tobias said, thinking for himself for a change. "That just isn't smart, Miss—say, what's your name, anyhow?"

"As if you didn't know it, you sweet li'l ol pizza pie, you!" Hattie said. "After all th' *fun* we'uns had up there in Chicago that summer I went up there to see whether y'all city slickers could learn a gal a li'l sumpin. An' y'all couldn't. Yore ways is too complicated. What th' hell I wanta organize myself a mob fur 'n have to divy up my take? This way when I pulls a heist hit's *all* mine, baby!"

"Look, Angie!" Tobias thought desperately. "I'm going to get rid of this Tony Mariposa alias, right now! Far as I can see it's a perfect synonym for 'X marks the Spot' or 'Target For Tonight.' "

"Right," Angie thought back at him. "Ye may reassume yer own true identity, Toby, me boy."

"I take it, then," Tobias said politely, "that you're acquainted with this Antonio Mariposa, aren't you, Miss?"

"What's wrong with yore *haid,* honeychild?" Hattie said. "After all th' nights—not t' mention, mornin's, afternoons 'n evenin's—we done turned each other ever which a-way but *loose,* you ain't got no call to ax me a fool thing like that!"

"Then I'd suggest," Tobias said, "that the next time we stop for gas, you take a good look at me, Miss. Because I'm not only *not* Tony Mariposa, I have never even seen that gentleman in my life. In fact, the only thing I know about him is that his popularity leaves a good bit to be desired. And that the people who don't like him have a tendency to play awfully rough!"

"Ain't *that* th' truth!" Hattie sighed. "But saaay! You doan even *sound* like 'em, come t' think o' hit! You sho Lawd talks all fancy 'n prissy 'n fine. Jes like a prof o' sumpin. 'N *he* couldn't shoot shit off a outhouse floor. Main reason he wuz always whittlin' on folks, o' poundin' 'em into a mush wit lead pipes 'n such like. Jes like he done Slow Dough Moe Green. Now hand me that theah flashlight. Hit's on th' floah right next t' yore seat . . ."

Tobias groped for the flashlight, found it, handed it to her. And was instantly blinded, as she turned it full on his face.

"Wal I be dawg!" she chuckled. Then: "Jes like mah po' ol Momma allus tol me! Hit's better to be born lucky than rich!"

"I'm afraid I don't understand you, Miss," Tobias said primly—and that he could *still* say things primly after Nancy, his dreams, anyhow, (and/or maybe) with Anne, L'Amour, and Conchita, was an accomplishment of no mean order, you must admit. "Would you care to elucidate, please?"

"Hot dawg! You *really* talks fine, doan you, hon?" Hattie laughed. "Look a heah—say what's yo John Hancock, honeyboy?"

"Tobias," Tobias said. "Tobias Tobit. But my friends call me Toby"

"Then *ah'm* gonna call you Toby, too, sugah. 'Cause we'uns is gonna be fas' frens o' I miss mah guess. C'mon now, snuggle up real closelike, 'n give us a kiss!"

"Going *this* fast?" Tobias gasped.

"Gotta be 'cross th' Nevada line fore daybreak," Hattie explained, "or else some nosey parker of a California copper mought stop us 'n ax whether we'uns had enything to do with th' stick up of th' Cattlemen's 'n Orange Growers' Bank in Dry Gulch, Californy. 'N since th' swag is hid under that seat you's a-sittin' in, that mought prove a mought embarrassin'. But in Nevada we'uns 'll be safe as in church. Nevada folks doan cotton to Californians none at all . . ."

"May I ask what your name is, Miss?" Tobias said quickly, before she could again suggest that they start playing kissing games at 60 mph.

"Hattie. Hattie McCoy. Folks calls me Hellcat Hattie on account o' that's th' kind o' disposition ah've got fuh a fact. Got a temper like greased chain lightnin' so doan yuh go'n make me mad, Toby, luv. Be a pity fer a fella as pretty as you be to wind up daid. A pity 'n a waste. 'Cause I got a sneakin' suspicion you's moughty fine in th' hay. Long, tall, skinny polecats like you most generally is, 'n that's th' truth! Now tell a gal sumpin: How come them Guinea torpedoes wuz tryin' to venilate *you,* seein'z how you sure Lawd ain't *him?"*

"A case of mistaken identity," Tobias said. "They thought I *was."*

"Yep. You do look a mite like th' Butterfly, for a fact. Jes' as skinny. Only you's taller 'n a helluva lot better lookin'. Good thing

I read that lousy newspaper, or I never would o' headed that fuh south a-lookin' fer Tony—"

"Thank God you did!" Tobias said fervently.

"Amen to that!" Hattie said.

They rode in silence for several hours. By then, in spite, or maybe because, of all the excitement he had been subjected to in the last few days, poor Tobias was so tired he couldn't keep his eyes open. He nodded, dozed, then plunged fully five fathoms deep into night and sleep.

When he opened them again it was daybreak, so for the first time he was able to see Hellcat Hattie McCoy clearly. She was a tiny little thing. He judged that facing him, her nose would be maybe six, seven inches higher than his belly button. She was as skinny as a rail fence, all angles, with a couple of lemon-sized (*small* lemons at that) protuberances breaking the absolute flatness of her blouse. Her wide, humorous mouth was clamped around a big, black cigar at least one-tenth as long as she was, from which arose a stench that would have floored a billy goat.

To have got even one more freckle on her face would have both violated and outraged the laws of probability, but that face itself was of that interesting type best described as homely-cute, though ugly-cute would have been closer to the truth of things. Her reddish blonde hair was so crinkly-curly that it missed being kinky by the margin of one sole unit of its component elements, and her little, screwed-up, green-blue eyes were full of every imaginable kind of hell.

In short, our hero found her both interesting and exciting. But then that was the main thing wrong with Tobias Tobit, the one incongruity in his basic makeup: He was completely and hopelessly queer for girls.

"So yuh're back with us, eh, Toby, hon?" Hattie chuckled from around the circumference of that mammoth cigar. "I'll be dawg effen you ain't th' sleepin'st critter I ever did see! You hongry yet, sugah?"

Tobias considered that. "Yes, Hattie, darling," he said.

"Wall, then, next hash house we'uns comes to, we'uns'll pull this heah bucket o' nuts 'n bolts up 'n put on th' feed bag. Doan you worry yore sweet li'l eddicated haid none atall. We'uns is in Nevada now—'n in Nevada we'uns is as safe as a flock o' mice at a tomcat's funeral. You see, hon, ah ain't *never* pulled a fast one in Nevada. That's usin' th' ol' bean. Allus keep at least one state as neutral territory—place where you kin hole up in if th' goin gits rough. You'll remember that won't cha ha, hon?"

"Yes, Hattie," Tobias whispered. "I'll remember. In fact it's already graven on my brain . . ."

But once again Fate was to prove that her basic malice is unrelenting. For long after having gassed, oiled, and watered the bucket of nuts and bolts—no easy matter in 1922, when "filling stations" as gasoline stations were still called, were few and far between—they finally came to an imposing establishment called "The Cottontail Ranch."

Now neither Hellcat Hattie nor Tobias in their pristine innocence knew what that sign implied. In fact only California businessmen and wealthy Nevada ranchers bent on changing their pace, or gait, or in any event their riding fillies, or merely obsessed by the desire to escape from their one and onlies for a weekend or a night truly understood the significance of that cryptic sign.

For the "Cottontail" was a "bunny" ranch. And the "bunny" is a venerable Nevada invention by now hardening or at least firming up into an institution. The good citizens of that state, moved by an exorbitant love for the long green, early hit upon the idea that oases in the desert, where erring and/or merely wistful dreaming wanderers from afar could be provided with cups that cheer, dice that roll, cards that flick, wheels that spin and well other commodities might well their several coffers fill as the Bard of Avon says.

The Cottontail Ranch specialized in other commodities, i.e., bunnies.

Now *Nevada* bunnies, and Hugh Hefner's sanitized, scrubbed, starched, perfumed modern versions, are, to put it mildly, two different breeds of female rabbits.

Tobias Tobit, as he limped into the place, gave one look, stopped limping, straightened up until he was at least ten and a half feet high, opened his mouth, and said:

"Wow!"

It was that arcane, erudite, and supremely intellectual remark that brought Hattie on the run. You see, she had lingered behind long enough to transfer some of the swag from under the front seat into her purse, and after that to lock the Hudson. But even in so short an interval in her sequential progression, so brief a hiatus in her and Tobias' cojoined inevitabilities, Our Hero was neck deep in bunnies by the time she entered that remarkable establishment.

And in Nevada, kiddies, bunnies grow wild. Besides which, the season having been, for several reasons including the post-World War I economic slump, rather slack, these bunnies were even wilder. In fact, sadly enough, the discussion over which of the dear little cottontails was going to drag poor Tobias up those stairs was rapidly degenerating into (well we can't say a screeching cat fight can we? That would be putting the elasticity of even *our* metaphor to too rude a strain—let's call it) a vulgar brawl, when Hattie got back from her car the *second* time.

The first time, of course, was just after she had heard Tobias give vent to that all-too-enthusiastic "Wow!" She had paused in the doorway just long enough to take in the scene, mutter: "Wal, I'll be shot with slops 'n hauled in fer stinking, if this heah ain't a *ho* house!" before whirling and running back to her car.

When she returned, she was armed with something more than outraged virtue; in fact, she had her trusty sixteen-gauge pump gun in her hands. And that mighty weapon was loaded buck'n ball. Which means that its shells were not only crammed full of buckshot, but had one close to .60 caliber lead slug rammed in on top of that.

The only thing that prevented a massacre that would have made Wounded Knee, Custer's Last Stand, and Andersonville look like Sunday school picnics was that Hellcat Hattie was so mad that she forgot to take her usual precaution—absolutely necessary for a person of her size (she weighed ninety-two pounds soaking wet) when firing a shotgun of that power—of bracing herself against a wall or a column. Instead she blasted away with the result that the recoil of the pump gun knocked her right back upon her scrawny derrière, while the slugs tore through the ornate crystal chandelier, snowing all and sundry with slivers of glass, which started all the bunnies *and* Our Hero bleeding from a mean average of two hundred tiny cuts each, none of which was dangerous, but that, altogether, were at least as spectacular as the tons and/or floods of tomato catsup in this week's slavish copy of *The Godfather.*

The bunnies started screaming so shrilly that all the windows shattered, which, according to musically inclined physicists, requires an F two full octaves above high C. Hattie picked herself up, dusted herself off, waded through three tons of wounded she-rabbits, all of them yelling (literally) bloody murder, caught Tobias—who, true to the basic heroism of his nature, had fainted outright at the sight of a couple of drops of his own blood—by the hair and dragged him out of there.

As she stuffed him bodily into the Hudson, Hattie gave vent to a remark that may serve us as a clue to the basic wellsprings of her (feminine) nature.

"I be dawg!" she crooned right tenderly. "Shore is a puny li'l fellow, ain't you, hon? Now doan you go 'n fret yore pretty haid none atall. Momma'll take care o' you, babyboy!"

Some hours later, Tobias, crisscrossed with enough sticking plaster to resemble a rather moth- and/or mouse-eaten, ragged, second-hand Egyptian mummy, dared address a question to Hellcat Hattie McCoy:

"Where're we going, Hattie, dear?" he whispered.

"Dunno," Hattie said from around still another cigar that looked like a short length of a transatlantic liner's tarred hawser and smelled like a long-deceased billy goat. "Outa Nevada enyhows. Ain't safe no mo' thanks t' you. I be dawg! Didya jes' hafta go 'n wrap yoreself up in *that* many hos?"

"Well," Tobias floundered, "I—"

"Doan make no nevermind," Hattie said calmly. "Jes' means you's a mite hard up. Come first dark, Momma 'll fix up thet mighty nicely. . . ."

And be it said, she kept her promise to the letter. Kept it, be it also said, in spite of the fact that "come first dark" they were at least nine hundred fifty-seven and two tenths miles, give or take an inch or two, from civilization's nearest outpost—a fact which fazed dear Hattie not at all. Very simply, she dragged the back seat and a couple of blankets out of the Hudson, turned to Tobias and remarked serenely:

"Tek yore pants off, hon. Yore underdrawers, too, you be a wearin' any. Ah ain't."

Which is why, Dear Children, those particular rites of spring were witnessed by seventeen prairie gophers, three jack rabbits, one long-legged bird of the species called roadrunners, and one diamondback rattlesnake, about as big around as Jack Dempsey's biceps, and as long as from here to the middle of last week.

For some reason or another, the diamondback rattler was peculiarly fascinated by all the general what Hattie called (with quite remarkable accuracy) "Whoopin' 'n hollerin' 'n sashshayin' aroun'," though it must be admitted, in defense of Our Hero's gentle birth and high breeding that *all* of the "whoopin' 'n hollerin' " and even most of the "sashshayin' aroun' " were on Hattie's part, not his.

In any event, the rattlesnake came slithering closer and closer, out of a desire, we must presume, to obtain a clearer view of an activity he must have found a trifle puzzling, until at last he drew up his sinuous sinuousness into a menacing coil exactly six inches from Tobias' nose, and swayed there in perfect rhythm with what was going on, his lambent yellow eyes boring into Tobias' dark brown ones, and his forked tongue flicking in and out, in and out, in and—

Whereupon, of course, Tobias was transformed into a greenish, bluish, petrified, unbreathing (and bareassed) statue. But, by then, Hellcat Hattie was much too busy to notice the difference, especially since the sudden paralysis affecting Our Hero was total, all parts of him retaining an essential rigidity that detracted not at all from the business at hand.

In fact, by fixing Tobias' attention upon other matters (such as the somewhat less than remote—six inches less, in fact—possibility of his abrupt departure from this vale of wrath and tears by means of snakebite, not exactly Our Hero's idea of either a charming or a cozy way to go) his sinuous sinuousness completely rid the well worn down anyhow young New England Yankee of any lingering tendency to go off half-cocked, as the gun manuals say. In fact, far from retaining his title of The Fastest Gun in the West there wasn't the slightest danger of Tobias' firing at all as long as that ominous triangular-shaped head swayed there six inches from his broken pug nose in perfect tune to Hattie's much more enthusiastic than graceful execution of "Le Sacre du Printemps" in double beat, forced marching time.

The result of which was—to Hattie's measureless delight—the anticipation on her part of one of Kinsey's most praiseworthy discoveries (later confirmed by Masters' and Johnson's cunning little super-voyeuristic machines) that if the male of the species is sufficiently well-trained, worn-out, or just plain *bored* with the whole essentially limited and repetitious business anyhow, to become the *slowest* gun in the west, the female rapidly transforms herself into one first-class replica of a Gatling gun, ecstatically firing off round after round.

And the result of that was that any chance of Tobias Tobit's separating himself from Hellcat Hattie McCoy while a rustle of breath remained in either or both of them practically disappeared. From then on, he would have to depend upon Blind Accidentality, Random Chance, and the Sheer Ass-backwardness of Human Fate to set one poor Ryland, New York, boy-child free.

Which, come to think of it, aren't the world's worst things to depend upon, being, Dear Children, a helluva lot more reliable than the rewards of virtue, the wages of sin, or Heaven as *anybody's* destination.

Thereafter, over the next several weeks, Tobias learned life's saddest lesson: that once it has palled on you, the only thing more appalling than For Unlawful Carnal Knowledging is For *Lawful* Carnal Knowledging. You see, dear Hattie, searching her memory, came to the conclusion that as far as she could remember, she really hadn't been *legally* married to anyone and gleefully dragged Our (totally *benumbed* by then) Hero before the first Justice of Peace she could find. So it was that Tobias Tobit first acquired himself a lawfully wedded wife.

Which, since, according to Angie, his inevitabilities were fully locked in, meshed, or what have you, with those of his darling little cousin Clara (or maybe Sara?) was sure to foul up matters more than somewhat.

The snake? *What* snake? Oh, *that* one. After watching the festivities for half the night, he wisely decided that if that were the way modern women go at it, he'd go back to Eve.

And did.

Twelve

"Angie," Tobias transmitted telepathically to his Guardian Angel, "if you're going to see the Auld Cuss anytime soon, ask him to make me a *monk* in my next incarnation, will you please?"

"Ha!" Angie snorted with unholy glee. "Ye think that monks *don't,* lad? Well then, what d'ye think that *nuns* are fer?"

"That's outrageous!" Tobias thought. "And unfair! And untrue."

"What ain't in this world o' sin, laddybucks? All three, I mean. Now leave me be. I forgot Hattie wasn't married. Now I got to figger out a *legal* way to get ye outa the clutches of that skinny li'l screwin' machine, afore she wears yer longitudinarious down to a useless *nub.* Which won't do. Especially since li'l Clara—or is it Sara? —has been savin' it all fer ye. Be a helluva a note to disappoint th' lass. Unfair. Unkind. Mebbe even *illegal.* Grounds fer divorce in several states, I'm told. 'Ye see, yer Honor, this here longtall goodfernothin' can't even git it up 'n—' "

"Oh shut up, Angie, will you please?" Tobias said.

"Hon—" Hattie murmured sleepily and reached for Our Hero—again.

"Oh, Lord, Hattie!" Tobias said, "I'm so damn tired that—"

"Doan worry 'bout that, honeyboy!" Hattie said gleefully, wide awake now. "Momma kin always *fix!*"

And she could. Only, by then, it was taking her from a half to three quarters of an hour longer every night. But since dear Hattie enjoyed the preliminaries almost as much as she did the main bout, that didn't trouble her at all.

"Git up," she said at last, after having reduced poor Tobias to limp exhaustion, or exhausted limpness, or both, "we'uns is got work to do t'day, baby boy. You's a expensive luxury, you is, Toby doll. Momma's plumb right outa cash."

"Oh, Lord, Hattie!" Tobias groaned. "Not again!"

"Now doan you worry yore pretty haid none atall, Toby, love," Hattie said tenderly. "You won't even hafta go inside this 'un. All you hafta do is stand guard outside 'n let me know effen you sees some pukin' polecat of a copper headin' that way in time for me to grab th' swag 'n scram. . . ."

"But, Hattie, I'm scared! I'm so damn' scared that—"

"Ah knows thet, honeyboy. I be dawg effen you ain't the gun-shyest critter I ever did see! Doan mek no nevermind. Ah loves yuh. Mebbe *'cause* you's so sweet 'n puny 'n good fer nuthin. 'Cept in th' hay. Be dawg effen I kin understand hit! A fraidy-cat, sissified fella like you be, Toby doll, oughtn't t' be worth goose shit on ice in th' beddin' department. 'N stead o' thet, you's right pert good. No, fact is, you's mighty fine! Now le's quit talkin' about it afore ah gits all steamed up 'n hafta wear you out some more! C'mon now, sugarplum, git up 'n git yore duds on, willyuh puleeze?"

Hattie's target for tonight—or rather for today, since robbing banks is essentially a daylight occupation considering the absolutely *splendid* hours that bankers keep—was The Merchants' and Farmers' Bank of Dustbowl, Kansas. Now the Merchants' and Farmers' was a large and flourishing bank, among whose clients were included the biggest wheat-growers round and about Dustbowl, some of whom owned tillable acreage bigger than the average county.

All of which dear Hattie knew, having cannily "cased th' joint" as her custom was. What she *didn't* know was that Dustbowl, through a pure fluke, had recently become a firmly established outpost of the motion picture industry.

The reason for that, kiddies, was its climate. One meticulous director had sent scouts all over the U.S.A. to find the *driest* place in the nation, with a view of making a picture to be called *The Grandson of the Sheik,* starring Rudolph Valentino. Now, for motives known only to Hollywood, that particular picture never got made, probably because Valentino had got to be a little too old and worn-out looking to play his own grandson; but several others, of the type known as hoss operas, were. In fact, by that point in Kansas's and the nation's sequential progression, a goodly portion of those epics which required a miner, forty-niner, my Darlin' Clementine, a desert rat-type prospector, or even a cowboy, to crawl in across the burning sands with his tongue hanging out like a yard and a half of red flannel (which is what it *was* most of the time, not even Hollywood being able to find an actor with a tongue of the required length) were being made in and around Dustbowl, Kansas. And *all* of those requiring sandstorms were. Somehow or another it appealed to a certain *je ne sais pas quoi* in the makeup of Hollywood directors to haul eight or ten war surplus, twelve cylinder, four hundred horsepower Liberty airplane motors, equipped with huge four-bladed propellers and mounted on dollies all the way the hell from Los Angeles, California, to Dustbowl, Kansas, in order to blow up the damnedest sand (or more accurately *dust*) storm anybody ever saw.

But what, you ask, has all this to do with Our Hero, Tobias Tobit, and our at least current heroine, Hellcat Hattie McCoy?

Strange as it may seem, quite a lot. For the very day that Hattie hit the Merchants' and Farmers' Bank, the famous director Wolfgang von Stiltiz (an apocryphal story has it that he once offered ten thousand dollars to anyone who could pronounce his name, and his own dear *liebchen* mama tried it—and lost) was making one of his really fine and sensitive oatburners in Dustbowl.

So it was that Our Hero, Tobias, posted outside the M and F as a lookout, looked out and saw a tall rawboned individual named Tom Mix (who Tobias, who *never* went to the movies, naturally didn't know) coming slowly up the street towards him. The tall rawboned individual was listing to starboard under the weight of the artillery he was carrying, and his lean, sun-browned hand hung menacingly close to that holstered railroad siege gun. Then the absolutely petrified Tobias saw that the tall, rawboned individual wasn't even looking at him. So, turning his petrified head on his petrified neck (the groaning grind of stone on stone was deafening), Tobias looked behind him and saw still another tall, rawboned individual canted to port—the side he wore his eleven inch bore, battleship-sized naval gun on—and whose name was Hoot Gibson, or maybe Fred Thompson, or maybe Hopalong Cassidy, or—which makes no difference because Tobias didn't recognize him, either, for the same reasons stated above, coming towards the bank from the other direction, while a woman named Marilyn Miller scurried for shelter, dragging a fifty-nine-year-old subcompact midget named Ronald Reagan who was playing the rôle of her child (yes, Berkley flower children, the *same* one. According to "a reliable source" he was *born* fifty-nine-years-old, and in full possession of all the bright, leftish, liberal ideas he's got right now) behind her, muttering through his set, store boughten teeth: "Gonna git them Reds!" Or maybe it was "Redskins," he said.

What was happening, of course, was a classic "walk down." But Tobias, of course, didn't know that. All he did know was that a couple of large, stern-looking characters were obviously bent on shooting each other, with him, Tobias Tobit, in the exact center of their line of fire.

So he let out a screech two and one half octaves higher and shriller than the bunnies at the Cottontail Ranch out there in Nevada had employed to shatter crystal, and dived into the Merchants' and Farmers' Bank just as Tom and Hoot/Fred/Hop or what have you opened fire. That they were both using blank cartridges was still another thing that Our Hero didn't know. And it wouldn't have made the slightest difference to him if he had. He just didn't *like* guns, that was all.

But as he dived into the bank, his own pearl-handled, gold-plated Colt .45 automatic—a wedding gift from his shy and blushing bride—fell out of his wildly trembling hands and accidentally went off wounding an actress named Maysie Pigeon in her left rubber falsie. Thereupon, *everybody* started shooting: Hattie, the bank guards, the movie extras, and the cameraman, which was why Our Hero's heroic action—he was crouched on the floor in Easter egg position with both hands over his eyes—was recorded for posterity on film, as was the inspiring spectacle of Hattie's dragging him out of the bank by his left foot, while he kicked and screamed and went into the most effectively dramatic hysterics you ever saw.

The results of this contretemps were twofold: For the first time since she took up bank robbery as a profession, Hattie was unable to heist even a torn three-dollar bill, and the newspapers all over the nation had themselves a picnic, headlining the event in such terms as: "HATTIE AND SIS!" and "GUN GIRL AND HE (?) MOLL!" and "HELLCAT HATTIE TEAMS UP WITH LITTLE LORD FAUNTLEROY!"

And the result of *that* was even stranger still: Tobias brooded over these deadly insults to his machismo (he didn't know what the hell his machismo *was,* but that it had been insulted he was absolutely sure) for two whole days, while gentle Hattie did her level (a synonym for "horizontal") best to comfort him. Then, at high noon of the third day, snarling at Hattie out the side of his mouth to "stay the hell home like a woman should, or I'll bat you right back on your bustle, so help me!" which so delighted Hattie's essentially unliberated soul (the woman's liberation movement being, anyhow, a rather forlorn response to the progressive swishification of American males) that she actually obeyed him, he stalked out into the street and headed for the Merchants' and Farmers' Bank.

When he walked into it, the bank guards (who were dressed as western-type sheriffs' deputies for the benefit of von Stiltiz's whinnying epic) collapsed upon each others' shoulders, weeping tears of uncontrollable mirth. The cameraman ground away, sure of getting enough footage on film to make himself filthy rich when he got back to Hollywood and sold it to Mack Sennett.

Seeing the laughing "deputies" and the grinning cameraman, Our Hero got mad. Madder than he already was, which was plenty. In fact, he was consumed with an absolutely bottomless rage, all the more cold and deadly because he himself headed the list of all the people it was directed at. His self-loathing, fed by a despairing recognition of his own monumental ineptitude, weakness, clumsiness, and above all cowardice, had reached suicidical proportions. Only he meant to take a lot of other people with him when he went, notably those who had laughed at him and scorned him. Seeing this, recognizing the absolute degree to which he meant it, his Guardian Angel—and what else are Guardian Angels *for?*—was moved to take a kinetic parapsychological hand.

"Better arrange this a wee bit," the Angel thought, to himself for a change, "or else th' li'l twerp'll go 'n commit a public nuisance—a small size massacre, say . . ."

At that precise moment, Tobias opened fire. His first shot scored a perfect bull's eye in the exact center of the camera's lens. His second bullet parted the hair of the first "deputy sheriff" and/or bank guard, and grazed the bald scalp of his partner. And his third hit the combination lock of the huge steel door of the bank vault at just the right angle to make it spin to the exact numbers of its combination and swing slowly open all by itself.

"Get down on the floor, all of yez!" Our Hero snarled—he was getting good at snarling by then, you will note. "And put yer hands behind th' back of yer heads! Or so help me, I'll drill th' lot of yez!"

(The above was Tobias' idea of how *real* gangsters talk. Not even *that* did he get right, but he was too mad to notice.)

"Even you, Miss!" he said to the banker's private secretary who was diligently trying to sneak out of there. "Or damn yer fanny to deep blue hell I'll—I'll *rape* you!"

"Oh would you, *really?*" the secretary said, in a pleased tone of voice. You see, kiddies, she was going on forty-five years old and *nobody* had been obliging enough to, so far.

Looking at her out of the corner of one eye, Tobias immediately realized that raping her was one dim-witted idea, but he knew better than to tell her that.

"Yep," he said menacingly, "with the barrel of my gun! Or better still, with a corncob!" (Thus anticipating Faulkner.)

Immediately the secretary flopped down beside all the others. "Corncobs hurt!" she muttered. Tobias was too busy to wonder how she knew. But afterwards when he did wonder, Angie had an answer even for *that.* "Th' electric vibrator still hasn't been invented," the Angel said.

Anyhow, the rest of it went off like clockwork. The hell it did! Clockwork goes tickiteetock! Tick-it-tee-tock! Tick-it-tee-tock boingggggh! It went off more like L'Amour McSimple Fearsome's black silk and lace step-ins. Sort of swooosh! Sweeesh—ohhh!

Anyhow, bent almost double under the weight of the loot, Tobias got out of there. In the doorway he turned and fired one last warning shot which, ricocheting off a brass spittoon, wounded poor Maysie Pigeon for the second time—in her *right* rubber falsie on this occasion so that the poor girl had to buy a complete new set. Then he loped off into the sunset. (Or anyhow he would have loped off into the sunset if it hadn't been one thirty in the afternoon, Central States Time.)

But when he got back to his—and Hellcat Hattie McCoy's—hideout with the swag and walked in the door, thunder and lightning exploded inside his head. He saw all the constellations, dwarf stars, planets, and spiral nebulae. Then, as he sank down through one of the black holes of outer space—time warps, Angie swore they were—he heard a male voice snarl—and a helluva authentic snarl it was!

"Geez, Hattie! You miserable hillbilly cunt you! Can you ever 'pick 'em! A hayseed like this hick, here, and you go and pass him off as *me!* As Tony, th' Butterfly Man, no less! Gonna take three pounds off yer skinny tail wit me belt fer th' insult—cause more than that, you just can't spare! And, as fer *'im,* I gotta good mind to mess 'im up so bad that they won't even be able to fingerprint him like they done Slow Dough Moe to find out who th' bastid *wuz!* In fact—"

"Oh, Tony, honey!" Hattie wailed. "Pulll-leeeeze doan do thet! He's harmless, I tell you! 'Sides—'sides—" she was really thinking now, desperation lending a razor edge to her wits. "He's mah ol' man! Legal, Tony! 'N since ah'm alreddy in th' family way 'n *you* sho Lawd ain't even fixin' to give mah pore baby *yore* name, I'd purely appreciate yore lettin' him *live.* Ah—ah'll go wit you, honey! Ah'll do whatever you says, but doan go'n rob mah pore chile o' th' only pappy it'll *ever* have!"

"Ain't that th' truth!" Tony, "the Butterfly" Mariposa, mused. "All right, Hat. I'll let th' poor bastid be. Just relieve him of all this here *lettuce* he seems to have plucked somewheres. Then you'n me'll git moving, doll!"

Now, Children, Antonio "the Butterfly" Mariposa was making a grave mistake by the procedure he was suggesting. Or rather, he was compounding the one he had already made. Now if you're a rackets guy like dear, sweet-natured little Tony Butterfly, you can't afford even *one* mistake, so *two* are likely to prove fatal. In fact, they did.

You see, among all the odd characters in that exceedingly odd metropolis named Chicago, Illinois, the large majority of whom had one *idée fixée* as far as "the Butterfly" was concerned, which was, to quote the chaste and simple language of Eliza Doolittle, and/or George Bernard Shaw, "To do th' Blighter in!" there was a minority of at least one mobster smart enough, or sufficiently less dim-witted than his fellow hoods, to figure out what Tony "the Butterfly" Mariposa would do next, to wit:

"By now he's outa cash. 'N he won't pull a heist. Not th' Butterfly's style. Gats he ain't good wit. He could pull a stickup wita lead pipe o' a baseball bat, he might. Or a shiv. But even th' Butterfly ain't dumb enough to figger he can pull somethin' that would net him more'n loose change wit blunt instruments o' a blade. So what'll 'e do? I ask ya? What? Why look up that hillbilly skoit he wuz layin' sometime back 'n pimp 'er outa a li'l foldin' money. 'Specially since this ugly little freckle-faced frail done made th' big time. Been knockin' off banks in tha sticks just like they wuz pins in a bowlin' alley. So all we gotta do is read the noospapers 'n see where tha broad is operatin'. . . ."

And where the broad—definitely a misnomer as far as a girl with a derrière as narrow as poor Hattie's was concerned—was operating, we already know: Dustbowl, Kansas, at the moment. The trouble was that a large number of gentlemen of unsavory reputations already knew it, too. In fact the carloads of characters arriving hourly in that part of Kansas had to be seen to be believed—not that that would do much good, for most of the plug uglies, torpedoes, hoods, gangsters, mobsters, and what have you holing up in and around Dustbowl waiting for the Butterfly to show up, you wouldn't believe even *after* you had seen them.

Not that the Dustbowlers paid them any especial attention. For, as we have seen, Dustbowl was already a movie mecca, junior grade. And the first things that the citizens of any movie mecca achieve is the suspension of disbelief. When you're accustomed to the kind of individuals that Hollywood could dream up, Dion O'Banion's Irish bully boys, the *Unione Siciliana*'s hoods (don't believe the Mafia, Kiddies, there *ain't* no sich animal!) Hymie the Wise's matzo balls, and Scarface Al's torpedoes, all of whom were present by then, aren't likely to faze you. The three terrible Gennae didn't send a representation. This was one rubbing out they meant to enjoy. So they came themselves.

Therefore it is scarcely odd that when Tobias woke up from the sweet sleep that Tony "the Butterfly" Mariposa's gentle love tap had induced in him (the Butterfly had bent a lead pipe to the exact contours of Tobias' cranium with that tap) the first sound that he heard was gunfire. At first that seemed perfectly normal to him. What with von Stiltiz's mustang melodrama being filmed in Dustbowl, gunfire was something that happened all day long. But then it came to him that this kind of gunfire was all *wrong.* Not even hammer fanning could make a Colt revolver shoot that fast. And even if the monocle-wearing, potbellied, bald-headed little fugitive from Krautland was filming a massive Main Street shootout between two rival cow-punching outfits, there would be some breaks in the shots, as one or another of the main characters slowly and coolly took aim.

Besides, Our Hero had heard that sound before, notably upon the occasion when Hymie the Wise's musicians had rubbed out a whole adobe hut, thinking *he* was in it. Or rather that Tony the Butterfly was. The only thing that could shoot that fast at that particular point in the armament industry development was a Thompson submachine gun, since neither the Bren, the Sten, nor the Schmeisser Burpgun had been invented yet.

"Not a Thompson submachine gun," he corrected himself sorrowfully, "at least a *dozen* Thompson submachine guns. All of 'em going at once. . . ."

Then it came to him who the character on the spot marked X probably was: Tony, the Butterfly Man. But considering all the pain, sorrow, trouble, and danger that Angie's accidental borrowing of that poison-mean little hood's name had caused him, his reaction to *that* particular thought was a broad and happy grin.

But then he remembered who was probably sharing the spot with Tony: his bride. His lawful wedded wife. Hellcat Hattie McCoy. Who in spite of everything was fun to be with. Who was a loving (a mite too strenuously) and tender spouse. Who forgave him all his faults up to and including his miserable cowardice, which was a thing no other woman he'd known before had been willing to do.

What hit him in the big gut was a combination of anguished grief and a rage so terrible that it actually floored him. But he came up off the floor almost at once, and ran out the door, his gold-plated Colt automatic ready in his hand.

He was too late. When he got to the spot marked X the Chicago delegation was already departing the scene in a mushroom-shaped cloud of dust. And the Hudson lay canted up at an angle in a ditch. It had so many bullet holes in it that he knew there wasn't a chance, but he went over to it anyhow. Stood there, looking into that car. The gold-plated Colt slid out of fingers suddenly without strength or feel, thudded against the ground. He didn't hear it. He hung there, eyes and mouth stretched wide, not even shaking yet, seeing it, taking it.

Tony "the Butterfly" Mariposa was draped gracefully halfway out the right front door. Or at least he assumed that was "the Butterfly." Insanely a thought rose up and went jerking like a spastic through his mind: "First damned time I ever saw hamburger steak with *pants* on it!" Then he turned to Hattie—or to what was left of Hattie, which wasn't much. But her head and face were untouched, making a rather peculiar spectacle since they sat atop a bundle of red-soaked rags, wrapped around hash. She had so many holes in her that some of the holes had holes in them. And not even Hollywood's "special effects" artists would have dared apply *that* much catsup. Only it wasn't catsup.

Still, she was smiling at him. Incredibly, she was smiling.

"C'mon heah, hon," she whispered, or rather whooshed, because all that catsup that wasn't catsup, but her life, was coming out her mouth: "Kiss Momma good-bye. Then tek—"

"Hattie!" Our Hero moaned, or screamed, or both.

"Th' swag 'n git!" Hattie said. Or tried to. Anyhow he understood her. By telepathy, maybe. The doomed and those by their own idiocy damned are close enough linked for that. And any kind of suffering is holy. He bent to that gallant head, set atop so much butchered meat, kissed those bloody lips (it was the bravest thing he'd ever done) without even shuddering (not to mention throwing up), straightened up and stared at her. But by then he couldn't see her, he was crying so hard.

"Doan cry, baby-boy, Momma'll tek care o—" Hattie said. And died.

He took the swag. But he didn't "git." Moved by some obscure impulse, he marched back into Dustbowl with it. Walked like a sleepwalker or a walking corpse into the Merchants' and Farmers' Bank. Went straight up to the teller. Lifted the bag of stolen money. Said: "Here. Take this. It's yours."

When the bank guards grabbed him, he made no resistance. They were puzzled at the fact that he was totally unarmed. (The answer to that puzzle was, of course, that he had dropped the gold-plated Colt next to the car when he had seen poor butchered Hattie sitting there.) But they were even more puzzled at the other fact that the bag, bank notes and all, was not only more full of holes than a piece of Gruyere cheese, but was covered with blood, because as far as they could see their prisoner hadn't a scratch on him.

Then the local sheriff came through the door. Told the bank guards (who were still disguised as deputy sheriffs in chaps, sombreros, and spurs for cinema purpose):

"Turn 'im loose. Y'alls go th' wrong man. Th' bank robber is still in th' car wit Hattie. O'anyhow, whut's left of 'im is. . . ."

They turned Our Hero loose. He started to get out of there. He hadn't a red Indian copper in his pockets and absolutely nowhere to go, but by then even nowhere looked a helluva lot more inviting than Dustbowl, Kansas, did to him.

But a fat, short, bald-headed man with a monocle in his left eye was blocking his way, and hopping up and down and yelling:

"Ist perfect! Donner und Wetter! Ist viel und sehrviel mehr dan perfect! Ist ein miracle! Der nose! I awsk you! Hast Du nichts gesehen? Der nose!"

"What about his nose, Chief?" one of von Stiltiz's aides-de-camp said.

"Dummkopf! Narr und Esel! Hast Du nichts gesehen? Ist *broken* der nose! Per-fect! Für die film vom gangster Ich bin gemaking am going to! Mit dieser Kerl in der rôle dem Al Capone! Ist viel und sehr viel *mehr* dan perfect! Don't let dieser Amerikaner Idiotischer get away! Even if er under Contract von der United Artists ist! Don't let 'im get away! Hören Sie nicht? Grab him!"

And that, Dear Kiddies, is how Our Brave and Gallant Hero, Tobias Tobit, became a movie star. And, directly as a result, met Roxane de la Rue, who starred opposite him in the great gangster epic, *The Man on the Spot.* And following naturally and of course his natural bent as in that poem by Rudyard Kipling, he—

But, for that, and divers other matters, as they said in the "Cliffhangers" of those days, Dear Children:

"SEE NEXT CHAPTER!"

Thirteen

"Cut!" Wolfgang von Stiltiz bawled. "Per-fect! Ist von und zu viel mehr vom per-fect! Ich bin vier und dreizig bedamnt und der schlafkamerad von der Frau Schicklgruber if per-fect nein ist! What ein *Actor* ist dieser Kerl!"

The *Kerl* (translation "Oaf") to whom von Stiltiz (don't even *try* to pronounce it; the last person who seriously tried to say "von Stiltiz" aloud had his lips in a plaster cast for three months) referred was, of course, Our Hero, Tobias Tobit. Or at least, a revised edition of him, screen credits to the make-up artist, Don Lucifero Angel Moreno. Yes, children, Angie. Who had arrived in Hollywood, California, bringing Anne with him. And, being Angie, had had no trouble at all convincing von Stiltiz that he was the greatest make-up artist that Hollywood had ever seen. Which he *was* even though his methods were a trifle unorthodox. Eschewing greasepaint, powder, eye shadow, putty, gum rubber and what have you, Angie simply touched his clients on the forehead with one horny finger, whereupon they immediately looked more like the characters they were supposed to represent than the characters did themselves. For instance, Tobias was a head taller and thirty-five pounds skinnier than Al Capone. What's more, he hadn't any scars except one on the top of his head where they'd dug that shell splinter out of him during World Smashup Number One. And that scar was well hidden by his thick black hair. But Angie touched him, and he shrank eighteen inches shorter, and swelled thirty-five pounds heavier on the spur of that one incredibly brief hiatus in his personal sequential progression. Not only that, but the scar of an old razor cut bloomed on his dark, porcine-looking left cheek. (Or on his dark, porcine-looking *right* cheek. Or wherever the hell it was Al Capone had *his* scar.)

Now, the only trouble with Angie's method was—as the actors and actresses found to their acute dismay—it wouldn't wash off. Whomever and whatever that most unangelic Angel made them resemble, or, more accurately, transformed them into, they went right on resembling, or, in fact, practically being, until Angie got around to touching them a second time, and thus restoring them to their ordinary selves.

Naturally, Angie saw the possibilities in *that.* Even quite opposite possibilities, to wit: He would reduce a whole gaggle of starlets into exact replicas of H. Rider Haggard's *She,* at the age of eight hundred years, and only restore them to their youthful little selves after they had signed an iron-clad contract to provide him with full and frequent use of a due portion of their dainty little anatomies—in a horizontal (though not necessarily supine, since Angie was far from hung up on the missionary, rather favoring, in fact, the prone) position, whenever and wherever he should so desire. But even more fruitful was the opposite: He would restore aging ("Aging" in this sense being any female star a day younger than the midwife who delivered God, who could crawl or be pushed in her wheelchair before a motion picture camera) movie queens to a dewy youth and freshness that most of them had never had, and then threaten to again make them look like the plastered-over grim deaths they actually did resemble if they also didn't suitably reward him. Only most of the time, he didn't even have to threaten. The poor old dears were so overwhelmed with gratitude that Angie practically had to fight them off.

But Angie soon fell victim to an unforeseen contingency. That unforeseen contingency grew out of his basic error of having married a girl who came equipped with one First-Class A-Number-One brain. For Anne, though rounding and bulging serenely into sweet motherhood, had not yet rounded nor bulged enough to incapacitate her for nocturnal activity. So she noticed how *tired* Angie was. How reluctant to engage in boudoir gymnastics, fun and games—with *her* anyhow. And to make matters worst (superlative; they had already gone past worse, comparative, in the initial portion of that particular sequential progression), Angie frequently muttered in his sleep that absolute gem of poetic wisdom:

> *"I love girls over forty:*
> *They don't yell;*
> *They don't tell;*
> *They don't swell;*
> *And they're as* grateful *as hell!"*

Which caused dear little Anne to think long, deeply, and, what was even worsssttt, accurately. So the next time Angie arrived on the set he found his blushing, rounding, and bulging little bride ensconced in the position of wardrobe mistress at a perfectly enormous salary. Don't ask how she managed that. The best guess is that some of Angie's Angelcraft had rubbed off on her. Or that she wasn't really, or at least not entirely, human either; because certain cryptic remarks she occasionally muttered in her sleep, and the weird but lovely gibberish that made up the lyrics of the operatic arias she frequently gave vent to when, to quote the Bard of Avon, "In the very lists of Love, Her Champion mounted for the hot encounter . . ." had caused Angie to seriously suspect that she was more a humanoid than human, and very probably from an exceedingly remote planet, circling an invisible dwarf star on the very edge of extra galaxial space.

Anyhow, humanoid, human, or witch—another of Angie's speculative theories about the nature of his bride—there his darlin' Annie wuz, blushing, rounding, and bulging simultaneously, or rather concurrently, and what was more, grinning wickedly at her erring spouse, while eating—also concurrently—a huge dill pickle, festooned with whipped cream, the traditional favorite dish of pregnant brides.

Which, as you can well imagine, put quite a crimp into Angie's hustle. His reaction to *that* was to try to pass off his little black book with all the names, addresses and telephone numbers to Tobias. But Our Hero wasn't having any.

"What kind of a heartless bastard do you think I am, Angie?" he said soulfully. "And my poor Hattie not yet cold in her grave!"

For Tobias Tobit still carried about with him a full supply of noble sentiment, a conception of basic ethics, quite a few notions touching upon morality, a whole trunkful of scruples, and a well-formed idea of personal integrity. All of which would have been at least harmless if he hadn't also retained the distinctly odd belief that all this curious collection of dusty emotional freight actually had something to do with what goes on in this world.

"Thereby proving," Angie sighed, "that ye're the dopiest dope what ever came down th' pike! Listen to me, laddybucks! The wages o' sin are a cool million bucks which kin be increased by playin' th' market—or th' bangtails. On th' whole, I recommend th' ponies as safer. And virtue is its own, and *only* reward. Now take this number. Beverly Hills—006 05–31. Cute li'l redhead. Got more wiggles than a jazz pianist and—"

Tobias and the Angel

"Oh go away, Angie, and leave me *alone,* will you please?" Tobias said.

He was sincerely grieving for Hattie. And, at intervals, also for Nancy, since the tragic death of his one and only ("ball 'n chain!" Angie shot sardonically into his mind) reminded him of the equally tragic death of his darling little playmate. What's more, his grief was compounded by his guilt-laden recognition of the fact that he had loved neither of them.

Which troubled him more than somewhat, because it pointed up a curious duality in his nature: With the lone exception of Conchita, he had never been able to *love* any girl whom he had For Unlawful Carnal Knowledged, probably because his own dear Mama, Anna Tobit, had firmly implanted in his cranium the quaint and curious idea that girls in general can be divided into but two great categories: *Good* girls and *Bad* girls. Good girls being, of course, the ones who wouldn't, and Bad girls the ones who would.

"Whilst, as a matter o' fact," Angie said, "they fall into three: Good, Better, 'n Best. No—four. Good, Better, Best and Ohhhhhhhh Brother!"

"You're a scoundrel," Tobias said. "Besides, when Mama said 'Good,' she damned sure didn't mean good in bed!"

"There're *other* ways o' being good? For a filly, I mean?" Angie said wonderingly. "C'mon, Toby, me boy, me boy! Take this li'l book 'n—"

"No," Tobias said firmly. And that was that.

But, along with Random Chance, Blind Accidentality, and the Absurdity Factor, there *are* a few other laws operating at least spasmodically in the Universe, among them being the Newtonian concept of the conservation of energy. And, at the moment, it was the chief thing that Our Hero had going for him. In a practical sense, it worked out like this:

Tobias Tobit was sad. He was sad because he was grieving for his departed soulmate. And his grief and his sadness gave him a gloomy look. Now, according to the Newtonian law of the conservation of energy, the human countenance conserves the living hell out of energy by reducing all emotions to five or six basic expressions, so alike that most people can't even distinguish one of them from the others.

So, applying this great Newtonian principle, when Tobias looked gloomy, the expression served well enough for also looking mean, and/or menacing, which, especially when Angie had transformed him into an exact replica of Scarface Al Capone, served to convince all and sundry, up to and including von Stiltiz, that Our Hero was the greatest actor ever.

The concrete result of Tobias' apparent talent in a profession where talent was not only unnecessary, but was often actually looked upon as a bloody nuisance, though, fortunately for Our Hero, von Stiltiz was not of this rather reactionary school of thought, was that Angie, who, naturally, had appointed himself as Tobias' agent and business manager, demanded and got huge raises for his protégé every time he horned in on von Stiltiz's supposedly private viewing of the "rushes" and "takes." The be-monocled little Kraut raised no objections at all. He was absolutely sure that *The Man on the Spot* was going to break all box-office records in history once it was released.

In fact, Tobias was making so much money that Angie was beginning to speculate upon the possibility of unlocking Our Hero's inevitabilities from Clara's (or maybe Sara's?) and going on with what looked like a very good thing indeed, when they reached that part of the picture where—in the interest of giving the moviegoers a little relief from two and a half hours of unmitigated and gruesome butchery (von Stiltiz had even filmed the sequence based upon the "rubbing out" of Slow Dough Moe Green in close-up and slow motion, using cold hominy grits dyed shocking scarlet to represent poor Slow Dough's splattered brains)—the "love interest" had to be introduced.

Now the "love interest," of course, was Roxane de la Rue. Born Tilly Higginfrother in Glasgow, Scotland, Roxane made her first claim on fame by actually and gleefully selling herself to the white slave trade. This, of course, will be instantly comprehensible to anyone who has ever spent two million years over one weekend in Glasgow, Scotland. But the *way* she got to Hollywood is worthy of note. A great director, who, for obvious reasons, will remain nameless in these chaste and simple chronicles, encountered her gracing the doorway of a bordello in the Old Port of Marseilles. And the main result of that encounter was that the great director, convinced beyond argument of the supremacy of her talents (nobody who ever enjoyed the only talent Roxane had to her name ever had breath left to argue about anything, not even her asking price), put her under contract and brought her back to Hollywood, not to make a star of her, but to protect his investment in a large, muscular he-man great lover, who was probably *the* fruitiest swish in the long line of closet queens over which whole generations of poor, benighted female moviegoers have swooned.

In those unenlightened days before anyone had even dreamed of such a thing as the gay liberation movement, for the general public to learn of the above-mentioned great lover's amatory predilections and/or peculiarities, meant the end of a promising career, because —and this *does* have bearing, as we shall presently see, upon Our Hero's, Tobias Tobit's, affairs—Fatty Arbuckle's excessive devotion to the missionary position had already cause Hollywood to call in Will Hays to remove the movie Mecca's fine excess of dirty linen from the public view.

For after an hour with Roxane, as Tilly already called herself— though the movie magnates, having been thoughtful enough to have the rest of her nom de guerre, "du Trottoir," translated, instantly rejected it and substituted "de la Rue" as being more elegant, a distinctly debatable point—the great director decided that if *anyone* could cure the great lover of his at least commercially unfortunate tendencies, it was surely dear Roxane.

As it turned out, the director was right. After Roxane had ripped the great lover's (1) long, (2) black, (3) silk, (4) lace-trimmed, and (5) delicately perfumed nightgown—the son of an overripe grapefruit even *slept* in drag—off him and treated him to a combination riding lesson and wrestling match, with a few delectable, delicious, and delightful variations upon the basic theme, so absolutely outrageous that even old swisheroo hadn't encountered them before, for the better part of an entire weekend, the great lover woke up roaring like Tarzan of the apes, and completely converted to heterosexuality.

The only trouble with that was an hour later he died of a heart attack.

Mighty rough li'l gal, that theah Roxane!

So, in order to cut his losses, the great director decided to give

Roxane a screen test. When he saw the rushes, he almost passed out from sheer joy. Because, you see, he had discovered a marvel: an absolute combination of exact opposites in the same barbed-wire and whip-cord tough, ice cold, poison-mean little bitch.

For Roxane had the kind of face that the Pre-Raphaelite artists painted onto lady angels, combined with a temperament that would have given Lucrezia Borgia pause. She hated men, women, children, babes in arms, directors, producers, publicity men, agents, cameramen, property men, grips, lighting men, Hollywood itself, the whole U.S.A., dogs, horses, ants, beetles, worms, ants—oh hell. You name it. Roxane hated it.

And yet—she *oozed* sex. That was what stoned the great director right out of his skull. She could turn those great big, baby-blue eyes on you, open those sweet, childish lips a little—and—Wow! Zowie! Boinggg! Supply your own sound effects. That was *it,* Brother. It was absolutely the damnedest thing. You could cast her in the role of the mother superior of the Transalpine Humpbacked Nuns, going to her death as a martyr for the faith, and it would come out with an X rating. Well, not an X rating, because they didn't have X ratings in those days. But the Hays office held up every single picture she ever starred in for months, and then *had* to release them because not one of them had an offensive word, gesture, or scene in them. But the minute they were released the American Women's Purity League (sponsored by Kelvinator, natch) and the League of Decency (sponsored by the Benevolent Brotherhood of Saloon and Brothel Keepers, Inc.) picketed them every one.

She could read the *Bible* and turn it into porn. But it was the contrast between the sweet, dewy-eyed innocence of her looks, and the aura of sensuality she effortlessly, even unconsciously, projected, that made Roxane so valuable in the *new* Hollywood where *every* contract—including our friend Tobias'—had a morals clause written into it; and pictures starring actors whose private misbehavior became public (c.f. Arbuckle, Minter, Normand, Reid, La Marr, etc.) got quietly shelved forever.

In the Hollywood of those days, with the Hays office riding herd on *every* picture in the interest of public decency, Roxane de la Rue was absolutely the hottest property anybody had ever heard of.

Because, you see, the movie moguls didn't have to *worry* about her pictures. They *couldn't* be banned because they were demonstrably as pure as the drifting snow. And yet, everything she'd learned in *les bordels du vieux Port de Marseilles* came over no matter what the script said, or the scene in question showed. She could play Little Bo Peep and have every poor horny frustrated illegitimate in the United States of America (ninety-nine and ninety-nine hundredths per cent of *all* American males at that precise point in the nation's sequential progression) lined up before the box offices, panting. She was indisputably the world's worst actress—and with Theda Bara and Pola Negri both still around, that took some doing. She played in what were beyond all question the world's worst motion pictures, including that epic that should have sunk the cinema forever, *The Man on the Spot,* costarring Tobias Tobit, and every single one of them made millions. If she hadn't lived, Mencken would have had to invent her, because she completely justified his dictum Khat "Nobody ever went broke underestimating the taste of the American public!" That lapidary phrase describes her essence perfectly. It should have been carved upon her tombstone.

It has already been pointed out that Roxane de la Rue hated everybody, and everything. But, Dear Kiddies, there was one outstanding exception to that rule. Our Hero, Tobias Tobit. Him, Roxane didn't merely hate; she loathed, despised, and passionately desired to—well no, not just murder—say to annihilate, to exterminate, draw and quarter him, subject him to tortures not even dreamed up by the Office of the Holy Inquisition, plus those which, in her extreme old age, she later passed along to the Gestapo. Why? you ask?

The best guess is that this happened because Tobias was an authentic gentle soul. And gentle souls—a euphemism for utter dopes—*normally* inspire homicical impulses in any woman with blood in her veins. But a soul gentle to the degree that Our Hero, Tobias Tobit was, or, if you will, as dopey a dope, brought out every drop of sadism in Roxane's sadomasochistic makeup, while leaving the masochism at home.

Which is why, on the evening of the first day that she came upon the set, after those first rarely touching love scenes your grandmothers swooned over had been filmed and were already in the cans, Angie found Tobias sitting in his dressing room (the one with the vile, vomit-green star on the door) and crying his poor little heart out.

"What did she do to ye?" Angie grinned. "Kick yer shins? Bite yer lip?"

"Worse!" Tobias groaned. "She chews tobacco. Old Boar Hog Black, in fact. Mixed with *fresh* garlic. Then when she's got a mouth full of th' stuff, she *soul* kisses me! And—"

"And what?" Angie said, happily.

"The *things* she says! That she wouldn't let me even if I borrowed *yours* to do it with, and—"

"Hmmmm—" Angie said. "Unnecessary. I'll lend it to her. Personal application free o' charge, of course. If I kin git me Annie outa me curly blond locks long enough, that is! Say on, Toby, me boy, me boy!"

"She wants to know what I'm standing up for, and pretending to be *human,* when any fool can plainly see that *crawling* is my natural mode of locomotion. No, creeping. She asks me if I was born or hatched? In a snake pit, that is. Or maybe wasn't I the result of a nightmare my poor Mama—"

"Whom th' blessed saints have with 'em in glory!" Angie added piously.

"Whom th' blessed saints, et cetera," Tobias groaned. "Where was I? Oh yes, whether I wasn't maybe the end product of a nightmare of my poor Mama's. The one where she dreamed she was the *pièce de résistance* at a gang bang in the monkey house at the Bronx Zoo. Say, Angie, what's a gang bang anyhow?"

"An anachronism. Th' term hasn't even been coined yet. Anyhow, skip it, laddybucks—'cause its meaning is unfit fer yer tender ears. Appears to me I better have a word with this li'l girl!"

"She won't listen," Tobias said. "All she'll do is swear at you. In Scottish. And in Marseillaise waterfront whore house argot. You know what she calls me most of the time?"

"No. What does th' li'l lassie call ye, Toby, me boy, me boy?"

"Queue d'huître," Tobias said.

Angie threw back his head and roared.

"Don't see what's so damn funny about *that,*" Tobias said.

" 'Tis an epithet of real class," Angie chuckled. *"Queue d'huître:* oyster tail. Kin ye think of a more repugnant object than the arse-hole of an oyster? Rather like clotted snot, what? Th' lass has imagination! Now tell me, Sir Toby Oyster-tail, what—"

"Oh, get out of here, will you?" Tobias said.

"No," Angie purred. "Listen to me, Toby lad, after this sequence is over, we kin head straight fer East Egypt Kentucky. An' in style. Ridin' in th' Pierce Arrow I jist bought ye: gold plated 'n with basketweave, wickerwork side panels, yet! Even th' numerals on th' dashboard instruments are gemstones, me boy! Rubies, sapphires 'n diamonds. Real ones. When Raguel—I mean Ralphie—sees that flossy wagon, with me in a field marshal-type uniform, a-drivin' it, and me Annie in black silk, and 'll starched white as yer maid, it'll rock 'im right back on *his queue d'huître* 'n—"

"Angie, I'm going to *hit* you in a minute!" Tobias howled.

"Whazzamatta, Toby, me boy, me boy? This lass *gits* to ye, right?"

"Yes," Tobias said miserably. "I—I'm afraid I've fallen for her, Angie. In spite of everything. In spite of poor Hattie, and poor Nancy, and little Conchita and—"

"Not 'little' Conchita," Angie explained with professional gravity. "That's what th' 'ita' part of her name means, me boy: 'little.' Catch? Therefore ye kin say 'little' Concha, but niver 'little' Conchita, fer then ye're sayin' 'little little' Concha, which is one little too many to me way o' thinkin'. So ye've gone 'n flipped fer Sidewalk Roxane, eh, lad? Hardly smart o' ye, I must admit . . . Lemme think, lemme think . . ."

"She sends me, Angie," Tobias groaned; "even if that is another anachronism, it's the only way to describe it, and—"

"Hmmmm," Angie mused. "Th' only trouble is, me boy, that I ain't sure that 'twould be safe to apply th' usual cure. After all, dear Roxie spent all o' three years in a Marseillaise bordello. 'N even grantin' ye that I'm contradictin' meself, 'cause time don't rightly exist, leastwise not in the precise way that ye humans think o' it, that's one helluva long segment o' anybody's sequential progression to have lingered in the world's third-worst cat houses, after the ones in Calcutta, and Algiers' casbah, I mean—"

"Angie—" Tobias said.

"Shut up 'n lemme think! I know, I know, th' *only* way to cure ye o' her would be to let ye bed with her. But then, th' risk is too great. To th' rest o' this particular sequential progression of yer *present* avatar, ye ken? How kin I be sure that yer poor, puny li'l longitudinarious won't *rot* clean away afore ye kin even pull it out o' her fuzzy li'l quim? Or drop off on the floor th' next mornin'? Nope. 'Tis up t' me to be a martyr fer th' cause! Hafta try her first, meself —who knows? Considerin' what puts into th' *vieux Port de Marseilles,* she may have Korean, Vietnamese, North 'n South in both cases, Arabian—Saudi Arabian at that which is the *worst* kind—Roosian, North American, 'n Israeli V.D. all combined. An' ye *need* yer poor li'l longitudinarious such as it is, such as it is! To even terminate yer present incarnation's sequential progression properly. No, I'll hev to be th' sacrificial goat, that's all . . ."

"What will *Anne* say to that?" Tobias said, "especially if *yours* falls off?"

"It won't. I'm an Angel, remember? Not o' th' same essence as ye humans. 'N hence unaffected by all th' disgustin' diseases—psychosomatic, wun 'n all!—that ye've made up to punish yerselves fer yer more interestin' type sins, instead o' relaxin' 'n enjoyin' th' way ye ought to!"

"You," Tobias said darkly, "are a mere figment of my diseased and distorted imagination! Hell, you don't even *exist,* you celestial whorehopper, you!"

"Hence even *less* likely to be affected by, or even *catch* th' three hundred 'n forty varieties o' V.D. poor li'l Sidewalk Roxie's got by now. Of course, 'tis possible that th' movie moguls have had some fancy pill pushers 'n or sawbones in to clean up th' works. Protectin' their business interests, ye ken? But I can't jist *awsk* 'er, kin I? Look, Roxie, La Moxie, 'ave ye a clean bill o' health? Hell, she'd smite me hip 'n thigh, I wuz to awsk 'er that! 'N lie about the whole matter in th' bargain. Gotta try 'er once. Ye see that, don't ye, Toby lad?"

"I see that you're a lecherous celestial scoundrel," Tobias said, "and that Roxane sends you, too."

"Right. Right as rain. But then, most young female humans, as well as some *not* so young, do that. Anyhow, I'm off. Wish me luck, laddybucks?"

"Oh go fornicate yourself, Angie!" Tobias said.

"With dear Roxane du Trottoir. I mean 'de la Rue'—around to do th' job even better? Not on yer sweet, innercent little life, Toby, me boy! By the bye, me Annie inquires, tell 'er I'm off on an advance publicity job fer *ye,* lad. Truth, what? Now ta ta, bhhoyyy!"

And the only thing wrong with *that* was that the next morning, Angie limped into the studios of Metacolossal Pictures, Incorporated, with *two* black eyes, and various assorted bruises.

"Th' *left* shiner, courtesy o' Roxane," the Angel groaned, "th' right at th' hands o' me darlin' Annie! Who *followed* me. 'N *both* of 'em jumped me, th' pair o' screechin' hellcats!"

"And afterwards engaged in the damnest clawing, spitting, hair-pulling contest anyone ever did see?" Tobias said hopefully.

"Not on yer life, boy-baby! Th' two of 'em discovered that they have certain affinities. That, like Rosie O'Grady 'n th' Colonel's Lady, they're sisters under th' skin. On the subject o' men, plural, 'n general, they're in perfect agreement. We, sez they, belong to the porcine species, with overtones o' male chauvinism, whatever th' blazes that be! 'N I—'n mebbe even ye—although they had th' goodness to doubt that ye're old enough to qualify—are prime examples of unsanitary senior citizenship. When I departed th' scene—in some haste, ye kin bet!—they were discussin' th' possibility of forming a League fer th' Liberation o' Young Females from our Senile 'n Unhygienic Clutches!"

"So?" Tobias said, "now what do we do, Angie?"

"We wait," Angie groaned, " 'til von Spiltscheisserstoff's gangster epic is over with. Then I figure out a reasonable way o' breakin' th' ironclad contract fer three more flicks he's got ye tied up into. Somethin' touchin' th' Hays office 'n yer morals clause should do that, quite nicely. But it's gotta be good. 'Cause ye really ain't up to doin' a poor frail in by For Unlawful Carnal Knowledging her to death like old Fatso did. Besides which, ye're much too skinny. Got it!"

"Got what?" Tobias said.

"We stage an orgy. A real, first-class smasheroo of an orgy. At that flossy pad in Beverly Hills I leased fer ye. 'N we *don't* invite yer neighbors. Which'll get 'em so pissed off they'll complain to th' law. So yer joint will get raided. 'N ye'll be caught in th' hay with a starlet.

A thirteen-'n-a-half-year-old *child* starlet, with a Grade A, Pasteurized Virginity Certificate in her pocketbook. Say, d'ye suppose there *are* any thirteen-year-old virgins in Hollywood? Mebbe we better look for an *eight*-year-old female child star 'n—"

"Angie!" Tobias said.

"All right. We'll leave *that* detail pending fer th' moment. But ye're throwing th' orgy—th' party—to celebrate the glorious termination o' *The Man on the Spot.* We can't wait around fer th' triumphal openin' night. Meanwhile, we lie low, Toby lad! We lie mighty, mighty lllooww!"

But as we have seen, the best-laid plans of mice and men, and even of mice-men, to which species poor Tobias indisputably belonged, not to mention those of the wild and weird figments of their diseased and distorted imaginations, that most angels, anyhow, are, seldom, if ever, come to a good end.

For, at the very moment that Tobias' magnificent orgy was at its zenith or its nadir, depending upon what *your* moral concepts are, Children, a huge, platinum-plated Rolls-Royce Silver Ghost drew up before Tobias' mansion in Beverly Hills, and out of it stepped both Roxane de la Rue and dear little rounding, bulging, pickle-eating Anne.

They couldn't have chosen a better moment, or a worse, again depending upon your point of view, for, as they walked into the garden, the first sight that greeted their eyes was a human daisy chain that Angie had arranged (and was participating in) all around Tobias' South Atlantic Ocean-sized swimming pool. At least *Anne* was startled at the sight of all those people in various stages of undress right down to *au poil* most of them, busily engaging in all sorts of mutually entertaining perversions and/or abominations, though truth, sad truth to tell, there were even a few sturdily rectilinear citizens who were going at it in several of the approved modes and positions, even in the case of one quaint couple, the missionary, considered entirely normal even in those dear, dim ages of antiquity.

What startled Roxane, who, naturally, found anything so tame, domesticated, *passé et déjà vu* as the kind of perversions and/or abominations mere Hollywoodians would know a matter for yawning over if that, was the only thing that could have possibly startled her: The sight of Tobias, fully—and decently—clothed, seated beside a darling little eight-year-old child star, also fully clothed, and feeding her ice-cream cones. That said ice-cream cones had been variously spiked with peyote, mescal, heroin, hashish, opium, marijuana, cocaine, and *bananas* (the absolute end!) was a thing that Our Hero didn't even know. And you may rest assured that he wouldn't have tolerated it if he had known, for decency had no stouter champion than Tobias Tobit.

But the highly opportune arrival of Roxane and Anne saved Tobias from even finding out just how filthy a trick his Guardian Angel had pulled off on him *this* time. Because the child star, stoned out of her childish mind, had just begun to lisp out an outrageously indecent and/or immoral proposition—(the *same* outrageously indecent and/or immoral proposition that *her* own dear Mama had taught her to lisp out to casting directors, with the result that at age eight—or slightly less—she was (A) (unquestionably) a full-fledged child star and (B) (maybe) the youngest casting-couch broad in Hollywood's history—when Tobias caught sight of Roxane and Anne and, dropping the ice-cream cone onto his well-tonsured lawn, rushed over to greet them.

To greet Roxane, anyhow, because by then Anne had already proved that what she was packing in her handbag was not—or at least not only—a pickle, for she had one of those, and of the dill variety, duly, and messily, garnished with whipped cream in the handbag, too; but a pistol. A large and exceedingly unladylike pistol of a perfectly enormous caliber. In fact, even as gunshy as he was, Tobias' first thought consisted in pure, scientific wonder as to just how she had managed to get a cannon of *that* size into her bag at all, though his second, it must be admitted, was to look for the nearest exit. But, at that precise moment, dear little Pistol-(and Pickle) Packing Annie opened fire.

Her markswomanship was perfect. In fact, it was miraculous. The only thing *more* miraculous was the speed at which Angie's various female partners in extravagantly carnal sin invented simultaneously the art of streaking, departing the vicinity of that heavenly miscreant at a velocity roughly approximating, if not actually doubling, that of light. But Anne wasn't even aiming at *them.* In fact, every one of her bullets hit Angie in what would have been, under ordinary circumstances, a vital spot.

Which, of course, because Angie was: (A) (perhaps) an Angel; (B) (surely) not even human; and (C) (indisputably) a figment of Tobias Tobit's diseased and disordered imagination, did him absolutely no harm at all. But Angie was much too smart to allow his irate, rounding, bulging, pickle-eating, pistol-packing bride to see that she hadn't, to again quote Eliza Doolittle and G.B.S. "done 'im in," and, what was worse, since Angels are presumably immortal, couldn't *ever* accomplish that most satisfactory of all feats to any wife with blood in her veins, so he immediately began to bleed rivers and fountains of gore, to writhe, twist, groan, moan, jerk, thrash about, in short, to present so heart-rending a spectacle of a man in the throes of his ultimate agony that poor little Anne threw away both pistol and pickle, and ran screaming to gather her poor dying spouse in her tender arms.

"Well, that's that," Roxane said, calmly. "Now tell me, Toby, why didn't you invite *me* to your obscene and what's rawther a bit worse, *vulgar* brawl?"

"Thought you wouldn't come," Tobias got out. He was strangling. That was one of the milder of the various effects that Roxane had upon him.

"You thought right," Roxane said, "but I'm glad I did."

"You *are?"* Tobias gasped.

"Yes. Gave me a different slant on you, Toby. Bit of all right, aren't you, luv?"

"If you say so, Roxane," Tobias said.

"I do say so, Toby, luv," Roxane said. "Now come on."

"Come on—where?" Tobias breathed.

"To yer bedroom, luv. Or anywhere else that's private. This *is* an orgy, isn't it? D'ye know anything *else* a couple can do at an orgy?"

"No," Tobias said.

"But in private. Cozy, what? Object to public previews of private emotions, luv. Object violently. Not done. Rum show, rawther. Not U. Somewhat less than pip-pip, tickiboo 'n tophole, wouldn't you say?"

"Raw-ther!" Tobias said. "Carry on, Roxane, lass! Britannia rules 'n God save th' King!"

"Better awksh th' old sot to save *you,* Toby, luv! You're going to need 'im!" Roxane said.

Which turned out to be the understatement of that, or any year. For, once they had retired to Tobias' bedroom and divested themselves of their garments (now *there's* an elegant turn of phrase if I ever heard one!), dear Roxane reached into her handbag and produced a piece of artillery bigger, if anything, than the one Anne had used to (supposedly) do poor Angie in, and shoved the muzzle of that somewhat less than dainty phallic symbol up under Our Hero's (by then wildly quivering) chin.

"Embrace me, luv," she cooed, "but no mannish tricks, my beamish boy! Had a hard day. Bit of fatigued, don't chew know? Tuckered out, rawther. So here're the ground rules for this rugby match: You may kiss, stroke, pet, or what have you—*above* midcenter field, luv. But ploughing, harrowing, tunnelling, and all such vulgar arts of husbandry are *out.* Absolutely no probing in the bushes by the fork. Bad form. Distinctly non U. Indulged in *only* by the lower orders . . ."

"But *I'm* a lower order!" Tobias groaned.

"I should say you *are!* The bee's knees. Maggot's belly button. *Queue d'huître . . .*"

"Oh God!" Tobias said.

"Oh, come now! Hardly the fate worse than death, Toby, luv! Now snuggle up to muther like a good lad. D'you know, you really aren't half bad? A bit on the skinny side, but you'd do. Definitely —if I felt in the mood, which I don't. . . ."

Tobias, always the perfect gentleman, complied. But, as you may have expected, Children, he found snuggling up to a shapely (and stark-naked) young woman who was pressing a .38 caliber Smith & Wesson firmly into his Adam's apple to discourage any attempt on his part to tactilely explore the more interesting and tropical areas of her personal geography, somewhat less than cozy. To make matters worse, dear Roxane proceeded to kiss, stroke, pinch, and (gently) bite him, with the inevitable result that, even as gunshy as he was, she very quickly achieved her basic objective, which was to drive him right out of his ever lovin', cotton pickin' mind.

After about ten minutes of *that,* he groaned.

"This isn't *fair,* Roxane! And I thought that the Anglo-Saxon peoples *invented* fair play!"

"Rawther!" Roxane said. "Must be true to the playing fields o' Scotland, what? Roger. Can do. Wait right where you are, luv!"

Whereupon, she skipped blithely into his dressing room. When she came back, her aspect was somewhat startling. For, as any serious study of the refinements of sensuality shows, the only thing nakeder than a naked woman is a not-quite naked woman. Because, Girl Children, if you want to drive Boy Children crazy, don't take it *all* off. Leave something on, but in the wrong places. Such as wearing, as dear Roxane did, when she came back into Our Hero's bedroom, a sombrero; chaps (strapped to bare thighs); a gunbelt garnished with two pearl-handled Colts buckled around her slender, and bare, midriff; and cowboy boots. Between the gunbelt and the boots, she wore absolutely nothing but those chaps, and if you know how chaps are made, you will realize that they, by sheer contrast, only improved the view. But, in one slender, gloved hand, she bore a new riding crop, or quirt. And the boots, Dear Children, were duly equipped with spurs.

Thereupon, after adopting one of the more modish of the woman superior positions and chanting (A) "I got spurs that jingle, jangle, jingle!"; (B) "Home, Hhhhoame on th' Raaange!"; (C) "Git along, Little Dogie, Git Ahhhhlawngggg!"; (D) Firing off both Colts at intervals; (E) quirting her mount bloody; and (F) spurring the poor beastie into pure, foam-flecked exhaustion, she played fair. Moughty, moughty fair, Pard!

Anyhow, when Beverly Hills's finest finally arrived upon the scene, they found Our Hero, or the flayed, mangled, striped, foam-flecked, wind-broken remains of him sleeping the sweet sleep of total, tender satiation in Roxane's loving arms.

The very next day, Tobias, Angie—who hadn't a scratch on him despite all the gunplay and/or gore—and pickle-packing Anne (she'd thrown the *pistol* away by then) headed eastward in the Pierce Arrow. After von Stiltiz had reluctantly invoked the morals clause. With tears in his eyes. Having no other recourse after *every* scandal sheet in that lotus eaters' paradise had trumpeted Our Hero's misdeeds to the four winds.

Which was just as well. Life has its own inevitabilities built in. Plus Random Chance. Plus the Absurdity Factor. Plus Blind Accidentality.

Plus the Machiavellian mechanisms of—an Angel.

End of Chapter

P.S. It didn't. Drop off, that is. So maybe Angie was right about the movie moguls having had pill pushers and/or sawbones in to protect their investment. So therefore this book goes on for a while. In fact, it even turns serious. What's that? The *book,* Children, the *book!* Not poor Tobias' longitudinarious.

What *it* turned was *blue!*

Fourteen

Roads.

Endless, winding, dusty roads. Stretching from west to east, across the nation.

At first they went up. Into the towering grandeur of the Rockies. Then they went down again, crossing the great plains. And then—

But it didn't matter where they went, because to Tobias Tobit, they all ran through an utter desolation, a private map of hell, a blasted moonscape of that region of the heart, that dark night of the soul where, as poor Zelda-haunted Scottie said, "It's always three o'clock in the morning . . ."

Tobias wasn't doing anything so simplistic as mourning for all the loves he by then had lost. In fact, he embarked upon a much more dangerous process: At long last, with his twenty-eighth birthday but a month of nonexistent time away, he was growing up. And it can be logically argued, Dear Children, that growing up is a thing you should *never* do. For, not only is the process painful beyond all bearing, as dreams, hopes, illusions, belief, faith, and even fond desires are ripped bloodily from your hearts by that sadistic surgeon, Experience, who *never* employs anesthesia, assisted by an ugly, bare-assed witch of a nurse called Truth; but in the end it is always fatal, since maturity is a disease life will not tolerate, the final cancer that we die of. Or, to put it another way: Who eats of the fruit, must perforce leave Eden.

He thought: "All suffering is Holy. Hattie's was. And even Nancy's. In spite of—of the ugly way she went. They died for me. Or at least because I failed them . . ."

"Horse droppings!" Angie's raucous voice jarred through his mind, a little louder than usual because the Angel, clad in a field marshal's uniform at least as gaudy as one of Hermann Goerings's, was driving the Pierce Arrow, while little Anne, completely bulged, and *very* round by now, snoozed on the front seat beside him.

"Then why did they?" Tobias thought at his *soi-disant* chauffeur.

"Because their time was up," Angie telepathed. "Their inevitabilities had run out on them."

"But," Tobias sighed into vast vacancy, "what did it *mean?* Their deaths, Angie? What does anything mean? Life, even?"

"Life? That the Absurdity Factor has been For Unlawful Carnal Knowledging around with Random Chance, got knocked up and given birth to Blind Accidentality. How's *that?"*

"No good," Tobias communicated. "You can do better than that. Try again, Angie!"

"Lemme think, lemme think," the Angel mused. "What cosmology are ye ready for by now? Shall we try th' Hindu?"

"Why the Hindu?" Tobias asked, or rather thought, which between him and his Guardian Angel amounted to exactly the same thing.

"Because it's so damn *peaceful,"* Angie said. "Kind of a quietism, Toby lad. Teaches a bloke to give up th' struggle, stop bein' reincarnated over 'n over ag'in th' way ye've been, reach Prajna—enlightenment to ye, me boy, accept Nirvana, 'n cease to be. . . ."

"That's for me, then," Tobias said. "But is it *so?"*

"Ye ask th' damnedest questions, blinkin' idiot that ye be! Of course it's so! All religions are. Everything some poor bastid really believes is so. Even great wickednesses 'n stupidities. Which is why *Das Kapital* and *Mein Kampf* are also holy books. . . ."

"Now, An-gie!"

"They are. True Samhitas,* like the Vedas—"

"Angie, you've *already* lost me."

"I know. Poor dull ignorant clod that ye be, Brahma help ye! But then ye *are* Brahma, or ye'll get to be, when your Atman reaches Prajna, and learns its true identity. That's all the Upanishads teach anyhow—"

"What?" Tobias thought.

"Th' unity of Brahma and Atman. Th' final cojoining of the Oversoul and yer individuality. When yer Atman, yer *Self,* lad, realizes that it *is* Brahma, th' world soul, an' sort o' merges with it, ye've got there. To Nirvana, I mean."

"Which is death," Tobias sighed.

"No it *ain't.* Not exactly. 'Cause, ye see, there's a built-in escape

*In Sanskrit, Samhita means to gather together, to compile. Presumably, as in the Four Vedas, the truth.

hatch. Convenient cosmology, th' Hindu. Works like this, laddybucks: Even *after* ye've attained enlightenment 'n are jest burstin' out all over with Prajna, as it were, 'n thereby 'ave freed yer poor stupid self from bein' reincarnated over 'n over ag'in to do th' same tomfool things—or mebbe *worst*—foriver, which is what the reunion of yer Atman with Brahma, the Oversoul, boils down to in practical terms, ye kin always pull a Bodhisattva, 'n postpone Nirvana in order to help th' res' o' th' poor bastids to get there. . . ."

"But it's *still* ceasing to be, isn't it?" Tobias said.

"Who knows? Maybe it's sittin' around in Brahmaloka, th' highest part o' Kamaloka—Kamaloka's Tartarus, actually, or Hell, or maybe even Heaven—'n blissfully contemplatin' Brahma foriver. 'N occasionally pullin' on th' teats of Kamadhenu, th' Sacred Cow, whose milk is life, and one of whose milkings formed the visible world—"

"But, Angie, this is bloody nonsense!"

"What religion *ain't?* Don't ye believe th' Father is th' Son, 'n th' Son, the Father, 'n both of 'em th' Holy Ghost?"

"That's the Trinity," Tobias began, "and—"

"No it *ain't.* The Trinity, or the Trimurti, is made up of Brahma, the Creator; Vishnu, the Preserver; and Shiva, the Destroyer—"

" 'I am become Death, shatterer of Worlds.' Who said *that,* Angie?"

"Robert Oppenheimer. Quotin' th' Rg Veda—in reference to Shiva, natch. Only he *hasn't* said it *yet.* Ye're rememberin' forwards ag'in. Told ye to quit it. Drive ye batty, sure!"

"I believe in Shiva," Tobias whispered. "Unchristian of me, but I do. Maybe because I've seen him operate."

"Yep. Ugly cuss, ain't he? With all them arms, dancing on th' poor, prostrate world . . ."

"I wouldn't postpone it," Tobias said slowly. "Nirvana, I mean. If I could reach enlightenment—what's it called, Angie?"

"Prajna. And ye're a damned sight too close to it, now. Gives me the shivers. Ye git there 'n I'll be an unemployed Angel. That is, if th' Auld Cuss don't assign me to somebody else. Wouldn't like that. Grown too fond of ye, ye dumb bastid!"

"So you wouldn't *want* me to reach Nirvana, Angie?"

"Don't think ye could. Ye're too caught up between Kamamara —th' God of Lust—and Death. Yer poor ol' Dharma is all mixed up. Kama and Mara who're two beings in one—almost as wild an idea as yer Holy Trinity, ain't it?—would kick th' stuffins out ye down there in Kamaloka, then turn ye over to Kali—the Creative aspect of her, anyhow, 'n she'd reincarnate ye as a billy goat. . . ."

"Angie, you don't really *believe* all this stuff, do you?"

"Natch! Don't ye?"

"Holy Mother of God!" Tobias said.

"Who was Isis," Angie said. " 'N her child was Horus—in the Egyptian cosmology, anyhow. She resurrected him. Stopped th' boat of millions of years dead in th' sea of Heaven, made Thoth climb down out o' it 'n draw Set's poison outa th' poor kid. Set is Death, y'know. An' she resurrected Osiris, too—her husband. Only she fanned the breath of life back into his nostrils with her wings, 'n plagued th' dog-faced god, Anubis, into goin' down to Amenti, tha's Tartarus, too, or Hell, 'n bringing 'em both back—"

"Angie, you can't! Talk about all religions as though they're exactly the same, I mean! You can't!"

"Why not, laddybucks? Since they *are?* Wasn't Mithra resurrected too? And Dionysus? Don't they *all* have holy mothers? And fertility cults? Take Astarte, now—"

"No," Tobias said. "Stop it, Angie. I have to believe what I was taught. I have to."

"Of course. That's the second meaning of Dharma—conformity to yer own religious law 'n customs, lad. Nobody's stoppin' ye from believing yer own brand o' Judeo-Christian nonsense, or even arguing that it ain't so. 'Cause it *is.* Everything ye poor mixed-up bastids believe is so. All I'm tryin' to git ye to see, or at least to accept, is that ye've no right to reject th' other fella's bloody nonsense, deny him the right to believe it, or try to convert him to *yers.* Mohammed *did* go up to heaven on a horse with a woman's face 'n a dragon's tail. An' the Prophet Elijah in a chariot of fire. K'ung Fu-tzu *was* eighty years old when he was born, 'n could be seen shining through his mother's womb like a light. Ye see?"

"Yes," Tobias said sadly. "You don't believe anything."

"Ye're wrong there, lad; I believe *everything.* Including coexistent contradictions. Fer instance, look at the road ahead, will ye?"

Tobias looked. As he did so, the road abruptly faded out of the twin illusions of time and mind, and he saw the tiny figure of the three-year-old girl child, tottering through that wind-whipped, storm-tormented desolation. She was crying. The rain came down in sheets, and battered her helpless little form. She hadn't even a raincoat on. She stumbled ahead, falling, getting up, finally not getting up, crawling under those palmetto palms, that were bent almost double by the lashing gale.

Tobias could see the pond before her now. That icy, rain-stippled, fatal pond.

"Stop her!" he screamed at Angie, "she's going to—"

"Fall in 'n drown. 'N three, four days from now, th' crows'll be at her. Like ye saw it the first time. A little further along in this sequence. Poor li'l Clara!—or is it Sara?—D'ye believe *this,* Toby lad?"

"Yes," Tobias whispered, "I believe it. Only make it go away, will you? It's—too awful, Angie."

"There *are* worse things. Like th' ghost poor Edna has created in her mind. Take care ye don't marry th' *ghost,* Toby. That would be a sight too much. Choose th' right one, will ye? Which ever th' right one is. Sara—or Clara. Or neither. Or both. Who knows? All right! All right! It's gone!"

And when Tobias looked again, it was. But another thing had taken its place. The man, and now Tobias could see he *was* a man, sat on the edge of the bed. He was naked, except for a pair of B.V.D.s, pushed down around his hips. He was as hairy as a great ape, and his face was clearly the face of one mentally retarded. Not —mad, Tobias decided; subnormal. The face was much younger-looking than his huge, hairy body was, as though it had stopped when the mind behind it had stopped, about age twelve, Tobias guessed.

"I didn't make ye see *this,"* Angie said. "Stop it, Toby! Stop it right now, d'ye hear?"

But there was no stopping it. The road poured itself into that dark, circular room, jamming itself and the illusion of time to a halt, pooling the sky into a soft, pearly glow around the hairy monster/man/child who was holding the slim, hauntingly lovely blonde girl on his knees. She was trying to push away his huge, hairy, and exceedingly busy hands. Trying, but not too hard. Then she gave it up. Let him take one of her small, firm, conical breasts out of her blouse. Paw at it. Kiss it. Suck at the nipple, greedily. She sat there, slack mouthed, her eyes lid-hooded, while he pushed his other huge paw up under her skirt. All the way up. Fondled her, there. She lay back on the bed. Put her own slim hands down to the hem of her skirt. Pulled the skirt up around her waist, herself. Tobias saw then that she hadn't on any underwear. Realized what that meant. Saw her stretch her arms up luxuriously to the hairy monster. Lock them about his neck.

"Don't blame me!" Angie said angrily. "Each man invents his own version of hell!" Then, more quietly, his angel's voice finding its own true tone, almost silvery, vibrant, somehow, with pity:

"Could ye—forget *that,* if ye had to, lad?" he said.

"Angie, for the love of God!"

"Could ye? Or even *forgive* it? If *she's* th' one yer inevitabilities be locked in with?"

"Is she?" Tobias whispered.

"Don't know. If th' poor li'l tyke who got drowned was one o' th' twins, she *has* to be. Ye see that, don't ye? If not, yer chances are fifty-fifty. But even so . . ."

"Even so, what?" Tobias got out.

"Don't know. Anyhow, it's gone now. So fergit it."

"I can't," Tobias said. "You *know* I can't!"

"Oh yes ye can. A man ken do eny bloody o' blessed thing he *must,"* the Angel said.

"Angie," Tobias said, a couple of days later, while they were crossing the Mississippi on the ferry, "why'd you do that—get me mixed up with all those wild women, I mean? To demonstrate to me that—that life's a farce? Or that love is?"

"No. Not neither one. 'Cause they *ain't,* laddybucks! A farce is an absolute. And life ain't. Nor love. I was just exercising yer dichotomies, a little. Gittin' 'em into foine workin' order. Ye're gonna need 'em, lad!"

"But, Angie! Dichotomy *consists* in the division into mutual exclusives! So how—"

"Don't know. Mebbe ye better explain it to *me,* Toby, me boy, me boy. Tek Nancy, now. Randy li'l whore, wasn't she?"

"Well—" Tobias said.

"She *wuz.* Ye can't deny *that.* A nach'l born tail-peddlin', bustle-hustlin' li'l—"

"Angie, you stop it!"

"What're you two arguing about *now?*" Anne said.

"Nothin', hon. Go back to sleep like a good lass, will ye? Conserve yer strength. Ye're goin' to need it. . . ."

"All right, darlin'," Anne said, and kissed him. Then she curled up into a delicious little bulging roundness and went back to sleep. A tear stood and glittered in Angie's eye.

Which Tobias saw. No, that's not right. He *couldn't* see it.

He was sitting on the *back* seat of the Pierce Arrow, remember. Say—he felt it. Running molten through his Guardian Angel's heart. And thereby through his own.

"Angie!" he screamed telepathically.

"Yep," Angie said. "Hers too. All played out on her. Oh th' Auld Cuss take inevitabilities enyhow!"

"Oh, Angie, no!" Tobias wept.

"Oh, Angie, yes!" Angie grated. "It's the damn brat. Mine, all right. A point I wasn't sure about at first. 'Cause it could o' been yers, Toby. Got a helluva lot o' ape in its bloomin' make-up. A streak o' randy billy goat. From *her* side, I suspect. 'Cause them ain't angel-type characteristics. . . ."

"Huh!" Tobias snorted, "if they aren't, then you're no Angel!"

"I'm *yer* Angel, laddybucks. 'N partake o' yer nature. But I wuz hopin' th' brat wuz *yers,* lad. 'Cause that way, it wouldn't have been a giant. When Angels o' th' Auld Cuss mate with th' daughters o' men—'Course me Annie ain't exactly a daughter o' *men,* but she *is* a humanoid, so the end result is th' same far as th' Auld Cuss is concerned—their offsprings is always outsized, jes like th' Good Book sez—"

"*Which* Good Book?" Tobias said. *"Das Kapital? Mein Kampf?"*

"Dunno. Th' Sama Veda, mebbe. Or th' Yajur Veda. Or mebbe one o' th' Norse Eddas. Sounds more like one o' them. They don't give nobody a decent break. Not even th' Aesir, th' gods. 'Cause even Asgard is gonna come tumbling down into ruins. Tha's what the Nibelungenlied is about. Only them krauts got th' hero's name wrong. It's Sigurd, not Siegfried. But, anyhow, a *Gotterdämmerung* in th' end. Makes sense, don't it, when ye come to think o' it?"

"Angie, for the love of God!"

"Can't help it. Th' brat's too big. A giant. From Jotunheim, likely. Tha's where giants come from. In the Eddas, anyhow. Of course, th' titans were even bigger, and they were always here, leastwise after earth 'n heaven give birth to *them.* Until that horny li'l bastard Zeus threw his own pa, Cronus, out 'n—"

"Angie, you quit it, damn it all!"

"All right. What were we talkin' about enyhow, before?"

"Dichotomy. Dichotomies, plural. But, first, does she—does she *have* to die?"

"Yes. Should o' let ye screw her, damn my jealous hide! That way th' brat would be a puny li'l mouse like ye. Only I've been round humans too damn long. 'N some of it rubbed off. Stupid notions, I mean. Like jealousy. Far as me Annie is concerned, enyhow."

"Angie—you said you thought the—the kid could be mine. What made you think a thing like that? You *knew* I never touched her!"

"Neither did I 'til *after* she was knocked up. Just used a li'l kinetic sexual parapsychology on her. 'N, since ye did too, 'cause ye sure wore yerself down to skin 'n bones a projectin' th' damn finest humpin' enybody iver heard of onto me Annie *every* blessed night, but even more because on that damn planet she actually comes from it takes *six* o' their kind o' males working on *one* o' their fvonia, or females, and in correct sequence at that, to get 'er in th' family way, I thought mebbe ye had a share, enyhow, in his makin'—"

"Only," Tobias pointed out sadly, "she wouldn't cooperate. She always dreamed it was *you.*"

"Yep. An error she's gonna die of. A pity, ain't it? Mighty sweet li'l duckie, me Annie. In her *human* form, leastwise. 'N th' kid would of been th' greatest basketballer iver. Siven 'n a half foot high 'n—"

"Him, too?" Tobias whispered. "Oh Jesus!"

"Don't call on th' Essenes' dreamboy. Hell, he couldn't even keep th' Romans from nailin' him to a tree 'n—"

"But you said he didn't *exist!*"

"Ye believe in 'im, don't ye? So now he *does.*"

"Angie, you drive a fellow right out of his mind!"

"Wit ye, laddybucks, that don't take a *drive.* A putt, mebbe. A two-inch putt on a level green. Where *wuz* we, enyhow?"

"Talking about dichotomies. You were using Nancy, of all people, to explain them."

"No I wasn't. 'Cause they can't be. Explained, I mean. Nothin' can. Or be solved. 'Cause if they could, life would make sense. 'N it don't. Not a damned bit."

"Then what *were* you doing?"

"Pointin' out to ye that everything's a *part* of everything else. Yin 'n yang. That good is evil, 'n evil is good. That th' Auld Cuss 'n Auld Nick is Siamese twins. Say! D'ye have any *spade* blood in yer veins, laddybucks? Eny o' yer ancestors changed his luck—or *her* luck, that happened sometimes, too, though ye palefaces don't want to admit it. . . ."

"Goddamn you, Angie! Why—"

"Did they? Kinda swarthy-lookin' bloke, ye be, laddybucks."

"Not that I know of," Tobias said, "and, anyhow, wouldn't *you* know it, if so?"

"Nope. I'm *yer* Guardian Angel, not yer ancestors'. When ye 'n me git together, in whativer avatar, ye're already *ye,* catch? So I don't know it."

"Nor do I. But I don't think so. Damned few spades where I come from. Why do you ask?"

"Africans have got a thing about *twins.* In half the black countries, they're considered a curse, 'n infanticided right off th' bat. In th' rest, they're sacred. So sacred that if one of 'em dies, th' other has to carry the fetish o' his dead twin around his neck th' rest o' his life, the poor double-dipped bastid! Ye know, *tha's* what Edna could of done! Forced poor Clara, or mebbe Sara, to carry th' other one, her ghost, her mental image, a recreation of what she would have been like if she hadn't fallen into that damn pond—around in her head, her heart, foriver! That would account fer it! It would, why damn me for a sinner!"

"Account for *what?*" Tobias said.

"Asmodeus. Lettin' him screw her. Deliberate violation o' the created image, 'n hence its ritual destruction. Makes sense, don't it?"

"No," Tobias said, "but then nothing you say *ever* does. At least not to me."

"Right. Don't have to. Hattie was a bank robber. Nancy was a whore. L'Amour was a hypocrite. Conchita was a pepperpot. 'N ye, damn yer bonny brown eyes, *loved* every one of 'em."

"Yes," Tobias whispered, "plus *your* Anne."

"Ridiculous, wasn't it? Pure farce. Say, I forgot Roxane!"

"I didn't love *her.* I merely—"

"Got a hard-on iver blessed time th' mere thought o' her crossed yer feeble mind. If that ain't love, what is it?"

"Lust," Tobias said.

"Yin. Yang. Good. Evil. Love. Lust. Th' Auld Cuss blast me if yer dichotomies ain't workin' overtime!"

"Angie, so help me I'm going to—"

"Sit right there on yer narrow arse 'n listen. To wit: Nancy wuz a whore. Proved that, didn't she? Went out 'n hustled her nicely rounded li'l bustle so *ye* wouldn't have to sleep in packin' cases 'n eat swill no more. Th' method was a mite rough, but th' intention, lad? 'N that cruel Auld Cuss upstairs let her get knocked off the worst way he could think of 'cause he jes' can't stand ye poor humans enjoyin' enything as foine as screwin' is! But Hattie kicked off real great, now didn't she? Gallant as all get out, th' way she went. Smilin' at ye. Vowing to take care o' ye fer iver. 'N she *will,* Toby lad. Got yerself a patron saint. First-class santa patrona t' intercede fer ye before th' Auld Cuss's throne!"

"But—a bank robber and—"

"A gun moll, 'n no better 'n she should of been. So what? Like Saint Thelma of Egypt who—"

"All right, all right! Angie—nothing's going to happen to—this one, is it? To Sara? Or—to Clara, if it's Clara? I couldn't stand it if it did! Especially if she's the one I saw in that little house. *Not* the one in that damned castle! Because the one in the little house is a *good* girl, and—"

"Is she now?" Angie said wonderingly. " 'N how, me saintly master of all dichotomies, th' livin' hell d'ye know *that?"*

Tobias bowed his head. Whispered:

"I don't, do I? How could I?"

"Now ye're gettin' there!" Angie said.

"Now I'm getting where?" Tobias got out.

"To Prajna. Enlightenment. Because the first thing that Prajna teaches is what's within th' reach o' human knowledge, or more important still, what's within its grasp, 'n what's not . . ."

" 'A man's reach should exceed his grasp, or what's a heaven for?' Who said that, Angie?"

"Browning. Robert Browning. Now one more test 'n I'll let ye be. *What* is within th' reach 'n grasp o' human knowledge, Toby, me boy, me boy?"

Tobias thought about that.

"Practically nothing of any importance," he said sadly.

"Knowin' *that,* is important. 'Cause when ye do, ye don't fry, fricassee, boil o' otherwise mess up other folk fer not bein' o' like mind. O' because ye don't like their noses, or their camouflage job. Or because some black-robed stupid damn fool old croakers have taught ye that they did in a bloke who niver even existed, maybe. So ye kin close yer glimmers too, now, me boy. Wouldn't do t' over work yer so-called mind—"

"East Egypt, Kentucky, Two Miles," the sign said, finally.

"Now, how're we going to find the castle?" Tobias said.

"Find some drunk, or bum, or rural-type slatternly slut what kin *see* me," Angie sighed. "Or a kid. Brats kin *always* see me. Don't know why. Mebbe 'cause grownups ain't tampered with their sense o' reality enough to ruin it, yet. . . ."

"Look, hon, isn't that a tavern over there?" Anne said.

"Yep. Sure is," Angie said. "Now jes th' two o' ye wait right here 'til I go find out—"

"Angie—" Anne said darkly, "don't be *too* long, will you please? And—and ask them where the nearest *doctor* lives. Or the nearest midwife. . . ."

"Annie!" Angie said.

"No," she whispered. "Not yet, darling. Well, maybe—a twinge or two. But we've got time. This time tomorrow, though—we'd better have *somebody* on hand to help us. And he—or she—had better know what he's doing. 'Cause this here brat of yours is *so* damn big! Kicks like a mule, too."

Angie leaned forward and kissed her.

"I'll be right back, duckie," he said. And his voice, speaking, was the saddest sound that Tobias had ever heard.

But he didn't come right back. He stayed in that tavern almost a half hour. And when he came out, he was accompanied by a woman. In some ways, she reminded Tobias of Nell Brightwell. She was the same kind of faded, washed-out blonde. Only, he saw at once, you *could* tell the front of her from the back. In fact, the front of her was sort of nice, except that even from the five or six yards separating her from the Pierce Arrow, he could see that she hadn't washed any of her in the last fifteen or twenty years.

She came on with Angie up to the car. While she was *still* a yard or two away, Tobias found himself forced to hold his breath, because she stank in about fifty-seven ways at once, her aromas running the gamut from the merely awful to the absolutely unbearable. She smelled of liquor, tobacco—a huge plug of which she had tucked into one cheek, visibly bulging it—kitchen grease, sweat, and plain damned unwashed female. There were black lines of dirt ground into the creases of her scrawny neck. Yet, Tobias could see, once cleaned up—which would necessitate boiling her in lye soap and water for at least five or six hours—she would be a rather pretty woman, no, a decidedly pretty one.

"Howdy, Ma'am," she said to Anne. "Yore hubby done tol me you's gonna need a midwife. Hmmm, moughty right, ain't he? 'N soon. Well Ah'm the onliest one hereabouts. Right pert good at hit folks say. . . ."

"But, but—" Anne got out, "isn't there a—a doctor?"

"Nope. 'Ceptin' ol Doc Merton. 'N you cain't depend on *him.* Blind, stinkin' drunk most o' th' time. Doan nobody call on him fur nothin' serious like. Specially not no birthin'! Doan you worry none atall honeychile. You kin trust in me. Ain't lost a brat nor its ma in th' las' ten years. . . ."

"Oh, Angie, no!" Anne wailed inside her mind.

Tobias realized that her telepathic communication came over stronger and clearer than ever. Then he realized why, and pity tore him. In the doomed and damned that particular faculty sharpened and intensified almost beyond belief.

"She'll—kill me!" Anne thought at her nonhuman husband. "With hands as filthy as hers she'll give me post-parturient fever sure as hell. There *has* to be somebody else! There *has* to be, Angie!"

"No there ain't," Angie thought back at her sadly. "But don't ye go 'n worry yer pretty head, me duckie! I'll make th' slattern wash. . . ."

He turned to the combination tavern wench and midwife.

"Tell me, Sal," he said, "is there some sort o' castle hereabouts? Like in th' storybooks, ye know?"

"Oh," Sal said, and winked at him, "you mean Schloss's schloss, don'tcha, hon? C'mon round back 'n I'll *show* it to you—"

"Why around back?" Anne said sharply.

Tobias wondered if she had heard Sal's thoughts as clearly as he had heard them: "C'mon round back, you long tall, mighty han'some hunk o' pants-wearing sin! Back theah us kin do a li'l bussin' 'n tetchin' 'n feelin' each other up 'n general messin' around. 'N tonight, after *she's* a sleepin' 'n mah ol man is drunker'n a skunk, th' worthless ol coot!—we kin really git down t' business! Lawd Gawd—I ain't been bedded decent in so damn long!"

She said, smiling cheerfully at Anne:

" 'Cause you *cain't* see it from heah, honey. This heah grove o' trees gits in the way. But round back you kin see it plain. Up on top o' th' mountain. Schloss's mountain. Named after th' ol German fella wha built th' castle. Wuz him learned we'uns to call it Schloss's schloss. Said that's what schloss means in Dutch: castle. On hit turns out that when he wuz sayin' Dutch what he *meant* was German. Crazy ol' coot, he wuz—but in a nice way, not like them Tobit bastids what've got it now—"

"What's wrong with the Tobits, Ma'am?" Tobias said then.

"They's loony. Every livin' one of 'em. Course nobody doan see 'em no more since they sold their coal mining business 'n moved way up there. Jes' as well. Th' old woman, Edna Tobit, is jes plain daft. 'N ol Ralph—ain't quite there. But that theah daughter o' theirs—"

"Isn't it—daughters, Ma'am?" Tobias whispered.

"Yep. But we'uns done got outa th' habit o' countin' Clara with th' rest o' them. She's our school marm. Quiet, decent li'l thing. Quit livin' wit 'em three years ago. 'Lowed she plumb couldn't stand thet gloomy ol rock pile. She ain't tellin' th' truth, though. . . ."

"She isn't?" Anne said.

"No 'm. what she cain't stand, th' po' li'l critter, is whut goes on up theah."

"And what does go on there, Ma'am?" Tobias said.

"Doan know, fer a fact, Mister," Sal said. "But there's been talk fer years. Sary—she's th' other one—th' one that doan nobody ever see—not nobody, Mister, cause she doan set foot outside th' walls o' th' schloss—is a maniac, folks say—a homey—homey—damn me fer a sinner if I doan disremember how you says thet word!"

"Homicidal," Angie supplied.

"Thet's right, hon! A homicidal maniac! You see—ever livin' year fer the las' six o' seven years—ever since those twin girls Clara 'n Sary is keen ol' enough to wed—citified fellas been comin' up theah. To co't one o' th' other o' th' twins, you know? 'N—they—they plumb disappears! Them Tobits put out that they'd done gone back home in they fancy motor cyahs. But th' *family* o' one of 'em sent detective fellas up heah a-lookin' fer him. Couldn't find him, nary a trace—"

"That doesn't prove that Sara—murdered him," Tobias got out.

"Knows hit don't, Mister! Them theah Tobits is too damn smart to git caught. Didn't turn er hair. Invited them theah detective fellas in. Let 'em search th' place. Went over it with a fine-toothed comb they did—'n didn't find *nothin'*. Not hair nor hide o' them po' fellas. . . ."

"Isn't there," Tobias said suddenly, "any other *man* on the place except Mr. Tobit?"

"Not that ah knows of, 'ceptin' th' hired help 'n they only works daytime. Scairt t' stay up theah nights. Swear th' place is h'anted. A h'ant what howls worse'n a snake bit hound dawg at th' dark o' th' moon. Sounds like he's up theah in th' tower. Th' keep, ol' Schloss useta call hit. . . ."

"Isn't he?" Tobias said.

"Cain't be, Mister—less en he's a h'ant fer real. Ol' Schloss had them twistin' stairsteps goin' up to th' tower bricked up. Filled 'em in with *rocks* 'n cement after his ol' woman fell outa th' tower room winder in a dizzy fit 'n kilt herself. 'N them detective fellas 'lowed they *wuz still* bricked up. So enything *human* would starve to death up theah. 'N perish o' thirst t' boot. . . ."

Angie stared at her. Then he said:

"Th' twins. Identical, ain't they? I mean they look just alike?"

"Doan know, honey. Ain't never seen 'em together. 'N ain't never heard tell o' enybody what has. Not even my sister-in-law, Sue. 'N she works for 'em."

"Isn't that—well—odd?" Anne said.

"Everything them damn Tobits do is odd, honey," Sal said. "Course Clara don' live with 'em no more. But when she goes to visit, 'cording to Sue, Sary goes 'n shets herself up in her room, 'cause she hates her po' sweet sister so damn bad. Does hit even afore po' li'l Clara gits theah. Sez she kin *feel* when Clara's gonna come—thet she kin *heah* Clara thinkin' bout visitin'—worryin' her po' li'l head over it, 'cause she only do hit 'cause she thinks she's obligated to. Lot o' craziness! Folks can't *heah* each other think, now can they?"

All three of them, Angie, Anne, and Tobias looked at each other and smiled.

"C'mon now, hon," Sal said to Angie. "Gotta show you th' schloss—"

"I'd suggest," Anne said coolly, "that you keep your filthy paws off my husband, Sal. While the two of you are around back, I mean. I grant you he's a long, tall, mighty handsome hunk of pants-wearing sin. But he's also my baby's papa, so I mean to keep him. So no—bussin', I think you called it, or touching, or feeling him up or general messing around. And as for tonight, after I'm asleep, you can forget it. *Now* are you so sure that people can't hear each other think?"

Sal stared at her, her pale blue eyes opening very wide. Then she spat a quid of tobacco juice into the dirt. Made the sign of the cross above her breasts.

"Witches," she said. " 'N you kin git yo'self somebody else, Ma'am. 'Cause I ain't even fixin' to help birth no witch chile. As for you, hon—I mean Mister, you doan need me to show you th' schloss.

Find it yo'self. Man what marries hisself a witch woman, ah doan want no part of—"

But Angie's eyes were on her, compellingly. His voice came out bronze toned, tolling, sweet as deep bells plunged in the wind and drowned.

"But I *want* you to show it to me, Sally me darlin'!" he purred, "so now c'mon!"

Anne's dark eyes leaped, and blazed with sudden fury; but before she could say anything, Angie's voice rang matter-of-factly through her—and Tobias'—minds.

"Something I've got to find out, duckie, 'n she won't tell me front o' ye 'n Toby. Don't worry yer pretty head none atall. I like fillies what smell o' good soap 'n fine scents, not sweat 'n she-goat. Wouldn't touch her with *Toby's.* Got too much respect fer that. 'Cause it would rot 'n drop off 'n I couldn't even give it back!"

"C'mon now, Sal—" he crooned.

They were gone a long time. Too long. Tobias could see the doubt and misery getting back into poor Anne's eyes. He strained, stretching the invisible antennae of his mind, trying to hear Angie's thoughts. But he couldn't. That was another thing the Angel could do—put them onto another wave length, beam them into a celestial frequency spectrum so high that no human mind could tune them in.

But then Angie came running around from behind the tavern. After him bounded a big, black-haired man, his ill-shaven and exceedingly ugly face contorted with what was clearly murderous fury. He had a lumberjack's broad axe in his hands. At each bound he swung it, trying vainly to chop Angie in half.

After them, Sal came. Her nose was bleeding and one of her eyes was already swollen shut. Compliments of her husband, Tobias thought.

Then Anne got out of the car. Bulges and all. Smoothly. Gracefully. Silky fast. Pointed her finger at the man.

"You stop that!" she said.

"Doan go nigh her, Ridley!" Sal moaned. "She's a witch woman! She hex you so damn bad thet—"

The man stopped. Stared at the three of them. He was even dirtier than his wife. And smelled worse. A damned sight worse.

"You can't move," Anne said slowly, icily. "You're frozen. You're frozen stiff. You won't thaw out 'til this time tomorrow. Neither one of you."

And they were. Both of them.

"Because they *believe* it," Tobias thought. "I see what you mean now, Angie. Whatever people *believe*—truly believe—*is.*"

" 'N I believe me Annie is a witch!" Angie groaned. "But then, what married woman ain't? Well damn me fer a sinner, Toby lad, le's go!"

Fifteen

Going away from the tavern, the road made a complete U turn, doubling back upon itself, and then they saw the waterfall. It was something to see, a narrow torrential whiteness plunging down a vertical rock face for eight hundred feet, a thousand, to smash into a rocky gorge with an explosion of spray that, when the light was right, as it was now, was rainbow hued, iridescent, splendid, making a noise that was like no other sound on earth: a long tearing scream and smash and thunder, pounding their ears deaf even from that distance, boiling up blindingly into shriek and slam and whistle, leaping, racing, going on, to disappear at last into a forest—pine and fir and balsam—that was inky, lightless, midnight black, even at high noon of that limpid day.

The castle, Schloss's schloss, was directly above the falls, though at least two or three hundred feet higher than the place where the torrent began its plunge. The single window of the keep, or tower, looked out over the waterfall, centered above it with a precision that was almost mathematical as though it had been planned or designed with the idea of dominating the view of the cataract below, except that a single tree, its roots clawing precariously into the rotted cement and accumulated earth between some of the rocks in the castle's wall, jutted out beneath the window, about halfway down between it and the place the falls began, extending far enough, Tobias guessed, to at least partly spoil the view.

But when the castle had been built, that tree hadn't yet been even an acorn or a seed or whatever, to be lodged by the wind in the crevice it had sprung from. So the idea that the window's location could have been deliberate was not to be lightly discarded. Placed where it is, the thought jarred icily through Tobias' mind, so that anything thrown from it would be swept away by that torrent. After being battered to bits by the rapids pounding over those rocks. Like —bodies, for instance . . .

"Which is *why* th' detectives couldn't find hair nor hide of them siven poor divils, likely," Angie thought at his protégé. "Smart operator, ol' Asmo. So they wuz probably lookin' in th' wrong place. Wouldn't be a mite o' conclusive evidence in th' schloss, come t' think o' it. Should've looked in Emmy's Pool. But since th' Pool's down there in them woods, at the first spot where that there mill race of a river slows down enough fer anything in it to sink or get caught, permanent, anyhow, that's the *last* thing that would iver occur to them. . . ."

"Can the pool be seen without going into the woods?" Tobias said.

"Don't know," Angie said. "Doubt it. 'Cause, if it could, we'd see it from *here.* This is the clearest view on the road, 'cording to Sal—"

"So," Anne purred, "you *were* talking with her all that time, Angie?"

"What else, Annie, me darlin'? I admit nobody in his right mind would plaster me over 'n stand me up in a niche longside th' altar in th' cathedral. But I've got a keen nose 'n a weak stummick, both, duckie. 'N round Sal, they're jest about as good a substitute fer a chastity belt as ye're likely to find, nowadays, that's fer sure!"

"Could the pool," Tobias persisted, "could—*whose* pool, Angie?"

"Emmy's, Emma Schloss's. She—ag'in 'cording to Sal—wuz th' first to go outa that there window. In a fit o' dizziness. She wuz in th' family way. 'N that *wuz* an accident, 'cause she wuz all alone in the tower room—"

"Unless our horny friend was up there even *then. . . .*" Tobias said.

"Our horny who? Oh you mean ol' Asmo. No. He's a *family* demon. Belongs to th' Tobits, exclusively. Always has. Always will. In whativer collective avatar ye Tobits find yerselves, there's *always* ol' Asmodeus. Only I always manage to sidetrack 'im far as ye're concerned, laddybucks! What wuz it ye wuz askin' me about Emmy's Pool? Besides its name, I mean?"

"Could it be seen from the castle? From that window, for instance?"

"From th' window—mebbe. But since th' stairs is bricked up, nobody lackin' a pair o' wings like mine is gonna do much lookin' from up *there.* From th' rest o' the castle, not likely. 'Cause then them detective fellas would of seen it, 'n unless they wuz utter dopes, it would of occurred to them to look into it. 'N it didn't. 'Cause *everybody* hereabouts knows that that's where poor Emmy's corpse wuz found—"

"But if they *told* the detectives about that—" Anne began.

"Who said they *did?*" Angie said. "Mountain folks ain't given to diarrhea of the jawbone, duckie—'specially not while talkin' to th' *law.* 'N I'm certain sure of one thing: Toby, here, is likely the first person to come up with a *workable* idea o' how ol' Asmo disposed of them bodies. 'Cause Sal said over 'n over ag'in that the local yokels think they're buried in the courtyard o' th' schloss, *under* th' pavin' stones. Couldn't be. Wouldn't work. Screw th' time element all to hell. 'Cause Asmo'd have to pry up a helluva lot o' pavin' stones, dig a grave, toss in th' stiff, cover him up, put th' stones back—all twixt midnight 'n dawn, without making noise enough to wake anybody up, and without *nobody* noticin' that th' courtyard had been messed up more'n somewhat. Not bloody likely, duckie!"

"But who says there *are* any bodies?" Anne said. "All you're going on is the word of that walking chemical warfare department —I mean factory—and from the looks of *her,* I'd never confuse her mouth with a prayer book, Angie!"

"Bacteriological, duckie, bacteriological. Startin' with spirocheta treponema pallidum, 'n workin' on up. Or on down. With a good dose o' ol' neisseria gonorrhea, thrown in, natch. Th' ol' claperoo. But there've got to be. Bodies, I mean. 'N siven of 'em. No more 'n no less. Th' Auld Cuss is set in his ways. Once he takes a likin' to a sequence, he goes on repeatin' it foriver. And tha's how many there wuz th' *first* time. In th' Book o' Tobit. Tha's in th' *Old* Testament, me doll. Or in th' Apocrypha—dependin' on which brand o' solemn tomfoolery *ye* hold to. First occasion I iver laid me glimmers on poor Toby, here. During th' Assyrian captivity, that wuz. Ol' Sennacherib had carried off all th' Jews and—"

"But, Angie!" Anne protested, "that was *thousands* of years ago, and anyhow, Toby's not Jewish!"

"He wuz in *that* sequence," Angie said. " 'N time don't exist, duckie-love."

"If it doesn't, what *does* it do?" Anne said.

"Coexists. In layers. Like water levels of different temperatures. 'N them there layers is *always* breakin' through one another, me darlin', which is why words like then, now, 'n later on, to reasonable beings, which ye humans *ain't,* come out as blah, blah, blah. Don't *mean* anything. Th' present 'n th' past 'n th' future are all imaginary states dreamed up by th' *human* race. Don't exist. Or rather, they coexist. Simultaneously. You see?"

"But, Angie, that doesn't make a damn bit of sense!" Anne said.

"What *does,* duckie? Now le's git a move on. . . ."

"To the castle?" Tobias said.

"Not yet. First we gotta go down there to Emmy's Pool 'n catch ourselves a fish . . ."

"A fish!" Anne said.

"Yep. Good fer smokin' out demons. Th' guts enyhow. 'N fer curin' blindness. 'Specially th' kind cause by hot bird shit droppin' into yer glimmers. Th' kind that Toby's Pa—"

He stopped short, stared at Tobias.

"Tha's right, tha's right," he muttered. "Yer ol' governor's dead, ain't he? This sequence is *way* off, ain't it? Don't like this a damn bit! Fer one thing, me Annie niver wuz in it before, wuz she? A new variant. 'N neither yer ol' fadder nor yer Momma *ought* to be dead, *yet.* Fault o' ye Protestants—leavin' th' Book o' Tobit *out.* Confused th' Auld Cuss even *more.* 'N he wuz confused enough to start with. But we better catch that damn fish or else things'll really git outa control. In case th' Auld Cuss remembers *that* much. O' how this sequence ought to work, I mean. . . ."

Anne shook her head. "You're crazy, Angie," she laughed. "Crazy as a loon! But maybe that's *why* I love you so. C'mon, let's go fishing then!"

"But *after* we catch the fish?" Tobias said.

"Th' castle. No! After the fish, th' dish. Clara, the li'l schoolmarm. That is, if Sal ain't mixed up, too," Angie said.

"Don't cheat," Tobias said to Angie. "No miracle-working this time, you celestial scoundrel!"

"Don't mean to," Angie said solemnly. "Pull a fast one, 'n it'll rob th' poor beastie of its magic powers, likely . . . C'mon, Toby, me boy, me boy, take off yer shoes. 'N yer socks. Ye've got to wash yer blinkin' feet."

"But they're clean," Tobias protested, "so I don't see why—"

"Ye niver do, ignoramus that ye be," Angie sighed. "If ye'd iver read the Good Book—the *Hebrew* Good Book, not th' Egyptian, th'

Chaldean, th' Moslem, th' Greek, th' Hindu, th' Norse, th' Roosian o' th' Kraut—although *Das Kapital* was Kraut to start with, wasn't it—before them Rooskys borrowed it, I mean?—ye'd know why ye *have* to wash yer blinkin' feet in this here blinkin' pool. As I said before, this sequence is too damn far out o' kilter *now.* Wouldn't do to throw it any further off, or mebbe this tune ol' Asmo jest might win out, after all. Ye heard me, Toby, take off yer shoes 'n wash yer feet. Feet 'n arseholes is human parts what *can't* be overwashed to me way o' thinkin'. Ah, tha's the good lad, now!"

"Brrrrrr!" Tobias said. "My God, but it's cold!"

"And—and gloomy," Anne whispered. "I—I don't like this place, Angie. There's something—something—oh Lord! What *is* the word I want?"

"Sinister?" Tobias suggested.

"No. But that's close enough, I reckon," Anne said. "I was thinking something more like—ghastly, ghostly—haunted. The—water's so—so still! And it shouldn't be! Not after the way that millrace of a river comes pounding down into it. Look at Toby's reflection. How clear it is! And yours and—"

She stopped short. Her breath made a strangling sound. Slowly she got up. Moved haltingly, heavily to the edge of Emmy's Pool. Stood there. Turned to face her maybe heavenly, perhaps immortal, surely nonhuman husband.

"Angie—" she whispered, "where—where's *mine?"*

"Duckie—" Angie groaned.

"The light's the same," Anne said, her voice taut, harp-string vibrant, but sinking, sinking down a tier of chords into silence's own bleak echo, "I'm standing right—right beside—the two of you. So—the angle that—that the sun's rays come down between those trees—those black, black, black and *awful* trees, Angie—is the same. And yet—I—I *haven't* any reflection! I'm not *there.* Why, Angie? Oh, Lord, Angie, tell me why!"

Angie bowed his head. Looked up again. The tears on his face were rubies, red-fired anguish, blood. He reared up, towered up, skyward shooting, taller by miles than Schloss's mountain, bigger by immeasurable mass and bulk than the castle, the ghostly forest, than all the visible world.

They could hear his big voice making an echo chamber of the Universe, rocking heaven with its mighty roar:

"I defy You! Kill me Annie and I'll tear the floor outa yer fake, imaginary heaven! Throw ye down where ye belong, ye cruel monster! She's gotta *live,* ye hear me! Live out this avatar 'n a trillion, trillion more! At me side foriver ye damned Auld Cuss! Or else—"

Silence. Heavier than a collapsed dwarf star. Than antimatter. Than the black holes of outer space where time is warped back upon itself and parallel lines twang around spiraling figure eights to meet, and meet, and meet.

Angie closed his two-mile-wide mouth. Shut his immense and tear-bleeding eyes. Bowed the ponderous immensity of his Angel's head. And—

Shrank to his human size, or maybe a little smaller.

"Angie—I—I'm going—to die, aren't I?" Anne said. "That's it, isn't it, darling?"

The Angel nodded, not trusting himself to speak.

She came to him, moving heavily, slowly, unsteadily—like a she-thing—'Wounded unto death!' the thought crashed unbidden into Tobias' mind. Put up her arms to this being—this achingly beloved being—beyond the grasp of her reason or her flesh, said, whispering the words, through the white fire flash and spill and fall her merely human eyes were pouring down:

"It—it's all right, Angie. Any time with you—any time at all—a day, an hour, a minute, a second, half a heartbeat, one single breath—was worth—my life. Worth all the pain. The terror. And the dark. The everlasting dark. So don't—"

He crushed her bloated body to him, weeping. His angel's tears dissolved the stones they fell on, made brilliant ruby lasers boring down to earth's own core.

"Oh, God, God!" he cried. "Just this once, please? Just this once? In all of eternity to—to pardon—one small life? Just *one,* Great God?"

The silence was a bone-powdering weight. A pulverization of this stuff of being. An implosion of the entire Universe until its whole vast mass occupied less space than the proton of a single atom does.

And it was then that Tobias felt the teeth of that big fresh-water carp clamp down upon his toe. He leaped from the pool, yelling bloody murder. Angie turned Anne loose. Came over to Tobias. Hooked one big finger into the carp's gills. Tossed the fish up on the shore.

"Leastwise we got *this* much right," he said.

"Now cut it open, Toby lad," Angie said. "Take out th heart, th' liver 'n the gall."

"What for?" Tobias said.

"I told ye that before. Because the Good Book, the *Hebrew* Good Book, better known as the Bible, says ye've got to. The Book of Tobit, Chapter Six, Verses one through ten . . .

"But *why* does it say I've got to?" Tobias persisted, trying to keep his eyes away from the resigned and lovely horror that was Anne's face.

"Th' heart 'n th' liver ye use to smoke ol' Asmo out. He'll be hidin' somewheres near yer nuptial couch, waitin' fer a chance to do ye in, jest like he done them other siven poor blokes. Th' gall—oh shit!"

"Why, Angie!" Anne said.

"Sorry, duckie. Didn't mean ye no disrespect. But this is what I *don't* like. Toby's old fadder should be livin' still, but with cataracts on his eyes caused by hot bird shit droppin' into 'em as per that same damn Book o' Tobit, Chapter Two, Verses nine through eleven. And yer ol' governor's *already* dead, ain't he, Toby lad? Which throws this whole sequence out o' shape. So throw away the gall. Ye won't be needin' it. Throw away th' guts, too. Th' rest o' th' beastie, we kin eat. Wait a sec, now, 'til I build a fire. . . ."

But none of them ate of that fish. Not really. They couldn't. There was a weight of darkness lying on their hearts. A silence that was more than the mere absence of sound. That was its negation—its annihilation. A clutch of icy fingers at the very roots and source of life. Two reflections not even shimmering in a pool both lightless and much too still. *Two,* not three. Three beings, each of different natures, tottering on the brink of that chasm where the mere knowledge of the mind is engulfed, washed out by the transcendental knowledge of the soul.

"Taste it, enyhow!" Angie said. "Ye've got to! We've got to

repeat th' sequence as exactly as we kin or—"

"Or what, Angie?" Anne said gently. *"I* can't repeat it. I wasn't in it before. And I won't be in it again. Not ever. You *know* that, don't you, lover?"

"Oh God. Oh blast and damn!" the Angel said.

Tobias tasted the fish. The exact segment of his progression that he did so, that other pool, that pond beneath two palm trees, slid into focus through an oblique time-tangent before his eyes. The crows. That obscenely stinking female girl-child's corpse. Because that was what the fish tasted like, rotting flesh. Maybe even rotting human flesh. He did not, could not, know.

He opened his mouth to spit it out, but the Angel roared at him: "Swallow it, ye fool!"

Tobias swallowed manfully. It stuck in his throat. Hung there, green-slimed and putrid, choking off his breath.

"Swallow it, Toby!" the Angel said.

Tobias swallowed it. Sat there sweat-drenched and reeling until now, quite meaningless now, crashed back again.

"All right," Angie said. "Tha's part o' life, too, laddybucks. Eatin' a ton 'n a half o' putrid swill. Gettin' it down. Goin' on. C'mon now. Le's make tracks. To the schoolhouse. Li'l Clara's there a-waitin'. . . ."

At the sound of the Pierce Arrow's motor, all the children came boiling out of the door, yelling their grimy, idiotic little heads off.

"Timed it jest right," Angie thought at Tobias. "We wait here five minutes 'n all these here impossible li'l buggers will be gone. . . ."

"Why, Angie!" Anne said, "you think such awful things, sometimes. Children—are lovely. I was—planning to give you a—a dozen! Only now—"

She bent her head and cried.

"Now, now, duckie—please!" Angie groaned.

Then, at that precise segment of their collective sequential progression, Clara Tobit came out of the one-room schoolhouse and started walking toward a little, cherry-red Studebaker roadster that was parked in front of it. Then she saw the big Pierce Arrow.

Turned. Came walking toward it. Tobias sat there. He couldn't move. Or breathe. Or even think. He could only do what he was doing, which was to sit there on the back seat of the Pierce Arrow and stare.

She was taller than he had thought she was going to be. And her hair was lighter—a silvery, ash-blonde shade, piled up on top of her head in an arrangement of plaits, topped by a bun. Her coiffure was obviously homemade, because wisps and sprays of light-blazed blondeness escaped it here and there. In sober fact, it was a mess. A glorious mess that stopped his heart. She wore glasses. Huge, unfashionable, silver-rimmed granny glasses. But, behind those glasses were her eyes. Magnified by those curving optics until they all but eclipsed her face. Blue. All right, say blue. Milk blue. White blue. The edge of the sky on a flag-banner October day. Out there where the world melts and the universe drowns—in softness, paleness, mist. The mists above a fjord. Freya's eyes. Norse goddess's glory. A turned up little nose. Pert 'n perky. With a freckle or two on it. A mouth that—

That didn't belong to her. That would have been shocking in Nancy's face. In Roxane's. A great big nigger-lipped, full-fleshed mouth that—that a man would go on screaming for forever in the dungeons beneath the seventh and final circle of bitter hell, Tobias thought. Or rather, knew.

Oh, it was pale enough. Shell pink and primrose—but that didn't matter. It—suggested scarlet. It projected crimson. It invited madness. It pan piped rut and riot all along his guts, his veins.

He forced himself to look at the rest of her. At that prim and proper shirtwaist dating back to well before the War, trying in vain to keep his eyes, his mind, his imagination off what it moulded, contoured, displayed; at that ankle-length skirt of a type that absolutely no girl at all wore anymore in A.D. 1922, a date by which hemlines had already reached midcalf, and were climbing steadily toward 1928–29's shocking exhibitions of female flesh. On Clara, those quaint, old-fashioned clothes—her mother's surely, he realized, for when shirtwaists and hobbleskirts like these had been in style this girl had not only been too young, but even too *small* to wear them—were provocations. Gross provocations. They clung to that figure he had already seen (Had he? Was such a thing possible?) stark naked through one of Angie's destructions of distance, place, and time—and only emphasized its absolute perfection. In that little house, he remembered now, he had seen her like that, preparing to take a bath. Or—

Oh Lord! Oh God! Oh Jesus, Buddha, Mohammed, Brahma, Vishnu, Isis, Aphrodite, Eros, Astarte, Freya—anybody! Don't let her be the one in that Tower Room he prayed!

But the Tower Room was bricked up. And had been since even before the Tobits had bought the castle! So how—

She came towards the car. The way she walked was indescribable. Tautly, with tension in her stride. A tiny hip sway all the more enticing for being held in check, for being deliberately restrained. Weightlessly. No footsteps sounding. As though her feet didn't really touch the ground.

He got out of the car. He had his hat in his hand. His heart. But not his mind. Her mouth had reduced that to a quivering jelly at the exact point in his sequential progression that his stunned perceptions had flashed her into being. Created her anew out of joy, of wonder, shaped her to fill—and receive—his aching need.

"Howdy," she said. "You folks must be lost. . . ."

And damned, Tobias thought. "Not lost—found. Miss Clara Tobit, I presume?" he said.

"That's right," she said. "How'd you know?"

"I—I'm your cousin, sort of," Tobias said. "Your Yankee cousin. My name's Tobit, too. Tobias Tobit. In fact, I've come to—to visit you. And—and your sister, Sara—if I may. That is—if—you don't mind?"

"Why should I mind?" Clara said. "This lady's your wife?"

"No!" Tobias said. "She's not! You see—"

"Well," Clara said, "she'd better be *somebody's* wife, it appears to me."

"My chauffeur's," Tobias said. "Angie's. This is Angie."

"Who is Angie?" Clara said. "You sure you feel all right, Mister Tobias Tobit?"

"Oh Jesus!" Tobias wailed inside his mind. *"This* tears it! Angie, help me! Make her *see* you!"

"Can't," Angie thought. "People do—or they don't. And the ones who do—are among th' walkin' wounded, Toby lad. I'd kind o' thought that being a Tobit, she—"

"She's lying!" Anne snapped. Her thought went curling in black sulphuric wrath through Tobias' mind.

"What did you *say?*" Clara gasped.

"Didn't *say* anything," Anne said flatly. "I only thought it. And that you *heard* me think it proves my contention. You are lying, Clara Tobit. Or is it—Sara? Because you could be either of the twins. Or are you—both?"

Clara stared at Anne.

"Reckon I'll have to overlook what you're saying, Ma'am," she said, quietly. "Result of your—your delicate condition, I reckon. I take it that you—you *do* have a husband? And that he—your husband —*isn't* my cousin Toby?"

Anne didn't open her mouth. She thought slowly, evenly, carefully: "Would you care? If Toby did belong to *me,* I mean?"

Before Clara could get her guard up, or perhaps before she realized the necessity for controlling, editing her thoughts before these variants, these semimutants, by then reaching beyond humanity all three of them, a cry of purest anguish tore through her mind: "Oh Lord God, I'd die!"

Anne turned to Tobias with a bitter smile.

"There you are, Toby my friend," she purred. "She's all yours! What you came here for, isn't it?"

"Why, ma'am!" Clara said, "what makes you think that I—that I—"

"Have fallen in love with Toby, here?" Anne said. "Don't think —I *know.*"

Tobias smiled at his cousin Clara then.

"Have you, Clara?" he said. "Because I certainly have—with you!"

"You're—you're fresh!" Clara said, "and presumptuous and—and an egotist and—"

"Then you don't love him?" Anne said.

"No! Of course not! I'm not in the habit of falling in love with men I never laid eyes on before. . . ."

"Then, come on, Toby," Anne said.

"Come on where?" Tobias asked.

"To the castle, of course. To Schloss's schloss. Since it's written in your stars that you're to marry one of the twins, it will have to be Sara, then—since Clara is so positive she doesn't want you!"

Clara's face turned white. Even her great, big, glorious mouth. "Mister Tobit," she began.

"Cousin Toby," Tobias said.

"Cousin Toby—don't—don't go up there. Don't go to the castle. I ask you that. Please don't. I—I *beg* you not to."

"Why not?" Tobias said.

"Don't ask me to explain," Clara whispered. "I can't. It would be —disloyal of me—to—to my father, to my family, my mother—"

"But—*not* to your sister?" Angie said.

"Well—yes. To—to—my sister, too," Clara said.

"You see!" Anne said, or rather thought. "She hears—or communicates with—and therefore, on some level, perceives—Angie. Proves my original contention: This little girl is lying!"

"Please don't, Cousin Toby!" Clara said.

"He won't die," Angie said then, flatly. "Not like them siven other blokes. Tha's me mission, lass—to guard 'n protect 'im. 'Gainst all harm, down to 'n includin' demons. Sich as ol' Asmodeus, fer instance. Better known to ye, me sweet, as Harold . . ."

"Oh my God!" Clara said. "Who are *you?* And—and *where* did you come from?"

"I'm Angie. Angie th' Angel. Tobias Tobit's Guardian Angel. Name o' Rafael. Don Rafael Angel Claro at yer service, *clarita mía.* 'N I came, presumably, from Heaven. Or could be from Hell. Depends upon yer point o' view. Where d'*ye* think I come from, me wee 'n bonnie lass?"

"Don't know," Clara whispered, "that depends . . ." Then, her mind, her heart, her being all tearing, her essence becoming the feel and texture of a scream, throat-ripping and bloody raw: "Oh please! Please! Whoever you are! Whatever you are! I *am* good. I *am.* That wasn't me. That was *Sara.* You—you understand that, don't you? Don't—don't show me—heaven—and then—and then—"

"Slam those pearly gates in your face?" Anne said. "He won't. He won't—because *I* won't let him. So you've got your chance, you poor, miserable, triply abused little bitch. Courtesy—of a dying woman, whom you don't even like, and who falls a damned sight short of cottoning to *you,* either—"

"Then—then—why?" Clara got out.

"Call it—Sisterhood. The Sisterhood of the Downtrodden—and the Damned. The East Egypt, Kentucky Chapter of Not-Yet Liberated Roundheels and Pushovers. A legacy from one who remembers how being considered—or maybe even *being*—just a convenient piece of ass, feels. Toby is—a good boy. A goddamned fool, of course, but maybe the two things are even synonymous, aren't they? So make the best of him. Something less—than heaven, Clara-Sara, but still—mighty fine. To have and to hold. To love and to cherish. And you can skip that 'obey' business. It won't even come up . . ."

"Won't somebody explain even a *little* of this to me, please?" Tobias wailed.

"No," Clara said absently. Then: "Anne—that *is* your name, isn't it?"

"Yes," Anne said.

"All right. Then don't let him go up there. To the schloss, I mean. Because if he does, *she'll* get him sure. And that'll be the end of him, I tell you!"

Anne stared at her. A long time. A very long time. Then she said slowly, softly: *"Who'll* get him, dear?"

"Sara. She's my twin. But she's *so*—beautiful! Not plain like me, and—"

"Plain!" Tobias said.

"Shut up, will ye, Toby lad," Angie said. "This is interestin'. Mighty, mighty interestin'!"

"Then—then there *is* a Sara, dearie?" Anne said.

"Of course!" Clara said, and her pale eyes opened very wide. Her astonishment was unfeigned. Even Tobias could see that. "What did you think?" she said.

"That she drowned in a pond," Angie said quietly. "Down in Beaufort, South Carolina."

"Oh no! That was Edna! She was a year older than Sara and I,"

Clara said. "Papa named her after Mama. She was only three years old—when she died. In a storm. In one of those awful storms they have down there. So, of course, we—Sara and I—don't remember her. But it—Edna's dying like that, I mean—affected Mama's mind. She hasn't been right in the head, since. When we were born—Sara and I—Mama was calm, so her—her craziness didn't do us any—much—harm. But she had a hard time with Harold. Seventy-two hours in labor. That's why he—Oh my goodness! There I go! Talkin' too blame much again! Anyhow, you *mustn't* let Toby go up there, you simply *mustn't!*"

"Because ol' Asmo'll get him? Do him in, like he done them other siven blokes?" Angie said. "He *won't,* Clara. I promise ye that."

She turned and stared at Angie. "Can you—also promise—that he—that Toby won't just—go away?" she whispered. "After he has seen—what my family's—like? Papa and Mama—and Sara—and—and Harold? Harold most of all. That is, if they even *let* you see him. But Sara's not far behind him. . . ."

"And what are they like, child?" Anne said gently.

Clara bowed her head. Looked up again. Said it then. Flatly, clearly, without emotion.

"Crazy. They're—crazy. Every living one of 'em."

Anne moved closer to her. Stood there, gazing into her eyes. As though she were trying to read something there, Tobias thought.

"And—*you're* not?" she said.

Clara's eyes went out behind a rush of water. Those huge, ugly glasses steamed up, causing them to disappear.

Dumbly, numbly, she nodded. "Yes. Me, too. But—*less* than they are! Long as I stay away from the schloss, I'm all right. I *am,* I swear it! And if I could get away forever—"

"Even at the cost of taking on a husband you don't love?" Tobias said then, bitterly.

She stared at him. Said: "If I *ever* take a husband, it'll be *because* I love him, Cousin Toby. You can be certain—sure of *that.*"

"Which rules me out, doesn't it?" Tobias said, even more bitterly.

Clara sighed then. It was a windy gust of pure exasperation.

"Didn't say that," she said quietly. "If you're doing all this pushin' and shovin' and displayin' the home trainin' you sure Lord *haven't* got to find out how I feel about you right *now,* I'll tell you: I *don't* love you. Haven't known you a whole half hour yet, Cousin. And that's not long enough. Which isn't—isn't the same thing as sayin' I couldn't learn to. You're tall and soft-spoken and good-lookin' and —gentle. All that—shows. So why don't you give me a chance, huh? A couple of weeks, anyhow, to get to know you? And for you to get to know *me?* But the main catch to those two weeks would have to be that you spend 'em down *here,* with *me.* Not flittin' back and forth between here and the schloss—a tryin' to make up your mind 'twixt me and my twin sister!"

"Why not?" Anne said then, sharply. "It seems to me that such a comparison would be entirely fair, wouldn't it, Clara?"

Clara glared at Anne, then. Her pale eyes made winter lightnings, became hoarfrost and flint, all twelve of Niflheim's iron rivers freezing up.

"It wouldn't be, and you know it! Unless I were willing to use *her* methods. And I'm not. 'Cause, if I did, the difference 'twixt us would be gone. Or don't you hold that Cousin Toby—I mean that *any* good man—is entitled to—to a *decent* wife?"

Anne smiled then. And Tobias, who had believed that she, at least, was without female malice, was shocked to his guts by that smile.

"Harold—" Anne purred. "Your—your brother, I believe you said. But what did you say was wrong with him, Clara, dear? There was something—well, odd about him—wasn't there?"

Clara's eyes brooded over Anne's face. Frost-maiden's eyes, misty with questioning, with doubt.

"He—he's backward, sort of," she whispered. "Because of the hard time Mama had, giving birth to him. It—affected his mind. Never did develop. . . ."

"But his—animal instincts—are in fine working order, aren't they, dear?" Anne said.

"Anne!" Clara gasped. "That—That's *mean!* And you said you were on my side! Oh, how hateful women are!"

"Annie, me darlin'," Angie said sorrowfully, "she's right. Ye're bein'—hateful. 'N unless I kin find some way o' savin' ye, ye can't afford that now. Ye want to go to th' Auld Cuss—to yer Maker, with th' sin of—of wantin' mercy, of bein' uncharitable upon yer soul?"

Anne bowed her head. When she looked up her dark eyes were tear blazed.

"You're right," she said. "Because—she's—she's innocent, isn't she? Because *sin,* true sin, involves one's will, doesn't it? Therefore she has never sinned, has she? Been victimized, yes. The sinner was always—Sara, right? And Clara, the victim. Poor little thing. Poor little lost, mixed-up thing! How're you going to—to—straighten *this* dreadful mess out, Angie?"

"Don't know. Beg her pardon, Annie!"

"I do," Anne whispered. "Will you forgive me, Clara? And—and let me kiss you, too—if I may?"

"Yes," Clara said. "Both. 'Cause you know—that time—that one awful time, wasn't my fault. To blame me for it would be like hanging a dead man for letting himself get murdered. And you're *not* mean, are you? Deep down, inside—you're sweet."

"So are you," Anne said, and kissed her.

"I—I *have* to go up to the castle," Tobias said suddenly. "I have to—sometime—even to ask your father for your hand—"

"I haven't accepted you yet, Tobias Tobit!" Clara flared. "And anyhow, go! Better like that! 'Cause if she—if Sara can—drive you wild—just like she did the others—*I* don't want you. Not even—if he—if your Guardian Angel—can save you—from the—the Devil—that possesses my poor brother! I'm going to—to come to my man clean—" she stopped, glared at Anne. "Yes, yes—clean! Butchered, maybe—but *not* dirtied, 'cause *I, me,* the *real* me stayed out of it!—and he's got to come to me as clean as he can, too. Oh, I won't fault you for the strayin' you did before you met me, Toby! But if you get mixed up with that whorish bitch of a sister of mine I—"

"Clara," Tobias said then, reasonably enough, "why don't you come with me—with us? Up to the castle, I mean? See for yourself that I won't, haven't!"

"Can't," Clara said. "I go with you up there, and *nothing* will be decided. You'll never even *see* her if I do. She'll lock herself up in her room and not come out as long as I'm there. She *hates* me that damn bad. And now—"

"And now?" Tobias said.

"I *want* you to meet her. Because *this* time, things have got to be decided. Have to be settled once and for all. I can't live like this anymore. I can't go on."

"Because of—" Anne began.

"Yes, yes! But don't you say it! Don't you even *think* it! He'll hear you think it—and it'll give him too—much of an advantage, fool that I am! Oh Anne, honey, please!"

"All right," Anne said. "And don't worry. *This* time you're going to win!"

"Am I?" Clara wailed.

"Yes. But do as I say, now. Kiss him!"

"Kiss him?" Clara got out. "Kiss—Cousin Toby?"

"Yes. Set your brand upon him, child. Mark him with the innocence you think you have, the purity. Against which neither Sara, nor all the hosts of Hell, can prevail. Go on, Clara, kiss him."

Clara turned those Aesir eyes on Tobias. Freya's eyes. For, although Angie, with his mania for equating all beliefs, would have said Freya was Astarte, Aphrodite, Venus, in one way, she really wasn't. Because, according to the Norse eddas, to her belonged one half of the valiant dead. No valkyrie would bear Tobias' soul to Valhalla now. It would freeze in Niflheim, burn in Muspelheim, after this transplanted Norse goddess had created her own bright saga out of their cojoined and united lives.

He opened his arms to her. She came to him, fitted herself into his embrace. Into every hollow and contour of his body. By a sudden surge of that human faculty for wonder-working, for magic that men —lamely—call imagination, he had the abrupt and marvelous sensation that neither his clothes nor—better yet, more gloriously satisfying—*hers,* were between them anymore so that every pore of their cojoined flesh achieved osmosis, making that kiss total, or very nearly, extended, as it did from mouth to knee.

Then the top of his head blew off. His brains became a pinkish, greyish geyser, skyward spewing. He was aware, even without them, that he had *never* before in his whole life been kissed like this.

Her mouth became—what? A Venus flytrap? A blood-gorged, hot wet fungus-flower, cannibalistically devouring—no, absorbing—what little thought, spirit, mind, will he had left by then, while her serpentine, educated tonguetip raised both his temperature and his blood pressure to levels usually fatal to the human organism, the *male* human organism, anyhow, which, in every specific way that counts, is much the more delicate of the two.

He was aware that, in one more instant of pounding, racing, nonexistent time, he was going to disgrace himself, commit a small public nuisance, which, as loin-glued to him as dear Clara was, she would be sure to notice, sense, even feel. But she saved him from the minor catastrophe by the simple act of drawing her mouth from his, releasing him, standing back.

She smiled at him. Her voice, speaking, was throaty, purring, warm. "Now go. Up there, I mean. To the schloss. And—forget me. Forget me completely," she said. Then she added, very, very softly, "That is, if you can."

And turned, and walked over to the little red Studebaker. Got in. Drove away. Left him there. Left him—damned.

Or saved.

Who knows?

Sixteen

The castle, Schloss's schloss, was absolutely perfect. It was so right, sitting there atop Schloss's mountain, so weathered and old, moss-slimed, damp, bolt and chain rusted, its wooden parts, the drawbridge already let down across the moat, and the huge gates, likewise opened, so worm eaten and visibly rotting that Tobias was startled.

"Looks like it's been there forever!" he said.

"Well it ain't," Angie said. "But it *is* as old as it looks to be, 'n parts of it are even older. . . ."

"But, Angie," Anne said, "that can't be. Why even this country isn't *that* old!"

"Know that, duckie. But all th' same, that there gloomy old rock pile is close to a thousand years older than these United States of America, give or take a hundred years."

"How," Tobias asked, reasonably enough, "could a castle be a thousand years older than the country it's located in?"

"Easy, when a bloke's got as many millions as ol' Schloss had. Went back to Germany 'n bought th' damn thing from the descendants of th' ol' feudal barons who built it in th' first place. Only he didn't tell 'em why he wanted *that* particular castle. . . ."

"Why did he?" Anne said.

"Revenge, sort of. You see, th' lord o' th' castle caught some o' ol' Schloss's ancestors—they wuz villeins and serfs, natch!—poachin' rabbits on th' castle's game preserves. 'N hung th' poor bastids from a beam extended through th' tower window. As a warnin' to th' other peasantry, ye kin—"

"But, Angie!" Anne protested. "You don't mean to tell me that the baron hanged a man for stealing a rabbit!"

"Not a man. Three men. 'N I guess there wuz mebbe half a dozen rabbits involved. But th' principle's th' same, ain't it, duckie? Sweet lovable characters, them ol' feudal lords, come to think o' it."

"But if it—the schloss—was in *Germany,* how'd it get over *here?*" Tobias said.

"Steamboat," Angie said. "How'd ye think it got here, laddybucks, swimming?"

"But—but—"

"Auld Schloss had it took apart, stone by stone. 'N th' stones wuz numbered, as his workmen took 'em down. So, after he'd got it here, it wuz easy enough to put it back together. The only trouble wuz that parts of it wuz missin'—th' later barons wuz dirt-poor 'n lacked the wherewithal to keep th' auld ruin up. So Schloss went back to Krautland, 'n bought two more castles. Out o' th' three of 'em, he got enough junk to built that'un there. Tha's why he niver wuz sure jest which wan th' ghosts came from. My guess is from all three. Mighty heterogeneous set o' ghosts, come to think o' it. . . ."

"You mean it's—it's *haunted?*" Anne said.

"Why, to be sure, Annie me darlin'. Ye iver heard of an auld castle what wuzn't?"

"Now, Angie!" Tobias said.

" 'S a fact. That there auld Bela Lugosi-type vampire's nest up there has got three separate 'n distinct sets o' ghosts. First, there's th' baroness's lover. Th' auld baron had him bricked up into th' bedroom wall. Th' same bedroom he caught 'em in. Starved t' death, th' poor bastid. Tha's why his ghost is so skinny. 'N then there's th' headless, titless countess. Goes about wailin' 'n weepin' 'n moanin' —her head does, enyhow. She carries it in her arms along with her wee bairn, who is dyin' o' hunger. You see, she cain't feed 'im what with her not havin' eny tits, either. *Her* hubby had 'em whacked off when he tumbled to th' fact that th' li'l bastid wasn't his. An' then—"

"Angie, you stop it!" Tobias said. "There're no such things as ghosts, and you know it!"

"I don't know it. 'N you don't neither, laddybucks. Le's see if you kin still make an outrageously ignorant statement like that'un, this time t'morrow mornin'. I've known hundreds o' ghosts, personally. Most of 'em friends o' mine. . . . Now, c'mon."

"Angie," Tobias said, "you're sure that drawbridge can support the weight of this car?"

"If it can't, Toby, me boy, me boy, th' schloss is gonna acquire itself three more ghosts, pronto. Hold on now! Here goes!"

He slammed the Pierce Arrow into gear, double clutching. The big limousine shot forward as though it were trying to imitate the weapon it was named after. It fairly hurled itself across that ancient drawbridge in a thunder of bucking, rumbling, cracking beams, poured itself through the gate and under the menacing iron points of the portcullis, to come to a stop, in a shrieking of tortured brakes, in the exact center of the courtyard.

A uniformed butler opened the door of the car. He bowed grandly.

"Mr. Tobit?" the butler said. "Mr. Tobias Tobit?"

"Y—y—yes," Tobias got out. "How'd you know? That I was coming, I mean?"

"Oh, Miss Clara 'phoned the master from the village, sir! Your luggage is in the boot, I suppose?"

Tobias followed the butler—imported from England, surely, from his accent—into the castle. Angie, bearing the bags, followed Tobias. For the moment, anyhow, poor Anne waited in the car.

In the great hall, whose walls were hung with tapestries, and also with shields bearing crossed empty scabbards behind them, a detail which struck Tobias as odd, Ralph Tobit was waiting; but, to Tobias' acute disappointment, neither his host's wife nor his daughter was in sight. Mr. Tobit was tall, and as pale blond as Clara—paler, for his hair was nearly all white by then. He was very thin. And even though he looked straight into Tobias' face, the expression on his own distant and wintry countenance sent an eerie feeling creeping up and down the young New Englander's spine. Suddenly he knew how Anne had felt when she hadn't been able to see her own reflection in Emmy's Pool. He was being willed out of existence. To those hoarfrost- and fjord-colored eyes he was invisible. He simply wasn't there. Not as a person, living, breathing, suffering in this world, anyhow. As an idea, perhaps. An abstraction. A distinctly tenuous connection with a memory. An old and faded memory at that.

"Tobias Tobit," Ralph said with the vaguest of all vague smiles. "My cousin Henry's boy, I presume?"

"Yes, sir," Tobias said.

"Welcome to the schloss," Ralph said, and put out his hand to Tobias. It felt as if it had been stored beneath the same damp rock the butler had crawled out from under. For at least a couple of thousand years, Tobias thought.

"Martin will show you to your room," Ralph Tobit said. "You've time to freshen up a bit before dinner. But don't dress. We've rather got out of the habit in this benighted neck of woods—much to Martin's distress!"

Tobias stared at him. Then he realized what his father's cousin meant.

"I'm not much for formality either, sir," he said. "In fact I don't even know whether Angie even packed a dinner jacket for me. Did you, Angie?"

"Yes sir, Young Master! That I did, sir!" Angie said, and touched his forelock in the very finest old country style.

"I must say your man's well trained," Ralph observed. "But—the —the young woman, I saw on the *front* seat of your motor car? Struck me as being rather odd. Her being on the front seat, I mean. . . ."

"His wife," Tobias said. "Angie's. And, sir, since she's—in a rather advanced stage of gestation—I hadn't the heart to make Angie leave her behind. They have neither relatives nor friends in California. . . . I only hope there's a good clinic, or a decent gynecologist hereabouts?"

"There's neither, I'm afraid," Ralph Tobit said, and an edge of bitterness got into his tone. "We did have a fairly decent midwife, but she died three years ago—and left her practice to her daughter. Shouldn't care to recommend Sal, though. Bit of a slattern. And no better than she should be—in her personal affairs if you get what I mean. Of course there's Merton, but—"

"He's a drunkard. Or so we were told in the village," Tobias said.

"Unfortunately that's quite correct," Ralph sighed. "Of course some of our older women on the place should know enough to help out if everything goes smoothly. In any event, we'll do what we can. After your man's installed you, he can bring her in. We've rather decent quarters below. Then I'll have Martin 'phone around for the doctor. If we can get him here long enough before, we'll stand a fairish chance of sobering him up. . . ."

He smiled at Angie suddenly. "Cheer up, my good fellow!" he said. "I'm sure we'll be able to manage quite nicely!"

The bathroom was straight out of a Victorian murder mystery but, surprisingly enough, everything in it worked. Finding that the water was piping hot, Tobias took advantage of that wholly unexpected detail to have himself a good, long bath.

As he lolled in the soapy water, seeping the grime of travel out of his pores, and the ache of it out of his bones, he heard, suddenly, water gushing into what was evidently another bathtub, separated only by a wall from his own.

"Not surprising," he thought. "Castle sure as hell didn't come equipped with modern plumbing. So they did it the easy way—ran all the tubing up through the center—alongside the stairwell, likely. So all the bathrooms will be grouped. Side by side when they're on the same floor, and directly above or below one another when they're not. Makes sense. 'Cause running hot and cold water pipes, not to mention drains through stone walls thick as this creepy old joint has, would be one hell of a job. . . ."

The water in the other tub went on gushing for a longish time. Then it stopped.

A woman's voice rang out clearly, thus proving that the wall between the two baths was only a partition, a modern addition to the schloss.

"Miss Sara!" the woman's voice said. "You're bath's ready, missy!"

"Coming, Milly," a softer, lighter, far younger voice said.

"Put bath salts in, jes like you tol' me to," the woman called Milly said. " 'N yor clo's is all laid out. So this 'un'll make number eight, won't he?"

"Don't get smart with me, Milly," the younger voice said.

"I ain't," Milly said, "but lemme tell you one thing, Miss Sara. I seen this one when he was comin' up th' stairs. 'N he's different from the rest. Not th' bes' lookin'. Mebbe he's even th' *worst* lookin', I don' know—"

"So?" Sara said.

"Only he's got—sech a *good* face, Miss Sara. A real kind *decent* lookin' face. So it 'pears to me . . ."

"It appears to you *what?*" Sara said.

"That you—oughta—kinda sorta—let him *live,* Miss Sara. Mebbe you cain't help—what you do. Mebbe you ain't even clothed 'n framed in yore right mind when you does it. Mebbe, like you claims, you plumb doan remember a damn thing—afterwards. But seven dead men is a mighty heap o' dead men to my way o' thinkin'. 'N one day hit's certain-sure to occur to *somebody* to pry up a few pavin' stones down there in the courtyard 'n have theyselves a look. . . ."

"Milly," Sara said, quietly, slowly, almost whispering the words, "you're saying that I—that I *killed* those seven fellows?"

"If you didn't, who *did,* Miss Sara? They was each 'n every one of 'em all alone with *you,* just before they ups an' disappears. Who *else* had a chance to—to murder 'em? A real *good* chance? When th' idea that they wuz in peril o' gettin' kilt wuz the *last* thing they had on they li'l horny minds? Never so much as occurred to 'em that they wuz gonna pay for they—pleasurin'—with they lives?"

"Their—pleasure?" Sara said. "I—I don't understand you, Milly!"

"Honeychile, 'pears to me yore fergittery is plumb workin' overtime. Doan tell me you done gone 'n disremembered who do yore washin', namely *me?* Not only yore pretty, frilly li'l underdrawers, but yore bedsheets, too, Miss Sara, hon. 'N I been married—twice. So jes you go 'n pull that there sweet innercence on somebody *else.* Somebody a damn' sight dumber than one Mildred Sloames'll ever git to be. . . ."

"Milly," Sara whispered, "I don't even know what you're talking about. All I done know is that you have a perfectly filthy mind, and that I'm going to have Papa put you off the place this very day!"

"No you ain't, honey. 'Cause tetched in th' head though everlast one of you Tobits be, yore Pa, at least, ain't fool enough to want me walkin' round all th' towns 'twixt East Egypt 'n Lexington, say, 'n talkin' my fool head off, 'n tha's a fact. What you's a gonna do, Miss Sara, is to ax him to raise my pay. Twicet what I'm gettin' now. Or mebbe this heah nice sweet *rich* young gentleman of a cousin of yourn jes might find out that th' girl he come all this way to see is . . ."

"What, Milly?" Sara whispered.

"A whore to start with. An' a murderin' maniac to boot, mebbe. Or do you know some other way to put it, honeybunch? I'm jes a plain-spoken Kentucky mountain woman. I plumb doan know no fancy words. . . ."

"Milly—" the girl said, and Tobias, hearing her voice breaking up, even through that wall, hearing what had got into it by then, was torn and rent by anguished pity; by that, and by the searing bite of a feeling that he did not yet realize was hope. "I—I didn't kill those fellows. I have never killed even—a rabbit—or a chicken in my whole life. I *couldn't,* Milly! I purely couldn't! And besides—"

"Besides what?" Milly said.

"Who says they're *dead?* Nobody ever found any bodies. So—"

"Hmph!" Milly said. "So they jes spread their wings 'n flew away? An' afterwards they folks sent detective fellas a-lookin' for 'em jes for fun? An' them rumpled-up sheets o' yourn with them mighty peculiar stains on 'em? That happened all by itself, Miss Sara, ma'am? Did it, now?"

"I don't know," Sara said. "I—don't—remember. Far as I know, I—I've never let—a man so much as touch me in my whole life. Now get out of here! And you be careful of what you say or—"

"Or what, you pretty, lyin', killin' li'l bitch? Or what?" the woman called Milly said.

Tobias heard the door of the other bathroom slam. He wanted to get out of the tub, but he didn't dare to. For, if he could hear every sound that came from the other bathroom, it was an absolute certainty that she could hear him just as clearly. So he lay there in a tub of water becoming uncomfortably cool now, and listened to her crying.

"Oh Lord!" she sobbed. "I want to die! I don't want to live any more! Not one minute longer! I—I'll hang myself! No, I'll throw myself from the tower like poor Emmy Schloss did! And, anyhow, I'll be dead, dead, dead! That way I won't have to wonder if—if I'm crazy, too! If I'm wicked—and—and whorish—and a slut—like my sister Clara! Lays down and spreads her legs for everybody, the awful, awful little bitch! I didn't kill those fellows! I didn't! I don't even *know* what happened to 'em! First they were *here,* and then they were gone and then those—those what was it that Papa called 'em? Oh yes—those gumshoes came and—Oh Lord, Oh Jesus! What *am* I going to do?"

"Pray," Angie's voice stole through Tobias' mind. And through *hers,* the young New Englander was abruptly sure. That he could hear his Guardian Angel was because Angie wanted him to. He knew that very well.

"Pray?" his cousin Sara whispered in her own mind.

"Yes," Angie said. "Try this 'un on fer size, me wee 'n bonnie lass:

> You are blessed, O God of mercy!
> May your name be blessed forever,
> and may all things that you have made
> bless you everlastingly.
> And now I lift up my face
> and to you I turn my eyes,
> Let your word deliver me from earth;
> I can hear myself slandered no longer.
> O Lord, you know
> that I have remained—"

Abruptly Tobias heard Angie's telepathic voice change its tone: "Hmmmmmm—" the Angel said, "mebbe we better leave verses fourteen through seventeen out, lass. I know they're true by *yer* reckonin', but they jes might get th' Auld Cuss off his feed. 'Cause there're truths 'n truths, ain't there, Sary, me lass? 'N yer truths 'n th' world's, 'n th' Auld Cuss's fer that matter, don't necessarily coincide. Lemme see, lemme see. Got it. Le's quote th' Vulgate's version from here on in. Ain't as accurate as th' Jerusalem Bible, which, come to think of it, ain't even been translated yet; but suits yer purposes better, don't it, me lass? All right. Th' Vulgate, from verse eighteen on. But first verses seventeen 'n eighteen o' *this* version to keep things clear:

> I am my father's only daughter,
> he has no other child as heir—"

"What about *Clara?*" Tobias thought. "And Harold, alias Asmodeus, the Demon?"

"Shut up will ye, laddybucks," Angie said. "Ye're gettin' *me* confused, now. Tha's what the Good Book says. 'N th' Good Book's always right, ye know. Even when it's wrong. Like now, mebbe. C'mon, lass, repeat after me:

> He has no brother at his side,
> nor has he any kinsman left
> for whom I ought to keep myself,

Already I have lost seven husbands,
Why should I live any longer?

"And now, th' Vulgate, lass. The Book o' Tobit, Chapter Three, Verses eighteen through twenty-two:

If I consented to take a husband
It was not out of lust, but out of
awe for you—
So then, either I was not worthy of them
Or perhaps they were not worthy of me
Or else you had another husband
In mind for me?
Your designs are beyond man's reach
But all who revere you know that if
they have been tested, they will be crowned;
if in distress, delivered; if punished, free
to come to your mercy!
For you take no pleasure in our fall;
but, after the storm, you bring the calm,
After tears and weeping you give
abounding joy—Amen!"

"Amen!" Sara whispered, and Tobias heard the splashing as she got out of the tub. He could hear her thoughts trailing behind her as she left the bathroom, not even, apparently, waiting to dry herself. "Maybe—*he'll* be the one. The man for me. Oh Lord, let him be! I'll—I'll be good to him! I'll love him and cherish him forever. If only he—he can take the spell off! End the—the bad dreams. The nightmares. When she—Clara—gets into me and makes me—Oh, please, God, please!"

When Tobias came down to dinner, the Tobits were there waiting for him. Three of the Tobits, anyhow, which, according to that confusing version from the Old Testament that Angie had quoted, were all the Tobits maybe. Edna Tobit was almost as tall as her husband. She looked like a grand duchess. Her presence was regal. But one long look into her face, her eyes, showed Tobias that trying to talk to her would be a perfect waste of time. For tall, handsome, surprisingly young-looking, red-haired Edna Tobit was—one glance sufficed to show him—quietly and completely mad.

He looked at Sara then, and all his breath tangled in his throat. Became a ball of ice, of fire. He saw what Clara meant now when she had complained that in comparison to Sara she was plain. No girl, no woman, no *human being* ("Is she?" his startled mind demanded. "Can she be?") could possibly be *this* beautiful. And yet, she and Clara were identical. Except, his thoughts protested, all the ways they don't look alike at all! This hair now—reddish blonde, isn't it? Or is it the candlelight that makes me think—? And her mouth, her lips? Oh Jesus God!—Not shell pink. Wine red. Rose-petal scarlet. Blood crimson. But just as—huge. As big. As soft. As—

"Hello, Cousin Toby," Sara said.

"My God, but you're beautiful!" Tobias said, and took the slender, flowerlike, fragrant (What in the name of all seduction's diabolical arts is *this* perfume?) hand she offered him, and raised it to his lips.

"How nice!" she laughed. "He's a *real* gentleman, isn't he, Papa? Just like you said. Well, Cousin Toby, do you like me? Do you promise to fall madly in love with me? This instant? At first sight?"

"Do you want me to?" Tobias said.

"Don't be a clever Yankee, Cousin Toby!" Sara teased. "But, if you must know, of course I do! I just adore having men at my feet. Which can be rather unfortunate for the men, come to think of it. This is—my mother. Mama, say hello to Cousin Toby."

"Hello, Cousin Toby," Edna Tobit said.

"Don't mind Mama," Sara said brightly. "She's—eccentric. A bit odd. But harmless. That's where my sister Clara gets it from—"

Tobias stared at her. "Gets *what* from your mother, Cousin Sara?" he said.

"Being odd. Don't tell me you didn't notice?"

"Not a thing. Your sister seemed perfectly normal to me."

"Then she was on her good behavior for a change," Sara said. "Come on, now. You'll sit beside me. And gaze into my eyes—"

"And fall into them, and drown!" Tobias said fervently.

"Oh, Papa! Did y' hear that? Cousin Toby's a poet! And I *like* him. Oh I do! Truly!"

"New Englanders, my dearest Sara," Ralph Tobit said indulgently, "tend to be a trifle straïtlaced. I'd suggest that you don't flirt with your cousin quite so outrageously. By now he probably doesn't know what to think of you!"

"I think that she's beautiful and charming and that I want to marry her," Tobias said easily. "That's if she'll have me, and if you'll permit it, sir? Will you? Grant me your daughter's hand in marriage, I mean?"

"But of course!" Ralph Tobit laughed. "Be happy to be rid of the baggage! But I think you go too fast, young sir—for your own sake, that is! You'd better get to know my daughter better. *Much* better. She can be quite a pain in the posterior when she puts her mind to it!"

"Oh Pa-pa!" Sara wailed. "What an awful, *mean* thing to say!"

"Awful truth," Ralph Tobit said drily. "Now come on, all. Dinner's waiting . . ."

"Isn't—your son going to join us, sir?" Tobias said. "Harold, I believe his name is?"

Ralph Tobit stared at Tobias. Sara stamped her dainty foot. Her wide blue eyes (considerably darker than Clara's, Tobias decided, softer, more velvety—or could this, too, be the effect of the subdued light in here or—?) filled up with tears.

"Papa, you'll just have to commit her, that's all!" she whispered. "Don't you see—she's getting worse?"

"I—I'm afraid I don't understand," Tobias said. "But, anyhow, sir, if I spoke out of turn, I apologize. Humbly."

"No, Toby, dear," Sara said firmly. *"You* didn't speak out of turn. My darlin' sister Clara did that—as usual. And for the same reason as usual. To sink, or ruin all my chances. Because when the average fellow finds out that I have a sister—a twin sister—who is as mad as a hatter—he runs like a rat. But *this* time, I don't mean to let her get away with it. You see, Toby, dear, dear Toby—I—I like you. This is—outrageous, I know, and exactly the sort of thing a well-bred girl should *never* say. But now I have to say it. Papa, don't frown at me like that! I like you, Toby. I think falling in love with you would cost me—or any girl in her right mind—very little trouble. But hear me out: My sister Clara is—insane. The trouble may even be inheritable, since Mama's—a trifle odd, too. And your being a Tobit—would make matters worse—if you and I *should* decide to marry each other, one day. For our children, if any, I mean—"

"Now now, Sara," Ralph Tobit began.

"Papa please! Toby has a *right* to know the truth. After all, he's family, too, isn't he? And *his* mother, you always said—"

"Let's not go into that," Ralph Tobit said. "Tell me, son, did my daughter Clara tell you that my son Harold is—dead? That he died of spinal meningitis at the age of twelve?"

"No, sir," Tobias whispered.

"You see!" Sara said. "And did she tell you, Toby, dear, dear Toby—how she got lost when she was three years old and fell into a pond and almost drowned? And that she was dreadfully sick for *months* afterwards and that her mind hasn't been right since?"

"No," Tobias said stiffly. "She did mention the—the incident. But she said it happened to—your sister Edna—who was a year older than you two are. And that she—Edna, that is—drowned—"

Sara turned to her father and flung wide her arms in a gesture that was exasperation's very self.

"Oh, Papa! You've *got* to stop her!" she said.

"We—never had—a daughter named Edna," Ralph Tobit said gently. "The twins—and Harold, God rest his soul—were all our progeny. Poor Clara. Guess I will have to do something about her after all. Strange. She was always the brightest of our children—intellectually, that is. Her grades in high school, in teacher's college, were—"

"What's that got to do with her being mad?" Sara said sharply. "Crazy people are *always* bright, Papa. Maybe that's what saved me—too stupid to go insane, I reckon! Cousin Toby, I'm sorry! Guess we've spoiled your first night with us, haven't we?"

"Not at all," Tobias said, gallantly. "Besides, truth to tell, and as unromantic as it sounds—I'm hungry as a bear!"

The supper was a strain. Sara chatted brightly all through it; saying, Tobias observed wryly, absolutely nothing at all, but saying it with considerable art. "After all," he thought, "isn't one of the uses of conversation to *conceal* thought? If so—she's doing it beautifully. But deep down, underneath, she's scared stiff, the poor little thing! Of *what,* I wonder? Of me—or of what I might find out? Suppose I were to say, now, aloud: 'Sara, who is Mildred Sloames?' "

"Don't!" Angie's voice jarred abruptly into his mind.

"Why not?" Tobias said, or rather, thought.

"One o' th' aspects o' wisdom, Toby, me boy, me boy, is knowin' *where* to quit. Or to put it in a way a sweet li'l auld intellectual like ye will cotton to better, th' point at which knowledge—as opposed to wisdom—had damn well better be autolimited. 'Cause knowledge ain't nothin' more than a collection o' facts. 'N facts can be useless, nonsensical, and downright harmful, among other things. Fer instance, don't *nobody* really need to know how to make some nice spiffy nerve gas, and/or a foine atomic bomb. Not neither one—"

"Angie," Tobias thought. "Your example's not worth a damn. Oh it's true enough, but in this case it's inappropriate. Try again. Wait —let me suggest one. A wise old tired man with a pretty young lively wife will always telephone from the railroad station before returning home unexpectedly. How's that?"

"Perfect!" Angie thought. "Jes what I had in mind! Look, laddybucks—ye've a lifetime o' happiness before ye. *Great* happiness—as long as ye observe th' golden rule o' matrimony. . . ."

"Which is?" Tobias thought.

"Don't try to find out too much about yer partner. That works in either case, 'n both ways. Ye don't need to know *all* th' reasons that she married ye, nor where she was las' Wednesday 'twixt five 'n seven, say."

"In other words: 'Where ignorance is bliss, 'tis folly to be wise?' "

"Not exactly. Put it this way: 'A wise man knows when, where 'n how to preserve th' areas of blessed ignorance ag'in th' intrusion o' unlovely and/or harmful fact.' *¿De acuerdo?* Ain't she *worth* it, really? This one? 'N for also t'other? Seein' as how they're two aspects of th' same kind o' being?—or mebbe even o' th' same being?"

"Am I, Cousin Toby?" Sara said.

"Are you *what,* Sara?" Tobias said.

"All the strange—and lovely things you were thinking then? Oh, finish your dessert! Then let's go walking among the battlements and towers! Gaze at the moon . . ."

She leaned forward suddenly, whispered through a silver lilt and gurgle of laughter, "I may—even let you—*kiss* me! Would you like that?"

"Would I!" Tobias said. "Come on!"

"Finish your dessert," Sara said demurely. "Papa, I'm going to show Toby the view from the battlements. Hope you don't mind?"

"And if I *did* mind?" Ralph Tobit said.

"Fat lot of good it would do you!" Sara laughed. "Oh, leave that ruddy custard, Toby, and come on!"

There was a moon, and the view from the battlements was lovely, only—

Only there was something—chilling about it.

Below them the falls plumed—white as sorrow, pale as death; and the water neighed and whistled, making a sound like the charge of the valkyries' war horses. In the courtyard beneath them, light and shadow made geometrical patterns, hard-edged, abrupt, except, Tobias realized, the words he'd used to shape his thought were themselves wrong: There was no light; there was a gemlike icy wash of moon with no warmth or softness or glow in it; there were no shadows; there was only light's absence, its negation, the blackness of the pit—of before creation, the darkness of the Deep before God said "Let there be light!" and his hand troubled the face of the waters.

It came to Tobias suddenly that he didn't feel romantic. He felt uneasy, somehow. A vague disquietude crawled along his nerves. Sara was standing very close to him, and that perfume of hers that had seemed so intoxicating before made him feel, in some odd way, sick. Its scent was like no other he had ever known, and yet, it formed images in his mind: a scene. A fair maid upon her bier, death's frozen rigor sculpturing her young beauty into immortality. Romeo comes, and stands there stricken, amid the grave smells and tomb incense.

"Grave smells," he thought again. "Tomb incense."

"What's wrong?" Sara whispered.

"Nothing," he said shortly. "A fit of nerves, perhaps: This old castle of yours takes some getting used to—"

"The castle? Or—me? Or all the things—the awful, lying dreadful things—my sister Clara told you?"

"Your sister told me absolutely *nothing* about you," Tobias said, "except two things that I have been able to confirm for myself, independently. About those two things she told the strict, gospel truth. You, yourselves, have proved that to me."

"Oh!" Sara said. "Have I? And what were those two things?"

"That you were far more beautiful than she is. Which is true. And that you couldn't stand her. And that, to judge from your own remarks, is—"

"Something less than true. I don't dislike Clara; I—I'm simply—afraid of her—"

"Are you? I'll be blessed if I can see why!"

"Because—because she—does things to me. To—to my mind—"

"Now, really!" Tobias said.

"She does. I'm not afraid of her physically. I'm both taller and stronger than she is. Besides—she's not violent. I—oh Lord, how *can* I explain it! You *know* all the Tobits are—well—odd. Even your branch of the family, I'm told—"

"Its present representative definitely *not* excepted," Tobias said, ruefully. "I'm as nutty as a fruitcake, I've been often told. Go on, Sara, dearest—"

"How nicely you say that! And how I wish I *were!* Your dearest, I mean."

"You *are,*" Tobias said quietly, his decision taken now. Taken irrevocably, although he, himself, could neither explain it nor justify it. "I'm in love with you. Seriously."

"Then prove it!" Sara said. "Kiss me. I've been wanting you to, all night. . . ."

"No," Tobias said, "at the moment, I'd rather not."

"Oh!" Sara whispered. "Why—not?"

"Don't want to engage in—a mere flirtation with you, my dearest. For one thing, you're far too good at it, judging from that session at the dinner table tonight. Denotes—practice. An awful lot of practice. Allow me—in this one small detail, to stand out from the herd. I'll kiss you when it means something to you. As much as it would mean to me. In other words, my dearest, darling cousin, I haven't the slightest intention of playing children's games. . . ."

"Toby—who told you there'd been a herd? Clara?"

"No. Clara volunteered very little information as far as you were concerned. As I told you before, she said that you were by far the more beautiful of the two. And, as I also told you, she said that you couldn't stand her—to the extent that, if she accompanied us up here, as I asked her to do, you would have locked yourself in your room, and stayed there until she had left—"

"She was right," Sara said. "That's exactly what I would have done. But only out of my fear of—of being tricked, or hypnotized, or bewitched by *her* into doing, or saying one of *her* things. Into behaving like *her.* Which, of course, would make you so disgusted with me—that you'd leave me, preferably, for her—exactly what she has in her weird little mind. But didn't she tell you about my *seven* previous suitors? All of whom—according to her—met some unspecified, but *horrible* fate—and, again according to her, at my hands, at that?"

"No," Tobias said calmly. "But then, she didn't need to. I'd already heard that one, in the village."

"Oh!" Sara said.

"And gave it exactly the degree of credence it deserves, which is none. As you can see, I'm *here.* In your hands—and at your mercy. Just what do you plan to do with me?"

She came to him. So close that to have avoided touching her, he would have had to step back, which would have been at least gauche, if not insulting. So he did what he had to, what she was literally forcing him to do. He put his arms around her, drew her to him. She leaned forward against him so that the whole warm softness of her from her knees upward was in perfect contact with his own lean, sinewy body, except, of course, for the minor protection, and the major irritant, of their clothing. She buried her face into the hollow of his throat, said, her voice muffled, both by her position, and her tears: "Marry you, if you'll have me. Will you? Will you, please?"

He hung there, frozen, hearing the desperation in her tone, and knew with bleak certainty that it grew out of no such respectably normal emotions as love or lust. Then, abruptly, pity stirred in him. He remembered Angie's telepathically projected remark: "A wise man knows when, where 'n how, to preserve th' areas of blessed ignorance ag'in th' intrusion o' unlovely and/or harmful fact—"

"As now," he thought, "as now!"

"Of course," he said. "When, Sara, darling?"

"As soon as possible!" she whispered: *"Tomorrow,* if it can be arranged! Oh, Toby, dearest, I'll be ever so grateful to you!"

"I should rather that you *loved* me," he said.

"I do! Oh I do!" she burst out; but then she felt, and raising her face, *saw,* his eyes.

"Toby—you think I—I'm doing this—for—*reasons,* don't you?" she said.

He studied her face, her eyes; said, bleakly, "Yes."

"You're right. First—to get away from—the schloss. Second—to escape—from Clara. Third—to have—a life. A good, warm, *safe,* normal life. I—I want that life with *you.* Because the minute I saw you—I knew *you* could save me—even—Oh, you'll just have to permit me the indelicacy, dearest!—thaw me out! Because unlike Clara, I'm frozen all the way through. Those seven fellows she—accuses me of having done something terrible to, all left here because I—I gave them chilblains, Toby! That's all there was to it. Papa invited them—they were sons of friends and business associates, you know, and—"

"You don't owe me any explanations," he said. "In fact, I'd rather *not* have them, if you don't mind. Let's say that life—our life—together—begins tonight. And that nothing that went before matters. Agreed?"

"Agreed," she whispered. *"Now* will you kiss me? Meaning it? As I *do?* Truly?"

He kissed her. Her lips were wonderfully warm and soft and trembling, and then abruptly salt, with the sudden rush of tears.

He leaned back against the battlement holding her. He felt good. And sure. Very sure. For she hadn't even known how to kiss—not with the devilish expertness Clara had displayed. Her kiss had been clumsy, innocent, unformed. He had nothing to worry about—

Except—too damned many things.

He said, unexpectedly, even to himself, without having consciously meant to, and thus not even giving Angie's wise counsel about avoiding too precise knowledge of one's beloved's weaknesses, follies, sins, time to come to mind:

"Who is—Mildred Sloames?"

"A woman," Sara whispered, "who works for us. But who is—is

a Guelf instead of a Ghibelline, as it were. That is—she—she is one of Clara's most ardent supporters. You—must talk to her. You must! So she can tell you—how—how *awful* I am. That's only fair, isn't it?"

"No," Tobias said. "It isn't. And I don't want to. For I've just become the titular head of the Ghibellines as far as you're concerned. And if there were—if there *is*—anything—well, say, unpleasant in your past, I'd rather not know it."

She looked at him, oddly. Studied his face. Whispered very, very quietly, "Thank you for *that,* my love!"

He said then, lightly: "You know, I liked your sister. Liked her immensely. So why do you think you need to escape from her?"

"As a child—as the pretty little boy you must have been—did you ever read, or have told to you—the story of Sleeping Beauty? How Prince Charming came—and awakened her to—to life and love?"

"Yes," he said; "but I don't see—"

"I know. But allow me—the—the metaphor. I *am* your Sleeping Beauty. And you're my Prince Charming. But what they left out of that fairy tale is—that the sleeping Princess—had—nightmares. Caused by the Wicked Witch—namely—Clara. Horrible, horrible nightmares, in which the Princess—behaves in ways—totally foreign to her nature, and—oh dear! Please, Toby, don't make me explain all that! And—and let's go back in now—or Papa will be furious! It's awfully late and he—"

"All right, dearest," Tobias said.

And it was then, at that precise instant of meaningless, perhaps nonexistent time, that in the courtyard below, they heard the whirring of the Pierce Arrow's starter. The motor caught, roared into life. The big car lurched forward, gathered speed. Poured itself through the castle's gates.

"Angie!" Tobias projected his thoughts furiously. "Where in all hell do you think you're going at this time of night?"

But the Angel didn't answer him. Not even in thought.

Lying there on his bed in the guest room Tobias Tobit simply could not sleep. He was being battered from two directions at once by concurrent contradictions. By two hauntingly lovely contradictions one of whom was named Clara and the other Sara. Who, between them, were tearing apart his being, heart and mind.

Because the problem at hand didn't boil down to anything so simple as to whether Sara (*Why* had he chosen her? Why?) or her sister, Clara, was lying about her mutually despised twin, or even as to which of them was—or was the *more*—insane. Clara, after all, had admitted to a touch of madness. And Sara's behavior—too brittle and too bright—hinted clearly at some inner stress, some close-to-the-breaking-point neurotic strain. Two gloriously lovely mad women. Twins. His cousins. And he, God help him, was in love with *both* of them.

Nor was *that* the worst aspect of his dilemma. The worst aspect, actually, was how that evening had disturbed his, Tobias Tobit's, special set of realities—borrowed from an Angel. Or from a figment of his own distorted mind.

What was reality, anyhow? A baby girl-child's obscenely stinking corpse with those vile and greedy carrion birds, beaking out her eyes? The corpse of the *wrong* baby girl? Or of a girl who was—according to Sara, anyhow—very much alive? But he had seen that. He had. He had!

A hairy monster far older than twelve years of age—except, of course, for his face, his eyes—incestuously coupling with—whom? With which one of the twins? In the tower room. In that tower room neither of them could possibly have entered because the stairway was bricked up and had been since Emma Schloss died, *years* before the Tobits had bought the castle.

A hairy monster who, Ralph Tobit said, quietly, honestly, truthfully, had died at age twelve. Of spinal meningitis.

But he, Tobias Tobit, had seen that, too. He had. He had.

Clara Tobit had kissed him with unfeigned passion, with mature sensuality, with considerable, diabolically practiced art. Yet evil, foul-mouthed, slatternly Sal, midwife and tavern wench—hardly a one to be charitable!—had remarked with the casual lack of emphasis of plain, accepted fact that Clara Tobit bore a spotless reputation in East Egypt, a town too small for anyone's behavior to escape endless scrutiny.

Sara Tobit, on the other hand, had kissed him in a manner both virginal, and shy. With slow, sweet, crippling tenderness. And yet—

That voice from the other bathroom. That nasal twanging Kentucky mountain woman's voice, accusing poor Sara (his promised, now, his beloved!) of both sexual promiscuity and multiple murder. And if the woman, according to Sara, was Clara's most faithful partisan, he had to admit that Sara's defense of her own behavior had been more than slightly lame: That she didn't *know* whether she had gone to bed with, or had merely murdered, her seven suitors, or both. She didn't—couldn't—*remember* what had actually happened. She *believed* herself incapable of killing. *As far as she knew,* no man had ever touched her lissome flesh.

Dear God! What *was?* And what was not? Dead Nancy? Dead Hattie? Dying Anne? Were there any such women? Had there ever been?

Sister L'Amour? Conchita? Roxane? *Were* they? Did they live? Did *anyone* live? Or were all human beings but momentary flickering dreams in the mind of the Creator, as Angie swore they were? *Bad* dreams, at that. And history, destiny, man's fate—but obscene cosmic jokes? Graffiti scratched on Olympian lavatory walls by ribald and drunken gods?

Angie—if he existed—warped sequence. Destroyed the very concepts of temporality and tridimensional space. Let Tobias see what was, had been, would be; guarded him, Tobias Tobit, through all past, present, future aeons of nonlineal coexistent, nonexistent time.

Or—Angie didn't exist and everything was mist and dark and dream and there was no such thing as reality and he, Tobias Tobit, was—like *all* the Tobits—mad.

Thinking that—alone in that dreadful room in that transplanted hulk of a castle—Tobias buried his face into his pillow, rooting back into prenatal mindlessness, into the warm womb/tomb of before being, reason, responsibility, fear.

Or tried to. It didn't work. He surfaced into awareness once more. Twisted his head to stare wide-eyed into an inner space teeming with horrors. Shut tight the eyes of his mind against them. Bent his head.

And cried.

Seventeen

And, as if in answer to his hoarse-voiced, half-strangled, male-animal sobbing, Nancy came out of the solid stone wall before him and stood there staring at him with dead eyes. At first, she was entirely transparent. He could see the wall behind her. Then she began to solidify a little. She was naked except for whatever rags of clothing the hoboes had left on her, and great globs of blood and semen trailed slowly down the insides of her thighs. More globs of the same concrete evidence of those human animals' inhuman bestiality and lust stole down out of both corners of her mouth, and out of her anus which she was still transparent enough for him to see.

She was beginning to rot in places. Several large maggots worked busily at her navel. One protruded from her left nostril. When she opened her mouth to speak to him, he could see that it was crammed full of fat, blind, loathsome, crawling things, so that whatever she had intended to say to him came out as a muffled soup-sound, as obscene as it was unbearable.

She stood there gazing at him with eyes that either no longer had any pupils, or that were rolled so far upward that the pupils didn't show. She didn't move. She simply stayed where she was and froze Tobias Tobit to the ultimate incorporeality of the imaginary essence of the supposed soul he wasn't even sure he had.

Then Hellcat Hattie McCoy came out of the floor, rising up out of a pool, a fountain of blood that was spraying out of all the hundreds of machinegun bullet holes she had in her. She had a hard time standing up, probably, he realized, because that many heavy-caliber bullets must, in fact had to, have broken all her bones. But she managed it finally, and stood there smiling at him from around the end of a big black cigar whose smell was the prototype of utter vileness. By its eerie glow, he could see, with a gut-ripping stab of sadness that her smile was forlorn and gallant and tender, and that the way her lips were trembling in her efforts to maintain it, was causing the great bloody tears bisecting and clinging to the corners of her mouth to quiver, break free, flash ruby fire, and fall . . .

And, with no break in the sequence, Anne came strolling through the opened window, which, since the guest room was on the third floor of the castle, meant that she must have been walking on thin air at least forty feet above the courtyard. She had a monster in her arms. A huge, slimy, blood-covered baby monster. She was crooning to it tenderly. But Tobias couldn't hear her either. He had not yet mastered the art of communicating with the dead. But now, looking down a little, he could see her belly had been ripped open from navel to crotch, and that her guts were spilling out of it.

When he saw that, he opened his mouth to scream.

But, before he could get the scream out, he became aware of still another presence in that bedroom. Turning, he saw a woman standing behind him. A stranger. A woman he had never seen before in all his life. He didn't know how he knew that she was a stranger since her head had been crushed in so far by some huge and heavy object —a stone, he guessed—that the top of her skull coincided with her eyebrows, and both her eyes lay on her cheeks like malevolent, bloody onions, on fresh, and dripping strings.

And then he did scream. The sound of it went echoing through the castle eerily, terribly, making the windows rattle and his own eardrums ache. He screamed again and again and again, mad with utter terror. He only stopped it when Anne, or Hattie, or both, reached up pitying hands and pulled the night down over his head.

He came thrashing upward through a trillion aeons of utter dark. Opened his mouth to scream again, to say—

What? He did not, would never know. For there was a softness covering his mouth, a warm, sweet-sighing softness, pressing against his gaping terror, drawing it out of him, open-lipped on his mouth, osculant, adhesive, moist, exploring, until his arms came up and locked themselves about her. Then she drew back enough to whisper:

"A—nightmare, darling?"

"Yes," Tobias groaned. "Or a whole flock of them. Don't go, Sara! Stay with me, please!"

"I mean to," she said gently. "At least until you've calmed down. But first, we'd better lock the door."

"Why?" Tobias said.

"If Papa heard you, he'll come up here to see what's wrong. If he does—tell him without getting up that you were dreaming. I *have* to stay here until I'm sure everyone's gone back to sleep. Or else the chances are I'll run into Papa, or Mama, or Ha—or Martin, in the corridor. And—and they just might think . . ."

"Oh," Tobias said then. "Oh, my God!"

"I shouldn't care, particularly," Sara said with grave tenderness, "except that I shouldn't want my—our—wedding spoiled. Of course, shotgun marriages are a commonplace hereabouts, but—"

"Sssssh!" Tobias hissed. "Somebody's coming!"

She skipped from the bed in a flash of white. As she crossed the casement window, of that medieval type called an Oriel, Tobias saw that she hadn't taken time to put on a robe. Her nightdress was like a mist of moonlight, her body, within it, a silver flame. Then she disappeared into the shadows. Tobias heard the huge armoire's doors open, then close.

"She'll stifle in there!" he thought, but he hadn't time for more, because Ralph Tobit's voice came through the door, vibrant with concern—and with something else, something close to actual fear.

"Tobias, my boy," he said; "what's wrong?"

"A—a nightmare, sir," Tobias said, raising his voice just enough to be heard without strain through that heavy door. "Sara—was telling me—about hers, earlier, tonight—that she often had them, I mean—and I guess the idea stuck. I've—been reliving my sins, sir! And paying for them, too! But don't worry—I'm all right now—"

"I'll have Martin bring you up a nightcap. A hot toddy, say—to soothe your nerves. This old heap of ours takes some getting used to, doesn't it? Oh, I say! You've locked the door!"

Tobias got up then, at once, and opened it. He was conscious as he did so, how that damnable perfume of Sara's lingered on the air. But most people, he reasoned, didn't notice a scent they smelled every day. And, anyhow, he had to risk it. If he even hesitated too long in opening up, Ralph's suspicions were sure to become aroused.

"Been sleeping in too many hotel rooms lately," he said, with a rueful smile. "Sort of got into the habit of locking myself in. Some of the fleabags I was forced to stop at on my way here really didn't inspire too much confidence. Please—don't get poor Martin up. I've the regulation hip flask typical of today's flaming youth! I'll take a snort from that, sir. And I must say, I'm dreadfully sorry to have disturbed you!"

" 'S all right," Ralph Tobit said. "By the way, Martin tells me that your man took your car to look for Merton. No problem, yet. Seems his wife felt a twinge or two. I've two of our most reliable women sitting with her—though that took some doing. They usually go home nights—their theory being—the superstitious fools—that the castle's haunted. . . ."

"I'd agree with them," Tobias paused for a just right wry chuckle. "Except for the fact that all the spooks I dreamed about were all my own. Seem to have followed me here. . . . Well, good night, sir. I promise you I won't yell my head off any more tonight!"

"If you feel like it, do. It sometimes helps," Ralph Tobit said.

Tobias waited until he heard his host's footsteps die away before crossing to the armoire and opening it. In his haste, born of an especially bitter childhood memory of having accidentally been locked in one of the damned things, himself, he forgot to lock the guest bedroom's massive door again. But his concern proved not ill-founded, for as he jerked open the armoire, Sara all but fell out of it into his arms.

"Oh Toby!" she gasped, "I—I'm so dizzy! So—faint. There was no air at all in there and—"

He crossed to the bed with her, laid her down upon it, began to chafe her wrists, her arms.

"Open—the window, dearest," she whispered, "it's—stuffy in here. . . ."

He went to the bay window and opened it. Moonlight flooded through the opened casements, silvering all the room.

He tiptoed back to that vision on his bed.

She put up white arms to him. "Kiss me, Toby," she said.

He kissed her. A long time. And very thoroughly. With great tenderness, but also with considerable skill.

She tore her mouth from his and looked at him. Her eyes were —strange. They had grown much lighter in color. They seemed to glow in the darkness. Her hair seemed much lighter, too.

"Effect of the moonlight," he thought, but a feeling of unease stole through him. He stared at her. Then it hit him.

"Clara!" he said.

"No!" she said bitterly. "Don't let her—invade me, Toby! She's *bad.* Wicked. She wants me—to do—*that.* To make—love. To love you—with my body. I'm—Sara, Toby. A good girl. A decent girl. I—I'll let you, after we're married. But now, no. Please no, Toby? Please?"

He went on staring at her. *"Who* are you?" he said.

"Sara," she whispered. "We really are identical, you know. I—put stuff in my hair—a kind of colored powder to make it darker. But I brush it out at night. I—tried a dye once, but it looked *awful!* The powder's good. And I wear dark blue a lot—to make my eyes look a deeper blue than hers. But nobody can tell us apart. Not even Papa. Don't you believe me, Toby? Clara's—down there in the village, damn her! Only—she—she's trying to—to get into my body now—"

"How?" Tobias said.

"Don't know. But when she does, she—she makes me *do* things. Like this!" She pushed her hand inside his pajama top. Ran it over his chest. Her touch was maddening. He twisted sidewise so that she wouldn't see what was happening to him.

She brought her hand down slowly over his lean, in-hollowed belly.

"How—hairy are you?" she said softly. "Just like a monkey—or a bear!"

Then she kissed him. Clung that great wide wonderful mouth to his, played braille games with soft hot wet lips and tongue tip. Buried her face into his neck, whispered:

"Please don't take my nightgown off, Toby. Don't. I beg you not to. Please."

He had not so much as touched that moon mist of a nightdress with his fingertips. But now, of course, he did. She struggled briefly, feebly, then lay back and let him bare her body to the moon.

Her eyes were star sapphires. They were wide and soft and crystalline and very far away.

"Don't—make love to me, Toby," she said in an odd, brittle tone of voice. "I'm a good girl. A—a virgin. You—you'll—hurt me. You'll make me—bleed!"

He bent to her. She twisted her mouth away. Grated into his ear: "Don't—kiss my breasts. Please don't, Toby! That's—wicked. That's what—Clara—likes! Ah! Ahhhh!—Sweet! Don't, Toby. Please don't, Toby—I beg you—Toby! Please, please, please . . ."

He smiled grimly. "Play games with me, will you?" he thought.

"And—don't—touch me—down there. Don't. Or—or—kiss my belly. Or—Don't! Don't! Don't!"

He tore his pajamas off. Crushed her to him. Played with her. Kissed her. All over. She did not fight or push him away. She embraced him, caressed him, kissed him. But all the time she was crying, beseeching, begging: "Don't! Don't! Don't!"

To test her, he stopped abruptly. Rolled away from her.

At once her hands were wild on his body, clawing him, bloody-nailed, digging into his flesh, dragging him to her, writhing against him, while her hot wet salt mouth kept babbling:

"Don't, Toby! Please don't! Don't make love to me! It's wicked! It's bad! People—shouldn't—do this! Besides your—your *thing*'s too big, Toby! It'll hurt—hurt—hurt—make me bleed! Oh. Oh. Ohhhhhh—my darling. Oh, my love. My dearest, dearest love! But stop now, Toby. Don't ruin me. Don't—shame me. Don't make love to me. Make love to—Clara. She *likes* it. She—*loves* it! She—"

"But—" he got out. "Clara isn't here. She's—"

She turned her tear-glazed eyes to him. Smiled at him. It was the most pitiful smile he had ever seen. The most macabre.

"Yes, she is!" she said; then her voice changed completely, became a harsher, warmer, contralto sound. Became—he would have staked his heart upon it!—Clara's own.

"Yes, I am!" Clara's voice purred into his ear. "Right here with you, you sweet ol' longtall Yankee hounddog you! Now quit foolin' around. Get busy, will you? Do it to me, honey. Do it to me, hard!"

It was like nothing he had ever experienced before, nothing he'd even imagined. His dazed, bruised, assaulted mind, a prey to his body's sensations, fought for even a marginal, momentary clarity, a hiatus long enough to define this naked oestrual fury, this outright attack upon him, upon his manhood, by this writhing, gyrating, grinding, pounding, already sweat-drenched maenad, this screaming Astarte with cruel, flagellant thighs, who was—unbelievably—converting sex into torture, making it perverse, sadistic, obscene.

And—hateful.

So hateful that his own response was slowed to what was in him, at least, an unprecedented degree. He lay there all but frozen until she had three times curdled the blood in his veins with absolutely *the* foulest language he had ever heard issue from a human mouth, as her slender form, after incredibly brief intervals of comparative quietude, jerked, like a demented spastic's, with visible, awful violence through what seemed to him utterly algolagnic, truly destructive orgasms, before he was able to reach his own—become for him equally hateful—relief.

He lay there beside her, fighting for life, for breath. Saw, before he had entirely won either, her sit up suddenly, grope for her nightdress, find it, draw it with perfect grace over her fair head. Smooth it down around her matchless body.

Then slowly, gently, with aching tenderness, she bent and kissed his mouth. Drew back, smiled at him through the tears that were pouring down her cheeks.

"Thank you Toby, dearest," the voice of Sara said.

"Thank me?" he got out. "Good God, Cla—Sara, for what?"

"For being a gentleman. For not taking advantage of me. You could have, you know—and you—didn't. You won't be sorry, dearheart! I—I'll make it up to you on our wedding night!"

He lay there staring at her. And what got into him then was very bad. A coldness. A—horror. Because she wasn't lying. Nor pretending. As far as she was concerned, nothing had happened. They hadn't made love. She was—Sara. A good girl. Perfectly entitled to wear white on her wedding day.

He wondered, suddenly, if Clara did this, too. Projected the ardent nature she could neither bear nor face off upon her hated twin? Made of her the ritual fetish-idol upon whom to hang her never-to-be-acknowledged carnality?

He doubted it. Clara had impressed him as being—straighter, somehow. More basically honest. She had kissed him with frank passion that first day. While Sara's shy, girlish kiss had been—like everything else about her—a lie.

No. That was wrong. Not a lie. A denial. A refusal to look life in the face. Pity tore him. Maybe, he thought, once married to me, she'll no longer have to pretend, so—

But he knew it wouldn't work out like that. This neurosis—no, this psychosis—was far too deep. And yet, he had pledged his word. So now to keep that pledge. To link his life—with horror.

"Good night, darling!" Sara said, and kissed him, gently, sweetly, shyly. "Lord, I'm tired! Don't have any *more* nightmares, will you dearest?"

"I won't," Tobias said, and watched the stunning grace with which she swung her long, beautiful legs down from the bed. He lay there, utterly fascinated by her floating, gliding walk—so different from Clara's taut, controlled style of moving—as she crossed to the door. Then she paused.

Stopped. A shiver went through her. A harsh, throaty laugh burst from her mouth, a sound utterly unlike the sunny, girlish gurgle of her normal laughter.

"The hell with this noise!" she said in a voice that was sensuality's very self. "Li'l Clara wants more!"

She reached down for the hem of her nightdress, raked it up over her head in one wild sweep. Hurled it to the floor. Came back to the bed.

"Move over, Toby love," she laughed, "and make room for li'l Clara! Clara, the nympho! *Never* gets enough! So I hope you're long-winded—'cause if you aren't—"

He hung there, staring at her. Multiple images formed behind his eyes: Clara before the one-room schoolhouse; Sara putting out her hand to him before dinner. So alike—and yet, so different. So very different. And this one *was* Clara! She was! She was!

"What's the matter, Tobe?" she mocked, those Norse goddess's eyes alight with devilish glee. "Don't tell poor li'l hard-up, hot-natured *me* you're tired! No matter—your li'l Clara girl knows lots o' tricks!"

She pushed him over onto his back with a stiff-armed thrust that any varsity halfback would have envied. Stretched out full length atop him, flesh glued to flesh. Kissed him. Drew back. Grinned at him. Said:

"Open up, Tobe baby, 'n let Mama swab your tonsils for you!"

She went on "soul," "deep," "French" kissing him. Pushed her left hand down between them and toyed with his sex. When his detumescence—caused far more by shock, by confusion, than by fatigue—was overcome, she rose up, straddled him; then, closing her eyes, and drawing in through the horizontally flattened, slightly opened "O" of her lips a long long long endlessly unbroken soft fluting sighing whistling inhalation of ecstatic breath that was voluptuousness's very self, and the most completely *female* sound he had ever heard, she lowered herself—with an almost infinite, deliberately controlled slowness, designed, he was sure, to prolong to the utmost what obviously was to her a peculiarly exquisite pleasure—upon him, engorging his rigid and penetrant maleness, until she was entirely seated, fully impaled; and then, after luxuriating in what must have been a kind of autoravishment, an unbreathing, enraptured stillness, eyes shut and slack mouthed, the whole of her surrendered to interior, purely narcissistic sensations that excluded him almost wholly, at long last, and finally, she began to move.

She opened her eyes, grinned at him. A gamine's grin, replete with mischief and delight.

"Damn, but you're dumb, Tobe baby!" she chuckled, employing that droll, self-edited version of a Kentucky mountain accent, which she—if she *were* Clara; for, by this time, his confusion was total—as the most highly educated member of the family, should have been the last to use.

"Am I?" he said, noting without pleasure that the coldness in him, the utter horror, at least served to permit him the retention of easy sensatory and neural control. "Am I, Sara—I mean Clara?"

"Ho!" she hooted merrily. "Don't you go and get me mixed up with Sary—th' poor, miserable, frustrated li'l bitch! Keeps her tail in th' ice-box, Tobe-boy, for fear some hot'n lovin' fella'll thaw it out for her one day! But 'pears to me I gotta learn you an awful lot 'bout beddin', lover! 'Cause you ain't got idea *one,* have you, baby-boy?"

"This game must be played out, wherever it leads," Tobias thought, "for, at least, afterwards, I'll know, I'll know—"

"Guess not," he said in a tone of voice whose forced, faked cheerfulness all but choked him; "but I'm a doggoned willing pupil, if you want to teach me, Clara-doll. . . ."

"Right. And I'm a first-class schoolmarm, and don't you forget it! Reckon I've taught mannish tricks to every boy-child over fourteen years old 'twixt here and the blue-grass country—"

She felt him freeze, sensed him sicken. Bent, swooping like a swan, all boneless grace, and found his mouth.

"That's a lie, Tobe-baby," she murmured against it; "a goddamn stupid lie. Don't even know why I said that, nohows. 'Sides—" she chuckled, between huge, slow, wet, lazy kisses, "you were plain downright jackassical to believe it! How long you think I'd have kept my job, if I'd have tried *that* even oncet? Why th' *first* li'l horny bastid would've gone braggin' his fool head off all over th' damn' county if I'd even so much as touched his pore li'l puny pecker accidental like with my hand! Or don't you know *anything* 'bout menfolks, which boy-children *is,* seein' as how you're one? Kind of, sort of, anyhow?"

"Only sort of?" he grinned, relief in him like a sunburst, warming the very cockles of his heart, knowing that now, at last, she had told him the truth, even about her hated sister, the twin, who to her, was clearly almost a second self.

"Only kind of, sort of!" she laughed, and straightening up gave a boneless, spineless, unbelievably sensuous doubly sidewise slow writhe and wiggle, then ended it with a viciously abrupt, almost flagellate, pelvic roll and snap that moved past titillation into actual pain.

"Why goddddamn!" he howled. "What're you trying to do? Maim me?"

She smiled at him, those Aesir eyes light filled and dancing.

"Jes' thought I'd break it off short 'n keep it for a souvenir!" she mocked. "Ah g'wan, Tobe! Doan tell me Mama done hurt her baby boy?"

"Lord, but you're the limit," he said.

"I know. And yore a mighty pore excuse for a man. But I reckon I can learn you. Now put your hands up. Both of 'em. So's you can play with my tits whilst we're doin' it."

"Like this?" he whispered.

"Yep. Only squeeze 'em for me, Tobe, hon. Li'l Clara purely *loves* havin' her tits squoze. . . ."

He obeyed her instructions, humbly, worshipping her milky flesh with adoring hands.

"No! Not like that! Squeeze 'em hard! Make 'em hurt *good,"* she said.

Twice more during that long night she reached for him. Went to sleep finally, curled warmly, wetly, into all his hollows. That perfume of hers almost choked him. Mingled with her sweat and his, and all their other carnal odors.

Then sunlight was pouring through that Oriel window and blinding him. But it wasn't the light that had awakened him. He was dismally sure of that. He turned—a feat that cost him considerable effort, due consideration being given to the stranglehold she still had around his neck—and stared at the door.

Ralph Tobit stood in it. His face was grey. And utterly weary.

"You little bitch!" he said quietly. "I should have had you spayed long ago!"

"Mister—Tobit—" Tobias got out, "I—"

"Shut up, you horny young scoundrel!" Ralph Tobit said. "Get up, both of you. And get dressed. You've got five minutes. No more!"

"Papa—" the voice of Sara said, crying now. "Don't be angry! Don't be angry please! I—I had one of—of my bad dreams. Walked in my sleep. But—but nothing happened. I swear it! Toby didn't—didn't *touch* me! He was—a perfect gentleman! Weren't you, Toby, dearest?"

"Oh Jesus!" Tobias said. "Look, sir, I asked you for her hand. And I—I meant it. Anytime you say I—we—"

"We can discuss that later," Ralph Tobit said, and Tobias was sure he had never heard so much weariness in a human voice. "Though I suppose the two of you deserve each other. But right now, there's no time. Get up, both of you. And get dressed. You see, the police are here. They want to talk to all of us—but especially to the two of you, since these damned people of mine, who've got tongues loose on both ends and hinged in the middle!, told them you were up on the battlements last night. . . ."

"The—the *police,* Papa?" Sara got out.

"Yes. Somebody—murdered Mildred Sloames. Last night. Crushed her head in with a rock. Which conceivably could have been thrown—or dropped—from the battlements. Because the body was found just below. Here, on our grounds."

"Ohhhh Pa-pa!" Sara wailed.

He stared at her bleakly. "I wouldn't have the luck for them to hang you for it, Sara," he said. "Now goddamnit, you young fools, get dressed and come on!"

Eighteen

"I was asleep," Edna Tobit said. "I heard nothing. I didn't leave my room all night. May I go back to it, now, please?"

The two men from the county sheriff's office looked at each other. Then the big one, the one with ice-blue eyes and a belly hanging over his belt, said:

"Yes'm, Miz Tobit. Reckon you might as well. 'Taint likely *you* had anything to do with it. Sorry we had to bother you this way, ma'am."

" 'S all right, officer," Edna Tobit said and got up. She crossed the room. But when she got to where Sara sat, looking absurdly small and forlorn and lost in her out-of-season quilted bathrobe, she stopped.

"Who let Harold out, Sara?" she said. *"You?"*

"Ma-ma!" Sara wailed.

"Who's Harold, ma-am?" the little deputy Sheriff said. The thin, dark, too-quick one. With eyes like a ferret's—or a fox's, Tobias thought.

"My son," Edna said calmly. "He's crazy, officer. They've got him locked in the tower room. He howls at night sometimes, and won't let me sleep."

"Do he—kill folks, ma-am?" the big, fat sheriff's deputy said.

"Why yes. As a matter of fact he's a homicidal maniac," Edna said. "And a sex fiend. He raped my daughter, Clara, once. Before we could stop him. He's very strong. And hairy. And stinks something awful."

"Ma-ma!" Sara moaned.

"Go to your room, Edna," Ralph Tobit said.

"All right," Edna Tobit said. " 'Bye bye, all."

"Mister Tobit," the fat deputy said, "I reckon hit's clear to one 'n all that yore missus ain't right in th' haid. But all th' same, there's a dead woman out there longside that there drawbridge o' yourn where she's gotta stay, pore critter, 'til the county coroner gits heah. So I hopes you won't mind tellin' us 'bout this heah boy o' yourn. Harold, yore missus called him, didn't she, now?"

"Not at all. I—we—did have a son named Harold, sheriff," Ralph said. "But what my wife forgets, or rather refuses to remember, is that he died when he was only twelve years old. Of cerebro-spinal meningitis. You can find a copy of the death certificate in the county coroner's office, since the poor child died *here.* Signed not by this man, Harris—I believe?—but by one of his predecessors in the office, a man named Sloames. A relative of the dead woman, as a matter of fact. Or rather of her late husband's, I should have said."

"Ol' Doc Sloames," the fat Deputy said. " 'Members him well. Deaf as a gatepost 'n damn' near blind, to boot. . . ." He looked at his partner uneasily.

"But what about that 'ere howlin' noise yore missus claims she hears?" the thin, dark deputy said.

Ralph Tobit looked at him. With the exact expression that most people look upon noisome insects and venomous snakes, Tobias thought.

"Come with me, both of you!" he rapped out.

The two deputies exchanged glances.

"Oh, for God's sake!" Ralph Tobit said. "Neither my daughter nor her fiancé is likely to run away, gentlemen! Not with their wedding ceremony set for tomorrow. Besides, they can come along, if you like!"

"They'd better!" the fat one growled.

Walking along beside Sara, a little behind Ralph Tobit and the fat Deputy Sheriff, but before the thin one, which, he realized, was no accident at all, hot rebellion tore Tobias' mind, his heart.

"Got me tagged as the murderer, already, haven't you, you damned country jakes? A stranger. A 'furriner,' as you'd put it. And a damn Yankee to boot! And you, Cousin Ralph—have found your perfect solution, haven't you? Unload your nymphomaniac of a daughter—who somehow found the means to shut Milly Sloames up forever before she could tell what she knew—off on me! A multiple murderess. A female sex fiend. And—"

Then he felt Sara's eyes upon him. They were softly glowing. They were also filled with tears.

"Please, Cousin Toby," she whispered. "Don't think that. What you're thinking now. Please."

"And what am I thinking, my dearest Sara?" he said with icy calm.

All the more icy because his insides were quivering like a bowl of gelatin.

"That I'm—wicked. Bad. And that *I* killed poor Milly," Sara said.

The little ferret-eyed deputy moved up closer. Let him! Tobias thought.

"Well?" he said.

"You *know* where I was last night," Sara said. "With you. *All* night. Doing what we shouldn't have. What *she*—Clara—made me do. Before that on the battlements. Again—with you. The only way I could have killed poor Milly from there was to have dropped that rock on her head. At ten o'clock at night. After it was too dark for me to even *see* anybody down below. . . ."

"Or for me!" Tobias thought. Then another thought hit him. He slowed, drawing a floor plan of the castle's layout in his head.

"Can the drawbridge be seen from the battlements?" He asked. "No! That's not what I mean! Could anybody drop a stone onto it —or close to it—from the battlements? Seems to me that would be awfully hard to do. . . ."

"Not hard," Sara said. "Impossible. You see it's right in front of the tower. Oh! Oh, Toby! You've done it! You've just *proved* that neither you nor I—"

"Ssssh! Don't say anything else, darling!" Tobias said.

"Yes I will!" she said in an oddly broken tone of voice, "but not now. Not here. To you. And to Papa. What's got to be said. What *I* have to say, or I'll never be able to—to live with myself again."

"What y'alls sayin' " the thin, dark deputy said, "is that not neither one of y'all kilt Milly Sloames. That there wuzn't no way y'all could of. Then, tell me sumpin, Mister Furrin Fella, if you please, who th' hell *did?"*

"Damned if I know," Tobias said easily. "As a matter of fact, officer, we didn't even know she was dead, until you and your skinny friend came and told us. . . ."

The dark, thin deputy loosed a dry chuckle.

"Sho hauls a whole lot o' meat around with him, ol' Bill do, 'n that's a fact," he said. "To tell the truth about it, mister, neither did *we* when we come up heah—"

"What!" Tobias began, but Ralph Tobit's voice cut him off.

"Here we are. This, Officer Hendricks, is the stairway leading to the tower. The *only* stairway. And it's been this way since *before* we bought the castle. Old Schloss had this done. As a native of these parts, I'm sure you must know the reason. . . ."

"Yep," Deputy Sheriff Hendricks, the outsized officer, said. "His ol' lady, Emmy Schloss. Throwed herself from that winder up theah. Glad you showed us this, Mister Tobit, sir. Thet th' stairway's *still* bricked up, I mean. 'Cause I reckon that proves—"

"That neither Sara nor I *could* have killed Mildred Sloames, Officer!" Tobias said crisply. "We were up on the ramparts—the battlements—until about ten-thirty last night. If Mrs. Sloames were killed by a heavy object dropped on her head—the official theory, I believe—it would have had to have been dropped from the tower window, or from that tree that juts out a little below it, if her body is where you say it is, near the drawbridge. Which means that it had to be dropped by a creature who has learned to live without either water, or food. Or one who knows how to fly. By the way, did you find the object that crushed the poor creature's head in?"

Deputy Sheriff Hendricks stared at this glib, talkative damn Yankee with noticeable, even obvious, distaste.

"No," he said. "To tell the honest truth, we didn't. . . ."

"Another thing," Tobias said, fully in command now, and even more fully enjoying that, for him, unusual experience, up to and including the look of grudging respect in Ralph Tobit's eyes; "how did you *know* she was there? *We* didn't. It's an awfully long way from here to the village, Officer—Hendricks, I believe the name is?"

"Tha's right," Hendricks said. "Fact is, Mister—?"

"Tobit. Tobias Tobit. A—cousin," Tobias said.

"Yep. Got th' family look, ain't you?" Hendricks said, and won some ground back again. "Th' fact is that we didn't know about pore Milly when we started out. Thet ain't why we come—"

"Then why did you?" Ralph Tobit said, sharply.

"Complaint o' Ridley Tyler. Y'all know *him.* Keeps th' tavern down th' road apiece. Swore thet a big, light-haired furrin' fella—a chauffeur—drives a limousine—big flossy cyah with headlights built into th' front mud guards—fer somebody stoppin' up heah—"

"Me," Tobias said at once. "My chauffeur, Angie. And my car, a Pierce Arrow. Go on, sheriff, please."

"Ol' Ridley charges thet yore chauffeur dragged his ol' woman off by main force. Sez th' she'd done 'lowed she weren't gonna attend no witch woman's birthin'—which 'cording to her—Sal Tyler, I mean—yore chauffeur's ol' woman *is.* An' this heah chauffeur o' yourn got mad 'n—"

He stopped short, halted in midflight by the heavy irony in Tobias' smile.

"Officer Hendricks," Tobias said quietly, "was Ridley Tyler *at home,* when all this happened?"

"Yep. Leastwise, 'cording to him, he wuz. 'N—Goddamn! C'mon, Tim!"

"C'mon where?" the little dark deputy said. Then: "Lawd God! We's been sold a bill o' goods, ain't we? Never stopped to figger thet ain't *nobody* gonna carry Sal off by main force long as that jealous fool o' a Ridley was to home! With *seven* shotguns, a deer rifle, a hawg-killin' knife, not t' mention—"

"That woodsman's broad axe of his," Tobias suggested quietly. "By the way, you'd better have a look at that axe. See whether it hasn't some blood, and hair—woman's hair—and even some human brains on the blunt end of it. If it does, you can consider the case of Mildred Sloames closed . . ."

"But—but—" Bill Hendricks spluttered, "why th' livin' hell would ol' Ridley kill Milly Sloames? Ain't no bad blood twixt th' Sloameses 'n th' Tylers, fur as I ever heard . . ."

"Don't know. My guess is that she saw something, or heard something that Ridley didn't want her spreading all over from East Egypt to Lexington and all points in between," Tobias said. "Such as, for instance, what *really* became of Sal Tyler. Or, better still, you might ask yourselves *why* Ridley Tyler sent you up here. So that you'd find poor Mrs. Sloames's body, wasn't it? And go baying off on a false scent. A very false scent—"

"I git it," Hendricks growled. "Ol' Ridley wuz fixin' up a smart cover-up, 'cause—Lawd Gawd! Tim, you reckon thet damn fool got likkered up 'n *actually* kilt pore Sal? Like he's been a-threatenin' to, fer years?"

" 'N Milly saw him do it. Accidental. 'Cause she'n Sal wuz

friendly, sort of," Tim said. "Yore daughter Miss Clara, too, Mister Tobit. Always swore that Sal wuz to wash her filthy hide she'd be a mighty nice woman . . ."

"But one more thing, Young Mister Tobit," Hendricks said; "we wuz told that yore chauffeur fella wuz seen down in th' village last night in yore cyah, so—"

Tobias looked at the fat sheriff.

"I'll ring for him. Then you can question him about that," he said.

When Angie came into the living room, Tobias was shocked at his looks. It came to him then that if Angels had greater capacity for wisdom, life, joy, than men, they also had more for sorrow. Angie, Tobias saw, sensed, felt, was being literally torn apart by grief.

"She ain't got a chance!" Angie thought at him. "Not a chance, Toby, me boy! This damned auld jackass we've got downstairs knows less medicine than the inside o' me arsehole does! 'N that goddamn filthy slut o' a Sal wouldn't—"

Then he saw the two deputy sheriffs, and pulled himself together. Touched his forelock in fine old country style.

"Yessir, Young Master?" he said.

"These gentlemen," Tobias said quietly, "want to ask you some questions, Angie. I charge you to answer them truthfully, and to hold nothing back. I charge you upon what you hold most dear—"

"Which is me Annie's life!" Angie said with a strangled sob. "Right, sir! I swear t' tell th' truth, th' whole truth 'n nothin' but th' truth! I'm at your disposition, gentlemen!"

It was quickly done. Yes, Angie declared, he *had* gone to the tavern looking for Sal to come to attend his wife who was entering into labor. What happened? Sal had refused to come on the score that Anne was a witch, and she didn't want to help deliver a witch's child. Had there been a quarrel? Yessir—a loud, profane, and prolonged quarrel, which was ended when Ridley Tyler shoved a double-barreled sixteen-gauge into his middle and put him off the place.

Had he gone? Yes. Taking Sal with him? Not on his life! That drunken crazy old coot up there would have killed him before permitting that. . . .

At this point, Tobias intervened. "May I suggest a question, Officer Hendricks?" he said.

"Why shore, son—I mean young Mister Tobit! Enything whut kin help us git to the bottom o' this we'd be mighty thankful for. Ax away!"

"Angie—" Tobias said, "when you came out the tavern, did you *see* anyone? Anyone else besides Sal and Ridley, I mean?"

"Yessir, Young Master," Angie said, "I saw Miss Sara's personal maid. Mrs. Sloames, I believe her name is."

"Lord Gawd!" Hendricks bellowed. " 'N where wuz she, young fella?"

"Sittin' in Miss Clara Tobit's car. A little red Studebaker roadster. All by herself, though. Miss Clara wasn't with her. Seemed to be waiting for Miss Clara though. . . ."

"How'd you know that, fella?" Tim, the other deputy, said.

"Because she wasn't behind the wheel, sir," Angie said. "Besides, does she know how to drive? Mighty few women do."

"Miss Clara is th' onliest one what do, hereabouts," Hendricks said. "Mighty smart li'l girl, Miss Clara—" Then seeing the face that Sara made, he added jovially, "You'n her oughta mek up, Miss Sara. Ain't right fer sisters to stay on th' outs so long. Well, that settles it. Me'n ol' Tim heah'll go 'n have another talk with Ridley. One thing though—I'd like to have young Mister Tobit's word thet he won't leave heah nor let his chauffeur fella leave neither 'til this heah is straightened up. . . . Wha's thet?"

Martin had come into the room.

"Doctor Harris is below," he said. "He says that you may—remove the body. He says the woman was killed—between twelve o'clock and five this morning. And that she *wasn't* killed here. Somebody brought—brought the corpse here—and dumped it. Those were his exact words."

"Now how'n hellfire would he know *thet?"* Hendricks bellowed.

"Took the precaution of awsking him that, sir!" Martin said. "He says, because of the blood. Had she been killed where she was found, there would have been a fair-sized pool of it beneath her head. And it seems that there wasn't. So Doctor Harris deduces that she was killed somewhere else, and that the corpse remained there long enough for the blood to congeal before—"

"Ugh!" Sara said.

"I quite agree, Miss Sara!" Martin said, then went on imperturbably. "For the blood to congeal before the cadaver was brought here. Of course there *was* some blood beneath the head, but not nearly enough, according to the good Doctor, not considering the extensive damage to the woman's cranium. . . ."

Tobias looked at Sara then. She didn't, he thought. Not this one —nor the others. She couldn't—just as she told the Sloames woman. And—the other? Aren't you indulging in a stupid male prejudice? So—she wasn't—virgin. So she's a bit of—of a nymphomaniac. And that's *bad?* When you've spent three quarters of your life surrounded by deep-frozen tails and moaning that there wasn't a piece to be had between wherever the hell you were and Lapland? This screwing spree Angie sent you on—you don't think that was *normal,* do you? Hell, it may all have been one of his out-sized illusions! If you checked back over the places you've been, would you find they existed? They or the girls you laid in those places? Figments of your distorted imagination. Stuff of your dreams. Or rather of your nightmares. Except—Anne, maybe. No. Not even excepting Anne. Because she's a *double* dream image. Yours *and* Angie's. Which makes her a *little* more real maybe. Oh Lord I—"

"Well, young fella?" Officer Hendricks said.

"What's that? Oh. Oh yes. You have my word. Neither Angie nor I will leave here 'til the case is settled," Tobias Tobit said.

After the two deputy sheriffs had gone, having promised to telephone Ralph Tobit if there were any interesting developments, that cool and distant gentleman turned to Tobias with a heavy sigh.

"Well, young fellow," he said, "you and I have some serious talking to do, I sadly fear. . . ."

Sara stood up then, but she didn't leave the room.

"No, you don't, Papa!" she said. "First, you're going to listen to me! You and Toby, both. I *won't* marry him. I simply won't. Nothing you or he could say or do would make me consent to being the bride at a shotgun wedding. You can—beat me to death, if you want to. Put me off the place—to starve. Commit me to an insane asylum, 'cause Lord knows proving that *any* Tobit's crazy is nobody's hard job! But marrying my cousin Toby is the one thing I will not do. I hope that's mighty clear!"

"Because—" Tobias said, and the pain in his voice was real, "you don't, or no longer love me, Sara?"

She looked at him, and now he saw that in clear daylight her eyes and Clara's were identical, just as she had said. But then they changed, hazed over, went huge and brilliant with a wash of tears.

"No," she whispered, "because—I do."

"Sara!" he said.

"Hear me out. I love a man who believes I am—a murderess and a whore. Who thinks—I tricked him last night. Came to his room—to—to seduce him—with pretense, with lies. Who won't believe the simple truth—"

"And what *is* that simple truth, daughter?" Ralph Tobit said. "That Tobias here respected your—alleged virtue—although you spent the night stark-naked in his arms?"

She bowed her head. Looked up again. Said: "No. Because *I* wouldn't let him respect it. I—I wanted him too damn bad, Papa—in the way any *real* woman wants her man. But all the same, it wasn't my fault, Papa! It wasn't!"

"Then whose fault was it, Sara?" her father said, "Tobias'?"

"No! Of course not! He didn't come to my room, Papa. I came to *his.*"

"So I *saw,*" Ralph Tobit said drily. "Go on, Sara. Explain to me how a piece of outrageously immoral behavior like *that* is not your fault!"

"It isn't, Papa. It's—Clara's."

"Clara's?" Ralph said.

"Yes. She—she gets—inside me. Transforms me. Turns me into —*her.* That's when I'm *bad,* Papa. That's when I do awful, lewd, wicked things."

"That's impossible!" Ralph Tobit said. "You know it's impossible, Sara! Do you want me to tell Tobias here *why* it's impossible?"

"No. Please don't. And besides, it's not impossible. Even—if Clara *were*—where you think she is, she *still* comes to me. Invades me. Changes me completely. Makes me—*her.*"

"But," Tobias protested, "even a foul-mouthed slattern like Sal swore that Clara has a spotless reputation in the village. And surely if there *were* anything—"

Sara turned on him. Her face was white with fury. "Go on down there, then! Marry *her!*" she said.

"No," Tobias said. "I don't love her. I love you."

She bowed her head. Her big, soft mouth pouted sullenly. "Fat lot of good it'll do you *now,*" she said.

Ralph Tobit said sharply, "You *admit* that you—that you were—well—intimate—with Tobias, here, last night?"

Sara bowed her head further still. "Yes, Papa," she whispered. "Only—it wasn't me—who did that, really. It—was Clara—inside my body, using it, for her pleasure. For her dirty, dirty pleasure. Now that—she hasn't got any body of her own. . . ."

Tobias stared at her. "And—why hasn't she?" he said.

" 'Cause she's dead. Didn't you know that?" Sara said.

"Now, really!" Tobias said. Then he saw Ralph Tobit's face. The expression on it stopped him. The terrible weariness. The utter despair.

"Cousin Ralph," he said then, his native, bone-deep kindly pity, sentimental folly, clad in its rusty armor, charging every windmill in sight, "I'll *still* marry her. Don't you see it's the best thing? To—to put it as delicately as I know how—might not the mere fact of her *having* a husband available tend to—to calm her? Keep her—impulses—somewhat satisfied and therefore under better control?"

Ralph stared at him. Sighed. "You *are* a gentleman, aren't you? And I must—reluctantly—give my consent. Not because of the *very* doubtful reasons you suggest but for a better, sadder one. Last night's affair wasn't planned. Not by *you* anyhow, of that I'm certain. So I'm quite sure you hadn't any—well—contraceptives—on hand. And surer still that you had no chance to use them if you had any. So we cannot rule out—pregnancy, can we?"

"Pa-pa!" Sara gasped, then: "Oh—I do hope I *am.* I'd be so happy! 'Specially if it's a boy. And—looks like Toby!"

Tobias smiled at her then. Sadly. "Then you *will* marry me?" he said.

"Of course not! Now that you've given me a baby, what do I need *you* for?"

"Maybe I haven't," Tobias said, "and besides, one's not enough. I was planning to give you a dozen!"

She stared at him. Then her lips spread slowly, slowly into a smile of pure sensuous delight.

"Will you?" she whispered. "Do you promise? Cross your heart and hope to die?"

"Cross my heart and hope to die!" Tobias said.

"Then I will marry you, after all, Toby, dearest," Sara said.

Tobias put out his arms to her. She came to him, kissed him, curled bonelessly up in his lap with her arms around his neck. Looked up at her father.

"You'll—arrange things, won't you, Papa? Call the Justice of the Peace—Mr. Wilkins—to come up here? This afternoon? So that—" she blushed vividly.

"So that, what?" Tobias teased.

"We can start on that dozen tonight!" fair Sara said.

"Why, you shameless baggage!" her father began, without real anger, Tobias was sure; but Martin came into the room and cut him off.

"Mr. Tobit, sir—" the butler said, then his voice choked up on him, drowned. And they saw that he was crying.

"Good Lord, Martin!" Ralph Tobit said.

"Sorry, sir! I'm a bit upset! Cawn't help it, sir! The—the sheriff's office just called. And, sir, the tavern keeper has confessed. He—he killed his wife. The woman Sal. In a drunken, jealous rage because she *admitted* she was in love with young Master Tobit's chauffeur, Angie. Threw her body into Emmy's Pool. And, just as young Master Tobit here guessed, Mildred Sloames accidentally *saw* him do it. So—to—to cover his tracks, he bashed poor Milly's head in with th' blunt side of his axe—And, sir—sir—!"

"Get a grip on yourself, Martin!" Ralph Tobit said.

"Yessir! He—he dragged her out of Miss Clara's little car to do it. And now—both the car and Miss Clara have disappeared! So now they think—they think—"

"What, Martin?" Tobias said then, sharply.

"That he—killed—poor Miss Clara, too!" the butler said.

Nineteen

Tobias Tobit lay there on the bed in the guest room. Physically, that was where he was, in any event. But mentally, spiritually—if those two words had or could be given meaning—he was an immeasurably great distance away from the demonstrably meaningless human concepts of here and now, wandering through a nightmare landscape whose nearer frontier was the loss of hope, and whose central regions were all bleak desolations, wild mountain ranges of utter grief and pain.

Because now he knew which of the twins he truly loved, knew it at long last, and fatally too late. That there was no actual proof as yet of Clara's death brought him no comfort at all. She had known both of the victims of that drunken, murderous madman; one of them had been a friend of hers; and this friend, partisan and supporter, namely Mildred Sloames, had been bludgeoned to death in or near her, Clara's, car. All of which led inescapably to the possibility—no, the probability, the quite appalling probability—that Clara, herself, had also been eliminated in one of Ridley Tyler's clumsy and stupid efforts to cover his tracks. And, to make matters worse—if worse were even possible—an hour ago, Hendricks had called again to say that the tire tracks of a small automobile had been found which led straight down into Emmy's Pool. And that they were dragging the Pool, now . . .

So, then, what to do? To live out his life as best he could—with Sara. "My bride-to-be!" he thought bitterly. "Soon my lawful, wedded wife, to love, honor and cherish, until death—or the lunatic asylum—do us part! Oh, Clara, Clara, my poor lost darling, forgive me, for I—"

Then one more memory hit him. He stopped short, realizing that metaphor was worse than inexact. It hadn't hit him, it had stabbed him. To his very guts, and with Laertes' poisoned blade.

Sara had said: "'Cause Clara hasn't any body of her own." Sara had said, in answer to his, "Why hasn't she?": "'Cause she's dead. Didn't you know that?"

"She's wrong!" he howled inside his mind, his heart. "How could she know a thing like that? That was *before* Martin had come up there blubbering like an overgrown baby and brought us the news! And he said 'disappeared' not 'murdered!' She couldn't know it! She couldn't! And yet—

"And yet, even before that, Cousin Ralph had said—in reference to what? In reference to Sara's insane claim that Clara somehow invades her body and forces her to do things foreign to her nature such as coming to my room in the dead of the night—but I *had* screamed, I had!—and screwing my poor, bony, willing, and perpetually hard-up ass off. In reference to that monstrous claim he said: 'That's impossible. You know it's impossible, Sara. You want me to tell Tobias here *why* it's impossible?' Emphasizing that *why* so sharply that the only interpretation I can put on those rather cryptic phrases of his now is that he too, believed, or *knew* that poor Clara was already dead!

"But, how could he know that? Unless—unless—dear God!—he and Sara between them *hired* Ridley Tyler to murder that poor, sweet, lost—angelic girl! No. Impossible. Why would they do a thing like that? Because they believed Clara was herself mad, and therefore a danger to the family's fair reputation? Believed that in spite of the fact that she has—had, dear bleeding Christ, *had!*—a spotless reputation in the village. And in any small town the schoolmarm—not to mention a young, pretty one to boot!—is always the target of all eyes. Hell and death! A stunning blonde like Clara would have found herself fired for lighting up a cigarette in public, let alone getting involved with her male pupils. And Clara kept that miserable job three long years. Kept it and won the friendship of tough and realistic lower-class women such as Milly Sloames and Sal Tyler—dead now, both of them, God rest their souls . . . And those deputies now—when they mentioned Clara, their voices were warm with genuine admiration . . .

"But, forget that. Forget Ralph's and Sara's motives for eliminating my poor, sweet Clara. Ask the right question, Tobias! And that question is, how could they have arranged it? And the answer to it is: Absolutely no way at all!

"Why this very afternoon, apropos of exactly nothing, Martin told me: 'The master hasn't set foot in the village in three long years, sir!' And Sara—*never.* Except for the servants, no citizen of East Egypt has so much as even seen her. You know, you jackass, that they haven't left the schloss since you've been here. So they would have had to 'phone, with the girls in the Central listening in like mad, and most of the telephones in the village being on party lines to boot, if I know anything about telephone service in rural districts and towns this small. So, the only other alternative would have been for them to send somebody with a note to Ridley Tyler, who, I'd bet my bottom dollar, can't even read his name, and their messenger would have to be a person they could trust not to stick their necks into the hangman's noose by giving away their plot against Clara whom everybody loves, which, by my lights, would have been the roughest chore of all, since nobody, as far as I can see, loves either Cousin Ralphie or little Sara a good goddamn!

"So chuck that theory straight into the nearest latrine. Don't you know by now that the Demonic Theory of Human History *never* stands up? Not because people aren't wicked enough, but because they're too weak and stupid to accomplish what their evil nature drives them to!

"And you hereby acquit Cousin Ralph of murder. And Sara. Except in her own mind. Because her crazy statement that Clara was dead was maybe her deepest wish given hopeful voice. Because she couldn't have known it—any more than you—"

He stopped then, his face greying almost out of life.

"Any more than you knew—you *knew!*—a blonde baby girl was dead, long ago dead with crows beaking out her eyes in a pond in a stinking pond in

"Beaufort, South Carolina. With palm trees around it.

"And—please, no! Dear God, no!—you know that Harold alias Asmodeus has been incestuously humping, screwing, fucking Sara for years, with not only no resistance on her part but with her delighted and enthusiastic cooperation, if the whole thing wasn't, isn't vice versa. Vice, surely; versa, who knows? And maybe—oh, Jesus, no!—even Clara as well—to judge by what Edna, who is the one member of this goddamned family who absolutely does not lie, said:

" 'Raped my daughter Clara before we could stop him.'

"She said that. I heard her.

"And Asmoharold's alive. And stinks something awful. And looks like a silverback gorilla. And doubtless howls at night.

"From the tower. From the tower whose stairs are bricked up so tight that not even an ant could climb them.

"Sara lied! People cannot know the future. But Angie says there is no future present past they're all the same slow rolling motionless or very nearly sea of co-existent concurrent contradictions obvious impossibilities such as the fact that

"Mildred Sloames whom you had never laid eyes on came up here through that wall behind you that solid wall behind you and stood there with her skull crushed down into the brain pan and gazed at you with her two eyes popped completely out of her head and lying on her cheeks like bloody malevolent onions on dripping strings long before

She

had

even

died. . . .

"I dreamed it! It was a nightmare! It was—

"The hell you say. You never fell asleep, Tobias Tobit. You were wide awake when all that crew of by-your-grievous-fault-slaughtered ghosts drifted in like smoke. And if battered to death by a drunken madman, Milly isn't enough to convince you that there *are* time faults through which what we call the future extrudes, protrudes, oozes, creeps, walks, how do you account for the fact that Anne came strolling in on thin air through that Oriel window forty feet above the ground bearing her by-an-Angel-sired blood-slimed monster of a baby—'For there were Giants on the earth in those days'—in her arms and with her belly ripped open from navel to crotch and Anne isn't or is not yet

"Dead.

"Anne!" screaming the name aloud. "Dear kind merciful God, Anne!"

He tore open the door. Hurled himself down those stairs.

It was a long way to the servants' quarters. He had time to think to torture himself a little more:

"The Tobits are mad. I am a Tobit. Ergo—*quod erat demonstrandum.* What? That any day now I'm going to wake up in the Veterans' Hospital in Alexandria, Virginia. That I never drank a bowl of rotgut with a .38 caliber police special dissolved in it, or took part in an aerial dogfight between Angels and Demons while riding stark naked on an Angel's back between his horizon-to-horizon sweeping wings with an equally stark-naked girl at my side.

"That I never wandered all over a private map of Hell in my present being nor as my eight-and-one-half-inch-high homunculus. That I never visited a mythical country called California by way of outer space nor returned there by way of a place called Dustbowl Kansas as a movie star after having humped all kinds of exciting women and girls such as L'Amour, Conchita, Hattie, and Roxane, I who never in my life have been able to screw *anybody,* not even Nell Brightwell, and I

"Surely never *dreamed* poor Anne into a state of pregnancy with the devoted assistance of an (by my warped, shell-shocked, bomb-casing-pierced and wounded mind created nonexistent absolutely outrageous) Angel."

But when he knocked on the door to that room in the servants' quarters he saw—to his great relief, for even if Angie really were only a figment of his diseased and distorted imagination, he could no longer contemplate or even imagine life without him—the Angel bending over that grossly swollen, obviously dying figure on the bed.

Beside them were three or four women, whose faces, figures, dress, or for that matter, *anything* about them that would have served for future identification, simply did not register in Tobias' mind or memory at the time.

And, beside him, was the doctor.

"I need a drink, Angie!" he was whining. "A quick snort, anyhow. I gotta do a Caesarian—hit's her onliest chance! 'N th' way my hands be a tremblin' now since you folks went 'n committed th' crime o' dryin' me out, I'll kill th' pore critter, shore!"

"Shut up, ye blinkin' whisky sop, 'n lemme think!" Angie groaned.

"Angie," Tobias whispered, "she—she's in a bad way, isn't she?"

"I'm—dying, Toby" Anne said, in a ghostly husk of a voice. "So far from home. So many billions and trillions of light years from my home. . . ."

Tobias stared at her. Turned sorrowing eyes upon Angie.

"No, she ain't," Angie said. "Ravin', I mean. Nor lyin', Toby lad. Tha's th' main trouble. When her one-sixth fadder transformed her into human form, he didn't get her insides right. Tha's why she *can't* give birth to me brat. O' *your* brat. Or both of ours."

"Now, Angie—" Tobias said.

" 'Sa fact. Me Annie's a denizen o' th' planet Yllyia. Tha's the ninth planet out o' th' fourteen orbitin' th' dwarf star Xfemon in the ninety-seventh galaxy. Th' ninety-seventh, that is, beyond th' place where *our* Universe jes kinda sorta *stops.* Tha's so damn far away that th' light from it ain't got here yet, 'n mebbe niver will. . . ."

"Then how'd *she* get here?" Tobias said.

"In a *soucoupe volante.* A flying saucer. Except that it don't *fly,* neither. It bends yer concepts o' space 'n time, creatin' black holes which ain't nothing but fourth-dimensional time warps, especially th' spiral figure eight kind, around whose curves parallel lines always meet, in th' direction th' Yllyian drivin' it wants to go. Takes care o' distance 'n the concurrent coexistin' confusion that ye humans call time quite nicely. Th' Yllyians had to quit usin' their hypergalaxial drive though. Too many of 'em wuz gittin' to their point o' destination a few million light years afore they'd started out which For Unlawful Carnal Knowledged up matters more'n somewhat—"

"I need a drink, Angie," the Doctor said, "a drink, damnit, a drink!"

"Shut up, ye damn old soak!" Angie said mildly. "Where was I, enyhow?"

"Don't know. Talking nonsense, as usual," Tobias said.

"No, he isn't, Toby," Anne whispered. "Come here, will you? I—I've got to tell you something."

"Me?" Tobias said.

"Yes, you. Anything I had to tell Angie, I've already told him.

Besides he—he's an Angel—with the stuff of immortality in him, so he's in no danger. But you're human, or maybe, humanoid, just like me, which isn't enough. All you've got is immortal longings in you, and they won't help you worth a damn when the big bang starts—"

"Anne—" Tobias groaned, and bent toward her. He was crying so hard that her outlines were blurred. Crying like a fool and child which are the stuff of innocence really, and are to come unto salvation finally are not to be forbidden and will maybe inherit the Kingdom of Heaven and the earth, too, for all the goddamned good it'll do them. . . .

"Don't cry, Toby," Anne said, "I love you, too, so listen carefully. I'm going to die. But that's not the important part."

"Then what is the important part, Anne?" Tobias whispered.

"That I am a Yllyian."

"A what?" Tobias said.

"A Yllyian. A humanoid from the planet Yllyia, the ninth planet from the sun Xfemon, a dwarf star in the ninety-seventh galaxy beyond the place where *this* Universe stops."

"Anne—" Tobias said, "don't talk. I—"

"You don't believe me. Look at me. Look at me hard!"

He looked at her. Her outlines blurred even more. Glowed. Wavered. Flickered like soft green flame. Then she *was* green. Absolutely the loveliest green he'd ever gazed upon. Very quickly she dissolved into a flower. A huge, soft green glowing flower that—No. Because what he had thought were her petals or her stalks were her eight arms and her twelve legs. They were very beautiful arms and legs, exquisitely shaped, of very lovely glowing shades of green. Then, being Tobias Tobit, which meant a human male of planet Earth, the third planet out from the dwarf star Sun, in the galaxy Milky Way, and therefore obsessed with sex, he noticed that she had perfectly normal female genitalia between each pair of those twelve beautiful green legs except that its natural foliage was a deeper green and looked rather like seaweed.

But her face was, or remained decidedly human except that she had six mouths, marvelously distributed so that kissing them involved no contortions whatsoever on the part of the six lover-husbands who had to make love to her simultaneously in order to procreate one Yllyian child, because no one male Yllyian had enough chromosomes in his chromatum spirem to do the job by himself. But she had three eyes, emerald green eyes that glowed tenderly as she gazed upon Tobias' face.

"Lovely!" Tobias breathed. "Gorgeous! Heavenly!"

"You see?" she said to Angie. "He is among the elect. Maybe even a mutant. If he were only a mere Earthling I'd be—repulsive to him, a monster."

"I love you, Anne," Tobias said. "Always have—always will, no matter what form you take!"

"Thank you," she whispered, and became Anne again. A grotesquely swollen earthwoman unable to give birth to the giant child of an Angel.

"Listen!" she said, her voice taut with earnestness. "I—came here —by mistake. One of my six fathers crashed his flying saucer into this planet with Mama and me aboard. Mama was killed. I hadn't a scratch. But my one-sixth father was so badly hurt that he knew he couldn't live. So he transformed me into an earthchild. Yllyians can do that. Yllyians can do all kinds of things. They mastered kinetic parapsychology millions of years ago. Some people found me—and I grew up to be a human. Only I wasn't. My one-sixth daddy didn't get my insides right. He never got *anything* right, not even piloting flying saucers, which was why my mama—the most feminine creature you ever saw—loved him so!"

Tobias sat there listening to her, and grieving.

"But that's not the main point—" she paused, fighting for breath.

"What is the main point?" Toby whispered.

"The sun Xfemon is a dwarf star. A *collapsing* dwarf star. In fact, the whole ninety-seventh galaxy is collapsing in upon itself. And I —am of the stuff of that galaxy. So when it has collapsed, which could be *any* time now, *I* will collapse inward upon myself with it. Each atom of my being, each proton, neutron, electron will become antimatter, weighing trillions and trillions of tons! So—get out of here! Take Clara and run away as far as you can! Because I'm sure to cause an implosion that will make everything for several *miles* around me vanish into a black hole in space and—"

"Not—Clara," Tobias got out. "I don't know where Clara is, Anne. She may be dead. And I—I've promised to marry Sara—"

"Oh you fool!" Anne screamed at him. "You can't! She's dead! Sara's dead! She drowned in a pond when she was three years old and—"

"Then, if I'm dead—Anne," Sara said, "what am I doing here, now?"

"Looking for Toby," Anne whispered. "To drag him down to—to madness—and to Hell, with you! You—you figment of your Mama's diseased and distorted imagination!"

"Toby," Sara said gently, "Mr. Wilkins—the justice of the peace—is here, now. To—to marry us. That is, if you haven't changed your mind. That's why I came down here looking for you . . ."

Tobias looked at her.

"Now?" he said, "with—with Clara lost? Maybe dead?"

"I know," Sara said. "Sounds—awful, doesn't it? But Papa says—that if she *is* dead, it wouldn't look right for us to get married right after the funeral. And if we wait too long, people might be able to see *why* we had to get married. Besides, they pulled that little red car of hers out of Emmy's Pool, two hours ago. If she's in *there,* at the bottom of the Pool, which is what Officer Hendricks thinks, it'll take *weeks* for her body to come to the surface, and that will be too long, and I—I'll be disgraced. You wouldn't want that to happen, would you?"

"No," Tobias said, "I wouldn't want that to happen."

"A drink!" Dr. Merton said, "I jes' gotta have a drink!"

"Wait!" Angie said, and picked up the receiver of the wall telephone.

"C'mon, Sara," Tobias said morosely.

"No!" she said, "I want to hear this! What your crazy chauffeur's going to say! *Whom* he's going to call!"

"Operator!" Angie said. "Gimme a hot line to Heaven. I want to have a word with God. Wha's that? Th' hell you say! To be sure there's such a line, sich a connection me wee'n bonnie lass! Jes' ye try it! There! What did I tell ye?"

One of the faceless, shapeless anonymous women crossed to the window and looked out.

"Look!" she gasped.

They all looked. A zigzag bolt of lightning stood up from the town of East Egypt, Kentucky, and lanced the heavens. It didn't flash or flicker. It stood like a flaming spear, a *crooked* flaming spear, and poured ice-cold brilliance over all the world. Around it thunder crashed and rumbled. It was approximately four o'clock in the afternoon but the sky was midnight hued, cloud covered. From those clouds rain hissed down. It wasn't until afterwards that they learned that what it rained during that awful hiatus in the workings of nature was hot, sticky human blood.

"God?" Angie roared into the mouthpiece, "Ye've got to save her, ye damned Auld Cuss! Ye've got to! Wha's that? Ye *can't.* Why in hellfire can't ye, damnit all! Are ye omnipotent or aren't ye?

"Oh—I see. Yer omnipotence don't extend beyond *this* here Universe. Th' ninety-seventh galaxy is in Universe Number Five 'n tha's th' jurisdiction o' another God? Wan ye ain't even on speaking terms with? Oh Hell! Oh Damn, Oh—then take away me immortality! Lemme die with her! 'Cause without her, without me darlin' Annie, I can't don't want to live!

"Wha's that? Ye can't do that either? Th' laws o' th' Universe is fixed and even Ye—We'll see about that! 'Cause me Annie dies I'm a gonna wreck your hustle! Throw down temples, churches, synagogues, mosques! Wake th' rottin', stinkin' dead! Send skeletons dancing down Main Street 'n—"

"C'mon, Toby. Before he messes up things *that* much, we'd better get married," Sara said.

Standing beside her before Mr. Wilkins, the justice of the peace, with Martin and two of the faceless, all-but-invisible serving women as witnesses, and Cousin Ralph, wrapped in his icy, maniacal calm, waiting to give the bride away, Tobias finally noticed what was strange about Sara: She was wearing a shirtwaist and a circa 1916 hobble skirt, of the kind that Clara wore—had worn.

She saw his look. Squeezed his arm.

"Yes, they're *hers!*" she whispered. "Since she can't be here—I—I wanted her to have some part in my—our wedding. Y'know. Something old, something new, something borrowed, something blue. This is—the—the borrowed part; Clara's clothes."

Mr. Wilkins raised his hand. Began to read: "Dearly Beloved, we are gathered together upon this happy occasion—"

"Happy!" Tobias groaned inside his heart.

"To witness the union o' this man 'n this woman in th' sacred bonds o' holy wedlock—"

Tobias didn't listen anymore. He closed his mind to it. His heart. But it went smoothly enough for all that. Cousin Ralph had even thought to bring some rings from the family jewel box, for the double-ring ceremony. They even fitted reasonably well.

"I now pronounce you man and wife!" Mr. Wilkins said. "Kiss your bride, young fella!"

Tobias bent and did so. The feel of Sara's lips got to him finally. They were warm and soft. And the tenderness they conveyed was almost crippling. They were also salty and wet with tears.

And it was then, at that precise hiatus in their collective, now cojoined sequential progression that that awful, demented howling started. It came from far above them. From the tower, Tobias guessed. But—but—the tower stairs were bricked up! He had seen them! He—

"That's Harold," his bride whispered in his ear. Her voice was filled with sad, sweet resignation. "I'll have to go—calm him, I'm afraid. Or else he'll howl all night, and nobody'll get any sleep. Of course," she giggled girlishly, "I don't mean to let *you* get any, but Mama and Papa need theirs. Walk me as far as the cellar stairs, will you? So Mr. Wilkins won't notice anything. . . ."

But Mr. Wilkins already had.

"Wha's that awful noise?" he got out.

"The wind," Ralph Tobit said matter-of-factly. "On stormy days like this one, it blows through the tower window, and makes that dreadful racket. One of the reasons that superstitious idiots think the castle's haunted, I suppose—"

"Lemme outa heah!" Mr. Wilkins gasped.

Which, Tobias guessed, was exactly what Cousin Ralph had wanted him to say, what his remark about the castle's being haunted had been calculated to put into Mr. Justice of the Peace Wilkins' all too credulous and fearful mind.

"Show Mr. Wilkins out, will you, Martin?" he said. "And be sure to pay him his fee, and a bit extra, will you? That's a good fellow. I'll settle with you later."

Tobias followed Sara to the head of the cellar stairs.

"This is far enough!" she said. "You see, I don't know exactly *where* Harold is by now. He may even be in the storage room where Papa has all that blasting powder hid. Barrels and barrels of it. To blow the castle up. The castle—and us. If the police ever find out and come to arrest us. You know? And, besides, Harold's awf'ly dangerous, even without that gunpowder. He'd kill you just like that. Only *I* can calm him. I'm the only one who ever could—"

"But—but," Tobias got out, "your father said—"

"That Harold was dead," Sara said calmly. "That he died when he was only twelve years old. Of cerebro-spinal meningitis. Oh well, you're my dearest, darling hubby now, and that makes you family, too, doesn't it? But then you always *were* family, weren't you?"

"Yes," Tobias said. Or rather groaned.

"Well, that business about Harold's being dead is just another one of Papa's pious lies. One of the family—arrangements. Designed to keep Mama as well as possible. Doesn't really work. Never has. But it did serve to keep poor Harold out of the state lunatic asylum. . . ."

Tobias stared at her.

"Tell me something, Sara," he said harshly, "did he—did Harold—kill—those seven fellows?"

She bowed her head. Looked up again. Whispered:

"Yes, Toby, dearest. And he'll kill *anybody* who looks at me sidewise. That's why I *have* to calm him. You *do* understand, don't you, love? Doesn't mean anything really. You go to our room. I—I'll come to you—as soon as I can—"

On his way to the guest room, Tobias noticed again something he had already noticed several times before: Though the many ancestral shields hanging from the Castle's walls had crossed scabbards behind them, there were neither broadswords nor daggers in those scabbards. And now, suddenly, he knew why.

"If that murderous maniac had ever got his hand on a blade, there would have been hell to pay," he thought.

He reached the guest room, put his hand on the door, pushed it open. Doubled in half as the first wave of nausea hit him. Followed by a blade of ice, pushed slowly through his guts. For he knew how his blushing bride was going to go about calming her maniac brother. Without even thinking about it, he knew.

He whirled, already running towards those cellar stairs, which proved what a hopeless, sentimental idiot he was. If he had dashed for the schloss's gates, for the drawbridge, there might have been some hopes for him. But he had to follow his natural bent, as Kipling put it, prove again the abysmal truth of Angie's dictum that each man invents his private hell.

So he dashed for those stairs, went down them. They were feebly illuminated by a string of bare bulbs of very low wattage that Sara had left on to light her own return, he guessed. At the foot of them was a dungeon, whose interior was made barely visible by the same kind of tiny light bulbs, though here they were set in iron-grilled niches—to keep Asmoharold from breaking them, he was sure. The dungeon's barred door was open. He entered it.

The floor was literally covered with human excreta, much of it fresh, and gnawed, broken joints of meat, most of them raw. The stench was indescribable. And unsupportable. But Tobias went on, slipping and sliding in that rich compost of rotting food and fresh man shit, until he had crossed the dungeon. On the other side of it was another room, its door agape, and barrels around all its walls. One of the barrels had been broken into, and a thick black powder spilled out of it, and poured in a neat spiral all around the room and out the door. But Tobias was too upset, too frenzied wild, to then realize what that powder was.

At the far side of that lethal room, there was a little door of solid iron. It had been torn from its hinges. From its huge, solid, medieval iron hinges. Tobias didn't even stop to think of the degree of herculean strength it had taken to do that. He went up those tiny, curving stairs behind it. Upward into utter dark, climbing from below it, up to the floor of hell.

Long before he reached the tower room, he could hear poor Sara screaming. Those screams were the distillation of the purest anguish he had ever heard. And yet, they were curiously muffled, as though she were trying to keep her tortured voice from carrying, as if she were attempting to prevent her agony from being heard.

Tobias hurled himself up those narrow stairs to the utter ruin of his clothes, and the loss of several square inches of his skin. Reached the top of them. Leaped through that opening into the Tower Room. Hung there, death in him like a blade.

Because now, he *saw* why Sara's screams were muffled. Her brother Harold—a huge apelike monster a full five inches above six feet tall, and broad almost out of proportion to that immense fur-covered height—had simply pushed her over forwards so that her forehead, pillowed on her own shapely arms, rested on the foot of the bed, yanked up her long skirt, and thrown the tail of it over her shirtwaist-clad back and shoulders, so that it completely covered her head (or had she done that, herself, Tobias wondered; dragging the skirt over her own face, her eyes, so as not to have to witness her own physical and moral destruction?), ripped off the step-ins that lay in shreds about her feet, and mounted her from behind as a stallion mounts a mare. Penetrated, impaled though she was, she remained doubled-over forward, half leaning on her own arms, half standing, her lovely legs spread wide, submissively receiving that brutal maleness, too big for any normal woman, as was clear from the bright blood trickling slowly down her thighs.

And she was still screaming, but now her screams were changing, changing. As Harold-Asmodeus plunged into her, snorting, roaring, bucking like the frenzied beast he was, she screamed louder than ever, but, Tobias realized—and a thousand thousand furry bat-winged loathsome things exploded outward shrieking and gibbering in his gut—what was causing her to scream was no longer horror, anguish, pain. In fact, she was saying it now, his tender bride of but one half an hour, her words panting, fluting, panpiping, shrilling through the stuff of her skirt:

"Give it *all* to me, Hal, darlin'! Every randy inch of it! Tear me apart! Split me in half! Harder! Harder! Got no strength, you delicious brute? Hurt me! Oh, please, Hal, *hurt* me! Hurt me gooood! Like that! Only harder, damn you! Harder! Faster! Harder! C'mon! C'mon! C'mon! Do it to me, Hal, do it to me, fuck your baby, ram it up, hurt Ah! Ah! Ah! Ahhhhhhh! Thaaat's it! Thaaat's—"

She ripped her skirt down from her face with clawing frantic fingers and Tobias saw her eyes. They had gone glassy as blue marbles. A titanic shudder whipped visibly through her slender body like a shoreward-racing wave; her mouth tore open, desperately gulping air. Then she racked hearing out of existence with a scrape of steel on glass so high and terrible that Tobias felt it in his ears, his throat, his guts like a banshee's—no, death's own—keening wail, a screamshriekshrilling of such pure shething bitchthing tortured ecstasy, an orgiastic transmogrification of orgasm's very—endless, multiple—self, into such unbelievable intensities of sound that he reeled under the impact as though it were a blow, and hung there trembling, watching her collapsing forward onto the bed, lying there, mouth opened, gasping, sobbing, shaking, her tongue protruding, the foam of utter madness flecking the corners of her lips, her eyes senseless, wide-stretched, unseeing and—

Her brother Harold, that obscene retrogression down the evolutionary scale into unmitigated apehood, or further still, into demonic possession, lying on top of her, snorting, panting, salivating, quivering, until

Tobias, driven into another kind of madness less bestial, more human, and thereby perhaps more *evil* than theirs, tore down a dagger from its scabbard on the wall—for Ralph Tobit had never reached the tower room to remove its ancient weapons—and plunged it through Harold's immense and hairy back.

But he aimed the blade badly, or Harold was too strong, or Random Chance, the Absurdity Factor, Blind Accidentality or his own woeful ineptitude at anything requiring bodily skills, force, or even an instinct for violence—people who hate the mere idea of killing are never good at it—intervened. For it was immediately clear that his murderous stroke, delivered out of so primitive and indefensible an emotion as plain rut-dog sexual jealousy, had failed.

Harold exploded up from that bed, floored Tobias with one easy backhand blow that, even though it didn't knock him completely unconscious, left him too stunned to move or think or do anything but lie there and helplessly witness the denouement of disaster.

Harold scooped poor Sara up from that bed. Leaped with her, as though she were weightless, as to him she surely was, just as that dagger buried to its hilt in his huge back was only a minor irritation, into the long-ago smashed, broken tower window, and hopped up and down there showing his huge yellowish teeth in his curiously handsome totally unapelike face, before leaping with her through it, out, and down.

And Tobias Tobit, true to his basic nature, fainted outright, then and there.

When he came to himself, the tower room was filled with voices. One of them was Cousin Ralph's, another was Martin's, another was the gardener's, perhaps, others were female, but none of them was the only one that counted, that might have done something. None of them was Angie's.

"The tree!" Martin cried. "The tree! He's caught onto it, sir! They're saved! They're saved! I'll go get a rope. Oh! Oh my God! The roots—the roots—"

"What man? For God's sake let me see!" Cousin Ralph's voice said.

"No. No, sir! Don't look! It—it's too awful! The roots are pulling loose—from the wall. We—we cawn't save them, sir! There's no time—"

"Let me try, sir!" the gardener said. "I could work my way down the wall. Lots o' gaps in those stones—and—"

"You'd only go with them when they go," Ralph Tobit said tonelessly. "Poor Sara. Poor—Hal. On her wedding day at that. Oh. Oh. Ohhhhh God!"

Tobias heard that awful tearing splintering crash. Reeled to his feet. Staggered to the window.

"Don't look," Ralph Tobit said gently. "It's too damned awful!"

"Mr. Tobit, sir!" a woman's voice shrilled. "They—haven't gone over the falls! The tree's caught broadside the river! And they—they're alive, sir! I kin see 'em strugglin'!"

Ralph Tobit leaned far out. Drew back in. Whirled. Roared:

"Come on!"

But that stairway was too narrow. There were too many of them. They had to go down it single file. In the dark at that. And even afterwards they had to get out of the castle, race across the drawbridge, down and around all the curves of that road until they reached the place where the road came closest to the falls. And when they would have got *there,* they'd still be two hundred yards away from that roaring whistling crack and slam and thunder. There wasn't a chance, and all of them knew it.

But, as they raced around the final bend, they saw that they were wrong. Half wrong, anyhow. For Angie came up that road, dragging Harold's unconscious bulk behind him by the hair.

"This critter's yours?" he said to Ralph Tobit, his angel's voice shaking with icy, more than human fury.

Ralph nodded, dumbly.

"Take it, then," Angie grated. Then he saw Tobias Tobit, saw his eyes.

"Go pack yer duds, Toby lad. We're widowers now. Both o' us. Ye heard me, Toby! Go get packed!" the Angel said.

And at that moment, listening hard, you might have heard his fellow Angels weep. For Raphael, the Angel. For his loss. For Angels weep, you know.

There's only one Celestial Being who doesn't. Who's forgot how.

The Auld Cuss.

Alias God.

Twenty

Leaving the castle for the last time, Tobias sat beside Angie on the front seat of the Pierce Arrow. Neither of them said anything, very likely because there was absolutely nothing to be said. They had got down as far as Ridley Tyler's tavern, closed now, boarded up, where this singularly disquieting sequence in their collective, and may be eternally, cojoined progression through the superimposed illusions of time, space, life had begun, when they saw the first of the troupe of human skeletons dancing up that road.

"Angie!" Tobias said.

"Told 'un I'd do it, th' damned Auld Cuss!" Angie said grimly and went right on driving.

"Oh, Angie, look!" Tobias moaned.

And there was Nancy—a little more rotted away, a little more horrible, and Hellcat Hattie McCoy smoking one of her absolutely vile-smelling cigars and grinning at them and spraying the whole damned road with blood and dragging the hindquarters that were all there was left of Tony "the Butterfly" Mariposa along behind her by one foot, and the tiny blonde girl-child with no eyes and the crows fluttering and cawing around her head, and Milly Sloames with her head crushed in and her eyeballs bouncing and dangling on their optic nerves on her cheeks, and Sal Tyler with her throat cut from ear to ear and dripping pond water from her clothes, and several young well-dressed male—from their clothes anyhow—skeletons who were tap dancing and soft shoeing and cutting bucks 'n wings and gesticulating upward towards the schloss as if to make clear where they had come from.

"So," Angie said, "they wuz under them pavin' stones after all. Reckon yer cousin Ralph must have helped that big murderin' ape bury 'em. Maybe even Martin too. Loyal enough. Ol' family retainer 'n all that sort o' bloody rot, donchew know. . . ."

Then there were dozens of dead people in various stages of putrefaction, and the skeleton of a tall woman with greyish blonde hair clinging to the top of her skull who, Tobias guessed, was Emma Schloss, and another skeleton in old-fashioned clothes who kept taking two big gold watches out of his waistcoat pockets and looking at them with his gaping eye sockets because he no longer had any eyes.

"Ol' Schloss," Angie said.

"Angie, you stop it!" Tobias screamed.

"No, goddammit!" the Angel said.

Then he was jamming the big car to a stop and jumping from it and running forward with his arms outstretched and tears streaming down his face, because there before them was Anne.

"Annie, me darlin' " Angie wept. "Oh duckie, love, I—"

She came towards them very slowly. She had that huge, greenish, bluish, blood-stained monster of a child in her arms. She was naked and her belly had been ripped open from navel to crotch and her guts were spilling out of it.

She paid them no attention at all. She went right on crooning to her dead child, but they couldn't hear her. When she got to the place where Angie was, his arms outstretched to embrace her, she walked into his arms, through his arms, through his body, out the back of him, through Tobias who was standing just behind Angie, through the car which had skidded broadside the road blocking it, on up the road, and, without increasing her pace at all, reached the castle, at once, instantly, with no apparent lapse in that curious illusion that men call time, drifted like green smoke like a flower like a huge green glowing flower with eight arms and twelve legs and six mouths and three emerald eyes and hair like lovely green seaweed into the big gates under the portcullis—

And then the castle blew up.

"Angie!" Tobias screamed "The powder! The blasting powder! He had barrels of it down there in the room next to the dungeon and—"

"No," Angie said. "Even if he had, he didn't get a chance to use it. Did ye hear any noise, laddybucks?"

"No—" Tobias whispered.

"Didn't blow up. Blew in. Imploded. Look."

There wasn't anything there anymore. No castle. No mountain-top. Only a big black hole that reached almost down to where the falls began. Then the black hole closed up leaving the mountain truncated. There was no sign that Schloss's schloss had ever been there, not even a trace of debris.

"Maybe it never was," Tobias thought.

"Maybe *what* never was?" Angie said.

"The castle," Tobias said.

"Now ye're learning, laddybucks. Things is, 'n they ain't. Concurrently, that is. Or as ye'd put it, simultaneously. All depends."

"Depends on what?" Tobias said.

"Ye ask too damned many questions, sometimes! It collapsed, ye ken. Th' ninety-seventh galaxy collapsed. Taking Xfmenon 'n Yllyia with it. Making antimatter o' all me duckie's folks. A pity. Nice li'l ol' humanoids, th' Yllyians—"

"Angie," Tobias said. "Leave the dead in peace now, will you? Huh, please? She's gone. Anne is—and what you're doing is no good. Hell, it isn't even intelligent—"

"Right. I couldn't win, anyhow. Th' Auld Cuss is too much fer me. In peace it is—all ye rotten, skinny hunks o' carrion! In peace!"

Then the night was very clear and all the stars were out, and the headlights of the big car made a broad swath of gold as they crawled down that twisting mountain road. Tobias bent his head. A tear stole from under his eyelids.

Which was why the top of his head and not his face crashed into the windshield when Angie slammed on the brakes.

"Why goddamn!" he howled. "Are you crazy or something?"

"Far from it," Angie said solemnly. "Look!"

She was sitting on a fallen tree trunk by the edge of the road. She had a white bandage wrapped around her head. In the glare of the headlights, Tobias could see that she was crying.

"Angie!" he grated. "You said you'd stopped it! You said you were going to leave them in peace! And now you go and—and bring her back! What good is it, you fool? We can't communicate with them. We can't! You couldn't even keep Anne—from vanishing—and you're an Angel! Besides—"

"Besides what, laddybucks?" Angie said.

"I don't *want* her back! She—she was horrible! Mad as a hatter. A—a nympho—and—"

"Ye've got me wrong," Angie said. "I didn't bring 'er back—fer th' simple reason *this* one never went. Get out o' the car 'n see fer yerself."

Tobias got out of the car. Walked over to the weeping girl. Peered into her face. A long time. A very long time. But even then he wasn't sure. She paid him no attention. She went right on crying as if she didn't even notice he was there.

"Clara—?" he said tentatively.

She looked up. Stared at him. "Who're—you?" she whispered.

"Your cousin Toby," he said.

"Oh!" she said. "Oh, yes—I—I remember now! Cousin Toby. I met you before, didn't I? You—you came to—to the school. I—I tried to keep you from going up to the schloss. But—but you went, didn't you?"

"Yes," Tobias said. "Come on, Clara, get into the car. . . ."

"All right," she said tiredly. She got up. Took his arm. He helped her into the car.

"Cousin Toby," she said. "You wouldn't have—something to eat—with you, would you? I'm so hungry!"

"No, I haven't," Tobias said, "but there's a restaurant in the village, isn't there, Clara?"

"Yes. But it will be closed now. It's much too late. No matter. Tired as I am, I'll just curl up and go to sleep. Tell me, where are you taking me, Cousin Toby?"

"My place. Ryland. New York. When we get there, we'll get married."

"Oh!" she said. "But—but didn't—didn't you—marry—my sister, Sara? In the village, they said—that Mister Wilkins, the justice of the peace, went up there—and—"

"Yes," Tobias said. "I married her. Only she—she's dead now. Your brother, Harold—jumped out the tower window with her in his arms—"

She peered at him. It was too dark in the car for her to see his face.

"You—don't seem—very grieved, Toby," she said.

"I'm not," he said. "But then, neither do you."

"I—don't remember her," she said softly. "I'm afraid I don't remember much of anything, Cousin Toby. *You*—yes. Your face. It's such a good face. Gentle. Kind. You'll—have to—to explain—everything to me. You see—I've been hurt. My—head, that is. Affected my memory. The people in the village think—a man named Ridley Tyler—oh now I remember him! He was Sal's husband, wasn't he?"

"Yes," Tobias said.

"They think he tried to kill me. That he—hit me on the head with something—something heavy. Some people—strangers—found me—lying on the road—unconscious. Quite near Emmy's Pool. They took me to—to Lexington. That's where they were going. To the hospital there. But the doctors wouldn't keep me when they found out my skull wasn't fractured like they'd thought. Just concussion, they said, and—a scalp wound. They're having an epidemic there, so there weren't—any—beds. Anyhow when they asked me who I was, I said 'Clara Tobit,' just like that. But I don't remember her—*me*—much, either—though the doctor in Lexington says my memory will come back with time. In the village, they told me I'd been a schoolteacher and that my family lived in the castle, and I said, 'Oh yes, Schloss's schloss,' and started to go up there. But, before I got there, some people came down the road in a car—they wanted to take me back down to East Egypt, but I wouldn't go with them—and—and anyhow they told me the schloss had blown up—and that my father, and mother, and—and Harold had been killed. But they didn't say—Sara had. Why didn't they, Cousin Toby?"

"Because—she was already dead. She went over the falls. On a tree trunk. She and Harold were in that tree when it fell down the mountainside into the river. *Above* the falls. Only—Harold managed—to get ashore before it went. But Sara—"

"Poor Sara!" Clara whispered. And started to cry again.

Tobias put his arms around her. Drew her to him. She smelled strange. Then he realized what that strange smell was. She smelled of medicines. Disinfectants. Hospital odors. Pity moved in him. He tightened his grip around her.

She moaned a little. Said:

"Turn me loose."

He did so. Sadly. Took his arm entirely away from around her.

She stared at him. Her eyes were very wide and soft and tender. Her lips moved, whispering, shaping words.

"Put your arm back. I *like* you to hold me. Makes me feel good. Warm and safe—and protected, somehow. But—but don't hold me so tight. You see, I'm—so sore. From the way that crazy man beat me up," she said.

When they got to East Egypt, she was asleep, with her head pillowed on Tobias' shoulder. By the streetlights they passed under, he saw that that part of her head that wasn't covered by the bandages had been shaved, so he knew her injuries must have been quite grave.

"That murderous crazy bastard!" Tobias thought.

Angie slowed the car, drew back the glass partition between them and the chauffeur's seat.

"She got her handbag with her?" the Angel said.

"No," Tobias said.

"Then you better wake her up. Ask her if she's got a key—somewheres. Round her neck on a chain, mebbe. To that little house. She's gonna need clothes, y' know. 'N papers. Her college diploma. Her teacher's certificate."

"Why?" Tobias said.

"Ain't likely she's got her birth certificate handy." Angie said. "Nor her baptismal one, neither. Most folks don't—"

"But why would she need *any* of those papers?" Tobias said.

"Proves *who* she is," Angie said. "Less explainin' to do that way, Toby, me boy. Hard to marry a girl who ain't got no proofs of her identity. By th' way, laddybucks, when ye do it, I wouldn't mention that ye was hitched to Sara before—"

"Why not? She's dead, isn't she?"

"Yep. But then ye'd need a death certificate to *prove* ye're a widower to th' competent authorities issuin' ye yer marriage license. 'Nain't *nobody* gonna issue ye one o' *them,* 'til poor li'l Sary comes floatin' to the top o' Emmy's Pool. Habeas corpus, ye ken? That might take weeks. 'N it jes might take feriver. She might be caught under sumpin on th' bottom. In which case, if I know me common law, ye'll have to wait seven *years* for a certificate o' legally presumed defunction—"

Tobias stared at him, but he went on, calmly:

"Ye see, Toby, me boy, me boy, *I* wuz th' first bloke outa that damned ol' rock pile when it happened. I grabbed me poor Annie, wrapped her in a blanket 'n run out to bury her. She *wuz* beginning to transmogrify, ye yen? Go back to her nach'l Yllyian form 'n substance—'n, unlike *ye*—who've got a sort o' special grace—most *humans* is just too damn stupid to see how beautiful Yllyians are. Didn't want 'em to see her like that. They'd of armed a scandal sure as ol' Hell when they seen she had all them extra mouths 'n eyes 'n arms 'n legs. So I sort o' froze 'em all 'n took off. 'N I was coming back from doin' that—buryin' me Annie, I mean—when I seen yer hairy ape o' a brother-in-law—fancy havin' a kid what looks, 'n worse still *acts* like him! Could happen, ye know—"

"I'll drown it!" Tobias said. "Go on Angie. Get to the point, will you?"

"Th' point is I seen ol' Darwin's proof positive strugglin' in th' water. Strugglin' feebly, by then. Say, who slipped him that shiv in th' back? Ye?"

"Ssssh!" Tobias said. "For God's sake, Angie!"

"Thought so. Niver could do anything *right,* could ye? Not even doin' in a thing like that un, whose pa should o' strangled it in its cradle. Enyhow I seen him strugglin' 'n pulled him out, sweet li'l ol' Angelic fool that I be! 'N by then, laddybucks, by the time *I* got there—'n I wuz the first by long odds—that clinkin' tree wuz *already* gone. That means that not *nobody* saw poor li'l Sary go over—"

"Angie," Tobias whispered, "you don't think—"

"That she got ashore, jes like ol' Asmo did? No. She wasn't nowhere near as strong. Besides if she had of got out, where'd she go? She'd have been lyin' on the bank somewheres, wouldn't she? Or you think she fell—or was throwed—outa th' tower window, hit a tree, crashed in th' damn tree all th' way down to th' upper river, swam ashore without a scratch 'n jes' blithely strolled off to visit friends?"

"But—but that maidservant saw her moving! In the tree! After it was already in the river, I mean. Her and Harold, both!"

"Yep. But I found Harold, Toby lad. 'N I damn sure *didn't* find Sary. So where *is* she?"

"Don't know. In Emmy's Pool, I guess. Angie—do I *have* to wake this poor little creature up?"

"Be th' best thing. Among other things, do her good to get a whole night's sleep in her own bed, laddybucks. *Alone,* that is. . . ."

"Why you evil-minded celestial scoundrel! It never crossed my mind to—"

"Know it didn't. I wuz jes plaguing ye. Now wake her up," the Angel said.

But in the end, they had to force the lock—which Angie did by pointing his index finger at it and muttering sonorous Hebrew curses. That night Tobias and Angie bunked in the car, since East Egypt had neither a hotel nor an inn. And the next morning after a tremendous breakfast of buckwheat cakes, sausages, eggs, and coffee, the three of them drove northward. By then, Clara was beginning to look slightly human again.

On that trip to New York state, Angie took his own sweet time, for at that stage in its sequential progression the nation's roads were still nearly all dirt and gravel, and the best they could do was between eighty and one hundred miles a day without running the risk of killing poor little Clara from sheer tiredness. They also averaged from three to seven punctures daily, and though Angie repaired those flat tires with a little profane, Hebrew-swearing, miracle working, they still delayed them considerably.

By the time they got to New York City, Clara's hair had grown out enough to make her look like a very pretty little boy. As they were crossing the Hudson from New Jersey, Angie suggested:

"Look, kiddies," he said. "Why don't th' two of ye get hitched in th' Big Burg?"

Clara looked at Tobias with a startled expression. Then she whispered:

"Do you *want* to, Toby? Marry me, I mean?"

"Of course!" Tobias said. "Just you try and stop me—" Then he saw the expression on her face. In her eyes.

"The question is," he said bitterly, "whether you want to marry me. And the answer to that is obvious—to judge from your expression right now. You *don't,* do you? Not really."

"Toby—" she said, and her eyes filled up with tears. "Will—you kiss me? Right now? This minute? Please?"

Then she saw Angie grinning at her.

"And you close that little window, Angie!" she said wrathfully. "And—and turn your back! 'Cause I want to—to kiss Toby. And to —to tell him something that's none of your business!"

"Natch, Miss Clara, ma'am!" Angie said, and did so.

Tobias took her in his arms. He remembered suddenly the other time she had kissed him. With frank passion. With considerable art. The disturbing thought stole into his mind:

"How had she learned all that? With whom?"

But now she astonished him again. Her kiss was soft and sweet and shy—and almost cripplingly tender. It also tasted salt from the tears that were pouring down her cheeks.

"I—I love you, Toby," she whispered. "With all my heart. You're the first man I've loved in my whole life. And—if you—you'll let me be your—your wife, you're going to be the only man I'll ever love. The father of my children, too—I hope—But it doesn't depend on me. It depends on—you. . . ."

"Good God!" he said. "You *know* how I feel about you! As far as I'm concerned, we—"

"Wait!" she said sharply. "This is very hard to say. I—I don't even know how to. Yet I've got to, haven't I? Put it this way: Would you care—very much—would it hurt you—terribly—if—if a man—another man—had had me—first? Before you? I mean—had my—my body?"

He sat there frozen. Said finally:

"You mean you've had—a lover? Lovers?"

"Oh Toby!" she wailed. "What a horrible, horrible thing to say!"

"Maybe I put it badly," he said. "You're trying to tell me that you let a man—one other man—make love to you? That you—you went to bed with him?"

"No!" she shrilled. "I'm trying to say nothing of the kind, Tobias Tobit! Oh, how *dense* you are! I have never *let* anyone make love to me in my whole life! Nor gone to bed with—"

Then it hit him. What the late Edna Tobit had said. Her mother. And the things she, herself, had said to Anne on the first day that they'd met.

"Harold," he said, "your brother. And—it was—rape wasn't it?"

She nodded, dumbly. Whispered: "I was—only twelve years old.

No—thirteen. He—knocked me unconscious—with his fist. When I came to—he was—doing that. It hurt—something awful—I—I almost bled to death—"

He said: "Then I *do* care."

She stared at him.

"Oh, Toby!" she wailed. "That's not fair!"

"But only because it's surely left you with the impression that men are brutes. And that love—physical love—is ugly. It's not, darling. Between two people who love each other—love each other in *all* ways, not just that one—it's—very beautiful. . . ."

"I—I—think it would be—with you," she said softly. "But you'll—have to be very patient with me. That is, if you *still* want to marry me, knowing that—Do you?"

"I'll think about it," he teased. "Maybe if you proposed to me very nicely and sweetly, I just might—"

She smiled at him, but her eyes were misty, still.

"All right," she said, "will you marry me? Make an honest woman out of me, as the saying goes? It's no fun being an old maid, you know. 'Specially when one isn't even a maid! And I'm twenty-six years old. So you better make up your mind, right now!"

"Of course!" he laughed, and kissed her.

"When, Toby?" she whispered.

"Today. Tomorrow. As soon as we can get the license," Tobias said.

Angie opened the partition again.

"Everything settled, kiddies?" he grinned. "Good! Better like that! You bring her up to Ryland not married to you 'n Nell Brightwell'll eat her alive. With you for dessert, laddybucks!"

Clara turned to Tobias. Her voice was very, very quiet, but her shoe toe made a drumroll on the limousine's floor.

"Just *who* is Nell Brightwell, Tobias Tobit?" she said.

He bought her an enormous diamond engagement ring at Tiffany's, and also, a wedding band encrusted with diamonds. But when, in the chambers of the justice of the peace, she put out her hand to slip it on, he saw, to his vast astonishment, that she already wore a wedding ring. A simple, plain gold band.

"Clara!" he said.

She stared down at her own finger. Her pale blue eyes opened very wide.

"I—I don't know *where* that came from, Toby!" she said. "I don't ever remember wearing a ring, before—Not this kind of ring—and not on this finger. It must have been—Mama's, maybe. She—must have given it to me—"

The justice of the peace stared at her.

"Young lady," he said, "you're *sure* you've got the right to marry this young fellow?"

"I—I don't know," Clara faltered. "I—I had an accident, sir. And I've lost my memory. Not completely. Partial amnesia, it's called. But I don't *think* I ever married anybody before—"

"She didn't," Tobias said. "She's—my second cousin, sir. I know her—know her branch of the family. She was a schoolteacher down in Kentucky. There're hundreds of people down there who can vouch for the fact that she's unwed. But I hope you'll take my word for it, sir. Delay things something awful if we have to get written proof. . . ."

The justice turned to Angie. "You know her, too?" he said.

"Yes, sir! And she ain't married. No point in your asking this young lady though—" he nodded towards the waitress from the restaurant they had eaten lunch at the day before, and whom he had easily persuaded to serve as the necessary second witness to the ceremony. "Cause she *didn't* know Clara before. She's a local girl, friend o' mine. . . ."

"Oh, your honor, can't you see my friends are telling th' truth?" the waitress said.

The justice smiled.

"Yes. I can see they are. Among other things—a lady bigamist would have thrown that ring in the East River before she came here," he said.

But the incident troubled Tobias, all the same. And it wasn't to be the last. For Angie had reserved a table for the four of them for the wedding supper in the dining room of the Waldorf Astoria. And a suite there for Tobias and his bride. A room for himself, on another floor. At the moment, he was chiefly concerned with getting rid of the waitress. Strange as that would have seemed to Tobias, Angie was still grieving for his darlin' Annie.

Now seated at their flower-bedecked table, Tobias kept staring at Clara. She was radiant. Heartbreakingly lovely, even with her close-cropped hair. And yet, yet—

Then the headwaiter handed her the menu. She read it easily, swiftly, without even squinting.

Then it hit Tobias. Why it hadn't before, on the long trip north, he simply didn't know. And perhaps it would have been wiser of him, or at least more cunning, to have kept his mouth shut. But Tobias Tobit simply wasn't made that way. He would never learn cunning, which, after all, left him some hope for attainment of wisdom, because cunning and wisdom are absolute dichotomies, and mutual exclusives.

"Clara!" he gasped. "Your—your glasses! Don't tell me you can read without them now?"

She stared at him. Her mouth trembled.

"Oh, Toby! Don't tell me I wore *glasses* too, before! Why I must have been a perfect fright!" she wailed.

Most normal men approach their wedding night with decidedly mixed emotions. Tenderness, love, desire, anticipated bliss seldom win out over screaming nerves, jittery, and usually well-founded fears that their performance as lovers is going to leave a great deal to be desired, and the sinking feeling that they have made a grave and practically irreparable mistake in undertaking matrimony at all. But Tobias Tobit was surely unique in the sense that having married the girl of his choice, and married her out of a pure and abiding and noble and completely honorable love, he stumbled towards his nuptial bed convulsed with awful dread, and practically frozen with an all-pervading feeling of horror.

"Nobody," he thought dismally, "*saw* that tree go over those falls. It went, all right—but was she in it? And if she *was,* did she—die? Jesus, Tobias! That's a drop of eight hundred feet! Nobody could survive it! But suppose—she was caught—among the branches in such a way that—that they protected her—from the worse blows—buoyed her up and—

"No! It's simply impossible! She's—down there in Emmy's Pool, all right. Or—is she?

"Suppose she got out of the river *before* Angie got there? Wandered away in a daze—from a blow on the head caused by the fall from the tower itself? A fall you *know* she survived, because that maidservant saw both her and Harold struggling in the tree, in the river!

"Say she walked off down the road half out of her senses and those people in the car—oh! Her clothes! She had on *Clara's* clothes! And that ring! The one *I* put on her finger when I married her the first time! And she can see perfectly without glasses! And that business about losing her memory is a goddamned lie and the perfect cover up and—"

She came out of the bathroom. Her negligee was new, bought that very morning. It was quilted, maddeningly chaste, voluminous enough to hide even the outlines of her lovely, perfect body. She was fairly floating on a cloud of perfume. She was also trembling like the leaves of *Populus tremuloides,* the white aspen, which quiver in the faintest breeze. Rosy blushes climbed her throat, her cheeks.

Then she saw him sitting there, fully clothed. He hadn't even taken off his shoes.

"Oh!" she gasped, and then: "Toby—what's—wrong?"

He knew better than to lie.

"Don't know," he said slowly. "Except that I'm having the damnedest attack of—of nerves, you ever saw. I've been sitting here wondering—all kinds of things. Including whether you—are really you."

"If I'm not *me,"* she said wonderingly, "then who *am* I?"

"Sara," he said, his voice a shudder.

"Why, Toby!" she got out. "You—*hate* her, don't you? You *hate* my poor dead sister, who was your wife! You *do,* don't you?"

"Yes," he said grimly. "She gave me reasons to. Within the single day that we were wed. And you? The two of you never got along, I've been told."

She came to where he sat, put her arms around his neck, looked into his eyes. Her own were very deep—and troubled.

"You know—I don't remember that at all," she said quietly. "In fact, I don't remember Sara. I've tried, and tried, but *nothing* about her comes back to me. Strange, isn't it? Because now I remember —Papa and Mama—and—and Harold. And Martin. And Mildred Sloames—she was so good to me, Milly was! Or at least to the girl I *think* I was. And I—remember *you,* from before. Your face, anyhow. But not *where* I saw you and talked to you, or anything. But all I have to go on about Sara is what you've told me. And you say—"

"That the two of you were identical. Not even your father could tell you apart."

"And *that* bothers you, doesn't it?" she whispered, plaintively. "So much that—that you're beginning to—to hate *me,* too!"

"No," he said. "I could never hate you, Clara. That is, if you *are* Clara. Put it this way: There were two sisters, identical twins. Say that one—disappeared, and the other—died. But under such strange circumstances that no one can, or I fear, ever will, be able to prove which one disappeared, and which one—died. Not even *you.* Are you sure that you are Clara?"

She stared at him. Thought about that.

Bowed her head. Looked at him again, her eyes misting over.

"No," she said quietly. "I'm not sure, Toby. Because, you see—I don't remember much—No! That's not true, either! Oh, Lord, I'm so mixed up! I don't remember *anything* about me—about Clara—either. They told me in the village that I was Clara. When I came back, I mean. Because I was wearing my—her—Clara's clothes . . ."

He stared at her. Whispered:

"Sara was wearing Clara's clothes—the day she disappeared, or—died."

Her eyes opened very wide. Her mouth trembled.

"She was? Why was she, Toby?" she said.

"A fluke. Or maybe to plague me. You know the old refrain for weddings? To bring good luck, I mean? 'Something old, something new, something borrowed, something blue—' That's what she borrowed: a whole outfit of Clara's. Right down to the underwear, I do believe."

"I see," she said, so low he had to bend forward to hear her. "Then—everything's—spoiled, isn't it? Our wedding—our life together . . . Because—you—don't know—who I am—and I don't—either—"

"Don't you?" he said.

"No. I *think* I'm Clara. Given a choice that's the one I'd like to be. She taught school, didn't she? Was—decent. Loved children. Wanted to get married—mainly so she could have some of her own, since actually, deep down—she's—afraid of—men—even of—a nice, gentle fellow like you, Toby—'cause she—she's damaged. Oh, not her body, but her mind—her—her heart—because of that time that Harold—"

He said, sharply, accusingly: "But you *remembered* that!"

And she, sadly: "Yes. But that's no proof of—identity, is it? That could have happened to either of—us. Or to—both. And Harold—being the way—he was—it—it probably did . . ."

There was a silence between them. It went on and on and on. Tobias' ears ached with it. It lay upon him like a stone of darkness. Crushing him—guts, mind, and heart.

He thought: "Those glasses that she doesn't need. That ring on her finger this morning that damned well shouldn't have been there. Those scars on her head that could be either the marks of a madman's blows, or of a thundering luciferian fall. Oh, God, I—"

Then he saw how she was crying. Put out his arms to her. She came to him. Stood close. Buried her face in the hollow of his throat. He could feel her lips moving against it scaldingly, Braille-coding her words into his very flesh:

"Couldn't you—just—take me on—on faith, Toby? Isn't that what any man takes any woman on, after all? And—and—on pity, maybe? On love? My love for you, anyhow? Giving me a chance—a fighting chance—to teach you—to—to love me again? Whichever I am? Whoever I am?"

He put his fingers under her chin, lifted her suffering, tear-streaked face. Said, very, very softly:

"Which do you want to be? *Who* do you want to be?"

"Clara! Oh, Toby, let me be Clara! So that I can be good, and you can love me! Oh, God, Toby, please!"

A strain from a medieval rondeau poured through his head, played—he would have sworn it!—on lutes, violas, virginals.

Without a pause, grave woodwinds shaped the bard's immortal words: "Call me but Love, and I'll be new baptised! Henceforth I never will be—"

He smiled at her, whoever she was, whichever she was. Bent and kissed her mouth. Drew back.

"All right. Be Clara—and all my own," he said.

Twenty-one

Coming back from the mailbox near the gate of his farm just outside Ryland, New York, with that letter in his hand, Tobias Tobit, gentleman farmer, could hear his wife, Clara, singing. She had a clear, bell-like soprano that was absolutely true and right on pitch. She could do all kinds of things with her voice, flute notes, run, trills, warbles, imitate bird song. And she sang for the same reason that birds sing: because she was happy.

"Why shouldn't I be—when I've got the nicest, finest, best, sweetest husband in all the world?" she often said.

"And I—my dream of fair women!" he thought with awe, and wonder. "The epitome of feminine perfections—a garden of delights—in one small and dainty form. Lord, I never know what she's going to do or say next! All I do know that whatever it is, it will make me happy. Happier than I am now—which is almost sinful. Positively indecent for a fact!

"And to think I ever dreamed, thought, or even imagined that she was, or could have been that poor, insane, bedeviled witch-child. Or that she might even share her twin's nature, might one day turn upon me the distorted, foam-flecked, ravenous face I saw that last day in the tower. The face of—Sara. The definition of—horror . . ."

But, as always, he pushed that thought quickly from his mind. Even yet, he didn't want to dwell upon it. It had taken him too damned long to rid himself of that particular nightmare. In fact, he never did rid himself of it. Rather, Clara exorcized it. Made it go away.

And she did that, performed that minor miracle, by her behavior towards him. Especially by her behavior in bed. Because it was precisely in their tenderest, most intimate moments that she first began to rid him of his fears that she could be (there was still the mysterious business of that extra wedding ring, and those glasses she no longer wore, or needed, that she wouldn't or couldn't explain) Sara; or even that she might one day prove to be too much like her twin. In all aspects of love, she was so perfectly normal. She had none of Sara's obviously sadomasochistic (he'd learned those terms by then) tendencies. Sex was *not* the be-all, and end-all, of her existence.

She put up with it with mildly exasperated good humor most of the time, enjoyed it tremendously some of the time, and refused him firmly when she really and truly didn't feel like it.

Strangely enough, it was her refusals that reassured him most of all. For, brief as his relations with her sister had been, he came out of them with the awed, and not a little fearful, conviction that Sara would never, under any conceivable circumstances, refuse a chance to engage in sexual activity, and that she considered the wilder that activity was, the closer it bordered upon at least certain forms of perversion, the better. Therefore Clara's clear, firm, and sometime ringing "No!" actually made him, despite his momentary disappointment, happy.

Clara was much too smart not to soon notice this. About the fourth or fifth time it happened, she said, her tone quizzical, and even a little annoyed:

"Tobias—you *like* for me to say 'No,' don't you? Why do you? Are you play-acting? I mean pretending to want me when you really don't?"

"Why should I do a thing like that?" he said.

"Don't know. Maybe as a cover up. So I won't find out you're having an affair with another woman on the side! Maybe even with that ugly Nell Brightwell!"

He threw back his head and roared.

"Don't laugh! I wouldn't put it past you! And I certainly wouldn't put it past *her* the way she looks at you, at times!"

"I'm a mighty pretty boy, y' know," Tobias said solemnly.

"You are," she said with a gamine's grin. "Now, come on!"

"C'mon where?" he said.

"To bed, of course. I'm going to call your bluff, Toby boy! And besides—"

"Besides, what?"

"Maybe that's *why* we haven't started little Toby even yet," she said sadly. "We don't do it enough."

"We don't do *what* enough?" he said, teasing her.

"Oh you know! *It,*" she said. "Now, c'mon!"

That was another way she was different from her twin. She *never* used profanity or employed a slightly risqué expression. He enjoyed forcing her into weird circumlocutions to avoid any of the Anglo-Saxon, barnyard, earthy, even humorous expressions for sexual activity, or even normal bodily functions. But he was glad she didn't. He had heard Sara sound off exactly twice; but her wild, demented screaming, the utter obscenity of her language were engraven forever upon the very tissues of his brain.

Only one trait, as far as he could see, did Clara possess in common—or rather had possessed in common while Sara lived—with her dead twin: her maternal instinct. Clara's was, and, in fairness, he had to admit that Sara's had been, deep and true and real. In sober fact, the *only* shadow existing upon the happiness of Tobias Tobit, Esquire, and his young second wife, was their failure to have a child. Clara had twice made him take her down to New York City, where eminent specialists had examined her with microscopic thoroughness, and afterwards him as well, then shook their heads and blamed it all on God, saying that there was absolutely no physical or biological reason that the Tobits couldn't have twenty babies if they wanted to.

In all other ways, their relations were very close to perfect. Mainly this was because they actually *liked* each other, which, between two people of opposite sex, is a great deal harder to get to than mere love. Not that they didn't occasionally quarrel; they were, after all, human beings. But their quarrels—which centered around the question of whether to adopt a child or wait for one of their own, Tobias being for adoption, Clara against: "It wouldn't be *ours!*" she stormed. "Not really!", were seldom prolonged and never serious.

So by that spring day in 1924, a year and a half after their wedding, she had rid him completely of all his doubts and fears. He didn't know as he loped toward the house with that letter in his hand that it was their potential destruction that he bore homeward with him—death, hell, and utter desolation.

"What is it, Toby, love?" she said, as he came up to the kitchen door.

"A letter—addressed to you. Why, I like this! It says: *"Miss* Clara Tobit, care of Mr. Tobias Tobit, R.F.D. 14, Ryland, New York!"

"Oh!" she laughed. "Looks like somebody thinks we're living in sin! Who's it from, Toby?"

"A law firm. Merryweather, Thornton, Greenspan, and Merryweather in—say!—Beaufort, South Carolina!"

"Where *we* came from, originally. My family. Open it, Toby. Read it to me." She was baking. Her hands were full of flour. Her cooking, sad, unromantic truth to tell, was nothing to brag about, but then, neither was Tobias' appetite, so the two things cancelled out.

Tobias opened the letter, read:

"Dear Miss Tobit:

We have been advised of the tragic deaths of your entire family on the eighth September 1922, said deaths being caused by an accidental or deliberate explosion—"

"Neither," Tobias said. "Wasn't even an explosion. It was an implosion. Caused by Anne's body turning into antimatter."

"Tobias, you're crazy! Comes from hanging around with Angie. You even sound like him at times. Go on! Read me my letter!"

"All right.

an accidental, or deliberate explosion which destroyed their residence on the outskirts of the township of East Egypt, Kentucky.

We are also most pleased to have been recently informed that due to your absence from said residence at the time, you fortunately escaped sharing your family's tragic fate.

Having in our possession a last will and testament drawn up by us on second April 1900, at the request of your late father, Mr. Ralph Anthony Tobit, and duly signed by him in the presence of witnesses, notarized, and sealed, it becomes incumbent upon us to inform you, Miss Clara Eleanor Tobit—"

"Didn't remember that was my second name," Clara said. "Oh Toby, d'you suppose my memory will *ever* come all the way back?"

"Don't know. I hope not. Lots of unhappy things you can do without remembering, it seems to me. Where was I? Oh yes—

incumbent upon us to inform you that your father's estate, 'Bellevue,' some fourteen miles beyond the city limits of Beaufort, was, under the terms of that will, to be divided among his three children, Sara Elaine Tobit, Harold Anthony Tobit, and yourself."

Clara stared at Tobias.

"His *three* children?" she said. "Wasn't Edna still alive in 1900? Let me see—let me see . . . No. She wasn't. She drowned when she was three years old. And she was a year older than Sara and I. And we were born in 1896. So she died in 1898. Two years before poor Papa made that will. Accounts for her not being mentioned, naturally. . . ."

Tobias studied her face. Said slowly:

"It might. And then it might not. There could be another reason, a much better one. Such as the fact that Ralph and Edna Tobit, your father and your mother, never had a daughter named Edna."

She stared at him. The astonishment in her clear blue eyes was real.

"Why Tohhhh-beee! Who *ever* told you a thing like that?" she said.

"Your father," Tobias said drily, "Ralph Tobit, himself."

"My father--told—you—that he—that he and Mama never had—"

"A daughter named Edna. That they had had only three children: you, Sara, and Harold. Sara also said that it was *you* who fell into that pond, my dearest Clara, and that you were dreadfully sick for months afterwards, and that your illness—affected—your mind—"

Her eyes were doe-things, mortally stricken.

"Why—are you—doing this?" she whispered. "Are—you—are you *trying* to drive me—crazy?"

"No," he said, and put his arms around her. "That's the *last* thing I'd want to do. I was only repeating things your father and your sister —dead now, God rest their souls!—said to me. I don't know whether they were telling the truth or not. For your father, also in my presence, solemnly swore that your brother Harold died at age twelve of cerebro-spinal meningitis. I believed *that,* too. But on my wedding day, Harold started howling from the tower room, Sara went up there to calm him, I followed her, Harold and I had a fight, and he jumped out of the tower window with Sara in his arms. . . ."

Her eyes were perfectly enormous now.

"Toby—do you *know* how—how Sara calmed Harold?" she said.

"Yes," he said grimly. "Do you?"

She shook her head. It was the motion of a dying swan.

"No," she whispered, "but I—I suspected—I believed—that she —that she let him—make love to her. That's *why* I left the schloss.

Got that job teaching. So I—I wouldn't find out for sure. So I wouldn't have to know."

"And you still don't," he said gently. "I haven't told you. I promise you I never will."

"Thank you for that, darling. You know I *still* can't remember her at all? And what I *think* I remember about her is wrong, at least according to you. It seems to me she was taller than I am—

"She wore *very* high-heeled shoes," Tobias said.

"And that her hair was reddish blonde—"

"She put colored powder in it to make it that color."

"Oh! And her eyes were a darker blue—"

"Because of the colors she wore, deliberately, she told me, to make them look darker—"

"Ohhhh! And she was very, very beautiful!"

"She *was.* Because the two of you were identical. You are very, very, very beautiful Clara. More beautiful than she ever was."

"But you said we were identical! So how could I be more beautiful than she was?"

"Because," he said quietly, "you're something that she wasn't. You're both beautiful and good. Which means you're beautiful all the way through. From the heart."

"Ohhhh! Tohhh-beee!" she wept. "Now I've got to kiss you! I've just got to! And my hands are all floury and I'll get you all messed up and—"

"Go on," he grinned, "mess me up. I'll love it!"

She kissed him. Said: "Now will you please finish reading this doggoned letter before you make me spoil the whole rest of the afternoon? So I won't get my baking done, and my letter won't get read, and you won't finish your harrowing or your seeding either one?"

"Hmmmn," he said, "harrowing, maybe not. But *seeding,* honey? Is that a hint, young woman?"

"Ohhhh but you're a naughty boy! Wicked! Read my letter, Tobias!"

"Oh all right!" he sighed. "Just when I had the dadgummed afternoon spoiled so nicely. Well here goes: 'As the sole survivor of your family, the estate, Bellevue, consisting of . . .' Lord, Clara honey, do I *have* to read all this? There're pages and pages of what it consists of!"

"No. Papa told me it was huge. More than a thousand acres. Doesn't matter. I don't want it. I love it here, Toby. You—you won't make me go down there to that horrible old place, will you?"

"No. Of course not. But you don't remember it. You can't. You were too little when your family left there. So how do you know it was horrible?"

"Papa said it was. And Mama. She—she hated it. Ever since—Edna—Oh, Toby! I *did* have a sister named Edna! I did! I did!"

"That's easy enough to check. When we go down there—"

"But I don't want to go down there. And I won't!"

"But honey, you have to. For the probation of the will. You or your legal representative, it says right here. . . . Afterwards we can put the damned place up for sale, or give it to the state for a poor farm, or a school for wayward girls—Saaay! That's a good idea. A school for wayward girls! And *I'll* be headmaster!"

"Ohhh, you! Aren't I wayward enough to suit you?"

"No. Far from it," he said, and kissed her. "But seriously, honey, we'd better go down there for a week or two. Probate the will. Put the place up for sale. And look up your sister's—Edna's—birth certificate in the county records. Or her baptismal certificate in the parish ones. And her death certificate. Clear that one doubt up for ever, right?"

"Yes," she said, "only you go, Toby. Without me. As my legal representative—which you are, anyhow, aren't you? To make sure I'll give you my power of attorney. That ought to do it, shouldn't it?"

"But Clara!" he protested. "I don't want to leave you here all alone and—"

"Dearest, you've got to. I—I—I don't feel up to travel right now. In fact, I'd better not. It—it might not be—good for me. . . ."

Dense as he usually was, Tobias got it.

"Clara!" he said. "Ohhhhh Clara!"

Then he kissed her as though she were made of crystal and held her as though she were made of cut glass, and moaned: "Clara! Oh Clara! Oh my darlin' Clara!" And kissed her again, and fool that he was, started to cry.

When she saw that *she* started to cry, too, which was so ridiculous that she started to laugh at the same time, which made him laugh and they were still standing there holding each other and laughing and crying like blithering idiots, young fools, or their exact synonyms, two people really and truly in love, when Angie came through the door and stood there grinning at them, and even wiped away a tear of his own with one huge and horny finger.

"But I warn ye," he said, "it'll be pale green 'n have six mouths and three eyes 'n seaweed hair 'n eight arms 'n twelve legs 'n its tits on its back if it's female anyhow 'n we're gonna name it Annie!"

"Ohhh you!" Clara said.

"Angie!" Tobias said. "You'll rally 'round and take care of things, won't you? I have to go down south to Beaufort, South Carolina. And I'd feel a lot better if you were here to see that nothing happens to Clara and—"

Angie grinned at them.

"Had me druthers, I'd much druther *help* sumpin' happen to li'l Clara—sumpin' mighty nice!" he teased. "Only she won't cooperate none at all. One time I tried to cop a nice gentle li'l feel o' all that softness on which she sits—by kinetic parapsychology only, laddybucks, 'n she hunted me all over the ding-danged farm in order to slap me winding!"

"Did you?" Tobias said to Clara.

"I sure did! And if I'd known that he really wasn't your chauffeur, I'd never let him on the place, the freshie! Calling himself an Angel!"

"But Clara, doll, I *am* an Angel. Haven't I proved that to ye yet?" Angie sighed.

"Well, you dig wells by pointing your finger at the ground, and plough our fields while lying flat on your back in bed, fast asleep. And nobody had ever even seen a crop like our first one in this cold, rocky country," Clara said. "So I reckon you *are* an Angel. A *Fallen* Angel. And I can't put you off the place 'cause Toby and I are going to need you more than ever now. But you behave yourself or—or I'll take an axe handle to you, so help me!"

"Yes ma'am! Miz Clara, ma'am!" the Angel said.

"And I don't just mean around *me,"* Clara said wrathfully. "Besides, you're much too loyal to Toby to get fresh for real. But you stay out of Dino's roadhouse, Angie! I just won't have a fellow who works for Toby and me consortin' with—oh heck, I might as well say it—with whores! You give our place a bad name, Angie!"

"Yes 'm," Angie said contritely. "I'll be good, Miz Tobit." Then, "Toby, lad, ken I have a word wit ye—alone!"

"No, you don't!" Clara cried. "Anything you say to my husband, you say in front of me!"

"Wimmen!" Angie sighed. "All right. I'll mek it short 'n sweet. Don't go down to Beaufort, South Carolina, laddybucks. Tell 'em to tek that ding-dang estate 'n shove it. In the Atlantic Ocean, fer instance—"

Tobias stared at him. "Why not?" he said.

"Don't know. Not for real. Th' Auld Cuss is mad at me for pullin' th' small-sized rebellion on 'im down in Kentucky. So he's cut my wave length. Don't reach that far south. But they's something *wrong* down there. Mighty, mighty wrong. 'N all that comes over to me loud 'n clear is that it's something *ye* don't need t' know—"

"Toby," Clara whispered, "he's right. I—I feel it! Don't go. Don't go, please!"

"But Clara—" Tobias began

"Besides—I'm not even *sure* I'm going to have a baby. I can't be. Not yet. Why don't you write those lawyers to—to dispose of the place—as best they can, and—"

But Tobias shook his head.

"No. Because there are at least two—well—mysteries, call 'em, that you don't even know about. That *have* to be cleared up for *our* security. For my peace of mind. And—for our baby's sake as well. I'm sorry, but I've just got to go down there. Believe me, it's for the best," he said.

Or for the worst.

Which was a point that he was sure he was going to die of old age of before he'd ever get to know.

Twenty-two

"A pity," Thomas E. Merryweather, attorney at law, had said. "We were looking forward to having Tobits on the old place again. But I can understand your wife's feeling, sir. The death of her sister—her twin sister, I believe—seems to have affected your mother-in-law's mental state adversely. Did you know her, Mr.—ah—Tobit?"

"I'm a cousin. Second or third cousin, I don't know which. And yes, I did know Mrs. Tobit, but very, very briefly. A day or two—only before the castle—blew up.

"Don't know why Old Schloss, the former owner, had all that miner's blasting powder stored in the basement. As a matter of fact, I discovered that powder, myself, by accident the day before—the tragic accident. But I've never had the slightest connection with mining so I didn't know what it was. And so much was going on at the time that I forgot to ask. A pity. A very great pity! For if I had asked Cousin Ralph—Mr. Tobit, that is—I might have saved them. . . ."

"An act of God," Attorney Merryweather said piously, "before which we can only humbly bow our heads . . ."

"Yes," Tobias said. "Then you—your firm will take care of the sale of Bellevue for my wife? It would be a comfort to leave the matter in such competent hands. . . ."

"Of course, my boy! And we'll get an excellent price for it, too. Valuable property, that. May take a bit of time—a year or two, say, to get what it's really worth. But you can afford to wait, can't you?"

"Easily. We're not rich, but we're comfortably well off, sir. I've a place of my own. Nothing like as big as Bellevue, though. But—three hundred forty acres anyhow. And I'm hoping to buy the neighboring place next year. Then we'll have six eighty."

Mr. Merryweather *was* impressed now. "Not bad! Not bad at all for such a young fellow!" he said jovially. "Anything *else,* we can do for you, Mr. Tobit?"

"Well—" Tobias said, "you could steer me in the right direction, sir. My wife wants some concrete information about her family. All the records were in the castle, sir. And were destroyed with it. For instance, could you tell me where to go to obtain copies of the marriage, birth, and death certificates of the family—while they lived here, sir? I'm particularly interested in finding out what I can about —Edna. Their first and oldest child, I believe—"

"Never heard of her," Attorney Merryweather said. "Which means nothing, of course. She may have died at birth, or before I became closely associated with the Tobits' affairs. . . ."

"Our information is that she died at age three. During a storm. Drowned in a pond on their place."

"That *was* before my time. My father was their attorney then. And he's gone to his reward now, too, Lord rest his soul! But I did hear him mention that incident once or twice, but seems to me he said it was one of the twins who drowned. . . ."

"No," Tobias said, "that couldn't be, sir. I—I met both of them. Confusing business. They were alike as two peas in one pod. I was thinking of embracing the Moslem religion so that I could marry *both* of them!"

"Were you now? Easier to move out to Utah and become a Mormon, I should think! Tell you what, Mr. Tobit, why don't you go in for a bit of tourism for a day or two? Sightseeing: old manor houses —the sea islands—our famous old plantations. Meanwhile I'll put some of my brighter young law clerks onto tracing your lady's family's records. Give th' lazy young devils something to do. Good practice for them. And they will do it much faster than you could. Know where to go and all. They've done this sort of thing hundreds of times. It's routine in will searches, property matters, inheritances and the like, you know. . . ."

"Would you, sir?" Tobias said. "That would help a lot. Of course I'm willing to pay them for their trouble and—"

"Not a red copper! Wouldn't do to spoil the beggars, young sir!" Attorney Merryweather said.

Two days later when the little mulatto bellhop came up with that note from Attorney Merryweather on a tray, Tobias found that he had considerable difficulty reading it. And the trouble was not the good lawyer's script, which was florid, ornate, round, but reasonably clear, but the fact that he, Tobias Tobit, had waked up that morning with absolutely the goddamnest hangover he'd ever had in all his life, topped off with the most abysmal sense of shame.

He hadn't even waked up in the quite respectable and exceedingly comfortable hotel he was staying at. He had opened his bleary, out of focus, bloodshot eyes in just the sort of disreputable establishment that Angie had always been luring him into earlier in their initial wanderings together; and turning his head very very carefully on his neck so that it wouldn't fall all the way off, he had found a black-haired girl, clad in black stockings—*net* stockings, naturally—and a black lace peek-a-boo envelope chemise, sleeping peacefully at his side.

That was when he had started to throw up. She had waked up and "tended to him" as she put it, bathing his face, holding the basin for him to throw up into, and being generally kind and cheerful.

"Doan worry 'bout li'l ol' me, honey!" she laughed, throatily. "You *didn't.* You wuz faithful to yore sweet li'l missus jes' like you swore you wuz gonna be all night. Brung you heah to keep them river rats in Dan's place from rollin' you. How come you *ever* strayed into a place like *that* anyhow, sugah?"

"Don't know—" he groaned. He didn't. But something had—well—compelled him to enter that horrendous dive on the waterfront, and to stay, after he'd got there. What had made him walk down to the waterfront anyhow? He hadn't had the slightest desire for a drink, and certainly not for feminine company. He was a happily married man and—

"Heah's yore wallet, sugah," the girl said. "Do you *remember* how much you had on you las' night?"

"Yes," he said tiredly, "fifty dollars."

"Well, you blowed twelve dollars on mint juleps fer you'n me. 'N two'n half for this heah room. 'N since you *didn't* avail yore self o' mah services—'less you wanta change yore sweet faithful li'l ol' mind right now, do you, honey?"

"No! God, no!" he said.

"Now tha's mighty uncomplimentary, but I doan mind—you doan *owe* me nuthin'. But since you did mek me waste mah time—you doan mind if I helps myself t' a sawbuck, d' you, honey? After all, a girl's gotta mek a livin' somehows. . . ."

"Not at all—take twenty. After all you probably saved me from getting my head cracked in that dive. . . ."

"Tha's *mighty* sweet o' you, honey. Heah—count it. In mah way, I'm an honest girl. . . ."

He counted his money. Accepting her accounting as accurate, as it probably was, he realized suddenly, his change was all there. While he was doing that, she'd pulled her knee-length silk frock over her bobbed and shingled hair.

"You wants me to call you a cab, honey?" she said. "Be th' best thing . . ."

"Yes," he whispered huskily, "do—"

So now he was back in his own hotel room, and trying to read Attorney Merryweather's letter. But he couldn't. The letters swam before his eyes. He gave it up, rang for room service. When the uniformed waiter came, he growled:

"Coffee! Black—and gallons of it, please! Make it fast will you—I've a million things to do. . . ."

And dived into the shower.

When he came out of the shower he felt considerably better, and after he had drunk that coffee, he felt better still in one way. His head still ached, but it didn't feel as if it were going to fall off and roll under the bureau if he moved it. And the lone fly creeping across the ceiling sounded a *trifle* less loud than a whole herd of rampaging elephants. But his own behavior, what he had done last night, was, if anything, more inexplicable than ever: He had walked away from the Port Royal Arms, the hotel he was staying at, gone down to the waterfront, entered the worse dive south of New York's Bowery and east of San Francisco's Barbary Coast, proceeded to get drunk as a Lord and to pick up a whore.

Why? In the name of God, why? He *never* drank of his own free will. He didn't even like the stuff, really. As for whores, a deep-seated natural fastidiousness, the same finickiness that wouldn't allow him to use another man's comb, not to mention his toothbrush, made them utterly repulsive to him. Angie, on two or three occasions, had fast-talked, smooth-talked him into taking one too many, and then pushed him into the arms of some of the less worn-out, beat-up daughters of commercial sin. But the only whore who had ever attracted him truly had been Nancy, probably because she looked like a sweet-faced plump and idiot child, and not like a poule at all.

Roxane? Where he'd known her, she'd been a movie star. And she'd looked like one, groomed, expensive, smooth as silk. Still—

Still he couldn't explain it. He wasn't even hard-up. He was still walking around in a rosy glow of perfumed bliss, accompanied by off-stage music at the thought that he was going to become the father of a child. He pictured Clara with their infant in her arms and tears came to his eyes. And now he'd—

Or maybe he hadn't. That girl said he'd refused. . . .

Groaning, he reached for that letter. A couple of minutes later, he was sitting bolt upright, his eyes almost popping out of his head, reading:

For not only did a search through the archives of our local Bureau of Vital Statistics fail to turn up *one single document* (the words had been underlined by Attorney Merryweather himself) relating to the Tobit family, which struck us as exceedingly strange since we, as you know, have been the legal representatives of your cousins for over forty years, but the clerk explained their absence by stating that he had delivered them to a gentleman who had then *made off with them* (again the words were underlined) a fact which was not discovered until young Sykes, our law clerk, asked to see and copy them yesterday. And when asked the gentleman's name the clerk replied "Lobit or Tobit"—something like that, and then proceeded to give a fairly exact description of *you,* sir. Therefore we must ask you to stop by our offices at the earliest possible opportunity—

Tobias was already on his feet, almost diving into his clothes.

But as he stopped at the desk downstairs to get some money from the funds he'd deposited in the hotel's safe—he was short of ready cash after his wild, wild night!—the desk clerk said:

"By the way, Mister Tobit, a telegram just came for you. We were just about to send it up to your room when we saw you crossing the lobby. . . ."

He took that blue envelope with trembling fingers, tore it open. It read:

Sara's body found. Ask that you stop—East Egypt identify her. Come home soon. Miss you. Love. Clara.

"Well," he thought, "that's one thing settled." Then he took his money, turned, and asked the bellhop to get him a jitney. That was what people down south called taxicabs in those days.

Half an hour later, he and Attorney Merryweather were standing before the puzzled clerk in the Bureau of Vital Statistics.

"I have never been here before in my life!" Tobias said, or rather roared.

"Shore did look like you, sir!" the clerk said. "Same build, same clos—same—wal now—Mister, would you mind sayin' sumpin else? In yore normal tone o' voice. Not yellin' . . ."

"Why?" Attorney Merryweather said.

"Sounds different, 'pears to me," the clerk said.

"I have never been in here before in all my life," Tobias said quietly.

"Reckon *you* ain't," the clerk said. "Yankee, ain't you?"

"Yes," Tobias said. "Why?"

"That 'ere fella warn't no southerner, though. But talked more like us than you do. Midwestner, likely. Chicago—out that way. You got any folks out theah?"

"No," Tobias said, "I haven't any living relatives, anywhere now—except my wife, who is a cousin. Why?"

"Shore did look like you, tha's why," the clerk of the Bureau of Vital Statistics said.

Back in the hotel room, packing his bags for the long trip home, with that shudderingly repugnant detour by way of East Egypt (how could a body that had been in a practically bottomless pond for a year and a half *be* identified, anyhow? By her teeth? He didn't know of any dental work that either Sara or Clara had had so—), it came to Tobias that other than putting Bellevue in the hands of the law firm, his trip south had accomplished exactly nothing. Then he straightened up, staring off into nowhere—thinking. Thinking slowly, carefully.

Bellevue! That was the key! On his sightseeing tour, he'd discovered that several of the bigger plantations had their own cemeteries, in which their owners and their families were buried. Their locations, usually twenty miles or more from the churches' or the cities' graveyards, and the intense, damp heat of the Carolina lowlands had made that necessary. Edna's grave, if she had a grave, would be out there. And her birth and death dates on her tombstone. He stopped packing the bags. Went downstairs. Had the bellhop call him a jitney.

But there hadn't been any infant's grave whatsoever in the Tobits' family graveyard. In fact there hadn't been a family graveyard at all.

All the way up to Kentucky, Tobias couldn't shake the feeling that there had been something—well—curious about his visit to Bellevue. Something more than curious. Something—strange. But for the life of him he couldn't figure out what something was. The house? No. It had been a typical ante-bellum southern mansion, in the then widely admired Greek-Revival style. Of course it had been a little too new-looking, not at all run down. But Merryweather and his legal partners had seen to its being well cared for, Tobias supposed. The caretakers—Uncle Ben and Ol' Aunt Sukie? Perfect old southern retainers—hair white as cotton bolls, lightish complexions—a cinnamon-ginger-cake color instead of black. They'd yassuhed him almost to death, bowed and scraped like Hollywood darkies in Civil War movie epics. "Yassuh, ah sho do 'members mah babies! Twin girls, suh—th' pruttiest li'l tykes you ever did see! What's that? Nawsuh! Ain't not neither one o' 'em got kilt in no storm. One o' 'em wuz los' Ah disremembers which 'un whether hit were Clary o' Sary, but us done found that angel—baby safe 'n sound—Edna? Nawsuh. Never had no girl chillen named no Edna. Jes' th' twins. An' th' boy—Harold. Yassuh, born—kind o' backward, him. But mah baby girls wuz th' sweetest li'l things, jes alike. Not even they Ma 'n Pa, Mis' Ralph 'n Miz Edna, could tell 'em apart. Nawsuh—they never had no different *ways,* suh, neither! They wuz jes' alike behavin' too—bof sweet as baby angels outa Glory . . ."

When he got off the train in East Egypt, Kentucky, after having changed trains several times because East Egypt, like many small towns in the Cumberland highlands, could only be reached by a narrow-gauge spur line that started in Middleboro, he had the feeling he had never been there before. And when he looked up at Schloss's mountain, towering above the town to a height of over three thousand feet, he was sure of it. Because there were the ruins of Schloss's schloss tumbled halfway down the slopes by the titanic explosion that had wrecked it. Which wasn't the way he remembered things: There hadn't been an explosion, but an implosion. He had heard no sound at all. There had been no ruins. The mountain had opened and swallowed the castle without a trace.

But when he mentioned his impression of how Schloss's transplanted castle had been destroyed to Bill Hendricks, full county sheriff now, and fatter than ever, the big man said:

"You's plumb rememberin' *wrong,* Mister Tobit! That theah explosion broke half th' windows in town. I wuz half deaf 'n had me a headache fur four days afterwards. C'mon now, suh. We's got th' body in th' icehouse so it would keep—"

And he standing there looking down at Sara's lovely, perfect face, looking as though she were asleep, except that her lips were a greenish-blue, at that ring on her finger, at those wrinkled muddy clothes that were the same clothes—he'd swear it!—that Clara had been wearing when they'd found her with her head shaved and swathed in bandages on that mountain road, and that ring the same ring he'd found on Clara's finger when he'd started to put the diamond-crusted wedding band on it in the wedding ceremony in New York, felt that strangeness rising in him like a scream of utter terror. But he mastered it, and said:

"But—but it's impossible, sheriff! She's been in Emmy's Pool a year and a half! She ought to be—"

"Plumb rotted away. Yep. But she ain't. Happens sometimes in these heah mountain pools. Water near th' bottom is close to th' temperature o' ice. So they don't rot. 'Course most in general them carps eats the hands 'n faces so bad you cain't even recognize 'em. But they didn't this time. I'd call it a miracle of th' Lord, suh, 'n be grateful fur it. Well, suh—this heah's yore missus? Yore first missus? 'Cause I heard tell you done gone 'n married Miss Clara, not long afterwards—"

The words were a reproach, Tobias realized, an accusation of levity. He said:

"I don't know, Sheriff. You see both my wife, my present wife, and her sister disappeared at the same time. My present wife turned up with a head wound that affected her memory. She doesn't know what happened to her. She thinks she's Clara. So do I. But she may not be. *This* may be Clara. Maybe Ridley Tyler hit her on the head and threw her in Emmy's Pool."

"Lord God!" Bill Hendricks said. "Ain't there no way you can tell, Mister Tobit?"

Tobias thought about that. Then he said:

"Yes. Will you be kind enough to turn your back, Sheriff? I want to look at my wife's underwear. I *know* what Sara was wearing that day. But by her outer clothing, I can't tell, because she had on an outfit borrowed from Clara. But her underwear were her own. I think I'd know them . . ."

"All right, have a look then, sir!" Bill Hendricks said.

It was Sara, all right. She hadn't on any step-ins at all.

All the way back to New York that feeling of strangeness persisted. By the time he'd got out to the farm, riding in a taxi, it was an icy hailstorm, bleak thunder in his veins. He saw Clara run out the front door come flying toward him, but her face was the strangest thing of all. It was dead white. Water was dripping off it. Her eyes were closed. Her lips were greenish blue.

"Angie," Tobias said slowly, clearly, "it isn't going to work. I don't want to be protected like a backward child. I can only live with the truth. Whatever the truth is. So quit this, damn you! Stop it right now, you hear!"

"Sure ye kin take it, laddybucks? Have ye got there? Achieved a state o' grace? Learned that forgiveness is *all?* Startin' with yer own miserable self 'n extendin' to her? O' will ye—save her? Are ye man enough—man but little lower than th' Angels—'n crowned—not with glory 'n honor—but reason, charity, humility, grace? Are ye Toby, me boy, me boy?"

"Why don't you try me, give me a chance? Stop fucking up my mind and my whole existence. Are you afraid I won't need *you* any more?"

"Ye don't *now,*" Angie said sadly. "N stopped it is, me beamish bhoy! Look!"

Then Clara was still running towards him but she wasn't making any progress. Instead she was receding, being borne backwards becoming doll-like, tiny, vanishing, and the taxi was hurling backwards through the twin illusions of space and time and he was in the train and it was shrieking backwards to East Egypt, Kentucky, and that was a flickering speeded up motion picture run in reverse and he was on another wrong way receding rearwards in time and space flying train and another and another and another and it was getting dark and a telephone was shrilling in his ears.

He picked it up. Opened his eyes. Saw with no surprise at all he was in the hotel Port Royal Arms in Beaufort, South Carolina.

"Mister Tobit? We've got your papers, sir. Yes, yes, all of them. Shall we send them over?" Attorney Merryweather said.

"Yes, please do, if it isn't too much trouble," Tobias whispered.

"Oh, no trouble at all!" the lawyer said.

Staring at those papers, those utterly damnable papers, Tobias Tobit realized that he was, if anything, more confused than ever. To start with, there *had* been a first-born child named Edna, just as Clara had believed.

She, Edna Tobit, the second Edna Tobit, had, indeed, been born in February, 1895. But she hadn't died in 1898, as Clara had said. Either she had died six months after her birth, for there was a copy of a death certificate, reading: "Child Tobit, Female, Daughter of Ralph and Edna Tobit, Bellevue Plantation, near Beaufort, July 8, 1895. Cause of death: Diarrhea," or she had died in August, 1899. Which meant that Clara was wrong, even so, for the second death certificate, as cryptic as the first—why the hell hadn't they put *names* on either of them?—read: "Child Tobit, Female, Daughter of Ralph and Edna Tobit, Bellevue Plantation near Beaufort, August 13, 1899. Cause of death: Drowning."

But, by August 1899, little Edna would have been four and a half years old, not three, as Clara had insisted upon. Clara's and Sara's birth certificate—there was only one issued for the two of them, he saw, likely because they had been born within minutes of one another—was there, as was Harold's, dated a year and five months after theirs, which meant that the huge hairy ape had been the youngest of the Tobits' children.

There was no record of Ralph's and Edna's marriage, which made him think it hadn't taken place in Beaufort at all. He phoned Attorney Merryweather about this point, who came up with a vague belief that he had once heard his father say that the Tobits came originally from Georgia. Atlanta, Savannah, Augusta, he wasn't sure.

But, Tobias realized, where the Tobits had married was totally unimportant. He'd found out the important thing: Cousin Ralph had lied when he'd said that he had sired no other daughters than the twins, just as he'd lied about Harold's continued existence long after that murderous creature was supposed to be safely dead. So Clara was right, was telling the truth. The only mistake she had made, an easy one to make, was in believing Edna had been only three years old when she died, instead of her actual four years, seven months.

But—there was that *first* death certificate. He picked it up, looked at it. Noted that date again: July 8, 1895. And ice-cold death and bitter hell wrapped iron fingers into his guts and dragged them slowly up his throat and out his opened soundless screaming mouth. He had to catch hold of the bedpost to keep from going down. Even so, to make sure, he laid the twins' birth certificate down beside that first death certificate on the bed, so that he could see the dates of both documents at the same time. Clara Eleanor Tobit, Sara Elaine Tobit, twin girls, daughters of Ralph and Edna Tobit, Bellevue Plantation near Beaufort had been born on June 2, *1896.* And who in insane gibbering stark-raving hell had died on July 8, 1895? Why "Child Tobit, Female, Daughter of—" Oh Christ. Oh God. Oh Jesus. *Before* Sara and Clara were even born. Almost a year before. And what female child dear bleeding crucified Christ in your crown of cruel thorns had been alive in 1895 so that she could so madly thoughtlessly obscenely die to wreck his life and—whose? He did not, could not know. Wreck it forever? Why *only* Edna Tobit.

Which meant that "Child Tobit, Female, Daughter of Ralph and Edna Tobit, Bellevue Plantation, near Beaufort, August 13, 1899. Cause of death: Drowning" was—*had* to be—one of the twins. Which one? It didn't even matter.

He was mad. Insane. Crazy. Howling. Stark raving. He had known Sara. He had known Clara. Grant from the outset that they were absolutely identical physically—right down, dammit, to the feathery spiralling crispness of their pale blonde pubic hair! That didn't matter, either. He had married *both* of them. Talked with *both* of them. Had sex with *both* of them. And as people, persons, women, they were *nothing* alike! Sara was a screaming sadomasochistic nymphomanical bitchy lying crazy mad horror. Who had incestuous relations with—Hell! Who screwed like mad, fucked like a she fiend—her own brother.

And Clara—*his* Clara—was an angel. Sweet. Normal. Gentle. A breath of spring. A delight. A glory.

But—had he *ever* seen them—in the same place, at the same time, together? Had *anyone?* What was it that Sal had said: that *nobody* had ever seen them together. Not even the people who worked for the Tobits. That when Clara went to visit her parents, Sara used to go lock herself in her room, *before Clara even got to the schloss,* swearing that she could *feel* when her despised, her hated twin was coming. Go in one damned door and out the other, pausing long enough to brush that reddish powder out of her hair, put on one of Clara's old-fashioned shirtwaists and hobble skirts which on his and *hers,* Saraclara's, Clarasara's—Jesus!—wedding day she'd proved she had access to, because—

But why? Why this lifelong, complicated elaborate charade? What sense did it make? What *reason* was there for it?

What sense, what reason is there for anything the mad do? Except their own interior logic?

He stared at those papers. A mistake? If one, just one of those two death certificates were a mistake! If some half-drunk blind sleepy old clerk had written "female" when he had intended to write "male" but—no.

You could confuse female/male, but the rest of it? Who could confuse the words son and daughter? Besides, where was the boy in question? Not Harold, certainly! The name. The family name. Possible. But the family name plus the given names Ralph and Edna? Impossible.

But—but! Ralph had managed to obtain a death certificate for a child who was *not* dead! For Harold! Why not, madman that he was, clever, clever madman, had he not pulled that same trick twice? Say he *had.* The question then became, why had he? Harold was a raving, monstrous beast. A rapist. A degenerate. Mentally retarded. A murderer. Though alive, he had to be kept hidden. To facilitate his hiding, he had to be represented as dead. Mad logic, perhaps, but logic.

But the twins were *not* kept hidden. All the world knew the Tobits had twin daughters. But no one, nobody at all, at all, at all, at all, had ever seen sweet gentle Clara, wild sex-mad Sara together.

He got up. Put on his jacket. His hat. Went downstairs. But as he stopped at the desk to get some money from the funds he'd deposited in the hotel's safe—he was short of cash after his wild, wild night! *What* wild, wild night? he thought with sudden wonder—the desk clerk said:

"By the way, Mister Tobit, a telegram just came for you. We were just about to send it up to your room when we saw you crossing the lobby. . . ."

Mad laughter tore him. He took that blue envelope with trembling fingers, tore it open, read it, crumpled it into a ball, was about to throw it into a nearby spittoon when what he had actually read this time came over to him. He smoothed it out against the marble desk top, read it again:

> Clara's body found. Ask that you stop East Egypt identify her. Come home soon. Miss you. Love Sara.

Exactly as before. But with the position of the two names in it reversed. Like his life. Reversed. Cancelled. Stopped. Driven right up the hotel wall. By its fingernails.

He went out into the street. Hailed a taxi. A jitney. A hack. Anyhow he hailed something. The boat of Charon, maybe, sailed down to where Acheron pours into Cocytus, and it into Phlegethon, and it into the Styx, and it into but no, he never got to Lethe, which is the river of blessed forgetfulness.

"Heah we be, Mister," his driver (boatman?) said finally. "This heah is Bellevue Plantation."

It was nothing like the other. It was older, shabbier, dilapidated, run down. The caretaker wasn't a ginger-cake-colored Hollywood movie darky. He was young and inky black. He neither scraped nor bowed. But, all the same, the name Tobit produced the desired effect.

"Which one is you, suh?" he said.

"Their Yankee cousin," Tobias said easily. "Or as you people say down here, their damn Yankee cousin, I suppose."

"Us don't. Only white folks say tha, suh. 'Sides, y'all done freed us kind of. You wants to see th' *whole* place? Tek you a couple of days. Mighty big, Bellevue. . . ."

"No," Tobias said, "only the house—and the graveyard, if any. And—somebody who worked for them when they lived here. An old retainer, you might say. Could that be arranged?"

"Jes' like fallin' off a log, suh. Ol' A'nt Sukie *live* heah, she do. Down in th ol' slave quarters. I lets you in th' Big House, or in th' graveyard, whichever you wants t' see fust, Mistuh Tobit, 'n whilst you's a-lookin' at anything you wants, I go git ol' A'nt Sukie. Seventy-seven years ol'. Damn nigh blind, but spry as a spring chicken, her!"

"Take me to the graveyard first. I need to copy down some names and dates from the tombstones. For my wife, who was born here. One of the twins, in fact."

"Wuz she now, suh? Didn't know th' family, myself, suh—Mister Merryweather, the lawyer hired me, after they'd done moved away. To Kentucky, wuzn't it, suh?"

"Yes, to Kentucky," Tobias said. "Go get Ol' Aunt Sukie, will you?"

There were the *two* infants' graves. The first was Edna's. It bore her name, her dates. Her pitifully brief dates. The second read: "Baby Girl Tobit, One of the Twins, June 2, 1896, August 13, 1899; Resting in the Bosom of the Savior." So he *still* didn't know which one of the twins he had married. Turning, he saw the ancient black woman standing there. A monument of quiet. Of dignity.

"Yassuh?" she said.

"Which one of the twins died?" he said. Like that. Without preliminaries.

"Dunno, suh. Doan nobody know," she said.

"Why not, Aunt Sukie?" he whispered.

"They bof got los'. They wuz wit that flighty yaller gal Carrie 'n a tree fell on her. Kilt her daid. Them po' chillem got scairt 'n run off. In that theah hurricane. In all that wind 'n rain. 'N one of em wuz found livin' t' other one—daid, suh. T'ree, foh days later. Half eat up by th' buzzards 'n the crows. But since Miz Edna dressed them two pretty gal chillun 'zactly alike, 'n since not *nobody,* suh, not me, not her, not they Pa could tell 'em apart, we never did figger out which one got kilt, Sary or Clary, 'n which one lived to grow up. Miz Edna, her, lost her mind a-grievin'. Tha's how come they boy, Harold, was born backwards kind of. Not right bright, you know, suh?"

"I know that! Get back to th' twins, Aunt Sukie, the twins. I—I married one of them, and I'd like to know—"

"Which one you married. You cain't, suh. Put hit this away, mebbe you done married 'em *bof.*"

"Both?" Tobias whispered.

"Yassuh. Mas' Ralph's fault. He wuz always mekin' us change that theah po' baby's clos. Takin' her in to see her po' Ma in one color dress then a lit' later in another. Mekin' th' po' li'l thing play-act like she wuz her dead sister. Got th' po', po' baby so confused she didn't rightly know who she wuz herself. When she got bigger, she wuz always play-actin'. Like she wuz *two* girl chillun, I mean. 'N one of her wuz a mighty naughty chile, I kin tell you thats Mistuh Tobit! But th' other one of her wuz a angel. 'N one day, jes' fo' they left heah, I whupped her li'l behind sumpin awful—Mas Ralph always made *me* chastize her, suh; reckon *he* didn't have th' heart—fur a thing she'd gone done: Took her pet canary-bird outa th' cage 'n *bit* hit t' death, suh. By th' neck. Hung onto it wit her teeth—'n it flutterin' 'n beatin' hits po' li'l wings 'til hit died. Then she stood there grinnin' at me wit her mouf full o' blood 'n feathers. So I whupped her. Darn neah bruk her po' li'l heart 'cause she could see I wuz mad at her for real 'n disgusted to boot. So after I done whupped her til I wuz too tired to hit her another lick, she throwed her li'l arms 'round mah neck 'n sez:

" 'Wasn't me! It was my sister! She killed my poor canary! A'nt Sukie—somebody's gonna kill *her*—gonna kill—Ah disremembers which 'un she said—'Gonna kill—Sary,' O' mebbe she said: 'Gonna kill Clary. One day 'n then I'm gonna be free! *Me*—The real me's gonna be free! 'Cause th real me's *good,* A'nt Sukie! She is! She is!' Me, I allus had th' feelin' that po' baby wuz right, suh."

He stood there. It had all been said now. Everything that mattered.

He gave her five dollars. She gave it back to him. Said: "Give it t' John. He th' caretaker. I doan need no money, suh. Ain't no buyin' 'n sellin' where I'm going. . . ."

He gave John the five dollars. Took the waiting jitney back to the hotel. Packed his bags. Drove to the station. Took a train. To Kentucky. To East Egypt.

This time the mountain was truncated, and there were no broken ruins of the castle. But knowing how Angie liked to play with human concepts such as time, space, motion, and even matter, he didn't worry about that.

But he couldn't identify the body, this time. It was too bloated, rotted away. The carp had eaten the face, the hands, the feet.

Looking at it, almost fainting from nausea, he felt Angie's raucous voice pouring words into his mind:

"Look at th' poor bitch's clothes, will you?" the Angel said.

Tobias looked. Shook his head.

"It's not my wife," he said to Bill Hendricks. "She wasn't dressed this way. She never worn aprons, for one thing. I think this is Sal Tyler."

"Why, gawddamn! It shore is!" Bill Hendricks said.

On the train that night, Angie materialized out of the wall of the drawing room compartment Tobias had taken and sat there grinning at him.

"What're ye gonna *do,* laddybucks?" he said.

"Don't know," Tobias said. "Angie, tell me something: Does she *know?* That she's Clara and Sara *both,* I mean?"

Angie stared at him.

"Who said she *is?"* he said.

"That old black woman! At Bellevue—down near Beaufort! And—"

"Why d'ye wanta go'n take *her* word for it?" Angie said in an exaggeratedly injured tone of voice. "Why not believe that ol' ginger-cake-colored woman? At that other Bellevue? Down near that other place called Beaufort? And—"

"But there *isn't* any such woman!" Tobias howled. "You made her up! And before that you made up that corn pone type bustle hustling little chippy with that sugar and molasses voice, so as to get my guilty conscience so worked up that I wouldn't figure things out.

Because you thought I couldn't *stand* the *truth!* And—"

"Who *kin?* 'N ye made up th' ol' black servin' woman. 'Cause tha's th' kind o' mind ye've got. Ye think th' truth's gotta be ugly. As a matter o' fact, me beamish bhoy—th' truth's eny damn thing ye believe it is—jes' like everything else."

"Angie!" Tobias said.

"I'll prove it to ye, laddybucks. Fer instance, when ye visited Bellevue number one or Bellevue number two, did ye cross water? Drive across a bridge? Tek a boat?"

Tobias thought about that.

"No," he said finally. "Not either time. Why?"

"Beaufort's on an *island.* It'n Port Royal, both. To git to *enywhere* from it, Toby me boy, me boy, ye've *got* to cross water. 'N ye didn't. Ye see?"

"I see you drive me craaaazy!" Tobias yelled.

"'N at th' risk o' borin' repetition, I told ye that that wasn't a drive. A putt, maybe. A two-inch putt on a level green."

"Angie, for God's sake!"

"He don't give a damn. Ain't ye had that demonstrated to ye enough yet, ye poor bastid? C'mon now, Toby! Sure there *wuz* an ol' black woman? A place called Bellevue? A town called Beaufort? A mythical country called South Carolina? Or ain't they, wuzn't they, 'n you'n me, laddybucks, hiven, earth, th' visible universe 'n th' Auld Cuss, himself—'sich stuff as dreams are made on, 'n our little lives rounded by—a sleep?"

"Angie, you stop it!" Tobias said.

"It's stopped," Angie said cheerfully. "But then, who sez it iver got *started?"*

There was a silence. That went on and on. Extended out to forever and beyond. Then Tobias broke it.

"Angie," he whispered, "she says she can't even *remember* Sara. . . ."

"She can't. Or mebbe it's th' other way eround. Mebbe Sara can't remember *her.* Gonna remind her, whichiver wan that she may be?"

"I don't know!" Tobias moaned. "I just plain don't know!"

"Time ye made up yer blinkin' mind, laddybucks!" Angie said.

"Angie—what *should* I do?"

"Decide fer yerself, Toby. Or else it don't count. Not valid. Cheatin'. Evadin' moral responsibility 'n stuff like that there . . ."

"Oh Christ!" Tobias said.

"Don't exist. Th' Essenes made 'im up," Angie said.

They sat there. The train poured itself out along the rails. Ran mourning sweet sad long lost lonely through the night: Whooooo-ooooo! Whoooo-eeeeee!

"Angie—was I ever in North Carolina, California, Nevada, Kansas, Virginia, Kentucky and—and New York?" Tobias said.

"Ain't no sich places. Mythical countries o' th' mind, jes' like South Carolina," Angie said. "Specially California. It plain ain't *there.* Not even the one that *is."*

"And *were* there those girls named Nancy, Anne, Conchita? Women called—Hellcat Hattie McCoy, L'Amour McSimple Fearsome, Roxane?"

"Dunno, wuz there? Do ye believe in 'em, Toby lad?"

"Yes. Oh, I don't know! Maybe . . ."

"Then th' answer's yes, dunno, 'n mebbe, as th' case may be. At eny given hiatus in yer sequential progression that is, I mean. Whatcha gonna *do,* laddybucks?"

"I still don't know," Tobias whispered.

"Gosh, but ye make me tired sometimes!" Angie said.

And vanished from that particular segment of the twin illusions of Space and Time.

When his taxi stopped before the gate of the farm, she came flying out to meet him. Her hair was loose. It streamed out behind her like distilled light, finespun mist silver, dream stuff, gossamer, pale white gold.

She hurled herself into his arms, kissed his face, his mouth, his eyes, everywhere she could reach, babbling, crying:

"Oh Toby Toby Toby Toby! I am! I really am! Oh dearest I'm sohhhhh happy! I'm—"

He drew her to him. Held her. Whispered:

"So am I—Clara."

He didn't lie. He was.

Then looking up, he saw Angie soaring skyward on huge, slow-beating, horizon-to-horizon sweeping wings, trailing glorious iridescent rainbow-hued contrails behind him.

"Where th' hell do you think you're going?" Tobias howled.

"Off to help create th' World," Angie chuckled. "Ye don't need me. Ye've got there. Reached Nirvana. Achieved th' state o' grace. 'N right now poor ol' Ahura Mazda's rubbin' on that rhubarb plant. Gotta go help 'im—th' poor Auld Cuss! He might not get 'em right!"

"Get *what* right?" Tobias yelled.

"Masya 'n Masyanag. Th' first man 'n th' first woman. In th' Zoroastrian cosmology, anyhow, that is," the Angel said. "So ta, ta bhoy! Take care o' me li'l Clara will ye? 'N also o' me darlin' li'l Annie when she's born! Gonna have a rough time ye know, living 'mongst humans wit her tits on her back 'n all them arms 'n legs! So take good care o' her, too! Take mighty good care!"

Tobias looked up towards the abruptly empty heavens. His eyes were wet.

"I will, Angie! Oh, I will!" he said.